Come As You Are

A Novel

Christine Weiser

PS
BOOKS

Regional Publishing, National Voice
A division of Philadelphia Stories

Regional Publishing, National Voice
A division of Philadelphia Stories

93 Old York Road, Ste. 1-753
Jenkintown, PA 19046
www.psbookspublishing.org
www.philadelphiastories.org

ISBN 978-0-9904715-6-1

Proceeds from the sale of this book support Philadelphia Stories,
which is a free nonprofit literary magazine publishing writers and
artists from the Delaware Valley.

Cover Image by Jim Eyles © 2016
Book Design by Andrew Whitehead

For Rob

CHAPTER 1

"Margo, report to makeup."

The disembodied voice of Margo's stage manager crackled through the dressing room intercom. Margo glared at the white box on the wall, resenting its hold on her, then glanced in the mirror for one last wardrobe check. Her ass looked good in the tight jeans, and a quick tug on her T-shirt amped up her cleavage. Not bad for a curvy woman in her thirties. She tossed her bottle-red hair over one shoulder and breathed in the sweet earthy air of her dressing room. She'd turned her love of gardening into a successful show on the Contemporary Living Network, her ratings were blooming, and she'd just signed for another season.

So why wasn't she happy?

Her dressing room was an oasis. Lush palms burst like fountains from the exotic pots she'd brought back from her travels. Colorful orange and yellow nasturtiums, glowing in the streaming white sunlight, dripped from baskets. On her way past the large window, though, she squinted at the scene below: a parade of gas-guzzling SUVs parked on the black macadam that baked in the June sun and suffocated the earth throughout the industrial park. No, this was not exactly the serenity for which she was searching. She took in one last lungful of the fragrant flowers and strode out towards makeup.

"Hey, gorgeous," Peter said, as he always did, when Margo

entered the room. He was her personal makeup artist and expertly masked her flaws. He was far too handsome to be straight, though he was, and he was on the very short list of her male acquaintances with whom she had not slept.

"Thanks for the lies, babe." She plopped into the makeup chair. "Just cover that last shot of Tequila and I'll give you a nice blow job."

"Promises, promises." He held her face in his hands and bent down to inspect. He studied her dark green eyes then turned her head to the right and left. "Looks like there was a little red wine to go with that Tequila."

Margo smiled. "You're good. Can you fix it, doc?"

"My powers can vanquish any alcohol." He picked through the rainbow of shadows and lipsticks and blushes on the brightly lit makeup table behind him. Each time he held a color against Margo's skin he shook his head. Finally, he put an emerald green liner to one side.

"Looks like another green day." He smoothed a creamy light beige foundation over her face and picked up the eye pencil. "Okay, look up." Margo turned her eyes to the ceiling. "So, who was the latest victim?"

"Wouldn't you like all the nasty details?"

"Of course. My sheets have been a little too clean lately. I could use some vicarious smut. Close."

Margo shut her eyes and felt the pressure of the pencil pulling against her lid. "Just some summer intern. He goes back to his safe little college bubble next week."

"A college boy? Surely you can find a better one-nighter than that. Open."

Margo opened her eyes and blinked against the bright lights. She stared at the shadowy stubble on Peter's upper lip as he leaned in to inspect his work. He picked up the green liner from the makeup table.

"Close."

"I don't need any more complications," she said as Peter tugged the liner against her eyelid. "This kid will go back to school, tell people he slept with me, no one will believe him, and he'll remember me fondly as that sexy older woman. Maybe I'll make it into his memoir."

"Or he'll start stalking you and you'll make it onto the evening news."

"Thanks."

"Open."

"I just think you need to be careful, that's all," he said, picking up a different shade of eye shadow from the table.

"If I wanted to get shit, I'd go visit my parents."

Peter shrugged. "Close."

Margo returned to darkness, enjoying the soft caress of the felt applicator against her eyelid. She knew Peter cared about her. She wasn't proud of her behavior, but she wasn't about to sit home alone either.

"I'm going on tour with my old band," she said, her eyes still closed. She could smell Peter's coffee on his warm breath—and the mint with which he'd tried to disguise it.

"Really? How does Warren feel about that?"

"I haven't exactly told him yet," she said.

"Open."

She squinted in the harsh fluorescent lights. "The tour doesn't start until after we wrap the season next week. I'll have to juggle a few publicity things, but I'll tell him it will be great for promoting the show. He should buy that."

Peter twisted around to grab a bottle of rose cream blush. He dotted some on his index finger and gently rubbed it against Margo's cheekbone.

"Warren is not a fan of interference," he said. "But from his hottie little garden princess, he might go for it."

"I can always dangle the wife card."

"I'd save that for a real emergency. Besides, I've heard Doris could care less who Warren flirts with as long as he brings home a big paycheck."

He dabbed on pressed powder then stepped aside so Margo could admire his artwork. He had done it again. He had transformed her face from hungover to Hollywood.

"You're a genius," she said.

"Hey, I didn't do this for free. I believe there was a wager on the table."

Margo stood and leaned in closer to the mirror. "And ruin this work of art? I don't think so." She smiled. "Maybe another time."

"Always." He winked.

She laughed. "Thanks. It's nice to have one normal person in my life."

He laughed too. "Glad you finally noticed."

Back in the gloom of the hallway she blinked and headed toward the glowing light at the end.

"Margo!" A deep voice boomed behind her and the ripe Tequila in her gut churned. Her executive producer's heavy footsteps and his familiar wheeze grew louder as he approached. Warren's odor—of coffee and cigarettes—was nearly as imposing as his large frame. He'd never have the courtesy to mask his breath with a mint.

"What's this crap about you going on some kind of music tour?" he said.

"Good morning to you, too, Warren." She smiled coolly.

He skipped a beat when he saw her face, as he always did. He was tall and eternally sweaty, his dark brown hair draping across his head in greasy slivers. He straightened. "Well? Carol tells me some guy left a message this morning about your old band going on tour? What's that about?"

"Word travels fast down these dank hallways."

"You can't leave. We haven't wrapped for the season and I still need you to shoot those publicity spots."

"We only have two more episodes to shoot. You know I won't leave you stranded. The tour doesn't start for two weeks. I'll make sure everything is set here before I go, and I'll do nothing but promote the show while I'm on the road."

He crossed his arms. "How do you plan to work gardening into a rock concert?"

"You'd be surprised. I'll only miss a few promo events. It'll be fine." She touched him gently on his shoulder. "I promise."

"You drive me crazy, you know that?" he said.

"But you've never seen ratings like the ones I bring you, right?"

"Don't be so sure of yourself, Margo. You might give one the impression of immodesty."

"I think they're waiting for me on the set."

"I did not say yes," he said.

"We'll talk about it later." She walked toward the outdoor set, feeling his eyes on her ass.

It was going to be so great to play with Broad Street again. There was just one small hitch—the rest of the band didn't know about it yet.

CHAPTER 2

Kit sat cross-legged, her back against the rough bark of the enormous maple tree and her old acoustic guitar propped in the crook of her leg. The umbrella of leaves broke the late morning sun into shadows, and she inhaled the sweet aroma of fresh-cut grass. Her ten-month-old daughter Elinor sat on the blanket next to her. Elinor turned her big dark eyes to her mother and waved her arms, pointing to the guitar. Kit smiled and nodded and began to strum. She wondered if Elinor would care, when she was old enough to notice, that her mother, with her tattoos and magenta-tinted hair, didn't look like the other well-dressed mommies at the park.

As she played, Kit drew the usual stares from the moneyed mothers and nannies. She didn't care. She missed the old days, playing bass guitar with her band, Broad Street. The name had been inspired by the busy street that slices through Center City Philadelphia but also by the irony of three "broads" contradicting the definition by rocking their original music. Her life hadn't evolved the way she'd expected it to since the band broke up eight years ago, but her daughter's smile always made things easier.

She started crooning an old Liz Phair song that always made her think of Margo, bulldozing her way through life to get what she wanted, Kit usually in her path. In the early years of the band Margo had taken charge as Kit tagged along. But as their friendship deepened the hierarchy had leveled, and at one point Kit even considered Margo her best friend.

Until it all fell apart.

Elinor bounced happily as Kit sang the familiar lyrics about not firing a loaded gun, the other person in the relationship taking back the power, "... *And then accused me of trying to fuck it up ...*"

Elinor clapped and wriggled in delight. Kit leaned over to kiss her chubby cheek, grateful for at least one remaining fan. She sat back again and closed her eyes, strumming softly until she found a slower song, one she'd written after the band broke up.

A shrill voice broke through her reverie. "*Excuse* me?"

Kit shaded her eyes with one hand and looked up. A blond in a designer tracksuit and heavy makeup, manicured hands on her hips, glared down at her.

"May I help you?" Kit asked.

"Do you really think that music is appropriate for children?"

"Probably not," Kit said.

The woman raised her perfectly plucked eyebrows. "Well. We're trying to enjoy a pleasant afternoon with our kids. We'd appreciate it if you played that somewhere else."

Kit glanced over at the huddle of moms and nannies glaring in her direction as the children, laughing and squealing, continued sliding, swinging, and digging. "The kids don't seem to mind," she said.

"That's because they don't know any better," the woman said. She looked down at Elinor. "It's up to us to teach them what's appropriate and what's not."

"Wow," Kit said. "That's a mighty Puritanical point of view for 2004."

The woman smiled icily. "I'm just expressing the opinions of our playgroup. Nothing personal."

Kit tilted her head and stared up at the woman. She was probably in her early thirties as well. And she was a mom. How could they be so different? Kit wanted the best for her daughter too. She couldn't believe that sharing the power of music with Elinor was harmful. But she didn't have the energy to fight.

She pulled her case over, put the guitar inside, and zipped it shut. "You're lucky," she said. "It's getting close to my daughter's naptime anyway."

The woman smiled. "Thank you. We appreciate it." She walked victoriously back to her posse.

Kit sighed. Would it kill them to invite her to join them? And what, she wondered, will happen when Elinor's older and wants to play with their children? She packed her daughter into the stroller with her diaper bag, swung her soft guitar case over her shoulder, and started walking back toward her house which, technically, was her dad's house. After enjoying moderate success with Broad Street and years of financial independence while working as a proofreader, her world had fallen apart when her mother died. She left the proof-reading job to move back home to take care of her aging father, and then discovered she was pregnant. She took a low-paying job at the American Society of Musicians and Performers thinking that would satisfy her love of music, but she was basically a coffee-fetching intern. She had become a single, motherless mom. Not the road she had planned at all.

She rounded the corner onto her street and breathed a sigh of relief when she saw her father's car wasn't in the driveway. She hurried inside, anxious to get Elinor down for a nap and maybe take one herself.

As she sat with Elinor in the old wooden rocking chair in the corner of the nursery, her daughter's eyes began to close and a familiar rush of emotion pulsed through her. How could her daughter, who meant so much to her, have been the result of an event that meant so little? It had been just another night of excess—too much to drink following too many empty nights.

"Kittimany!" Her father called from downstairs. "Where did you put the *Times Book Review*?"

Kit sighed. "Try the kitchen table!" she called. Elinor squirmed. "Shhh…" Kit whispered, willing her father to stay quiet so she and Elinor could nap.

"What?" he called back. Kit heard footsteps on the stairs, a dramatic cough accenting every other one.

Please don't come in, she thought. But the nursery door opened and Elinor startled and began to wail. Her father paused to take in the scene before him then turned and reached for the colorful mobile hanging over Elinor's crib.

"You should take this down," he said. "She can reach it now—
she might choke on the strings."

Kit lifted Elinor to her shoulder, shushing in her ear and
patting her back as she rocked. "Dad, can we have a minute? I'll help
you look for the *Book Review* when I'm done."

After her mother died, Kit had become her father's sole
companion. It wasn't supposed to be like this. Her mother had been
healthy, much younger than her father.

Elinor's cries quieted as Kit continued to rock and rub her
back. Her father opened his mouth to speak.

"Dad, please," she said. "I'll be down in a few minutes."

He reached over the crib and snapped the mobile from its
base. "I was just worried about Elinor, that's all," he said. He placed
the mobile on the floor with a groan and walked out of the room,
shutting the door behind him.

Kit cradled Elinor in her arms, grateful to see her eyes once
again drifting toward sleep, and hummed the chorus of an old Broad
Street song. It was definitely time for a change.

CHAPTER 3

Margo found the usual chaos on the outdoor set. Twenty-somethings clad in jeans and T-shirts toiled like hungry ants to create the illusion of a peaceful garden scene in a field of cameras, microphones, dollys, and lights. There was nothing in this garden that calmed Margo, so she reached into her purse for a cigarette.

"Jimmy, bring that box of purple flowers over here!" Amy, a young blond producer, shouted to an attractive, stubble-faced intern. Margo watched Jimmy glance around the set then reach down for a box of potted flowers.

"Not those, moron," Margo called. "The next box over!"

He looked back at her, flushed, and grabbed the right box. Margo smiled. They had been naked together in her bed just nine hours earlier.

Margo walked over to a silver-haired man standing behind a large camera shrouded by black metallic blinders. He was leaning over a script and making angry marks with a red pen.

"Hey, Gary," she said.

He jumped. "Jesus, Margo," he said. "Are you trying to kill me?"

"Impossible. Why are you trashing my script?"

"Because once again you've ignored my request for simplicity. This is television, sweetie, not a classroom."

"I'm sorry. Is it wrong to expect my viewers to have a few brain cells?"

"Yes. Men watch your show because they want to sleep with you. Women watch because they want to be you."

"A few may also want to sleep with me."

"Probably." Gary returned his attention to slashing long words from Margo's script.

"What about my mail? I actually get some semi-literate e-mail."

"Consider it foreplay."

Margo sighed and lifted her cigarette to her lips. The truth was, she didn't care about educating her viewers anymore. Few people understood what gardening meant to her. Certainly not her parents, who had been B-celebrities in the 1970s when their band Parallel's song, "Can't Fake that Smile," became a hit. Not her young lovers, who only saw her garden at night and after consuming too much alcohol. She thought Kit's mother Dana would have understood. She'd appreciated the escape a garden could offer.

She pushed the thought of Dana away and forced herself back to the moment. Jimmy was lifting tulips out of a cardboard flat and placing them wherever Julie pointed her finger.

"One more there," Julie commanded. "Oh, shit. Maybe that's too much. Margo! Can you come here for a second?"

Margo walked over to witness the disaster. Julie, who had come to the show—as most of them did—with a keen desire to be on camera and absolutely no experience, had mixed seasons and zones into a horrid horticultural orgy.

"What do you think?" Julie asked. "More red?"

"It depends," Margo said, inhaling. "Are you trying to create a murder scene or a postmodern ode to ruby?"

Julie ran her fingers through her long blond hair. "Is it that bad?"

Margo tapped her ash on the ground. "Yes." She turned and called to Jimmy, who sauntered over with a guilty smirk.

"Go grab those flats of yellow and white flowers over there and the one next to it with the purple flowers," Margo ordered.

"What's the holdup?" Gary bellowed from behind the camera.

"We can spare a few minutes for accuracy," Margo said.

Gary scowled and returned to the script.

When Jimmy returned with the plants Margo handed her cigarette to Julie and distributed pineapple flowers artfully among the sea of pink-purple Delosperma cooperi, creating a perfect balance of yellow and lavender. Julie stood watching the transformation, holding the burning cigarette like it was an M-80 that might explode at any moment.

"Can we start now, please?" Gary yelled. "The light is shifting."

Margo stood, hands on hips, surveying the improved backdrop. "Yes, Gary," she said. "Now we can start."

"Okay!" Gary shouted. "Everyone in position! Light Three, watch the shadows there on Margo's artwork. The yellow flowers are too hot. Two, you're going to need to check your white balance again."

As Gary continued to bark his commands, men and women scattered out of view of the cameras, leaving Margo alone in the center. As her eyes adjusted to the bright lights, she was slightly blinded to her surroundings. The commotion faded into a white noise of calm, and for a moment she could almost imagine serenity. A smile slipped onto her lips and a shadowy figure emerged from the light.

"Just have to cover a little shine," Peter said, waving a makeup brush in her direction. He dusted her cheek and the soft bristles tickled her skin. "There," he said. "Perfect."

Margo smiled, and he was gone.

"All right, Margo." Gary's voice boomed over the set. "Ready?"

Margo squinted toward Gary and the cameras and the scene took shape as her eyes adjusted. "Yep. Let's roll."

"Okay," Gary said. "This is Scene One for Episode Twelve. Everyone quiet!"

Margo watched Gary raise four fingers. "Four," he shouted, "three, two, and ..." He mouthed the "one" silently and pointed to Margo.

"Good morning, everyone." She smiled, imagining the thousands of viewers on the other side of that black window. Her eyes danced across the teleprompter. "Welcome back to *Guerilla Gardening*, where our goal is to eliminate urban blight one plant at a time."

    "I'm very excited about today's show," she said not quite
batting her eyes. "Today I'm going to introduce you to one of the
best-kept secrets in urban gardening." She leaned down toward the
bed of flowers at her feet, aware of the plunging neckline of her tight
black T-shirt. The camera rolled toward her. "This little guy," she
said, picking up one of the small plants and holding it at breast level,
"is a beautiful specimen with an unfortunate name: Black Scallop
Bugleweed. The dark green leaves and purple flowers make this a nice
alternative to pedestrian marigolds." She turned her eyes toward the
camera window like she was looking at a lover. "It may look delicate,
but this hearty plant is ideal for turning those ugly, bite-sized squares
of weedy dirt found in city sidewalks into stunning pockets of beauty.
It only requires proper attention. I'll show you everything you need to
know to make it grow."

✳ ✳ ✳

    After filming was over, Margo ignored the usual staff praise
and walked quickly to her dressing room, where she could enjoy a
cigarette in silence and muster the courage to call Kit, her old band
mate. She hadn't talked to Kit in over two years. When they'd formed
Broad Street back in 1994, they were still in the post-adolescence
of their early twenties—blindly partying, complaining about men,
holding each other up during the tough times. But after two years
of broken promises from producers and record labels, Margo had
decided she'd be better off leaving the band behind and had managed
to blend her secret passion for gardening with her love of the
spotlight. She'd been surprised by how easy it had been to sell her idea
of a "Guerrilla Gardening" show. Through the band, she'd made just
the right entertainment contacts to get a meeting with Warren, one
of the producers of the two-year-old Contemporary Living Network.
She wore a tight dress, turned her charm up to 10, and convinced
Warren he'd be crazy not to pick up a gardening show that, thanks
to the unique "guerrilla" twist, would be watched by housewives and
hipsters alike.

    Though Kit had been pissed off when Margo told her she
was leaving the band, she had eventually cooled down and they'd

remained friendly—until a couple of years ago, when Kit had stopped talking to her.

And now it was 2004, and Margo hadn't touched her guitar since the band broke up, and here she was sitting in the dressing room that she'd always wanted, thinking it would be a good idea to take this tour offer.

She didn't know why, but she knew she wanted to do it. Maybe she wanted to relive her twenties or rekindle a friendship that she missed—or maybe she just wanted to prove she could do it. It didn't matter. She had told the tour's manager she would make it happen.

She didn't have Kit's number, but she decided to start by calling her old home number. She could ask Kit's dad and catch up with him. She'd always liked Pierce.

She was surprised when Kit herself picked up.

"Hey, stranger!" Margo said, as if they'd parted as friends. "It's Margo." She pulled another cigarette from her pack and began tapping it against her dressing room table.

There was a moment of silence. "Uh, wow," Kit stammered. "Margo. How are you?"

"Oh my god," Margo said, pausing to light the cigarette. "I'm so busy with the show, I barely have time to take a crap. But, hey, I shouldn't complain. Ratings are good, even though my producer wants me to wear even tighter clothes. I'm sure my cleavage draws a few perverts, but come on, how many guys are really into gardening?" She cut herself off and took a deep drag. What kind of nonsense was spewing out of her mouth?

There was another silence.

"Anyway," Margo continued, "enough bitching. Listen, The Venturas' manager called me. He's putting together a Women of Rock Tour with some big names like Sam Starr. For some reason he thinks Broad Street would make a good addition to the bill. I'm sure he's exploiting me because of my show, but who cares? You up for it?"

She leaned back and sucked on her cigarette, bouncing her crossed leg impatiently. She imagined Kit sitting on one of the mismatched chairs in the hallway, the old landline pressed against her ear. What did Kit have to think about? Margo was offering her the chance to relive the rock dream she'd always said she wanted so badly.

"This is a little sudden," Kit said finally.

Margo exhaled. "The thing is, I really need to get back to this guy today."

"Today?" Kit said. "Jesus, Margo. You haven't even given me details."

Margo heard a small, choked gurgle in the background. "What's that noise?" she asked.

"My daughter. She's sleeping, but the baby monitor's right here."

Margo choked out some used smoke. "Your *daughter*? When did that happen?"

"Almost a year ago."

"Are you married?" Margo asked.

"Nope," Kit said. "It's just me and Elinor."

"Hmm. Well, good for you. Anyway, it's a three-week tour and it starts in a couple weeks, on the seventeenth. I know it's short notice, but they had an opening and The Venturas recommended us. It starts in Camden and then heads up the east coast and out west."

"Two *weeks*?" Kit said. "How am I supposed to get organized in two weeks? And we haven't even played together in like ..." Kit paused. "Has it really been eight years?"

"Look," Margo said, "I'm just passing along the message. If you don't want to do it, I'm sure there are plenty of other bands who will."

"Well, okay," Kit said flatly. "It's weird. I was just thinking about the band today. Why don't you get back to me when you have more details?"

Margo took an impatient drag on her cigarette. "Those are the details. I set up a practice tomorrow night at The Tritone, seven o'clock. I'm still in Philly, so that's about a twenty-minute drive for both of us. Are you in?"

There was another long pause. The gurgling sounds in the background grew louder. "I guess so," Kit said.

"Great. I'll see you then." Margo hung up and ground out her cigarette in a fit of frustration that felt familiar. Kit annoyed her. She'd never met anyone more determined to be self-destructive. But part of her missed the Broad Street days, when she and Kit would sit for hours smoking cigarettes, washing down cool beers, and sharing intimate details of their lives. How alike they had been. How different they had been.

The next call she needed to make was to Keri, Broad Street's drummer. Keri had also found some post-band success, with the publication of her graphic novel about a girl who comes out in high school. Margo had seen Keri and her partner Leah occasionally over the years. She scrolled through her phone's address book until she found her number.

"Hey, Keri," she said. "Blast from the past here—it's Margo. Sorry it's been so long since we've talked."

"Holy shit!" Keri said. "The garden princess herself! How are ya?"

"Oh, can't complain. The show's fun, got a nice place, blah blah blah. You know, grown-up stuff."

"Leah and I get a big kick out of your show. Nice outfits!"

"Oh, you know, we do what we can to keep up the ratings. Unfortunately not all my fans are dedicated gardeners. Listen, I'm sure you're busy so I'll cut to the chase. I got a call yesterday from The Venturas' manager, and he actually thinks people might want to see Broad Street again."

"What do you mean?"

"The Venturas are on the bill of this chick rock tour, and they invited us to tag along. Have you heard about the Women of Rock Tour?"

"Yeah! It's supposed to have an awesome lineup. That's the tour? Isn't that starting soon?"

"Yep—in two weeks. I know it's a crazy idea, but it would be fun. What do you think?"

Keri chuckled. "I'm a little rusty, to say the least. I haven't touched the drums in years."

"I hear it's like riding a bicycle."

"It's tempting. I'm on deadline for the next book, but maybe I could work around the schedule. I'd have to talk to Leah, too. What's the plan?"

Margo gave her the few details she had.

"What does Kit think?" Keri asked.

"Well, she seems into it, but to be honest I'm a little worried. Did you know she has a baby?"

"Yeah, Elinor's adorable. We get together every once in a while for lunch."

Jealousy twisted Margo's stomach. Why hadn't they ever called her? Her excitement soured and she lit another cigarette. "Yeah, well, anyway," she said. "Can you make practice tomorrow night?"

"It does sound like fun. Let me make a few calls and get back to you."

Margo stood at her window, watching the SUVs baking in the sun, her cigarette smoldering between her fingers. Did Keri even know that Kit had completely cut Margo out of her life? She wondered if it was too early for a drink.

CHAPTER 4

When Elinor woke up from her nap Kit rocked her again in the old wooden chair. Her mother had probably held Kit in this very chair. Had she felt this same affection? Kit rubbed her daughter's tiny hand between her thumb and fingers, the skin as soft and damp as a ripe nectarine. She missed her mother even more since Elinor was born. When she died Kit had been in New York for a long weekend, mostly drunk and sleeping with a guitar player she'd met through some mutual friends in the Philly music scene. It took her sister Nikki two days to find her to tell her about her mother's death. It took Kit almost two months to learn that Elinor was on the way. She knew having a baby would finish her dream of becoming a musician, but she couldn't bear the idea of losing another life.

Kit frowned and saw her daughter's smile fade. "It's all right, sweetie," she said softly. "I'm just crazy about you, that's all."

She sat Elinor on the edge of her lap and kissed her on the forehead. She had a tour to think about now. A national tour with real musicians—and she was invited. Elinor giggled as Kit bounced her on her knee.

"Kittimany!" her father called up the stairs. "Are you coming down?"

Elinor reached out and touched Kit's cheek.

"I know, sweetie." She sighed. "He's a pain in the ass. What do you think—should we bump him off and live off the pension?"

Elinor grabbed Kit's nose and pulled.

"You're right. That's not nice. Let's go see what the old guy wants."

The house still held the scent of Kit's childhood—cool and musty with the slightest hint of cinnamon from her mother's perfume. She breathed it in as she descended the stairs with Elinor in her arms. She hoped the smell never faded. In the living room, home to a potpourri of furniture including mismatched plaid love seats and an overstuffed chair, the coffee table was littered with newspapers, New Yorkers, and half-read fiction. Dusted light spilled through the windows and onto the emerald green walls, illuminating colorful abstract prints from neighborhood artists.

Her father sat in a faded armchair, the *New York Times Book Review* in his lap. He had been passionate about his work as an English professor, devouring literature like candy. Without students to impress, Kit thought he seemed bored. He had been twelve years older than Kit's mother and used to love grumbling about his decaying body while Dana cared for him and also nursed her other love, her garden. Her intelligent planting was still evident in the thriving garden of seasonal flowers. Kit did her best to maintain it, but knew she didn't have her mother's touch.

Seeing Elinor, her father smiled and tossed the paper onto the coffee table.

"I see you found it," Kit said.

He removed the glasses from the end of his nose. "Hey, little girl," he said to Elinor. He grunted dramatically as he pushed himself out of the chair. "Want to read the paper with Papa?"

"She's more into pictures, Dad."

He reached out and took Elinor. "Come here, kid. You might learn something." He carried her to his chair and sat down, placing the paper on his lap. He turned a few pages and pointed.

"This book is about a love affair between a seventeen-year-old sheepherder and a beautiful trapper in the Idaho high country."

Kit groaned. "Riveting."

Elinor grabbed the page and burst into a high-pitched squeal.

"Seems like someone disagrees with you," her father said.

Kit watched her daughter nestle into the lap of the man she'd never considered a nestler.

"Who was on the phone?" he asked, flipping the page again.

"Margo."

"Really? How is she?"

"She's fine. You know she has that show on the Contemporary Living Network."

He stroked Elinor's hair. "Your mother would have liked that."

Kit thought about the sunny day of her mother's funeral. It was a memory that crept quietly through her life, interrupting her at unexpected moments. She didn't own this memory in the same way she remembered falling off her bike or kissng her first boyfriend. The funeral lived with her in a hazy, detached sort of way, like the smell of gardenias that lingers in a room long after the flowers die.

She remembered the numbness. Her mother had been there at home just days before, laughing and alive, and then she was lying in a casket and Kit couldn't believe it. Aneurysm, the doctors had said, but Kit couldn't grasp this idea of an invisible bullet shooting through her mother's brain without reason. They had all sat through the funeral—Kit and her father and Nikki—staring as if they were watching a bad movie that could be turned off if they only knew how. Kit had not yet known about the life growing inside of her, the daughter who would never know her grandmother.

That was the last time Kit had seen Margo.

She'd arrived in a snug black dress. All eyes were on her when she entered the room and Kit had stared too, relieved that her friend was there. She had forgiven Margo for snatching away her dream of music when she left Broad Street six years before, and they'd kept in touch over the years. They weren't as close as they'd been when they were in the band together, but she enjoyed reminiscing with Margo over the occasional lunch or beer.

Margo had rushed straight over to Kit, leaned in to give her a tight embrace, and then stood back to dab at her streaming mascara. "Oh, sweetie," she said between dramatic sobs. "This is so awful. You know, I loved her, too."

The staged tone of those words pierced Kit like a bee sting. Was Margo really going to turn the most painful moment of Kit's life into an opportunity to be center stage? Memories flooded through her—of her mother sitting in the garden with Margo for hours, hours that were taken away from Kit. She wanted that time back. She wanted her band back—it was the only thing that had ever made Kit feel special.

Kit realized at that moment that Margo would always be about Margo. Kit had been charmed into thinking Margo's proclamation of friendship was real. But as she stared at this theatrical spectacle before her—with her tight dress and bright red lipstick, her perfectly styled red hair matching freshly painted nails—a light clicked on for Kit. Margo had used her. She'd used her family. Who knew why? Maybe she was lonely. But when she was done with them, she would move on. Margo could not care less how her selfishness affected Kit or anyone else. Kit decided then that she'd have nothing more to do with her.

Margo had called a few times after the funeral, but Kit ignored her messages. Eventually, she stopped calling.

Kit took a deep breath, steadying herself for what she was about to tell her father. He was pointing to a photo in the paper with his right hand as he cradled his granddaughter in his left arm. Elinor smiled and touched the page.

"Margo wants to get the band back together," Kit said.

Her father leaned back and cleared his throat. Kit knew he was waiting for more, for some sort of explanation that she couldn't provide. She let the silence pass.

"Why?" he asked.

Kit was amazed by how much weight one syllable could hold. "Because we've been invited to join a national tour of some of the biggest female bands in the country," she said. "It could be a great opportunity."

Elinor crumpled a corner of the paper and pulled it toward her mouth.

"No, sweetie." He released the paper from her ink-stained hand and tossed the *Book Review* back onto the coffee table. Elinor redirected her attention to her grandfather's glasses, which she attempted to pull off.

"Sorry, Dad." Kit walked over to rescue him, but he stopped her.

"She's fine." He removed his glasses and gave them to Elinor, who held them up to the sunlight. Tiny rainbows blinked on the walls.

"I haven't worked it all out yet, obviously. Margo just told me about it. But I'll think of something. Maybe Nikki could come on tour with me and help with Elinor."

Even as the words fell from her mouth, Kit knew how ridiculous they sounded. Her perfect baby sister lived in a perfect suburb with her perfect husband and two children—a boy and a girl, just to keep things perfectly balanced. Her sister could hardly leave her kids behind, even in the care of her full-time Dominican nanny. Kit flushed slightly at the notion of even suggesting it.

Her father stroked Elinor's hair.

"Or I could go," he said.

Kit laughed. She didn't mean to, but the thought of her father accompanying her on a rock tour flashed through her mind with ferocious comedy.

Her father's hurt expression halted her giggle. For a moment it felt good, powerful even, but then a more familiar guilt overwhelmed her. "I'm sorry, Dad," she said.

"It's a ridiculous idea," he said. "The whole thing is ridiculous. Your life is different now, Kit. It's time you think about growing up. You have responsibilities."

"I know." She felt stupid for even thinking it might be possible to play with the band again. Before her father could resume his analysis of this obvious fact, she walked out to the vestibule and started sorting the pile of mail on the small table—bills, catalogs, credit card offers. There was one piece of personal mail, a handwritten scrawl addressed to her. She opened the envelope and pulled out a piece of torn notebook paper that smelled of smoke. As her eyes ran across the page, her entire body froze.

> *You can't keep her from me. Have you told her yet that her mother is a whore? Have you whispered in her tiny ear fairytales about how easily you spread your legs? You think I don't know, but I do. I have some very powerful friends, and lots of them aren't very nice. You of all people should know about that. You can't hide. I will always be close by, watching. It's only a matter of time before I bring her home to me.*

Kit stared, scanning and rescanning the words. Although she didn't recognize the handwriting, she knew it had to be Damien.

Memories of the middle-of-the-night calls, mysterious hang-ups. and heavy breathing on her old cell phone, the number she'd had changed a few months after her mother's death, crept back into her mind. But how would he know about Elinor? He'd been a one-night stand. Well, technically a two-night stand—a stupid knee-jerk reaction to another of her failed attempts to start a new band. Self-pity had driven her into Damien's bed (that and a few six-packs), and when she'd returned from New York to face her mother's death as well as the sober reality of what she'd done, she could hardly look her father in the eye.

"Did we get the new issue of *Philadelphia Stories*?" her father called.

Kit folded the note and stuffed it into the pocket of her jeans. "Nope," she said. "Just the usual junk."

CHAPTER 5

At The Tritone the next night, Margo looked at her watch again. It was after eight o'clock, and still no Kit. Even Keri, who didn't fluster easily, seemed impatient.

Keri looked much the same to Margo—straight dirty-blond hair, no makeup, plain but pretty. She wore the same faded jeans and a T-shirt that hung loosely over her small frame. The practice space hadn't changed much either. The same stale stench of cigarettes and body odor hung in the air, a battered drum kit sat in the corner on a riser, and an army of amps lined two walls. In another corner, a P.A. dotted with red and green lights glowed like a bizarre Christmas decoration. Beside that, a halogen light bloomed to the ceiling and a dark slow burn had formed above it. The moss-green carpeting was covered with brown stains and cigarette burns.

Although Margo had been forty-five minutes late, she had a legitimate excuse. Shooting had run longer than planned, then she had to go home and shower to wash off the heavy stage makeup and change into something more comfortable. All this took longer than usual because she hadn't seen these two women in a long time. She'd finally settled on a flattering pair of black jeans and tight red floral top. Then she had to apply the perfect amount of makeup so she looked natural but not naked. Her signature red lipstick was always the final touch, and after applying it she finally felt good enough about her reflection to leave.

But over an hour late was unacceptable.

* * *

Kit watched the clock hands creep slowly toward, then past, seven o'clock—the time she was supposed to be at the studio with her bass tuned, ready to rekindle her old life. Her sister was late, and each passing moment was elevating her blood pressure. She paced the living room, bouncing a confused Elinor on her hip. Her father sat reading the paper, shuffling pages as the radio reported myriad world crises. Each crackle of the newsprint grated on her nerves; each muffled gunshot from the radio made her heart race faster. She turned off the radio.

"Why don't you just go?" her father asked. "Elinor will be fine."

Kit looked at him. Why didn't she just go? It wasn't like her father would let Elinor crawl into the fireplace, or fall down the stairs, or fall prey to any of the other thousand hazardous scenarios Kit could imagine. But it was the letter that stopped her. Could her father really keep Elinor safe? Damien obviously had her address. It was ridiculous to even think of leaving the house.

But she wanted so badly to play again.

"I'll give her a few more minutes," Kit said.

At seven-thirty, Nikki finally arrived. She was calm and unflustered, her blond hair neatly bobbed, her casual jeans and blouse pressed and tidy.

"Hi Daddy," Nikki said, walking past Kit and Elinor to give him a kiss. "How are you?"

He closed his paper to survey the sisters. His face changed when Nikki entered the room; everything seemed lighter.

"Same old aches and pains." He smiled. "You're looking good. How are Robin and John?"

"They're terrific. John already has a little girlfriend in his playgroup."

Kit shifted Elinor onto her other hip, inhaling deeply in a vain attempt to calm her anxiety. She would be over an hour late. She imagined Margo and Keri staring at the silent bass rig, Margo lighting cigarette after cigarette as her anger escalated.

"You're late," Kit said abruptly.

Father and daughter broke from their Norman Rockwell moment and looked over at her.

"Your sister's been a little frantic waiting for you."

"I'm not 'frantic,' Dad," Kit said. "I just have a responsibility to be somewhere at a certain time. Nikki said she would help me out, and being this late doesn't help."

"I said I'd do my best," Nikki said, in the tone she normally reserved for her two-year-old. "I'm here now, so go to your band practice. Everything's fine."

She walked over and tickled Elinor's toes. "Hi sweetie," she said in a high-pitched voice. "Do you have a kiss for Aunt Nikki?"

Elinor turned to her mother for guidance.

"It's okay, honey," she said. "Mommy won't be gone long."

Nikki reached out for Elinor, who erupted into a wail. Kit took another deep breath. Who was she kidding? She was a parent now. How could she possibly go on tour?

"Come to Aunt Nikki, sweetie," Nikki continued, trying to pull Elinor from Kit's arms. "Mommy has to go be a rock star."

Kit glared at her sister. It wasn't that long ago that her neat blond hair had been bleached white, shaved slightly longer than peach fuzz. Her nose, eyebrows, and ears had sparkled with silver hoops, and her small frame had been encased in tight black outfits. She'd been a student at Philadelphia College of Art, learning to design websites for the masses. But, after she met David, that Nikki faded away and she began to live the kind of life she used to mock— suburban, married, wearing designer outfits. The day she bought the SUV, Kit knew she'd lost her.

Elinor howled.

"Give us a minute," Kit said. She carried Elinor across the hall into the darkened dining room and held her in a cool shaft of light that bled through the window.

"Shhh …" Kit whispered into her ear, pressing her skin against Elinor's damp cheek. She ran her hand over the huge oak table that filled most of the dark room. They'd shared so many good times at this table when her mother was alive. Her favorite was always Christmas dinner, when her mother would open their door to any stray friend or neighbor spending the holiday alone. This room held years of laughter sparked by wine, strong personalities, and stories. Now the room housed only shadows.

Kit swayed with Elinor in her arms. "I'm so sorry," she whispered. The phone rang in the kitchen and she heard footsteps and her father's muffled voice.

Nikki appeared in the doorway. "Why don't you let me take her?" she asked.

Elinor breathed in one last feeble sob, and they stood for a moment in the calm blanket of darkness.

"I have to tell you something," Kit said.

Nikki cocked her head. "You're pregnant again?"

Kit rolled her eyes. "Thanks, no. I've learned my lesson." She paused, peering down the hallway to make sure her father was still in the kitchen. "I got a letter from Damien."

"That whack job? What did he want?"

"He didn't sign it or anything, but I know it was from him. He threatened to take Elinor."

Nikki reached out to touch Elinor's little foot. "What? How does he even know about Elinor? Skip told me he never sees him anymore. He said Damien became kind of a recluse after he left the band and started that bizarre solo act."

"When did you see Skip?"

Even in the darkened room, Kit could see Nikki flush at the mention of her ex-boyfriend. Skip's unofficial title was "The Mayor." He knew everyone in the scene.

"I bumped into him at a Starbucks a few weeks ago. He looked like hell. He's definitely back on something again."

Kit shifted Elinor onto her other hip. "You didn't mention my situation, did you?"

Nikki shrugged. "I may have told him you had a kid. But how could he possibly connect that to Damien?"

Kit scowled at her little sister, fighting the urge to slap the smug expression off her face. "It wouldn't take a genius to put it together. I don't want Damien to have anything to do with Elinor."

"Kittimany!" their father called. "It's for you!"

"Coming!" Kit called. She put her hand on Nikki's arm. "You have to ask Skip what he told Damien. How would he even know where I live?"

Nikki bit her lip.

"What?" Kit said.

"Well," Nikki said. "I may have mentioned you were living back home again."

"Kittimany!" their father called.

Kit narrowed her eyes at Nikki and carried Elinor out to the kitchen.

"It's Margo," her father said, the phone pressed against his chest. "We're having a nice time catching up, but she wants to talk to you."

With Elinor on one hip reaching for the phone, Kit balanced the receiver on her opposite shoulder.

"Hey," she began. "I am so sorry. I've had a little family emer—"

"Are you coming?" Margo snapped.

Kit felt the old defenses click inside her. "Yes," she said. "I'm leaving right now. I just had to find a baby—"

"Just get here," Margo said. "Frank still runs this place and he's as big a dick as ever. He says he wants us out of here at nine, but I'm working on buttering him up for some more time."

Kit glanced at the clock. It was already quarter to eight. "I'll be there in twenty minutes," she said.

Back in the living room Nikki avoided Kit's glare. "What time will you be back?" she asked. "I told David I'd be home by ten."

"I should be home by ten, but you can leave after Elinor's asleep." Kit glanced at the clock again. "Which should be about now."

"Daddy says you're going on tour."

"We're talking about it."

"What do you plan to do with Elinor?"

"We're just talking about it. I appreciate your concern, and thank you for helping tonight. I have my phone, so call if you need anything. Okay? I'll see you soon."

"I can take her," her father said. He reached out for Elinor, who snuggled into her grandfather's arms.

"Thanks, Dad."

He smiled. "See? I'm not so horrible."

"I never said you were."

"Didn't you?"

Kit ignored him. "There's a bottle of milk in the fridge if you need it. I should be home by eleven."

She kissed her daughter, inhaling her powdery fragrance. She almost kissed her father too, but instead she grabbed her bass and the makeup case she used for accessories and walked out the door.

✽ ✽ ✽

Kit popped an old Broad Street CD in the car stereo. She rolled the window down and let the summer night wash over her, singing loudly and driving eighty-five miles an hour down I-95. She tried not to look as the minutes ticked away on the dashboard clock, but when she finally arrived at The Tritone it was twenty-five minutes past eight.

The studio hadn't changed at all. It was still a dumpy row house attached to a dumpy bar called Whiskey Dick's. But the bar had a new sign—instead of choppy neon letters, a troll of a man smiling crazily behind a fisted beer mug glowed against a yellow background. She assumed this was Whiskey Dick himself. On her way in she ducked into Dick's to buy an apology six-pack.

CHAPTER 6

At eight-thirty, Margo turned as the studio door opened and Kit walked in—tall and slender, her old tattered blue makeup case in one hand, her sticker-laden black bass case in the other, a brown bag tucked under one arm. She'd grown her wavy brown hair long and tinted it magenta. Margo was a little annoyed that she still appeared so slim, without the pregnancy paunch she'd expected. In fact, Kit's usually small chest appeared to have benefited from motherhood.

"I am so sorry," Kit said as she dropped her bass and makeup case by the corner bass rig. She walked over to give Keri a kiss on the cheek.

Margo refused to be ignored. "Hey, sweetie!" she said, giving Kit a quick embrace and air kiss. "You look amazing!"

Kit stood back and smiled.

"Don't worry about Frank," Margo said. "I totally kissed his scrawny ass. We have the space until eleven."

"That's great, thanks."

Margo watched Kit as she set up her bright pink bass, checking the strings to ensure each one was in tune, adjusting the EQ on the bass head until she found the sound she liked. They'd been through so much together. Margo had always thought the band was just one piece of their friendship, but when Kit cut her off after Dana died, Margo had come to realize that Kit really only cared about the band. Apparently she was just like the rest of sycophants in her life after all, using Margo for her own benefit.

"Okay, ready," Kit said. "Oh—I got a six-pack. Anyone want a beer?"

Margo wanted one desperately but couldn't bring herself to accept it. "No thanks. Atkins."

Kit looked stung.

"I'll take one," Keri said.

Kit pulled two bottles out of the bag and brought one to Keri behind the drums. Margo watched them, imagining the lunches they'd shared while she sat alone in her dressing room eating salad.

"I thought we'd try a few from the old set," she said. "'Ugly Men' is pretty simple. Let's start with that."

The others glanced at her, surprised. She knew she sounded dictatorial, but she was hurt. She had a right to snap.

"Whatever you want," Kit said. "I'll just need a little refresher."

"Ugly Men" was one of the first songs Margo and Kit wrote together. "Follow the rule of the EDGA chords," her rocker ex used to say, and she applied this theory abundantly to their songs.

"It starts in E," she said. "I'll run through it; you can jump in or wait until next time through. Keri, I'm sure you'll remember it."

Margo started strumming, and the wall of noise from the amp washed over her. The sharp metal strings felt like dull razor blades on her soft fingertips, but it was a good pain.

Keri picked up the beat a few measures in, and the instant energy sent a shiver down Margo's spine. This rite of passage, initiating her virgin fingertips to the cool slice of guitar strings, tripped a hazy memory of the first time Kit and Margo had played together in her living room. It seemed like a million years ago.

Just as Margo stepped to the microphone to sing the first line, Kit began to play. The low, punchy thud of the bass added another textural layer to the song.

"Never pick a man who's prettier than you are," she sang. "He can even be rich, can even drive a fancy car."

She repeated the line and saw Kit step to the microphone to sing her harmonies. As the words spilled from Margo's lips, enhanced by the effects of the vocal PA, she felt the notes mesh with Kit's vocals. Margo allowed herself a smile.

"Throw him right out if he's stealing all your hair care," they sang. "Or if you walk in the room, and he's trying on your underwear."

Margo felt the fine hairs on her arms tingle. It had been a long time since they'd played together, yet the connection was still there. She could see on their faces that she wasn't the only one feeling it.

When the song ended, the room fell into a startling silence.

"Maybe I will take one of those beers," she said to Kit.

"I'd say you deserve it," Kit said, pulling a bottle from the bag and handing it to her. "That felt really good."

"You guys sounded awesome." She pulled a cigarette from her pack. "Do you guys mind?"

Keri shook her head and Margo held the pack out to Kit.

"Um, no, thank—," she began, then stopped herself. "I mean, yeah, I'd love one. Thanks. If Mayor Street has his way we won't be able to smoke anywhere soon."

"That's ridiculous," Margo said. "I have my rights."

Kit took the cigarette and leaned forward so Margo could light it. She inhaled and blew out a small plume of gray smoke.

"Should we try 'Slander You'?" Margo said.

Keri and Kit exchanged glances and nodded.

"Slander You" started out strong. Margo began swaying her hips to the groove, enjoying the sexual energy of their primitive sound. But, as they neared the chorus, Keri began to play too fast. Margo barely had time to squeeze in the lyrics, which threw Kit off and caused her to search in vain for the right notes. Margo's mind went blank on the chords. The magic in the room disappeared as quickly as it had come.

The third time through the song, Margo called for a break. She was discouraged and once again questioned the wisdom of playing for a large crowd. The last thing she wanted to do was make a fool of herself.

"We'll get it," Keri said.

"Maybe," Margo said. "Let's come back to this. I have to pee anyway. I'll be back in a few minutes."

She took the last swig of her beer and walked out into the

dim, smelly hallway and up the creaky stairs to the bathroom. She paused to listen to another band rehearsing in the third-floor studio. Despite the layers of foam that padded the walls, the floor throbbed with an energetic bass. A female vocalist screeched loud, fast punk rock. Young. That was how it sounded. Young and angry and much cooler than Margo had been since she bought her condo. The idea of the tour stretched out before her like a long awkward exercise in humiliation. What was she trying to prove? She had success. She had money. What would driving in a cramped van with two women she barely knew anymore add to her life?

CHAPTER 7

Kit exhaled as soon as Margo closed the door behind her. She felt like she'd been holding her breath for thirty minutes. She'd forgotten how Margo controlled the emotional tone of a room—and how most people tolerated that control. She didn't like it. But when everything clicked during "Ugly Men" she'd almost forgotten her new role as ex-friend. When she stepped to the microphone and her voice blended with Margo's, she was transported back to a time when she was younger and out on her own, when she could stay out all night if she wanted—when Margo was her best friend.

Keri tuned her drums. Kit envied her pleasant oblivion.

"I thought that sounded pretty good," Keri said, clamping a triangular key onto her snare and twisting the lugs tighter. "We always had trouble with 'Slander You.' Maybe we should move onto an easier one before we get discouraged."

Kit glanced at the door. "Do you really think we can pull this off?" she whispered.

"Sure," Keri said.

"I can't believe they actually want us on the Women of Rock Tour with Sam Starr headlining," Kit said. "I don't think she's toured in what—maybe ten years? She was awesome when she used to open for the Sex Pistols."

"We'll be fine," Keri said, tapping each drum again to test the tone. "Is your dad going to watch Elinor while you're away?"

Kit pulled her cord out of the amp and pushed it into her tuner to check her strings. "Please, the man can barely take care of himself. I'm going to bring her along."

"Oh?"

Kit stopped, realizing how irresponsible this sounded. What would she do with a one-year-old on the road? Who would watch Elinor while the band practiced and played? And what if Damien found out she was on the tour? "I haven't worked it all out yet," she said. "I'm kind of looking for someone to come with me to help me take care of her."

Keri paused her drum tapping. "This might be a crazy thought, but Leah's probably coming along for part of the tour. Maybe she could help with Elinor?"

"Really?" The idea of an easy solution made her feel lighter, more hopeful.

"I mean," Keri continued, "I'd have to talk to her about it, but I know how much she loves Elinor. It would all depend on her work schedule."

The door opened and Margo paused to stare at their tête-à-tête. "Talking about me again?" she asked.

"Always," Kit answered. She forced a goodwill smile.

Keri rolled the drums to warm up, and Kit and Margo tuned again.

"How about 'Things Work Out for Me'?" Keri suggested. "That one always came together pretty easily."

Kit and Margo shrugged. Keri clicked off four, and Margo's guitar burst into life with loud strumming. Kit's fingers remembered the song before her brain did, dancing through the introductory progression as if she had played it just yesterday. She was amazed at how rote playing was sometimes, how songs became patterns rather than notes. Her fingers walked in diamonds or triangles or rectangles.

Margo stepped to the microphone to sing this punk fairytale about a woman in control. Her guitar squealed as she slid bar chords high on the fret. Kit attacked her strings with the pick, slamming only on the downbeat to increase intensity. When they arrived at the chorus, Kit leaned into the mic and sang harmonies. Again, her throat remembered the song's movement and the vocals blended through the large speakers over their heads.

The rest of the practice continued on this sonic roller coaster. Some songs were rough; most were better than they should have been. By eleven o'clock, Kit was exhausted.

They made idle chat about the next practice as they packed up their gear, but no one mentioned the tour.

The door opened and Frank walked in. He had the physique of an aging basketball player, and time had not been kind to him. His darkened skin was carved with the deep wrinkles of sun damage and his blond hair had aged to the color of old straw.

"Helloooooo ladies." His voice, which was deep and rich, had not changed. "Glad to see you finally made it, Kit! You're lucky Margo's such a persuasive person. Celebrity sure suits her."

Margo tossed him a bored smile. "It's good to be back," she said. "And thanks again for letting us stay late. How's next Thursday night looking—seven o'clock again?"

"For you, Margo," he replied, "anything."

"Thanks, Frank," she said. "You're a doll."

The three women carried their equipment down the stairs and into the neon yellow glow of the Whiskey Dick's sign. Keri gave them farewell pecks and walked to her car.

"Well," Kit said, "I guess I'll see you next week."

"Yeah," Margo said. She started towards her car then stopped, set her guitar case and bags down on the ground, and turned. "Do you want to get a drink?"

Kit wanted nothing more than to go home and crawl into bed for the few hours of sleep she could get before Elinor woke at five. "Sure," she said. "Let me call my dad."

Margo waited at the entrance to Whiskey Dick's while Kit pulled her phone from her makeup case and flipped it open. Her heart stopped when she saw she had a missed call from her father.

"Shit," she mumbled. Horrible scenarios rushed through her mind as she waited for him to answer. Something had happened to Elinor because her selfish mother had decided to play in a stupid rock band that no one gave a shit about anymore and left her with an old man who couldn't take care of himself, let alone a small infant. What was she thinking?

"Hello?" her father's sleepy voice answered.

"What's wrong?" She held her breath, fear constricting her lungs.

"What do you mean?"

She took a breath. This was a good sign. "Did you call?"

"No." He paused. "Oh wait, yes. I wanted to check on what time Elinor should get the bottle, but I just gave it to her before she went to bed."

"You gave it to her? Where was Nikki?"

"She went home. Elinor wouldn't go to her, so there was no point in making her stay. Everything's fine."

In Elinor's short life, Kit had never left her alone with her father. "What time did she go to bed?"

"She was asleep by nine. What time is it now?"

Kit felt a familiar pang of guilt. "It's after eleven. I was going to grab a drink with Margo. Would you be all right?"

"Don't you have to work tomorrow?"

"I'm not asking you to lecture me, Dad. I'm asking if you would be all right with Elinor. She rarely wakes up at night anymore."

"We'll be fine."

"Okay, thanks. See you in the morning."

Her father grunted and hung up and Kit slipped the phone back into her purse.

CHAPTER 8

Images of Dana's funeral, the last time she'd seen Kit, flashed through Margo's mind as she waited in the doorway of Whiskey Dick's. She remembered the eyes on her tight dress and the momentary guilt she'd felt for wearing it. But what had really hit her as she walked in was the fear of her own death. The crowded pews had made her life feel empty. How many people, she'd wondered, would attend her funeral?

She remembered spotting Kit with her sister, who Margo never liked, and poor Pierce. She'd walked directly to her friend, through the gauntlet of stares, to give Kit a hug. She'd felt overwhelmed by sadness and couldn't stop herself from sobbing. It was awkward and surreal, and as she felt Kit's warm breath against her shoulder she realized how badly she would miss Dana.

"You know, I loved her, too," she had said. For some reason Kit had tensed when she said this.

But now, two years later, Kit was walking over to her in the yellow haze of the buzzing Whiskey Dick's sign.

"All set," she said. "Just had to make sure the baby was all right."

"Great. Let's go see how scary the regular Dicks are."

Margo pulled the heavy door open with a loud creak and a haze of smoke escaped into the cool night air. The room glowed red, and a handful of large white men sat at a circular bar, hunched over pints of beer and smoking ashtrays.

"This place is like a time capsule," Margo said. "It looks exactly the same as it did eight years ago." She led the way to a booth with cracked red seats in the corner. "I'll go get us a couple of beers," she said.

As she stood at the bar near one of the heavyset regulars, she wasn't surprised to feel his eyes move to her chest. She waved to get the young female bartender's attention. The bleached blond was resting her elbows on the bar, leaning toward a stubbly customer. She ignored Margo, who took a deep breath and thumped her palm against the bar several times. The bartender gave her a dirty look.

"I just need a few beers," Margo shouted over the bad jukebox.

The bartender rolled her eyes and turned her attention back to the man in front of her. Margo stomped around the bar until she was standing in front of the woman. "I'm sorry," she said. "Do you work here?"

The woman glared. "For polite customers, sure."

"I just need two beers." She looked at the tap selection, disappointed. "I'll take two Yuenglings."

The woman took a long drag from her cigarette, raised her eyebrow at the man, and meandered toward the tap. Margo tapped her foot as the bartender slowly poured two beers, stopping very short of the top of the glasses. She slid them, sloshing, across the bar in Margo's direction. "Ten bucks," she said.

Margo pulled a ten from her wallet and slapped it on the bar without her usual big tip. She grabbed the glasses and headed back to the table. Kit was sitting stiffly, both hands folded on the sticky table.

"You get the next one," Margo said.

She slid into the booth, pulled a cigarette from her pack, then offered one to Kit. They both lit up and sipped their beers as they sat in awkward silence.

"Looks like the show is doing well," Kit said.

Margo looked down into her pint, feeling lonelier than ever. Here she was, with the woman who used to be her best friend, and she was having the same banal conversation she had with everyone who saw her show. "Yeah. The hours suck, but the money's good. I

can't complain. How about you? Are you still at that music society?"
God, Margo thought, *I'm even boring myself.*

"Yeah, it's all right. I'm only working part-time, so the hours aren't bad, but the money sucks."

"Hmm." Margo took another swig and realized she'd already reached the bottom.

"I'll get us two more," Kit said, gulping down the last of her foam and grabbing the two mugs.

Margo watched her walk directly to the bartender, smiling pleasantly. The bitch shot Kit her cold glance, but Kit remained smiling and the cool drained from the bartender's face as she filled two mugs to the top, angling them for minimal foam. Typical Kit, Margo thought, always so sappily gracious while the world tromps all over her. Then she saw the bartender pull out two shot glasses and fill them with Tequila. Kit was still smiling as she walked back to the table clutching the two mugs by their handles in one hand and the two shot glasses in the other.

"I don't get out much," she said. She lifted her shot glass. "How about it. A toast with our old favorite to the big reunion tour?"

Margo clinked her glass against Kit's. "May we all survive." The warm, earthy liquor burned her throat. She licked the residue from her lips and took a contrasting swallow of cold beer. The soothing kiss of alcohol tickled her senses.

"I thought we sounded pretty good tonight," Kit said. She took another cigarette from Margo and lit it, exhaling smoke into the room's thick haze.

"Yeah, but it feels like a really long time since I wanted to be a rock star," Margo said.

"What do you mean?"

"I mean I get up, I go to the studio, I go home, I go to sleep, then I get up and do it all over again." She left out the part where she also got drunk and screwed the latest interns.

"I don't have much of a life lately, either," Kit said. "I get up at five o'clock every morning. I'm thirty-two, living with my dad, and for music I mostly listen to two-minute songs about duckies."

"It must be hard," Margo said, impressed with her own sympathetic tone.

"My dad drives me crazy," Kit continued, taking another long swallow from her beer. "I know he means well, but we're just so on top of each other all the time. He and I were never that close anyway, so it's just—I don't know—weird."

Margo nodded. She'd always liked Pierce Greene. He was grumpy, pretentious, and anti-social, but he was also funny and self-deprecating. The first time she met him, he'd quizzed her on current literature. Kit had warned her about the likelihood of a pop quiz, so she'd studied that week's *New York Times Book Review* before her visit. Once she and Pierce crossed that hurdle, they were just two stubborn people who butted heads on topics from politics to music. But she knew his daughters never played these games.

"Maybe it'll be good for you to get away for a while," Margo said.

"Yeah. I'm just a little nervous, with Elinor and everything. I don't exactly have a plan for her yet."

Margo drummed her manicured nails on the sticky table. "Are you sure you're up for this, with the baby and all? I mean, maybe a band doesn't fit into your life anymore."

Kit set her mug down. Hard. "I want to do this tour. I've wanted to play again for a very long time."

Margo leaned back against the cold vinyl, folding her arms in front of her. "Are you implying that I'm responsible for you not playing?"

"It's a little hard to have a band with no lead singer."

Margo felt her blood pressure rising. "Well I'm here now. Do you think I need to do this tour? I'm used to five-star travel now, not dragging musical equipment around crappy venues."

Kit frowned. "Then why are you doing this tour? You hated your parents' band. You hated the fact that they wanted you to be a superstar. I don't know how many times you told me you just wanted to live in your little garden and be left alone. Right? Do you see any irony here?"

Margo felt like she'd been slapped in the face. Kit had never talked to her like this before. She forgot how lonely she was, how much she'd missed Kit's friendship. She saw only that the whole thing now seemed like a bad idea.

"I guess maybe I heard about your situation," she lied, "and I felt a little sorry for you."

Kit's narrowed her eyes. "Don't do that."

Margo flushed. "What?"

"This is about you, as usual. Don't act like you care about me or my life suddenly."

Two beer mugs clunking down on the table and the low, smoky voice of the bartender interrupted their standoff. "Courtesy of Tommy," she said, nodding her head toward a flannel-clad man at the bar. He smiled and tipped his Eagles cap.

Margo smiled and gave the man a small wave.

"Thanks," Kit said. She handed the bartender a dollar. The woman stuffed the bill into the front pocket of her jeans and wiggled back to the bar.

"I could have done that," Margo said.

"I can still afford a dollar, thanks." She pulled the fresh beers towards them.

"You know, you're really not being fair," Margo said. "You're the one who stopped returning my calls, in case you don't remember." She looked out the barred window next to their table. The tilted sidewalk was cracked and the neighborhood was dark except for a few lights that shone from the row homes across the street.

"I was—" Kit paused. "Busy."

"Oh right," Margo said. "I guess that explains it, then. Just blow me off, even though I stuck with you through every one of your crises and then I had to deal with my own shit alone."

"What shit?"

Margo drank deeply from the damp mug. "Nothing. Don't worry about it."

"You can tell me. What happened?" Kit's voice softened. This was the voice Margo remembered.

"Just a little female trouble." Her head was light from the drinks. She wanted Kit back, but she wasn't sure she was ready to use her deepest wound to achieve that goal.

"What kind of trouble?" Kit persisted.

It seemed like it had happened so long ago, but it stung as fresh as a new razor blade. There had been so much pain. And blood. The doctors had told her that the fibroids would make it difficult, if not impossible, to get pregnant—even after the embolization.

Margo sighed. "Nothing I couldn't handle."

"Okay, well." Kit gazed out the window. "I should've called you back. I'm sorry."

The words melted through the abrasive guitar of a bad Bob Seger song churning from the jukebox. Margo had wanted Kit to apologize for so long. She'd often thought about calling Kit during that time. She'd even fantasized that Kit would surprise her by showing up after the operation with a bottle of their favorite Tequila. The booze arrived, but it was delivered instead by the too-tan hands of her ridiculous mother, who couldn't manage a single comforting word. "Don't worry about it, honey," she'd said with an air kiss. "Babies do nothing but ruin your figure and suck up your free time." Margo knew she'd meant to be kind.

"Forget it," she said. "I'm sick of looking back. Let's have a toast to a fabulous, glitch-free tour."

She lifted her mug for a toast, a ghost of friendlier times. But when they clinked their glasses together the melodic note rang false in Margo's ears.

CHAPTER 9

Kit's tongue was a foul, metallic slug in her mouth and her brain pounded against her skull, threatening to shatter it into a thousand messy pieces.

The sky outside her window was just starting to lighten and Elinor was crying in the next room. She glanced at the clock. Five a.m.

She pushed herself to sitting, causing the few trickles of blood left in her head to swim quickly to her feet. She braced herself on the mattress until the dizziness subsided.

Elinor cried harder. Kit had almost forgotten the sensation of alcohol and nicotine pumping through her body. She tried to envision herself rising to her feet, picking up Elinor, carrying her down the stairs, feeding her mushy cereal. Her stomach lurched.

As she tortured herself with these thoughts, her father flashed past her open bedroom door, silent as a phantom.

"Shit," Kit mumbled as she stood up, wrapped herself in a robe, and followed him into Elinor's room. Her father held the pacified child in his arms. His white hair was pressed flat on one side; his faded blue pajamas were rumpled. Elinor snuggled against his chest, wisps of brown curls circling her pink forehead.

"Sorry, Dad," Kit said. As she reached out for Elinor he stepped away.

"You stink," he said.

It was true. Kit could smell the cigarette smoke in her hair, leaking from her very pores. "I'll shower after I feed her," she said.

"I think you should take one now. I'll give Elinor her breakfast."

Elinor peered at her mother from the safety of her grandfather's arms but she didn't reach out for her like she usually did.

Back in her quiet bedroom, Kit listened to her father's footsteps descending the creaky stairs. She stripped off her clothes and wrapped herself again in her robe, the tickle of terry cloth soft against her skin. In the bathroom, she twisted the shower to life and stepped under the massage of hot water. She closed her eyes and moved her face against the stream, the smoky evening disappearing into pools around her feet.

She and Margo used to spend many hours drinking and smoking and talking, but at the bar last night she'd waited in vain for those moments of connection.

When her skin began to prune from the hot water she washed the last of the conditioner out of her long hair. She turned the water off and smiled when she heard the silence of a happy baby downstairs.

She took her time getting ready for work. As a contract employee for ASMP—the American Society of Musicians and Performers—she coordinated their special events. The society was best known for hosting an annual award ceremony that rivaled the Grammy Awards. The rest of the year they held talent shows, fundraisers, contests—events that brought together rooms full of mediocre musicians looking for a big break that would never come. Kit thought she would enjoy being involved with music this way, but it depressed her. She knew that most of these young musicians, like her, would end up succumbing to financial reality. It was a cruel manifestation of supply and demand: there were far more musicians than there were fans to support them.

She examined the red veins that tadpoled out from her brown irises, but gone were the days when a bottle of Visine was part of her makeup kit. Even the foundation and blush couldn't hide the sallow ashen tone of her tired skin. At least no one at work would judge her—most of her coworkers were usually hungover. But they were ten years younger and had the energy to work through it.

In the kitchen, Elinor was in her highchair and her father was feeding her small spoonfuls of cereal.

"Thanks, Dad."

Elinor turned away from the spoon and smiled widely. "Ma, ma, ma, ma," she said, holding her arms toward Kit.

Kit kissed Elinor on the cheek and sat down next to her. She ran her fingers through her daughter's fine curls and thought of the note she'd received in the mail. It had to be Damien, and she was sure her sister had pointed him in her direction. She would have to take extra precautions to make sure Elinor was safe.

"What time did you get in last night?" her father asked.

Kit sighed. "Late."

"How did it go?"

"It was a little rocky, but I think we'll be all right," she lied.

"Hmm." He pulled the top news section out of the morning paper and shuffled through the pages. "Any thoughts yet on what to do with Elinor while you're away?"

"Yes, actually," she said. "Keri's girlfriend is coming on tour with us and said she would watch her for me." Kit stared at Elinor's tray, unable to meet the eyes of either her father or her daughter.

Her father said nothing.

"Well," she finally said, "I'm going to make some breakfast. Want some eggs?"

Breakfast was long and silent. Kit cooked, ate, and cleaned up while her father read the paper and Elinor tossed Cheerios onto the floor. As the clock ticked closer to the time she'd need to leave to drop Elinor off at daycare, Kit grew more nervous. Damien knew where she lived. Elinor should be safe at daycare, but what if he followed her?

On the way to the sink, her plate fell onto the ceramic tile floor and smashed into tiny pieces. Elinor started to cry.

"What's wrong with you?" her father snapped. He pushed his chair back and lifted Elinor from the highchair.

"Nothing, nothing." Kit bent down on her knees and picked up the shards with shaking hands.

"I think Mommy had a little too much to drink last night," her father said to Elinor, who was still wailing.

"Dad, please."

"We'll be in the other room."

Kit was grateful for the silence that followed. She knew she should take Elinor away, somewhere Damien couldn't find them, but where would she go? She had no money, and after Elinor arrived she'd lost touch with all of her friends. Nikki would drive her crazy, and Skip probably knew where she lived anyway. She just had to keep her daughter safe until they left on tour.

She picked up the last pieces and vacuumed the invisible shards with a Dust Buster to keep little bare feet safe. Bending over and exerting herself made her feel even queasier, but she washed her hands and went to the living room.

"Ready, sweetie?" she asked, mustering some fake cheerfulness.

"Why don't you just leave her here today?" her father asked.

"No." She took Elinor from her father's lap. "I have to pay the center whether she shows up or not. It's silly to make you do all the work."

"I don't mind."

"It's fine."

Kit slipped on Elinor's tiny black patent leather shoes and left.

The center, which was attached to a local convenience store, was marked only by an abstract line drawing of a sun. Kit liked the couple that ran New Dawn Daycare, despite the fact that they and their staff seemed trapped in the wrong decade.

Holly greeted them at the top of the stairs near the main playroom with a big smile. "Good morning!" she chirped. She wore a tie-dyed shirt and her long braids nearly reached her thick suede belt. "How's our little Elinor today?"

Elinor began to reach out for Holly's bright green beads then pulled her hand away and hid her face in Kit's neck.

"Did you forget me already?" Holly asked in a bright high-pitched tone. "It's only been a few days!" Holly had recently moved from full-time to part-time at the center, and Elinor missed her when she wasn't there.

"Sorry," Kit said. "Listen, Holly ..." She hesitated, glancing over her shoulder for no reason. "I got a strange letter the other day. I don't want to worry you, but I just want you to call me if you see anyone suspicious near here, or watching if you go to the playground."

A cloud of concern passed over Holly's sunny smile. "What's up?"

"It's probably nothing, but I wanted you to be aware—please just call me if you need anything, that's all."

"No problem."

"Okay," she said to Elinor. "I'm going to work now. I'll be back this afternoon. You'll have fun with Holly and your friends, I promise."

She handed her to Holly. Elinor immediately reached out for Kit. "I'll be back honey, I promise."

Elinor began to cry.

"Just go, Kit," Holly said. "She'll be fine in a few minutes."

"You have my cell phone number," she said. "Please call me if you need anything."

"I will," Holly said.

When Kit leaned in to kiss her, Elinor grabbed her hair. She untangled her daughter's small fingers. "I love you, honey. I'll see you later."

Every bone in her body wanted to turn back to her daughter's heart-wrenching sobs, which faded as she descended the stairs.

Back in the car she adjusted the rearview mirror so she could inspect her splotchy reflection. Not too good, she thought, but who cares? I'm a musician and a mother and have every right to look haggard once in awhile.

"The tour," she said aloud to no one as she drove to Center City Philadelphia. She repeated the word over and over like a mantra. She'd be away from here with her daughter. She'd expose her to music and creativity and artists. It will be great, she thought.

CHAPTER 10

Kit was always one of the first to arrive. The society had a diverse range of responsibilities, from lobbying for the rights of performers to tracking down illegal use of material and maintaining a database of artists, agents, and labels. Despite the legal slant to many of the society's functions, there were only two lawyers on staff. The bulk of the drudge work was handed out to freelancers like Kit—mostly musicians willing to make phone calls or photocopies all day in the hopes of connecting with someone who could help their cause. Kit had started the job with the same aspirations, only to learn that being an ASMP employee meant developing a lot of contacts with agents and labels with an aversion to being hounded by ASMP employees.

The buzzing of the fluorescent lights high over her head was accompanied by distant tinny speakers pounding a punk song Kit didn't recognize. The space was enormous, spanning an entire city block, and workspaces were sectioned off by alternative versions of office cubicles. Employees brought their own dividers—Japanese tri-fold screens, old shower curtains hung from closet rods, milk crates stuffed with CDs. As Kit walked to her corner, the heels of her boots echoed through the room.

Her space was simple. She had built a makeshift wall out of black soundproofing foam, onto which she had taped an old Broad

Street poster from her favorite show with The Venturas and a photo of Elinor. She touched her daughter's photo, then checked her phone. No calls. She fought the temptation to call the daycare center.

She sat down on her trash-picked office chair and opened her e-mail, watching as the many messages downloaded. Today's debacle was the Lehigh Valley Pennsylvania Star Search. She'd been having trouble finding enough decent bands interested in participating in the talent contest, despite the prize of a label connection. And she still hadn't found a place to host the event. The venues were either too big and expensive or too small and without sufficient sound and lighting. Her job today was to complete both tasks, which meant more phone calls to unwilling club owners. She glanced at her watch. Eight-thirty. She doubted they'd be more willing if she called them now.

She scrolled through her work e-mails first, looking for priority subjects and names. When she didn't find any clubs begging to take the gig, she switched over to her personal AOL account and was surprised to find a familiar name in an e-mail address—that of her ex-boyfriend Charlie O'Donnell.

> *Hey Kit!*
> *How are you? I tried calling your old number and it said it was disconnected. Are you still in Philly? Hope this note finds you.*
> *Charlie*

Kit stared at the note, baffled by his chipper tone. She had totally screwed Charlie, one of the nicest guys she'd ever met, let alone dated. When she first knew him he'd offered a sympathetic ear when she was dumped by one of his friends, and he was always there to watch her shows, or give her a ride home, or take her out for coffee. When they started dating, he was the kind of romantic she had only read about: flowers, love notes, candlelight. In appreciation of his kindness, she'd gone on a self-pitying guy-booze bender when Broad Street broke up. Her relationship with Charlie hadn't lasted much longer after that.

She poised her fingers over the keyboard to type a chipper note back and then hesitated. Why was he contacting her now? The timing of surprise notes seemed too much of a coincidence. Was the e-mail really from Charlie? Or had Damien found her e-mail address on one of the band's old demo tapes? She decided to try a question that might help her confirm the sender's identity. She clicked "reply" and began typing.

> *Hi stranger,*
> *It's a surprise to hear from you. Last I heard you were still*
> *playing roadie for that girl metal band. Are you back in the area?*
> *Kit*

She stared at the note. No emotion, no information, and maybe she'd be able to find out where he was. She hit "send."

She sighed, checked her silent phone again, and made the trek to the coffee machine. She walked past the many empty spaces littered with empty beer cans and half-eaten doughnuts. Her hungover stomach churned.

As she neared the coffeepot, the aroma of freshly brewed coffee greeted her. She couldn't detect the usual burning odor that indicated it had been left on from the night before. The music grew louder, and soon she was standing in front of the cubicle of Ronni Sakai, a petite, perky Japanese-American drummer who had been working at ASMP for a few months. Her space was plastered floor to ceiling with posters from her hard rock band, Cat's Meow. Ronni's sister was the lead singer of the band, and two large white guys with dreadlocks played the bass and guitar. Kit had instantly pegged Ronni as a hungry musician who would exploit any connection to get her band signed.

Ronni was sitting back in her chair, silver go-go boots propped up on the metal desk. She had the new issue of *Tunes* on her lap, and she was using the points of a pair of scissors to cut the face out of a band photo. She startled when she heard Kit's footsteps, nicking the tip of her finger.

"Oh, shit!" Ronni said, sucking on her finger. "I didn't know anyone else was here."

"Sorry," Kit said.

"I was just ..." Ronni looked down at the magazine and quickly closed it, tossing it onto the desk. "Reading. What's up?"

"What are you listening to?"

"Oh this?" Ronni stood and walked over to the CD player to

turn up the volume. Screeching guitars wailed over a high-pitched girl's voice. "We recorded this last weekend! This is just the rough mix, but I think it turned out pretty good." She looked thoughtfully past Kit's shoulder, bopping her head to her own drumming.

Kit agreed it was pretty good. A little rough, but it had a nice hook in the chorus. That bothered her.

"I'm going to get some coffee!" she shouted over the noise.

"Cool!" Ronni said, turning down the volume. "I'll come with."

She followed Kit to the back of the room. Skylights painted large squares of sunlight onto the break room area, which was cluttered with dirty tables and folding chairs. Kit pulled a Styrofoam cup from the stack and poured a cup of coffee, inhaling the welcome fumes of needed caffeine.

"So we played an awesome gig last weekend at the Northsix," Ronni said. "It was like totally packed with kids, and they were all into it. We played with this killer chick band from the UK. They totally kicked ass."

Kit thought of the Little People's music concert she'd attended with Elinor last weekend. The crowd, mostly under age three, had demanded endless choruses of Old MacDonald. "That's great," she mumbled into her coffee.

"Yeah, and we partied after with these girls from the UK 'til like four in the morning, and they said they might be able to get us on a UK tour with them next fall," Ronni said.

If she said "UK" one more time, Kit thought she might slap her. "That's good. My old band's going on the Women of Rock Tour. Should be kind of fun."

"Holy fuck! How did you get on that tour? I mean, you guys totally rocked in your day and all, but ..." Ronni paused. "I mean, wow, that's fucking awesome."

Kit stifled a satisfied grin. "Yeah, we're kind of tight with The Venturas, and they got us on the bill."

"Morning, ladies."

Kit turned to see her boss Deirdre, her dyed-blond hair pulled into a bun as tight as she was.

"Hey, Deirdre!" Ronni said. "Did you hear Kit's going on the Women of Rock Tour?"

Deirdre turned to Kit. "No, I hadn't heard. Do tell, Kit."

"Well, nothing's been finalized yet," Kit stammered, suddenly feeling extremely hungover. "I was going to talk to you about it once I had all the information."

"Why don't you come over and give me the information you have so far?" She poured herself a cup of coffee and walked toward her office, the only enclosed space in the large warehouse.

As Kit followed her boss she glanced back at Ronni, who mouthed "sorry" through a sheepish smirk.

* * *

A large gray metal desk and two chairs sat in the middle of Deirdre's office. A dark gray carpet covered the concrete warehouse floor and a fake potted plant sat in one corner. No pictures, no color, no personality.

Deirdre, seated behind the desk, motioned toward the empty chair across from her. Kit sat on the hard wooden seat, trying not to think about how dry her mouth felt.

"So," Deirdre began, folding her hands on the desk in front of her. "What's this about a tour?"

"Nothing's set in stone yet, but yes, my old band Broad Street has been asked to go on the Women of Rock Tour. I just found out about it."

"What an honor," Deirdre said. "That tour's supposed to have some big names on it."

"Yeah, it should be fun. But I'll definitely have these projects completed before I leave."

Deirdre's eyes narrowed. "Have you found a venue for the Lehigh Valley event yet?"

Kit felt beads of perspiration form under her arms. "Almost," she lied. "The Sterling Hotel looks very promising. I'm just ironing out a few details."

"Really? I talked to Jeff from the Sterling on Friday, and he said they didn't have a big enough P.A."

Kit's shirt was growing damp. She would maim for a large glass of ice water. "I have a lead on a rental. Really, Deirdre, you don't need to worry."

"Do I look worried?"

Kit said nothing.

"That tour starts in a few weeks, right?" Deirdre continued. "We should have had the Lehigh Valley event logistics completed last week. That means we should have found a venue, put out a call for entries to bands, placed ads in the local papers, and sent a blast of press releases." She ticked off the items on her fingers as she talked, then switched to her other hand. "We also need the fall calendar of events finalized, including locations for all of the events and some big names to promote. I'm counting on you, Kit, to make sure this all happens."

"No problem," Kit said, trying to sound convincing.

"You do know how many people would love to have your job, right?"

Kit nodded.

"And you also know how long I've been dealing with musicians who think their careers come first? One of the reasons I hired you was because you seemed past all that."

Kit was growing annoyed. Thirsty, tired, and annoyed. For almost a year, ever since Elinor was born, she'd spent every waking moment trying to please other people: Elinor, her father, Deirdre. "It's a three-week tour," she said. "It's a vacation, not a new career." Her heart was pumping faster. "I'm a mom now. I'm very aware of my obligations, and all I'm asking for is a little break. I have no intention of neglecting my responsibilities here."

Deirdre leaned back in her chair, crossing her arms in front of her. "Bring Jay in to help you on these jobs," she said.

Kit inhaled. "Fine."

She stood up and walked out of Deirdre's office, trying not to think about how losing this job might mean living at home forever.

CHAPTER 11

"Let me guess—Sambuca?"

Peter leaned close into Margo's face again, his warm, sweet breath drifting into her nostrils.

"You got it, Einstein," she snapped.

"Somebody got up on the wrong side of somebody's bed this morning."

"I'm not in the mood, Peter," she said. She looked past his shoulder then sighed. "Sorry. I'm just a little tired. I went out with Kit last night."

"Who's Kit?"

"She's the bass player in my band," she said. "She and I used to be friends, so it felt strange hanging with her again."

"Margo Bevelaqua has a girlfriend? Now I've heard everything."

Margo was surprised. She considered Peter one of her best friends, yet he was right. She'd never mentioned Kit to him. In fact, she told him very little about what was really important to her. Why was that?

"Amazing but true," she said.

"Sounds like there's a good story behind this one."

"Not really. We were young and stupid and kind of bonded when we both got dumped. Typical girly shit. But, I don't know. I really liked Kit. Now we have nothing in common. She's got a kid and she's living at home with her dad and working some half-assed job with a bunch of loser musicians trying to be the next big thing. I think she's hoping this tour will make her famous or something."

Peter selected two small jars and began swishing a makeup brush between the two. "So, you miss her?"

"I thought I did."

The door opened and Warren burst in, his face speckled with sweat. "The New York office just told us they're moving our time slot," he announced. He paced the room a few times, frantically, before collapsing onto a soft leopard couch. "This is bad."

Margo's show had always run on Saturday mornings. It was late enough for moms to have finished dressing and feeding their kids and perfect timing for hungover guys to nurse their swollen brains while watching an attractive woman feel up plants. The show had blossomed in that time slot while other similar home and garden shows had withered into cable oblivion.

Margo swiveled her chair to face Warren. "Where are they moving us?"

Warren pulled a crumpled tissue from his shirt pocket and swiped it across his forehead. "Sunday. One o'clock."

"Fuck!" she said. "Why?"

"Because they're assholes. Because our show is too good. Because we've managed to build a weekend audience and now the station wants to exploit our hard work and throw some half-assed fucking dog-grooming show in our time slot."

He pulled out a cigarette, put it between his chapped lips, and lit it.

Margo paced the room for a moment then held out her hand. "Give me one of those," she said. Warren pulled another cigarette from his pocket and she leaned in so he could light it. His eyes moved to her cleavage. She blocked his view with her free hand.

"Can we keep our minds on the problem at hand, please?" she asked. He blushed.

"I need one, too." Peter extended a hand, into which Warren reluctantly placed a cigarette.

The three were silent, slowly filling the room with smoke. This was bad. Margo knew she had good ratings for a cable show, but she could never compete with the network institution of the National Football League. Her female audience made up about the same percentage as other programs on the network, but it was the young male audience that pushed her show past the mediocre home improvement shows. Margo had planned to use these ratings, and the desirable commercial demographic of the prized eighteen- to thirty-four-year-old male buyer, to negotiate a new contract at the end of the next season.

"Who's getting my slot?" she asked.

"Kitty Miller." Warren sighed.

"That little slut from the Oxygen network? What is she, like sixteen?"

Warren shrugged.

"When does this go into effect?" she asked.

"Right away," Warren said, taking a long crackly drag. "They're starting to produce the promos now."

Margo crossed her arms. "What if I tell them I'll walk?"

Warren turned a skeptical gaze toward her. "Walk where? To one of those chick networks that pays half our salaries? I don't think so. Believe me, I'm not ready to go back to producing old broads in the kitchen." He paused. "If we're going to make it on Sunday after-noons we need to introduce you to a younger audience. Maybe we should send you out to the late-night talkies."

Margo had made several appearances on some of the daytime talk shows, mostly the ones where groups of women sat around on couches and ogled B-celebs. They were tiresome and inane, but Margo did them out of obligation.

"You mean like D.J. Hamilton?" she asked.

"Yeah." Warren pushed himself out of a slouch, his expression turning hopeful. "Yeah, of course. Football season doesn't last forever. And this band thing of yours could be good to get the word out, too."

"Okay," she said. "Who can help get me on one of the late nights?"

The three began to strategize. Warren listed key network bigwigs Margo needed to schmooze. She wrote down the names— each moniker ringing with the entitlement of old white male. Peter hovered over her, offering helpful weaknesses for each of the names. The CEO, Phil Goldstein, was a leg man; she should wear a short skirt for that meeting. Dick Somers, the owner of the network, considered himself a breast sommelier; a tight shirt ought to cinch that one. And Harry Thomas, the top producer of the home and garden shows, was a rare leftie who fought for the rights of women and minorities. Turtleneck and a modest skirt, Peter suggested.

"You'll start by listing the reasons to keep the show in its current time slot," Warren said. "Ratings, good ad revenue—I'll get the latest numbers for you. Give them some examples of other successful shows that have flopped once the networks started jerking their times around. I know these guys, though, and they'll probably stick to their guns. If you can't persuade them to change their minds, stress the importance of getting you onto the late-night talk shows."

"Should I mention the tour?" she asked. A small fire was starting to burn in her stomach as she realized the truth: she wanted this tour to be a break from the pressure of carrying a TV show. Peter, Warren, Gary, Jimmy, the clueless assistant producer—all of these people were counting on her for their livelihood. Until now, it had come relatively easily; she stood out from the graying women cracking eggs and the bland couples cheerfully driving nails into wood. Margo had taken her rock music persona into something as innocuous as a garden and made it work. But having the best weekend time slot didn't hurt. She began to wonder if she was up for the battle—or if she even wanted to fight.

"I'd hold off on mentioning the band for now," Warren said. He stood up. "That's some good banter for the talkies. You need to get started on this ASAP. I'll see who's in this morning, and you can meet with them after the shoot." He stubbed out his cigarette in an ashtray. "All right, finish putting on the paint, and I'll see you out there."

When the door closed behind Warren, Peter put his hand on the back of Margo's chair. "This sucks."

Margo pulled a few antacids out of the bottle in her purse and popped them in her mouth, crunching on the chalky sweetness. "Yes it does."

"How can I help?"

Margo sat down in the makeup chair. "Barbiturates might work. Got any?"

"Funny." He picked up his brush.

"I don't know, Peter," she said after a pause. "I wonder if my heart is even in this anymore. This whole thing with the band has brought back a lot of memories. I think I was happier back then, plodding along at my advertising job, playing music with people I liked. There wasn't any pressure."

"I hate to break this to you," Peter said, rubbing circles of pink blush on her cheeks, "but the more successful you are, the harder it is. Why do you think you get that fat paycheck? If it were easy, everyone would do it."

"If I'm so important, why can't I even get a normal date?"

Peter stepped back, scrutinizing his work. "Have you thought about letting your guard down a little?"

"What guard?" she snapped.

"Exactly."

"Oh shut up and make me beautiful."

CHAPTER 12

After the show wrapped, Margo met Warren back in her dressing room. He had printouts of graphs and pie charts that illustrated increases in advertising revenue and audience since Margo had taken over the Saturday slot two years earlier. He had charts showing how revenue for other shows had diminished after moving to less popular slots. Her first meeting would be with hippie Harry Thomas, the one she thought would be the most difficult to convince in her usual way. She scanned her wardrobe for conservative outfits and settled on a long gray skirt and lavender blouse.

"That's good," Warren said. Sweat soaked the collar of his shirt. Margo had never seen him so nervous. "You clear on what you need to do here?"

"Warren, chill. I'll be fine."

He started pacing, shuffling through the charts again. "I hope these are straightforward enough. I tried to dumb it down to pretty pictures for these guys, but you never know what sort of limited imagination you're dealing with. Do you think these are all right?"

"Leave the papers. Leave the room. I'll get changed, go upstairs to Harry's office, and save the day. Okay?"

"You can get away with that attitude with me, but please don't use it upstairs."

"I'll be fine. Goodbye."

After he left the room, Margo sighed. Could she save the day? Did she even want to? Part of her still craved the kind of attention she'd received as an only child, being packed along on road trips like a special suitcase, displayed like a trophy by her bragging parents. She'd been wired for performance, but she also resented its hold on her. With the band, there had been so much more: creating the songs, clicking musically with her friends, sharing common goals. With the show, all the responsibility was on her.

She tried to envision how her life could change without the show. She could resume relative anonymity, work a nine-to-five job, find a nice handy husband, buy a home in the woods where she could garden on weekends.

Oh hell, she thought. Who am I kidding? That will never be my life.

She buttoned the blouse up high, wiggled the skirt over her hips, and looked into the full-length mirror. *Not bad.* She wiped some excess liner from under her eyes with a tissue and replaced the red lipstick with a subtler rose. She picked up the stack of charts and headed upstairs.

* * *

Harry Thomas was not bad looking. In pictures she'd seen around the studio he looked like a generic businessman, but in person his features were softer. His dark brown eyes seemed kind; his salt-and-pepper hair flattered his tan face.

When she walked in, he stood up from behind his desk and offered his hand. She noticed his ring finger was bare.

"Miss Bevelaqua," he said in a low voice, "it's nice to finally meet you."

She shook his hand. "Likewise. I'm surprised I haven't seen you around the studio."

"They don't let me out much. Please, have a seat. I'm sure this occasion was inspired by our recent decision to move you to Sunday."

Margo sat down, crossed her legs, and placed the small pile of charts on her knee. She took a deep breath. "Yes, basically. I've worked very hard to develop a good Saturday morning audience, and I think a move to Sunday afternoons would be disastrous."

Harry leaned back in his chair. "Why?"

Margo glanced at the charts in her lap but realized this man might find them patronizing. She looked back into his dark eyes. "Because, as you know, my show does not have a typical home improvement audience. We keep it fun and fresh so that people other than housewives will watch it."

Harry raised his eyebrows. "The urban focus of your show is a nice twist, I admit. But I'm not sure it draws a significantly different audience than, say, Betty's show."

Betty Davenport was a plump British gal who hosted a late Saturday afternoon garden show that was as plain as milk. Margo was insulted by the comparison.

"I'm sorry, but I have to respectfully disagree with you there," she said. "Many of my viewers are young urban types who like my tips for making even the smallest square of dirt beautiful. I don't tell them to go plant some boring marigolds next to their stoops. I give them exotic taxa options that they won't find anywhere else."

"Taxa?"

"Sorry, plants," she said, feeling her cheeks grow warm. "You get my point, though. My show has a very different message from shows like Betty's. People think of it as the 'alternative' gardening show. My background is very different from Betty's, too, and I think my audience can relate to that background. My parents were pseudo pop stars, I played in a garage band for years, I didn't study formally—"

Harry leaned forward. "A band? That's interesting."

Hooked, Margo thought. "Yeah, it was an all-girl band. I wrote a lot of the songs, played guitar, sang." She hesitated, then decided to take the plunge. "We're actually heading out for the Women of Rock Tour in a couple of weeks while the show is on summer break."

Harry smiled, but Margo wasn't quite sure how to read it. He paused for an uncomfortable moment. "That tour's getting a lot of press," he said. "Just the kind of free publicity we could use to promote the new Sunday time slot."

Her moment of power was gone. She had tricked herself right into a corner. "It could also make the Saturday audience bigger," she tried.

"Sorry," he said, standing. "Unfortunately the wheels are already turning on that one. The first promo airs tonight."

Margo remained seated. "If you weren't willing to even hear me out, why meet with me?"

He smiled again. "I wanted to finally meet our garden princess. I have to say, I'm glad to see you're more than your wardrobe."

She remained seated for a few more moments, not sure if she'd just been insulted or complimented, then stood to leave. Harry extended his hand again, which Margo shook. His palm was soft and dry.

"I'll bring up this tour promotion idea at our meeting this afternoon. We'll get marketing on it right away. Maybe we can book a few late-night slots before the tour leaves."

Margo started to walk out, then turned. "Did I just totally blow that?" she asked.

"Not at all," he said. "I don't make time for many people."

CHAPTER 13

Kit was on time for Broad Street's practice the following Thursday. Her father had agreed to take Elinor over to Nikki's house while Kit was out and Kit felt safer, knowing her daughter was in a crowd. She and her father seemed to have come to a silent agreement that he would help take care of Elinor, and Kit found herself believing that she might actually pull this off.

Keri was at the studio warming up when Kit arrived. She listened outside the closed door for a few seconds, impressed again by Keri's solid drumming. She and Margo had been lucky to find her. Audiences loved to watch the petite blond thrashing wildly against the skins, her head bobbing enthusiastically. It was after Keri joined them that Broad Street started getting noticed—first by a local producer who recorded their CD, then by an independent label who wanted to send them on tour to promote the CD. That was when Margo decided that music wasn't in her life plan, so five thousand CDs sat in the Greene's basement.

She pushed the door open, and Keri paused mid-drum roll.

"Hey!" she said, finishing the roll with a crash of her high-hat cymbals.

"No Margo?" Kit asked.

"Not yet, but you know Margo. It's only seven o'clock. She still has a good half hour before her usual arrival time."

Kit popped her guitar case open and lifted her bass from the soft black cushiony casket. It had been custom-made for her by local guitar maker Chris DiPinto, the deep Pepto-Bismol pink accented by a silver glitter pick guard. She pulled a cord from her makeup case and pressed one end into the guitar, the other into a tuner.

"Hey," Keri said. "Good news. I talked to Leah about helping with Elinor, and she is totally into it. She already got off from work for the whole tour."

Kit looked up from her tuner. "Really? That's awesome!"

"Yeah, she's pretty great." Keri stood, spun the drum stool to make it higher, and sat back down. "Do we have any idea what the travel arrangements are?"

The door crashed open and Margo stormed in, guitar and peripherals in hand.

"I'm doing Hamilton next Tuesday," she said, walking toward her corner of the room. "Fucking D.J. Hamilton. Can you believe it?"

Kit stared at her in awe. How did Margo constantly manage to trump her own small victories?

"You're kidding!" Keri said.

"Would I make that up? The assholes upstairs are moving my show to Sunday afternoons, so I have to promote the new time. They had to pull a shitload of strings to get the appearance so soon. Who knew the Contemporary Living Network had that kind of cred?" Margo dropped her guitar case and lit a cigarette. "And, here's the best part—though this is only a very, very remote possibility." She paused. "They may actually want us to play."

Kit's heart skipped a beat. "Excuse me?"

"You heard me. I mentioned the tour, and they thought the band was a great hook. You know, little old garden gal rocks out, kinda thing."

"This is happening next Tuesday?" Kit asked. "Like, in five days?"

Margo plugged her guitar into her amp and strummed, the strings singing metallically through the speaker.

"I did mention we hadn't played in a while," she said, "and that we're basically a sloppy garage rock band, but they didn't mind. We wouldn't be the featured music act—it would be more like a novelty thing."

Kit laughed. The whole idea was surreal. The thought of being on the same stage as D.J. Hamilton was just too much to swallow. Still, she allowed herself to imagine the audience. Her father would see her on national television. Deirdre would see she was more than a glorified intern. Joe Phillips, who had asked her best friend to the prom instead of her, would see what he missed.

But Damien might see her, too. He would find out Broad Street was back and that they were going on tour.

"I guess we need to set up some more rehearsal time," Keri said.

"I'm pretty swamped right now," Margo said. "I've been going straight out for over a week. We're wrapping the season tomorrow. I can't even believe I'm here right now. We can focus on 'Ugly Men' tonight; that seems to be our strongest song. I'm going to crash this weekend—with the show on Tuesday and the tour starting a week from today I need to get some down time. We can get together again Monday night, but that's the best I can do."

Kit tried to envision Margo's life, what "going straight out" even meant to a celebrity with no baby, no elderly father, no responsibilities besides getting her makeup done and her cleavage pumped up so she could flirt in front of the camera and lean over to move some plants around. She tried to remember what "down time" was like. She wondered if Margo could have any idea what this chance with the tour and the band meant to Kit. If they weren't going to blow it, they needed more practice time. "So we only have two practices before we're on national television?" she asked.

"Before we might be on national television. All the more reason to get started," Margo said, turning on the vocal P.A.

"And the tour leaves a week from today?" Keri asked.

"Look," Margo said, "don't think I'm not nervous about this too. You guys have no idea the kind of pressure I'm under right now. If my show flops in this new Sunday time slot, there will be a lot of people out of work—including a few I actually care about. You two may not even be on the show Tuesday, but I definitely will. Personally, I can't wait to get this tour started so I can finally relax."

Kit stared at Margo, feeling again the ocean of difference between their worlds. "Fine," she said. "Let's play 'Ugly Men.'"

CHAPTER 14

When Margo arrived in her dressing room the next morning, a bouquet of yellow roses greeted her. She found a card trapped between two thorny stems.

> *Margo,*
> *I enjoyed our meeting yesterday. Good luck wrapping your*
> *season today. I'm sure you'll handle the move splendidly. — Harry*
> *PS I hope you don't find roses too pedestrian.*

Margo stared at the card, wondering why the top producer would take the time to dictate this message to a stranger at one of those horrible flower factories. She prided herself on knowing men, and she hadn't picked up on any sexual interest from Harry. He was attractive, but he was way too old. If he wanted a good lay in exchange for her show, he'd have to think again.

She did like his postscript; it implied some respect for her knowledge. Maybe she was too cynical. Maybe he really just enjoyed their meeting and was wishing her the best.

The door opened and Peter walked in.

"Thank God you're here," she said, handing him the card. "What do you make of this?"

Peter stared at the card. "Who's Harry?"

"Harry Thomas. Your boss. Warren's boss. Everybody's boss."

"Wow," he said. "What did you do to him?"

"I just met with him about the show, like we talked about. I asked him not to move it, he said no, and I left."

"You obviously made an impression."

"What do you think I should do?"

Peter sat down on Margo's vintage red chair. "That's a tricky one. Ignore it, and he could get pissed. We definitely don't need him pissed. A thank-you note would be too formal." He tapped the card on his knee. "I don't know. All the other power mongers up there are easy to read. Harry Thomas is a mystery. He's the one who fought to bring on Debbie Evans because he thought the station was too white. He's pretty liberal for an executive. He doesn't seem like your type."

Margo crossed her arms. "What does that mean?"

"Oh, sorry, Gloria Steinem. I forgot about your wicked political streak."

"My whole show is about taking a political stand against urban blight."

"Planting a few flowers around the city is noble, yes. Sleeping with interns, not so much."

"Peter!"

"Oh, stop. I'm just busting your chops. Here's what you do. Call the guy when you know he's not there." He glanced up at the clock. "Like now. No big shots show up before eleven. Leave a quick voicemail thanking him for the flowers, but don't imply you want a call back. Keep it short and sweet."

"Good idea."

Margo turned back to the flowers. How long had it been since someone sent her a sex-free gift? Her last real boyfriend had wanted to be a rock star. He had no time for romance. He was tall and gorgeous, with a cool veneer Margo used to find attractive. She even thought she'd been in love with the asshole.

"I'll call him later," she told Peter. "I'm not in the mood right now."

The final taping before summer break went smoothly. Margo flirted with the camera and coddled rare flowers and gushed about the incredible transformation guerilla gardening can bring to any tired neighborhood. The show would air with a montage of

Margo's favorite clips: Margo supervising the rogue landscaping of an abandoned dirt pile in Detroit, planting a vegetable garden with schoolchildren in Newark, hijacking a park in Des Moines to prevent it from being turned into the site of another supersized discount store. When Margo had produced these segments, and watched herself on the monitor, she'd been impressed with the confidence of this persona who taught people from a variety of backgrounds about the beauty of gardens, using scientific language with authority even though she was almost entirely self-taught. Margo had created this life she now owned, and she knew she should feel prouder of herself than she did.

When she returned to her dressing room, she picked up Harry's card and glanced at the clock. He'd probably be in his office now so she couldn't just leave a voicemail.

She picked up the phone, dialed the operator, and asked for the office of the big boss.

"Harry Thomas's office," a nasal female voice answered.

"Hi. This is Margo Bevelaqua. I wondered if ..." she hesitated. Would asking for him by his first name be too presumptuous? Oh hell, she thought, I'm taking this way too seriously. "Is Harry in?" she asked.

"Who's calling please?"

"Margo Bevelaqua."

"Just a moment, Ms. Bevelaqua. I'll see if he's available."

Margo was clicked into the station's annoying on-hold tirade of self-promotion. She heard the tail end of a segment hyping Jack and Jill, the perky home improvement couple.

"... does home improvement better than this couple next door," the woman's voice said smoothly into Margo's ear. "No home project is too big a hill to climb for this dynamic duo ..."

"Give me a fucking break," Margo said.

"Excuse me?" a male voice replied.

Margo's heart skipped a beat. "Whoops," she said. "Please tell me this isn't Harry."

"In the flesh."

Margo's mouth went dry and her palms grew damp. "Um, this is Margo Bevelaqua."

"Who else but our garden princess would invent such a

greeting?"

"I was sort of talking to someone else, sorry."

"I figured as much. How did it go today?"

Margo was confused, but calmed, by his familial tone. There was something sensual in the belly of his deep voice.

"Fine, thank you, and thank you for the flowers. They were ..." She paused. "Unexpected."

She flushed as the word left her lips. She thought of a thousand better words: nice, thoughtful, considerate, touching, romantic. Wait—maybe not romantic.

"I'm glad you liked them," Harry said. "I enjoyed meeting you yesterday."

Damn, he's cool, Margo thought. Too cool. She felt her usual defenses begin to rise.

"As did I," she said flatly. "And I appreciate the flowers— although keeping my Saturday time slot would be an even better gift."

"Nice try." He chuckled. "But you know my hands are tied there. I'm not worried about the change, and you shouldn't be either. People will follow you to Sunday, especially after they see you on Hamilton, and then on tour. You need to have a little faith."

"I'm an atheist." Margo knew she was pushing it, but she couldn't stop herself. She was now bothered by his low, sexy voice. It seemed too practiced. It was not what she had hoped when she allowed herself to feel a little giddy about the flowers. For a few naïve moments, Margo had seen herself at a real dinner with Harry, with real candles, and only minimal wine to take the edge off—not the usual shot-and-a-beer foreplay her partners required.

But instead of getting angry at Margo's snide remark, Harry laughed again. "I'm sure Warren lets you get away with that, but you should really be nicer to the man who signs your paychecks."

"You're right. Thanks for reminding me of my position." *What the hell are you doing, Margo?* She felt herself digging a deeper hole, the light of opportunity dimming above her head.

There was a pause on the other end of the line.

"I really am just kidding you, you know," Harry said.

Margo flushed. "I know. I'm sorry. I was just calling to thank you for the flowers. They were a nice surprise, really."

"I'm glad. I get the impression you don't surprise easily."

She curled the corner of her mouth into a soft smile.

"So," Harry continued, with the first hint of hesitation in his voice, "maybe I'll surprise you at one of your shows. Do they let old farts into those things, or is there an upper age limit?"

"I suspect my band will be increasing the median age significantly," Margo said, "but I still might be able to pull some strings to get you in."

"I'd like that," he said. Margo heard a distant knock and then the sound of a woman's voice and Harry's muffled reply. Then he was back. "Sorry," he said. "I have someone waiting. Good luck on Hamilton next week. I'm sure you'll be great."

"Thanks."

"I'll see you again soon. When you least expect it."

Margo smiled. "I look forward to that."

She hung up the phone, letting her hand rest for a moment against the plastic receiver. She felt lightheaded. Her whole body seemed lighter. She hadn't felt this way since her musician boyfriend first played a song for her late at night, before they knew about their unhappy future, when it was still just the two of them in his chilly apartment. They had sat in his tiny living room, drinking whiskey to fend off the cold. He'd strummed his guitar and sang in his sweet, smoky voice about a man falling in love. She had let the words blanket her, reason draining from her thoughts, ignoring her friends' warnings about this guy's reputation. She had allowed herself to fall into his world, never realizing how long that fall would sting.

There was a knock on her door and Peter popped his head in. "You coming to the wrap party?" he asked.

She released the phone and turned away from the flowers. "Yeah. I'll meet you there."

CHAPTER 15

Kit was in the middle of a very pleasant dream. She was playing in a dark, smoky club that was somehow in the living room of her old house in South Philly. She didn't recognize the song that was coming from her bass, but she felt it ooze through her hips. The guitarist in front of her was a man, and from the back he looked like her high-school boyfriend, but when he turned around she saw it was Charlie. He looked good, and she stepped forward to greet him with a kiss, but then his face melted into something darker, his hair grew long and tangled, and she could no longer see his face, but he had hold of her, stopped her from moving, and there was a cry from somewhere, the high-pitched cry of a baby she didn't know she had, and it grew louder and louder until the man was gone and she had to open her eyes.

Dusty pink light seeped through her window. She turned her head to the clock. Six thirty. Better than five, she thought, trying to convince her tired body that she was lucky to have this extra hour and a half of sleep. She pushed herself out of bed and rushed to make sure Elinor was okay.

Elinor was standing in her crib, sleep pressed into her cheeks. She reached out excitedly for her mother.

"Hi pumpkin," Kit said, scooping her into her arms. Elinor looked up into her face and began tugging at her nose.

"Thank you," she teased, "that's such a nice way to wake up."

She sat in the rocker and cuddled her daughter, enjoying the serenity of the still-sleeping house. She often thought of her mother during these moments. Every day brought small reminders of how much emotional space her mother had occupied. Kit wanted to be wrapped in the cinnamon-tinted embrace that had always melted her anxieties, even if only for a moment. She wanted her mother to teach her how to hold Elinor that same way.

From downstairs, the phone's loud ring sliced through the silence. Who would be calling so early on a Saturday? Even telemarketers wouldn't be so ambitious. She listened carefully as the phone stopped ringing and the answering machine clicked on. There was a pause as the outgoing message played, then she heard a woman's voice. It sounded a little like Margo, but Kit couldn't make out the words. She looked down at Elinor, who smiled contentedly. She knew she couldn't sprint to the phone in time to answer it. Her heart raced. This could not be good news.

She lifted her daughter to her shoulder and made her way down the stairs. Shifting Elinor to one hip, she played the message.

"Hey, Kit, it's me, Leah. Keri was in an accident. She's better now, but she did get banged up. Sorry I didn't call you sooner—yesterday was really hectic. We're at Jefferson, room 1218. I think you guys were supposed to get together this weekend, so I thought you should know. Give me a call on my cell phone if you want."

Kit felt guilty about her first thought: *Would Keri still be able to play?*

"Okay, honey," she said. "We're taking a ride to the city."

Kit left a note for her father and drove to Jefferson hospital. It didn't seem that long since she'd visited her father there after his heart attack. The doctor had scolded him for not taking better care of himself, her mother had been worried, and Kit and Nikki had done their best to reassure her that everything would be okay.

Kit pulled into the parking garage and bundled Elinor into her stroller. When they walked into room 1218, she stifled a gasp. Keri looked terrible. Her face was bruised and swollen, her right eye almost closed, and tiny scars sliced her cheeks and lips. Her arm was in a cast. Leah was lying next to Keri in the bright white bed.

Kit pushed the stroller into the room. "Oh my god," she said.

"What happened?"

"Some asshole just plowed into her," Leah said. "She was driving home from practice and a car came out of nowhere, hit her, and drove off." Tears formed in Leah's eyes as she squeezed Keri's hand. "I don't even want to think about how much worse it could have been."

Keri looked down at her cast and then up at Kit. "I'm so sorry." Her words slurred through swollen lips.

"For what?" Kit said. "Don't be ridiculous. Is it just a broken arm?"

"They think so," Leah said. "They're keeping her here for observation to make sure there are no internal injuries or concussion. The airbag really banged her up."

"I was really looking forward to this tour," Keri said, "and you were counting on Leah to help with Elinor—and then there's the Hamilton show." She paused, staring down at her bandaged arm. "This just sucks."

Elinor began to whimper and Kit lifted her out of the stroller. "There will be other opportunities," she said, trying to sound encouraging. "Tell me more about what happened."

"I don't know," Keri said. "It was so strange. After practice I loaded my stuff into the car and drove down that steep hill toward the traffic light. The light turned green and I began to turn right onto Leverington and then, all of the sudden, I saw headlights heading straight for the side of my car. That was the last thing I remember."

"Did anyone see what happened?" Kit asked.

Keri shook her head.

"There was a guy who'd been sitting on his stoop who said he saw the car pull out from an alley behind Whiskey Dick's," Leah said. "He just said it was a dark car with New York plates, but no one got the number or a decent description."

Kit's skin turned cold. It seemed impossible, but a terrible thought occurred to her. Could the driver possibly have been Damien? No, she thought. Even he wasn't that crazy. Was he?

"You and Margo should still do the tour," Keri was saying.

"What?" Kit said, still dazed by the idea that Damien might hurt her friend. "No, no, we can't do it without you."

Her mind raced. What if Damien had been following her?

Was he so angry that he'd try to hurt her, or worse? If he'd been watching her at practice, he could be anywhere. The idea seemed ridiculous. But still.

"At least if you do the tour you can get the word out about Broad Street," Keri continued. "We'd have a better chance of playing other tours, or recording again, or whatever. If you don't do this tour, that's probably it for Broad Street."

"I'll talk to Margo," Kit said, looking again at her battered drummer, "but I don't know how we'd find someone. First of all, no one rocks out like you."

"This is true," Keri said, trying to push her swollen face into a smile.

Elinor reached for some tubes that snaked out from Keri's arm and Kit pulled her away before she could cause any damage.

"Can I hold Elinor for a minute?" Leah asked.

Kit handed her to Leah, who began humming and bouncing, making Elinor giggle.

"Do you have any other friends who could tag along with you and keep an eye on Elinor?" Leah asked.

Kit shook her head. She'd always had lots of friends, but since becoming a mother her life had changed while their lives had not. She shook her head again as she thought of the offer from the one person who was still in her life in addition to her daughter—the offer from the last person she'd want to take on a rock tour.

Her father would embarrass her and invade her personal space and generally make her life miserable. The whole idea was ridiculous. But she needed to keep Elinor safe, and she knew her father would never let anything happen to her. On tour, she would be surrounded by people she knew, people who would protect her daughter. She had to at least consider the idea.

CHAPTER 16

Margo was uncharacteristically perky for a Saturday morning. She'd made only a polite appearance at the wrap party, hoping that Harry might make a surprise entrance. He didn't, and after an hour or so of watching her coworkers get stumbling drunk, she slipped out. She had hazy memories of the wrap party last year, and she'd awoken the next morning with an unattractive young grip.

But this morning she woke up alone, refreshed, feeling cleaner than she had for some time. She walked out to the kitchen in her silk robe and leopard slippers and ground fresh coffee beans for her extra-strong brew. She sat at her cherry-red 1950s Formica table and breathed in the aroma of the coffee. She felt slightly sad about the end of another season, but not as sad as she had been last year, when she'd had nothing to occupy the large void of time that had stretched before her. She'd done some traveling, alone, and made a few tedious visits to her parents at their new home in Boca Raton. Her mother's eternally tan skin had taken on the texture of a worn handbag in her new sunny environment, and her father's inner tourist had emerged with a new floral wardrobe. Margo was mortified by them, and she had been since they dragged her on tour as a child. They always seemed louder and less civilized—not only than other parents she knew, but also than the other musicians who toured with them. Even as a small child, she'd understood at some level that they had no self-awareness, and as she grew up she became more convinced that their sole purpose, even before she was born, was to humiliate her.

They loved to tell the story—loudly and in public—of how she'd been conceived in the back of Gary Puckett's van on a night they opened for him in Brooklyn. They took a hiatus from the tour when her mother's water broke onstage in Kansas City, Missouri, and rested just long enough to get Margo acclimated in a small apartment in Downingtown, Pennsylvania. Four months later they were back on the road, passing their daughter off to odd roadies, musicians, and acquaintances with no discernible parenting skills.

Margo poured herself a cup of coffee, grabbed an Atkins bar from the fridge, and sat back down with a *People* magazine. She was on her second cup of coffee when the phone rang.

Kit's voice echoed, as if she were in a windy tunnel. "Margo, I have some bad news. Keri had an accident. She's basically okay, but she broke her arm."

Margo sat down. "What?" No Keri. No Hamilton performance. No tour. No break from the mundane days of her off-season life.

"Keri broke her arm," Kit said again, more loudly. "She's okay. She's still at Jefferson, but they expect she'll be released soon. Listen, I have to talk to you about something. Is it okay to stop by?"

Margo glanced around her messy kitchen and shrugged. "I guess so."

She gave her the address, and about fifteen minutes later the doorbell rang.

When she opened the door she found herself face to face with a small girl wrapped around Kit's hip. She didn't look much like her mother. Kit's skin was darker, slightly olive, and her daughter had fair skin and light brown curls. But she had Kit's dark brown eyes, and Margo caught herself shaking off the odd sensation of both of them staring at her.

"Hey," she said, and stepped out of the doorway. "Excuse the chaos—I haven't had much time to tidy in the last few weeks. The show's been crazy, but we wrapped yesterday, thank god."

Kit stepped into the vestibule, looking uncomfortable.

"Come on in." Margo gestured toward her living room. "What's up?" she asked as she cleared some magazines off the sofa.

"This is Elinor, by the way," Kit said.

"Oh, yeah, I figured that. Hi, kid." Margo sat down with her coffee. "What's going on? How's Keri?"

Kit tried to put Elinor down on the floor, but she whimpered, so Kit picked her back up and sat with her on a chair.

"I have a huge favor to ask," Kit said.

Margo sighed. She didn't like doing favors. "Yes?"

"I have a situation," Kit stammered. "I got this letter, and …" Her words caught in her throat.

Margo waited to see how this was going to affect her. "Go ahead—what happened?" she asked.

"It's Elinor's father, actually. I'm pretty sure anyway. I got this letter in the mail the other day threatening to take Elinor away." She paused to inhale a sob. "It's all so screwed up. I mean, I never thought he'd find out about her, and that was fine with me because he's crazy, or at least neurotic, and I thought I could handle everything myself, but now with the tour, and Keri breaking her arm, I don't know what to do."

"What do you want me to do?" Margo asked.

Kit turned her damp eyes toward her, the tinier version in her lap looking hopefully toward Margo too.

"Is there any way we could stay here, just until the tour? Until I figure out some options?"

Margo valued her time alone almost as much as money. "I don't know, Kit," she said. "This place is hardly baby-friendly. Don't you have a relative or someone else you can go to?"

Kit wiped her eyes with her sleeve then wrapped her arm around her daughter. "I don't have anyone. This guy knows where my sister lives, and he knows where I live, and it's pathetic, but I've lost touch with everyone. I know this is a lot to ask, but …" She paused and took a deep breath. "I think he may have been responsible for Keri's accident."

"What?"

"Leah told me witnesses saw a car with New York plates. That's where he's from."

Margo leaned forward. "Kit, you need to go to the police."

"With what? I have an anonymous letter and a hit-and-run with no evidence. No one will believe me."

"You need to try."

"I will, but in the meantime, I just don't feel safe at home."

Margo took a cigarette from her pack, looked at Elinor, and put it back. "I don't know," she said.

"I'm sorry. It was a bad idea." Kit stood and headed for the door. "Maybe we can borrow some money from my dad and stay at a hotel."

Margo closed her eyes and inhaled. "Just until the tour?" she asked.

Kit stopped and turned toward her. "Definitely. That gives me almost a week to figure something out."

"Okay," she consented.

Kit walked over and leaned into a hug, squeezing Elinor between them. "Thank you, thank you," she said. "I promise, we'll be quiet and neat and grateful. It will be the fastest few days of your life. I'll do all the cooking."

"Yeah, okay. We still have the drummer problem."

Kit paused. "I do know someone, actually. Someone I work with. Her name's Ronni. She's in an all-girl punk band. I've heard her play, and she's really good. She knows most of our songs already, and I know she would kill to go on this tour."

"What's she like?" Margo asked.

"She's all right," Kit finally answered. "She's very into the music scene. I think she'll fit in."

"Fine," Margo heard herself say. She didn't want to lose this tour.

"Really?" Kit said. "I mean, great. I haven't asked her yet, obviously, because I wanted to talk to you first, but I know she'll be totally into it."

"I'm going to miss Keri."

"Yeah, me too."

CHAPTER 17

Elinor fell asleep on the drive home from Margo's. Kit wasn't looking forward to telling her dad how her irresponsible behavior had put his granddaughter at risk, so she pulled off the road and got out her phone. She scrolled through her address book until she found Ronni's number.

The phone rang. And rang. Kit grew more anxious with each ring, writing and rewriting the speech in her head to try to sell this idea to Ronni when she wasn't sure she believed it to be a decent one. Finally, as she was about to hang up, a groggy female voice answered.

"Ronni? Hey, it's Kit from work."

"Yeah," Ronni said, the phlegmy echo of alcohol still in her voice. "What's up?"

"Remember I mentioned that Women of Rock Tour?"

"Yeah."

She detected the impatience in Ronni's voice but pressed on. "Anyway, we've had a sort of situation come up with the tour. Our drummer broke her arm, so we're sort of in a jam, and I kind of thought of you since you sort of know our songs, maybe—"

"Holy shit! Of course I'll do it. I'll totally do it!"

"That's great," Kit said. "But there's more. We may actually have a chance to do the Hamilton show."

There was a pause. "As in *D.J. Hamilton*? Get the fuck out." The phlegm was subsiding and Ronni's voice began to return to its usual grating chirp.

"The very same. Margo is going to be a guest on Tuesday night, and there's a chance—a slim chance—that we'll be playing one of our songs. It's just a novelty thing. We're not the musical performers or anything, but they thought it might be fun to show that side of the famous gardener."

"Wait. What day is it today?"

"Saturday."

"And we'd be playing the D.J. Hamilton show this Tuesday?"

"Yes." Of course, it's insane, Kit thought.

"Well," Ronni said. "I'm totally game."

Did she really have to say "totally" all the time, Kit wondered. She pushed the irritation aside.

"Okay, great. I'll talk to Margo, but we should probably get together later today, then maybe again on Monday night. I'll let you know."

"I can't stay too late today," Ronni said. "I have a gig tonight. Shit, I guess we'll have to cancel those DC shows next week. Oh well, the guys will understand. Hell, this will be great for them, too—their little drummer spreading the news about Cat's Meow on a national tour. Damn, this is totally awesome."

"Okay," Kit said. "So I'll call you later."

There was another pause. "Oh, cool. Hey, thanks for thinking of me, Kit. You won't be disappointed, I promise."

Kit hung up, hoping she was right.

* * *

When she carried a still-sleeping Elinor into the house she found her father in his robe and pajamas, slippered feet propped on the coffee table before him, a thick novel open on his lap.

"So," he said, pulling the reading glasses from his nose. "What's the latest?"

"She'll be fine. She broke her arm, but we've found a replacement drummer for the tour."

Her father raised one eyebrow. "And you think this replacement will be ready in time?"

Elinor woke at the sound of her grandfather's voice and reached out for him. Kit deposited her daughter on his lap and sat down heavily in the large overstuffed chair next to him.

"No, Dad," she said. "I don't. Honestly, I have no idea what I'm doing. I need to tell you something."

She told him about the letter and the accident and her suspicions, and when she was finished she felt as wrung out as a sponge. Her father stared back at her, his blue eyes still intense despite the wrinkled face that now framed them.

"So what do we need to do?" he asked. His tone had changed. For a rare moment, Kit did not hear accusation, or disappointment, or superiority.

She leaned forward to twirl her daughter's hair around her finger. "I need to go to the police and tell them what I suspect. And I think Elinor and I should stay somewhere else until we leave. Margo said we could stay with her."

"Who's going to watch Elinor on the tour?"

"Maybe you could, you know ... well, maybe you could come with me?" She braced herself for the sarcasm, for the force of her own words from the last time they broached the subject thrown back in her face.

"Okay," he said.

Kit kept her gaze on the braided rug, swallowing the tears before they could escape. "Thank you. That would be nice," she said.

The two sat in silence for several moments until Elinor started to whimper.

"She's probably hungry," Kit said, and she stood to carry Elinor into the kitchen to get her some lunch. Her father replaced his reading glasses and shifted the novel back into his lap where Elinor had been. Back to their routines. But the moment lingered as Kit settled her beautiful daughter into her highchair.

"Mama," Elinor said with a smile.

CHAPTER 18

Margo stepped out of the car and inhaled the sweet summer air cooling as the sun began to fade. Summer wasn't her favorite season. It didn't have the drama of fall's changing landscape, or the hopeful mystery of spring's new buds, but it did have a certain lazy appeal. The hard work of planting is finished by summer, so it becomes a season of maintenance, when the hard-working gardener can pawn off her watering and weeding duties to some kid in the neighborhood, put her feet up, and relax.

As the door beside Whiskey Dick's closed behind her and she ascended the stairs, the dark cave of the hallway swallowed the light and the odor of stale beer and cigarettes stamped out the fresh summer scents. Margo stood in the silence of the third-floor studio for a moment, listening for Frank's footsteps or the echoes of other musicians practicing, but she seemed to be alone. She began setting up. What was this girl Ronni like, she wondered. And what would Ronni think of her? She pushed away this twinge of anxiety by reminding herself that this was her band, she was a celebrity, and she had no reason to be intimidated.

Even so, her heart skipped a beat when she heard the distant sound of the door opening and street noises drifting into the room, followed by footsteps on the stairs and the clunking of equipment being dragged along.

It was Kit.

"Hey," she said. "No Ronni yet?"

"Nope. How did it go with your dad?" Margo asked.

"Actually, it went really well." She leaned down to open her guitar case. "He's taking Elinor to the library while I'm here and then I'm meeting him back home after practice. Then I'll pack up and head straight over to your place so I can get Elinor settled before her bedtime." She paused and looked up at Margo. "Is that okay?"

"I guess so." Margo pulled out a new pack of cigarettes and tapped it against her palm. "So you're moving in tonight?"

Kit stood up. "I thought you said that was all right?"

Margo continued to tap the pack of cigarettes against her palm. "Sure, yeah. I just have all my shit in the guest room. I don't even know if you can get to the bed."

"It will be fine, I'm sure." Kit pulled the guitar strap over her neck and began to tune.

The door flew open and Ronni burst in. "Sorry I'm late!"

Margo turned toward the petite Asian woman and her heart sank. Ronni was young and cute, her long black hair mussed around her shoulders, her jeans faded to the perfect shade of punk, her tight black T-shirt splashed with the fuchsia lettering of a band name Margo didn't recognize. She was lugging two drum cases almost larger than she was, and she looked adorable doing it. Ronni gave a quick wave to Kit and bounded toward Margo like a stray dog.

"I'm Ronni," she said. She held out her hand, gripping Margo's much too firmly.

Margo attempted a smile. "Hi," she said. She glanced at Kit, who looked embarrassed.

"This is so fucking awesome of you guys to let me play with you!" the Chihuahua of a girl continued. "I already know the songs from your CD, so I am totally ready to rock out!" She climbed up to the drum riser and started personalizing the kit.

Margo hated her. Pure, from-the-gut, hatred.

Margo finished setting up her microphone and tuned her guitar as best she could over the loud drum preparation. Keri never needed to tune the heads with such volume, and each crack of Ronni's stick against the drum jolted down Margo's spine. After an eternity of banging and splashing and thumping, Ronni announced she was ready.

"Let's start with 'Ugly Men,'" Margo suggested. "That's the one we'll play on Tuesday—if we play on Tuesday."

"Awesome!" Ronni said, followed by a ridiculous drum roll.

Margo waited for the ringing cymbals to silence. "Okay," she said, trying to sound patient. "How about a four count?"

Ronni lifted her sticks high in the air and clicked them together four times before bringing them down loudly on the toms. Margo and Kit simultaneously launched into the song, and the intro fused together pretty well. Ronni's approach was simpler than Keri's, but it worked with the primal beat of the song. Margo clung to that positive thought. It was about the music, the tour, reviving happy times with friends. It was better than Boca with her parents.

As Margo stepped into the microphone, Ronni pulled back on the volume tastefully. Nice, she thought as she began to sing the lyrics. As they approached the chorus, Kit sang her harmonies flawlessly, her bass driving along with the drums. By the time they reached the end of the song, Margo was feeling pretty good about their sound.

"That was good," Margo said. "You've obviously been playing along with the CD."

"Oh, yeah," Ronni said, thumping absentmindedly on her bass drum with her foot pedal. "It's easy stuff. Four/four time, straightforward approach. This is a piece of cake compared to the shit I'm used to playing. My guitar player has a hard-on for crazy time signatures."

"Yeah, we're not exactly art rock," Kit said, making Margo smile.

"You kidding me?" Ronni said. "This is fucking art in its highest form. The art of stripped-down, balls-out rock. Who wrote your songs?"

Margo smiled. "It was a collaborative effort," she said. "I'd usually bring in a riff, and then Kit and I would mess around with it until something came out of it. This was back when we had the time to mess around."

"Well, it's great stuff," Ronni continued. "The hooks are really strong, and the vocals pull the whole thing together."

"Thanks," Margo said. "How about we try 'Take That'? We

can come back to 'Ugly Men' and run through it a couple times at the end. Somehow we need to learn ten more songs by Saturday."

"No problem," Ronni said, raising her sticks above her head again. "Ready, gals?"

Margo disliked her bossy tone. "One second," she said. She leaned down to twist a few knobs on her guitar pedal, enjoying the moment of control. After returning them to their original positions, she straightened up and was happy to see Ronni still holding up her arms. "Ready."

Ronni clicked off again, but this time the tempo was faster. Too fast. Margo and Kit started to play along, but then Margo stopped.

"Sorry, that's too fast. Try taking it a little slower."

Ronni nodded, then raised her sticks to click again at what seemed like the right tempo. Margo and Kit played along, but something felt off. The timing was right, but the approach was wrong. It was too simple, too repetitive. Before they got to the verse, Margo stopped again.

"I'm sorry," she said into the microphone, looking over at Ronni. "That's not quite it. Keri used to play a little more fill before the verse comes in. Did you hear that on the CD?"

Ronni took a deep breath and nodded. "I did," she said. "I thought that part was a little busy on the CD, but that's no problem."

They started the song again, and this time Ronni emulated Keri's drumming better. The song mirrored the CD, right up through the big splashy finish. Our perfect wind-up drummer, Margo thought.

"That was great," she said. "I can't believe you learned that so fast."

"Thanks," Ronni said. "What's next?"

"How about 'Things Work Out for Me'?" Kit suggested.

"Excellent," Ronni said, stretching her arms in front of her. "I love the chorus on that one. It's like completely raw sexual energy."

Again, Ronni played the song exactly as it had been recorded. Kit flubbed a few times, and even Margo forgot a line or two, but the drummer had clearly studied their songs note for note, beat for beat, and had learned them all in less than 24 hours. By the end of rehearsal, Margo dared to hope they might pull this tour off after all.

"Great job," Margo said as they packed up their stuff.

"So," Ronni said, "are we getting together Monday?"

"I think we should," Kit said.

Margo nodded. "I'll talk to Frank."

"Sounds great," Ronni said. She stuffed her cymbals into a circular bag and zipped it closed. "I might have to work late, but I can come straight here. I haven't asked our boss for the time off yet, and I'm sure she's not going to like it since Kit will be out too. But so what? If she cans me, there are plenty of other low-paying jobs out there."

"Shit," Kit said. "I didn't even think about that. Deirdre's gonna have a fit."

"What else is new?" Ronni said. "The woman has no life. That's not my problem."

"I wish I could afford that attitude," Kit grumbled.

"After this tour," Ronni continued, "who knows? You may not need that stupid job. We'll all be big rock stars with labels beating down our door to sign us."

Margo tensed. She had no intention of making Broad Street a permanent thing. Did she? But it had been a great practice so she chose to ignore the comment.

CHAPTER 19

Kit struggled all the way through the practice. She'd really wanted to enjoy it, but every time Ronni opened her mouth she had the urge to strangle her. Not only was Ronni young and way too self-confident, but seeing a work colleague in her band only served as a reminder of the impossible task she had created for herself. There was no way she could finish everything Deirdre wanted her to accomplish before the tour started in less than a week. Broad Street rehearsals were supposed to be her escape—from work, from her dad, from worries about Elinor and Damien and money. And, to make matters worse, it was very clear that Margo was not happy about letting them stay with her.

As they packed up the last of their equipment, Margo lit a cigarette.

"So what's the latest for the Hamilton show on Tuesday?" Kit asked.

"They want me at the studio by four," Margo answered. "I plan to take the train up so I don't have to deal with traffic. I figured if I leave 30th Street Station by one, I should be there in plenty of time."

"How about us?" Kit asked. "I mean, if we're going to play— do you know when they'll make that decision?"

Margo bent down to pick an ashtray up from the floor and

tapped her ash into it. "I guess you should be there about the same time."

"Do you want to take the train up together?"

Margo looked back down at the blackened ashtray. "Yeah, I guess so."

"We don't have to," Kit said.

"No," Margo said. She flushed. "Of course we should go up together. I'm sorry I didn't think of it. I guess I'm just a little nervous. I have no clue what witty anecdotes to share. I just don't want to look stupid."

"You'll be great," Ronni said. She strapped a large drum bag of hardware over her tiny shoulder. "I might drive up. I can crash with some friends up there, so I'll probably just blow off the whole day at work. You should do that too, Kit."

Kit winced at the thought of seeing Deirdre on Monday morning. "Maybe," she said.

"All right," Ronni said. "I'm outta here. Still feeling a little woozy from our gig last night. It was amazing. There were like kids jumping onto the stage and throwing shit and we sold like twenty-three CDs."

Margo and Kit stared at her.

"So," she continued, "I guess I'll see you guys Monday. Let me know what time. Great practice."

"Yeah, you too," they said in unison.

As they listened to her footsteps on the stairs, Kit turned to Margo.

"What do you think?" Kit asked.

"She's very young," Margo answered, "and a little perkier than I usually care for, but I guess she'll be fine."

"Yeah," Kit said. "I think she'll be fine. We're not shopping for a new friend here, just a temporary replacement for Keri."

"Exactly."

"Do you want to grab something to eat?" Margo asked as she closed her case.

Kit flushed guiltily as she looked at her watch. "I promised my dad I'd be gone for three hours, tops. I better go."

Margo shrugged. "Okay. No big deal."

"But it won't take us long to pack, so I'll see you back at your place in a little bit? I promised to cook, so I'll make us something tonight. Okay?"

Margo stared into the ashtray, stubbing out her cigarette with studied concentration.

Kit looked at her old friend with a mixture of annoyance and desperation. "Margo? Does that sound okay?"

"Sure. Whatever."

＊　＊　＊

When Kit arrived back home, she left her equipment in the car and hurried in. The music had taken the edge off her worry, but at every red light on the way her anxiety about Elinor had increased. Her father's car was in the driveway, but the house was quiet.

"Hello?" she asked, panic rising in her throat.

"We're up here!" her father's voice called from upstairs.

Kit followed the muffled noises to her father's room, where a large battered suitcase lay open on the bed. Elinor was playing in a pile of shirts on the floor, lifting them over her head to hide her eyes, then pulling them off and giggling. When she saw Kit, she smiled and crawled toward her.

Kit picked her up into a hug. "Hi pumpkin," she said.

"I thought I may as well get a head start on packing," her father said.

Kit stared at the meager contents of the suitcase: a small pile of graying briefs, black socks, a pair of slippers. Old man clothes. What was she thinking, bringing her father along on the Women of Rock Tour? She had no idea where they'd sleep on the road and she didn't want to share a room with her father. It would just be too weird. If the tour didn't pick up the tabs for her rooms they might have to shell out money for two rooms, and her sagging credit would not allow her a card that would cover that much overhead. They'd have to tap into her father's pension. She sighed.

"Did you see anything unusual while you were at the library?" she asked, tickling Elinor with her nose.

"Nope," he said.

He walked over to his closet and slid some hangers together to create a gap at the collection of suits draped in plastic. "Goddamn plastic ruined my gray suit," he grumbled. "I knew I should have taken them out of these bags."

Kit was the one who had convinced him that the plastic would keep his suits from getting dusty.

"What do you mean they're ruined?" she asked.

He pulled the gray suit out of its bag. "Look. It's all yellowed now. I wore that suit for thirty years."

"Maybe it's time for some new clothes."

"Why?"

Kit sighed. "We should get going. There's some beef stew in the crock-pot."

Her father put the gray suit back into its bag, slid it to the side, and inspected another one with a grunt. "How are we going to be getting around for this tour?" he asked.

"I don't know."

He turned around. "Will it be some kind of bus, or are we expected to run up miles on our own car?"

"I don't know."

"What about accommodations? Will they be putting us up?"

"I'm finding out everything on Wednesday. All the bands are having a meeting at the organizer's office. I'll have all the details then."

"Doesn't this thing start on Thursday?"

"Yep."

"That's ridiculous. That doesn't give people enough time—"

"That's the way it works in the music business, Dad."

Kit put a squirming Elinor down on the floor. She crawled over to a hanger lying on the floor and started to put it in her mouth.

"Oh, honey," Kit said. "Don't do that." As soon as she'd taken the hanger away, Elinor darted over to a cufflink lying on the floor. Kit beat her to it, tossing the cufflink onto her father's end table. Elinor began to cry.

"She's tired," her father said, returning his attention to the closet.

"No kidding," she said. "Did she nap in the car?"

"No, she just wanted to play."

Kit took a deep breath. "Okay, Dad. We need to go so I can get her settled before she melts down." The thought of bringing a hysterical Elinor into Margo's house was painful.

"Okay," her father said. He seemed lost in his closet full of memories.

"You remember about the stew in the crock-pot, right?" Kit said. "Don't forget to turn it off. There should be enough to last a few meals for you, and then there are dinners in the freezer."

"Yup," he said.

It took Kit much longer than expected to pack up everything they'd need for less than a week at Margo's. She got all of her things into a backpack—mostly jeans and T-shirts—but her small companion required a portable crib, clean sheets, baby food, booster seat, stroller, bibs, medicine, extra pacifiers, and enough clothing to cover unexpected explosions. By the time she was finished, Kit was staring at a very large pile of baby paraphernalia. It would look like they were planning to move in permanently. Margo would not be happy.

CHAPTER 20

Elinor cried the whole drive to Margo's. She started when her grandfather gave her a farewell hug, and nothing could calm her down—not the pacifier, not her favorite CD of children's songs, not endless rounds of "Wheels on the Bus."

Kit parked in front of Margo's building and tried walking Elinor up and down the street, bouncing her and singing and doing her best to stay calm, but the shrill cries continued and Kit was running out of patience.

"What are you doing?"

Kit turned to see Margo standing on her front stoop, hands on her hips, glaring at them.

Kit walked over, shouting to be heard over Elinor's cries. "I'm sorry. I was trying to calm her down before we came in."

"Well," Margo said, "if you're trying not to disturb me, it's not working."

She turned and walked back into her house and Kit followed.

Inside the still peace of a single woman's home, Elinor sounded even louder. Kit held her closer, rocking her back and forth, but Elinor continued to wail.

Margo stared at them for a few seconds, then waved Kit into the living room. Margo walked over to a remote on an end table, flicked on the television, clicked a few numbers, and soon cartoons were dancing across the screen.

Kit turned Elinor away from the screen. "I don't let her watch television," she said, but she noticed a hiccup in Elinor's cries. She peered around her mother's shoulder and her damp eyes widened at the dancing colors on the screen. Kit sighed with relief and put her daughter on the floor.

"Thanks," she said. "I guess I can break the rules for a few days."

"I may not be a parent, but I do know the power of television," Margo said. She picked up a dirty ashtray. "I straightened up the guest room, but it's still a little messy."

"Hey, that's great. Believe me, I am so grateful for this, I don't want to be any bother." She turned to head toward the door. "I brought over some chicken—I thought I'd make us Chicken Marsala tonight."

"Thanks, but I can't eat the sauce. Atkins, remember?"

"Oh, well, I'll just grill it with some Italian dressing then, and make some vegetables."

Margo shrugged. "Whatever."

Kit leaned down to Elinor. "Mommy has to go out to get our things. I'll be right back." Her daughter, mesmerized by the cartoons, ignored her.

Kit went out to the car, popped the trunk open, and sighed. She decided not to bring everything in right away and selected the key pieces: the portable crib, food, diaper bag, Kit's backpack, and one bag of Elinor clothes. It was still a mountain of stuff, and she limped her way to the door and tapped it with her foot. Finally, Margo opened the door.

"Holy shit," Margo said. She stepped out of the way. "It's up the stairs and down the hall to the right, last room."

Kit dragged everything upstairs, her shoulders aching from the weight. The hallway was accented with tasteful artwork, and Kit realized that Elinor could do some expensive damage in this place. Margo had come a long way since Kit used to crash at her apartment back in the early days of the band. They would stay up all night watching old noir movies, drinking beer, bitching about their exes. They'd sleep until noon and Margo would make Kit's favorite hangover breakfast: sunny-side up eggs, perfect for dipping toasted bagels smothered in cream cheese. Kit's mouth watered just thinking about it.

When Kit pushed the door open with her foot, she realized that Margo had not been exaggerating about the mess. Clothes and shoeboxes were piled everywhere. A double bed pushed into a corner was clutter-free, but there wasn't enough floor space to set up Elinor's crib. It didn't even look like there was enough space to rearrange things to make room. The piles reached halfway to the ceiling and teetered precariously. Kit dropped the bags on the bed and returned downstairs.

Elinor hadn't moved, and Margo was sitting in a leather recliner with a Vogue magazine propped on her lap.

"Is it okay if I move some of the things into a closet or something?" Kit asked.

Margo kept her eyes on the page. "Sorry, no room."

Try to remain grateful, Kit told herself. It's only for a few days, and Elinor will be safe. "Okay," she said. "How about I start dinner?"

Margo looked up at a clock on the wall. "It's five-thirty."

"It will take me some time, and we usually eat around six."

Margo looked back at the magazine. "I'm not hungry, but suit yourself."

Kit squatted down beside Elinor. "Honey, do you want to help Mommy make dinner?"

Elinor stared at the screen.

It's only for a few days, Kit told herself several more times as she went back to the car, brought in the groceries and booster seat, and made dinner.

CHAPTER 21

Sunday had always been Margo's favorite day to sleep in, but as soon as a hint of sunlight slipped across her lashes she heard the sound of a baby crying. She lay in bed, waiting for Kit to deal with it, but the crying continued until she could take it no longer. She pushed herself out of bed and looked at the clock. Seven o'clock.

She rubbed the sleep out of her eyes and slipped her feet into fuzzy leopard slippers. Why did she have to be so nice? These were her only few days to rest before the tour. She wrapped herself in a robe and went down to make coffee, the echoes of the baby's piercing cries following her down the stairs.

As she waited for the brew, dying for a cigarette she was too polite to light, she thought about the Hamilton show. Playing guitar had never been her most confident endeavor. On stage, hidden behind the volume of Kit's solid bass and Keri's tight drumming, she could rely on her personality to mask any shortcomings in her playing—the rough bar chords that she slid sloppily up and down the neck of the guitar, the awkward picking on her few attempts at a lead. In the studio, they could cover up these flubs with computer tricks. But, as she well knew, the television camera can expose all kinds of errors in a close-up.

She took her coffee into the living room and flipped through her CDs until she found the Broad Street CD. She slipped it into the stereo and hit play.

She hadn't listened to it in a long time. The first song, "Things Work Out for Me," clicked off with confidence. She tapped her foot along with Keri's pulsing bass drum as she sipped her coffee. Her guitar, sufficiently buried in a wash of distortion, sounded fine.

Things work out for me, her old self sang. Always get it for free …

The memory of recording the CD was as clear as if she had stepped to the microphone the day before. She could almost feel the headphones clamped to her ears, the cord draping down her back, the intimate voice of the engineer in her head guiding her, instructing her. She closed her eyes and listened to the song. Nope, not too bad at all.

But then she remembered how the song had sounded before the engineer worked his magic—running her vocals and guitar through a pitch corrector, adding distortion and reverb to blend her less-than-perfect chords. They had to have that kind of technology on Hamilton, right? She'd heard plenty of bands on the show that sounded fine. But she'd heard plenty that sounded like crap, too. What was she thinking? She turned off the CD. Upstairs, the baby had finally stopped crying.

She heard footsteps and Kit and Elinor descended the stairs.

"I am so sorry," Kit said. "I can usually rock her back to sleep in the morning, and she's fine, but she's just really upset today. Why don't you go back to bed? I promise we'll be quiet."

"No big deal," Margo lied. "I'm up. There's coffee in the kitchen."

"Awesome. Come on, honey," she said to Elinor. "Mommy needs some caffeine."

"Mama," Elinor said as they walked away.

Margo followed them into the kitchen and sat at the table. "Did you sleep okay?"

"Um, yeah, pretty well, thanks," she said, her back toward her as she poured coffee. "Elinor woke up a few times. I think she's just a little freaked out about being in a new place. She's never been away from my dad's house. Plus, a pile of shoe boxes fell over during the night." She turned toward Margo. "I cleaned it all up."

Margo watched as Kit strapped Elinor into the booster seat

she'd attached to the chair and sprinkled a few Cheerios onto the small tray. Elinor proceeded to toss them onto the floor that Margo had just paid to have cleaned.

"Honey, please don't do that." Kit knelt down and picked them up. "I am so sorry," she repeated to Margo.

"What are you going to do with her tomorrow when you go to work?" Margo asked.

"I think she'll be okay at daycare. She'll be surrounded by staff members and other children all day."

"What about Tuesday when we go to New York? Daycare won't be open that late, right?"

Kit opened a jar of pureed fruit and began spooning it into Elinor's mouth. "I am worried about that. I arranged to take her to one of the daycare worker's homes. She's off that day, and Elinor really likes her. I've been careful to watch for cars that might be following me whenever I go anywhere, but I don't know. Maybe I can figure out a way to switch cars with my dad or something." Kit put down the jar and rubbed her eyes. "This is all so crazy, and I hope I'm overreacting. I just don't want to take any chances." She turned toward Margo, and Margo noticed for the first time that Kit looked exhausted. Her dark eyes were ringed in shadows, her skin pale.

"I'm sure everything will work out," she said.

Margo's phone rang, startling all three of them. She didn't recognize the number.

"Who would be calling this early on a Sunday morning?" Margo asked. "Hello?" she answered tentatively.

"Good morning," a formal male voice replied.

Margo hung up. "Fucking telemarketers," she said. The phone rang again. Margo ignored it.

Moments later, the phone chimed to let her know there was a new voicemail.

"Margo, good morning. It's Harry, from the station." Margo walked into the living room as she listened. "I hope this is Margo. Anyway, I wanted to congratulate you on a great final show. We watched the edited version last night, and the season wrap-up segment turned out really well. So, anyway, I just wanted to tell you that. So, I guess I'll see you later." There was a pause, then: "If you feel like calling back, my number is ..." She grabbed a pen and tablet from a small drawer and quickly wrote down the number.

She took a large swig of coffee and made her way out to her patio garden. She cleared her throat, smoothed her hair, and dialed the number.

Harry picked up on the second ring. "Hi Margo," he said.

The sound of his deep voice saying her name made her tingle slightly between her legs. *God*, she scolded herself, *keep it together, girl!*

"How did you know it was me?" she said. "My number's blocked."

"I have my ways."

"What, the network gets around the phone company's tricks?"

"Actually, I just guessed."

Margo racked her brain for a clever comeback but kept tripping over the fact that she was talking to the head of the entire network. Maybe he was still in his pajamas like she was, putting out a secret cigarette.

"Well," she said, "I'm glad you liked the show. I had fun doing that segment."

"It was great. The music was perfect."

There was a long moment of silence. Finally Harry said, "So, would you like to get breakfast with me this morning? I don't have an appointment until eleven."

Margo's heart raced and her mouth dried up. "Um, yeah. That would be great."

"Perfect, great," he said. "You're in Center City, right?"

"Is there anything you don't know?"

"Plenty, but I'd like to change that. How about we meet at Rouge, say, in about an hour?"

Margo had never gotten ready that quickly. "Sounds good," she said.

"Great. See you then."

CHAPTER 22

Back in the kitchen, Margo refilled her coffee. "I have to meet someone for breakfast," she said and walked upstairs to the shower.

In order to be at Rouge in an hour, she would have to leave her house in forty minutes, leaving twenty minutes to get to the Rittenhouse Square area and hunt for the rare parking space—and even that was pushing it if she hit any kind of traffic. She stripped off her pajamas and stepped into the hot shower, her mind racing. Her boss had just invited her to breakfast. She was going on national television the night after tomorrow. She was leaving on tour on Thursday with a drummer who may or may not drive her insane. Her old friend and her baby were staying in her house. How had her life become so chaotic?

After soaping and rinsing, she wrapped herself in a robe and strode barefoot to her walk-in closet, one of her favorite retreats. Colorful outfits flanked three of the four walls. On one side she had her business attire, mostly snug suits with a variety of contrasting bright shirts that flattered her complexion. Another wall showcased dresses, from sparkling cocktails to tasteful formfitting black in a variety of lengths and styles. The third wall had more casual skirts, pants, and tops. She began to inspect her options.

Rouge was a hip-casual restaurant on the upscale Rittenhouse Square in Center City, so she had to find something that wouldn't

look like she was trying too hard. She slid hanger after hanger
along the rails, but nothing shouted out to be worn. She looked at
the clock. Down to twenty-five minutes, and she still had to apply
makeup and dry her hair. Crap. She walked over to her closet and
zipped through a series of silk blouses, sliding rejects across the rail
like a factory assembly line. She paused when she came to one of her
favorites in a deep plum. Holding it against her, she looked into the
full-length mirror that hung on the back of the closet door. It was a
good color on her; she could match it with a pair of black pants that
would make her look slimmer and accent it with a colorful necklace.
Fine. She draped the blouse over her arm, grabbed the pants from
their hanger, and glanced at the clock again. Twenty-one minutes left.

Thirty minutes later, Margo was essentially ready. She walked
to the kitchen, glancing once again at the cursed clock. She was down
to nine minutes to drive to Rittenhouse Square, find parking—which
was just about impossible this time of day—and race to the restaurant. Why did she say an hour? What had she been thinking?

Kit and Elinor were still meandering through breakfast.

"I'll be back in a little while," Margo said. "Make yourselves at
home."

"Thanks," Kit said with a confused smile.

Margo drove down Broad Street, running yellow lights and
swerving to avoid hitting the occasional pedestrian who dared to
cross in front of her. She blared her horn at a daydreaming old driver
peering over his steering wheel. She honked again at a red Toyota
that started slowing down when the light was only just turning
yellow, swinging her car into the other lane to pass it and barely
missing another car trying to run the same light. Fuck, fuck, fuck,
she thought as the digital clock on her dash clicked away. It was two
minutes fast, which meant she was now three minutes late.

She turned off Broad and headed toward the restaurant. As
she approached it on her right, she saw the blink of red brake lights
from a parked car. She slammed on her own brakes, sending her purse
flying off the passenger seat, and threw the car into reverse without
looking behind her. Thankfully, the street was void of other vehicles
and small children. She waited impatiently to the clicking of her right
indicator as the young woman in the coveted space took an eternity
adjusting her mirrors, belting herself in, checking her lipstick. It took

all of Margo's strength to avoid beeping her horn. Finally, the woman left and Margo swung her car expertly into the empty space.

She was now seven minutes late. Not bad.

She took a deep breath, gathered her purse from the floor, along with the lipstick and wallet that had fallen out, and walked toward the restaurant. Her heart was racing, her palms damp. She felt like a ridiculous teenager.

She scanned the busy room full of the young and beautiful, wondering why so many were here early on a Sunday morning when they should be sleeping in. Harry's salt-and-pepper hair would certainly stand out in this crowd, but she saw only a sea of perfect highlights. She sighed and turned her attention toward the large picture window, bordered along the bottom with a tasteful arrangement of wild flowers. She could see the street in three directions from this window, and there seemed to be no sign of Harry. Her enthusiasm began to fade. He was standing her up. He probably did this to women at the studio all the time. He probably tossed his title around to get them into bed whenever it was convenient for him. Well, she was not that kind of loser. No man stood her up. She would leave his sorry ass . . .

"Hi," a low voice said from behind.

Margo turned to see Harry, looking far too dressed up for the restaurant. But he looked good. The dark navy suit and cranberry tie complemented his tan. His dark brown eyes seemed to stare right into her, so she looked away to jam her keys into her purse.

"I thought you were blowing me off," she said, returning her eyes to meet his.

He smiled. "I was here early. I just stepped into the next room to make a phone call."

She smiled back. "Sorry. I'm not the most prompt person. If it's any consolation, I'm usually much later."

"That makes me feel better. Hungry?"

"Starving."

Harry motioned the hostess over, and she led them to a corner table.

Margo picked up the menu and opened it, grateful for the small distraction. "The fruit pancakes are excellent here," she said, ready to abandon her no-carb rule for the special occasion.

Harry closed the menu. "Then pancakes it is."

When they placed their orders and the waitress removed the menus, Margo felt exposed. She was dying for a cigarette, but she'd intentionally left them on her kitchen table in case it might bother Harry.

"So," he began. "The show was great."

"I think we covered that."

"You're right. Are you seeing anyone?"

Margo laughed. "Wow, you're not one to beat around the bush, are you?"

"I thought I should be clear about my intentions. I like you. I think you're interesting, and I'm glad you agreed to have breakfast with me. So, it would be nice to know, if I asked you to dinner, if anyone would get upset."

Margo turned her eyes to the ceiling in mock contemplation. "Well, my fish died a few months ago, so that leaves me pretty clear for a dinner date."

"I'm sorry."

"We weren't that close, but thank you. How about you? Any mammals requiring your time and attention?"

Harry smiled. "Not currently."

"Good," she said, propping her elbow on the table and resting her chin on her hand. "I guess we can have two meals together then."

Harry folded his hands in front of him, inches away from her. She felt the electricity between them and wanted to reach out and touch him. His skin looked soft.

"So," he said, "are you ready for Hamilton?"

"Oh, I'll be fine. Any words of advice?"

"Are you kidding? You should be the one to give advice. The camera is a very good friend of yours. Just be yourself, and don't use any big words."

She felt her face flush. "You mean like eupatorium?"

"That would be one, yes. I've just found, in general, that not many people like to think while watching television."

"That sounds kind of cynical coming from a TV exec."

"I'm not saying it's a good thing. But I've learned some hard lessons along the way. You're right. You'll be fine."

They spent the rest of the hour chatting. She learned that he was born in Connecticut and lived in Blue Bell, an affluent suburb, and that he dabbled in sculpture and photography. Margo enjoyed his ease. He was smart, and funny, and he asked about her life in a way that didn't feel like prying. Of course, she wondered if he knew about any of the interns. She also wondered if he'd ever been married, and if not, why he'd gone so long in life without making that kind of commitment. But mostly she just enjoyed having a grown-up conversation with a man who wasn't headed back to college in the fall.

When they were finished, Harry grabbed the check as soon as it was placed on the table.

"We can split it," she offered.

"My treat," he said, pulling an expensive-looking leather wallet from his back pocket. She glanced at the many gold cards in its fold and wondered again why this man was single. Maybe he had a secret bedroom fetish for women's underwear or some other weird obsession. But she couldn't quite picture it. He seemed like a nice guy, which was normally an attribute she found boring. But Harry was different. She liked him.

"Thank you," she said, sorry the meal was over so soon. As they left the restaurant, he opened the door for her. These small tokens of chivalry were foreign to her, but she enjoyed them.

They walked out into the warm summer sun and Harry paused outside the door.

"So when can I take you up on that second meal?" he asked.

"I have practice tomorrow night and the show Tuesday. The tour leaves Thursday, so I guess that leaves Wednesday."

Harry's expression soured. "I leave for L.A. on Wednesday."

They stood awkwardly at the door. Margo imagined the young and beautiful staring at them through the picture window, wondering where they'd seen her before, wondering who the man was.

Harry reached out and touched her fingers, sending a tingle up her arm. His skin was soft.

"I'll see you soon," he said. "We'll figure something out."

"I hope so," she said, feeling hokey and happy and self-conscious. She wanted to kiss him. She hoped he would kiss her, but their fingers parted and they walked to their separate cars.

CHAPTER 23

Elinor was surprisingly calm when Kit dropped her off at daycare on Monday morning. She was grateful there were no tears—especially since she'd felt so jittery, constantly looking in her rearview mirror for any cars that might be following her as she took the most circuitous route possible from Margo's house to the daycare center. She was still nervous about leaving Elinor, but she knew her daughter would be surrounded every moment of the day with staff who were trained to keep her safe.

As she climbed back into the car and drove to work she realized how exhausted she was. Margo had been gone most of the day on Sunday, and Kit was starting to feel like a prisoner in her home. All night long Kit found herself startling to every small creak or noise in the unfamiliar house. The words of the letter kept running through her head: *You can't hide. I will always be close by, watching. It's only a matter of time before I bring her home to me.*

When she got to her cubicle, she flopped down in the chair and booted up her computer. What would happen if she lost this job? She liked the fantasy of being work-free, of leaving behind her many obligations here and setting off on a music tour without the haze of guilt shadowing her.

But the tour would be over before she knew it and she would be back without a job, living with her dad, and trying to raise a daughter with no money.

Her computer hummed to life and she clicked into her e-mail. Dozens of messages began to download, filling her screen with intimidating boldface type. She took a deep breath and decided she'd need a cup of coffee before wading through the digital muck.

After pouring herself a cup she stood still for a moment by the coffee machine, enjoying the vast silence of the room around her.

"Good morning." A curt female voice interrupted her thoughts.

Kit turned around. Deirdre was wearing her usual gray suit—she must have a dozen of them—and clutching her Monday morning gift of bagels in two stuffed paper bags. It was her only gift.

"Morning, Deirdre," Kit replied. "I was just about to tackle my e-mail."

"Why don't you come chat with me first? I want to see where we are with things."

Kit sighed and followed her into her dark office. Deirdre switched on the light and Kit wondered what it would be like to live in a world where every pencil was sharp and standing tall in an engraved silver cup, where every piece of paper sat tidied in an orderly pile.

"Have a seat," she ordered.

The two women sat on opposing sides of the desk.

"Fill me in."

"Well, I'll actually know more after checking my e-mail," Kit began. "The Sterling Hotel looks very positive, but I just need to confirm today."

"Looks positive? This should have been finished two weeks ago."

"It hasn't been that easy. It's not like I haven't been calling these people. The area just doesn't have many appropriate venues. If we'd decided to hold it in a different location, it might have been easier."

As soon as the words left her mouth, Kit regretted them. Allentown was Deirdre's hometown. It had been her idea to have it there, and she'd been enthusiastic since the beginning to support the local musicians. But Kit had had as much trouble finding talent as she had interested venues.

Deirdre narrowed her eyes. "So you've been saying. That's why I decided to make a few calls myself. I made three calls, and I have three potential places. It took me about twenty minutes."

Kit was shocked. "How? Who?"

"The Sterling for one. The Icehouse and Godfrey Daniels also agreed. I'm in negotiations with all of them, and the best deal wins."

"I called those clubs. The Icehouse and Godfrey Daniels don't have big enough P.A.s to handle the event."

"So we rent one. It's called problem-solving."

"I consider myself a very good problem-solver," Kit said, trying to remain calm. "You told me we didn't have the budget to rent a P.A."

"That was before I knew how little the venues were charging. If you had presented some numbers to me, I certainly would have approved it."

Kit stifled the urge to sweep everything from Deirdre's neat desk onto the floor. "I've been updating you on these venues several times a week. I told you how much each place wanted."

"Well, I guess you never asked them to negotiate. Once I told them how much publicity they'd get if they hosted the event, they were willing to work with me."

"Deirdre," Kit began, surprised by a warm calm. "I really feel like you're not being fair. I think I did the best I could within the limitations you gave me. It seems like you thought I could handle it until I mentioned the tour. I've worked very hard for you, and I know I've been one of your most responsible employees."

Deirdre curled her lips into a cool grin. "Don't flatter yourself, Kit. You're not that good. I feel sorry for you. That's the only reason I keep you around."

"You're not that selfless, Deirdre," Kit said, standing. "I appreciate what you've given me here, but I think it's time for me to move on. I can finish out the day if you want, but I won't be available the rest of this week. I'm sorry I can't give you two weeks' notice."

Kit enjoyed the faint hint of panic that rippled across Deirdre's usually stern expression.

"Just organize all of your projects and leave them on your desk," she said. "You've done enough already."

As Kit turned and walked out of the room, the calm slowly

dissipated and the more familiar anxiety crept back in. What had she done? She walked down the empty corridor toward her cubicle, her shoes clicking against the concrete floor. "Dead man walking" rang in her head.

She passed dozens of empty cubicles. No one to bid her farewell, no one to notice her absence. She'd worked at this job since she had Elinor almost a year ago, and when she left her memory would disappear after a few days of whispery gossip.

"Kit!" Ronni, carrying a huge retro purse disproportionate to her petite frame, walked towards her. "Hey, that was fun Saturday," she said. "Thanks again for letting me play with you guys. You totally rock."

"Yeah, you too," Kit said.

"So what kind of mood's the hag in today?"

"The kind to make me quit."

Ronni's eyes grew wide. "No way! What happened?"

"Nothing, really. It was time."

"Wow." Ronni shook her head. "Maybe it's time for me, too."

She was the last person Kit wanted as an ally. "I'm sure Deirdre will let you take some time off."

"Yeah, probably." She looked pensively over Kit's shoulder. "I do need the cash. I'll see what mood I'm in later."

You are so young, Kit thought. "Good luck with that. I'll see you tonight at practice."

Kit continued her career death-row stroll toward the tiny spot in this place where she had spent so much of her time. She sat down and looked at the long list of unread e-mails. She began deleting those whose subject lines revealed many creative spellings of "Viagra" and "penis," pausing to read only familiar names and subjects. There was nothing unusual—mostly boring industry news that no longer had an impact on her life. She forwarded some to Deirdre, deleted others. Then she came to the release about the Women of Rock Tour from Susan McKeown, the well-known director of Showgirls Entertainment Group.

> *New York, NY—The first annual Women of Rock Tours kicks off at the Tweeter Center in Camden, NJ on June 17. Headliners include Sam Starr, who made her name opening for punk bands*

like the Sex Pistols in the seventies, and then made her comeback in the nineties with her underground hit "Rising Starr." L.A.-based rockers The Venturas are also on the national bill, along with indie gal bands like The Crocodiles. An unusual addition to the bill is The Contemporary Living Network's Margo Bevelaqua of the urban gardening show Guerrilla Gardening, *reviving her nineties garage band, Broad Band.*

The Women of Rock Tour was inspired by the many talented women musicians who go unnoticed . . .

The release went on about female empowerment through art and a bunch of other crap in which Kit had no interest. She read and reread "Broad Band," wondering how they could spell Bevelaqua correctly but screw up a simple name like Broad Street. She knew the answer: Broad Street was a bunch of nobodies headed by a somebody. That was okay, she told herself. That meant people would come out to see them and would hear the music, and she would get to do what she loved. At least for a little while—until the real world came crashing home.

She printed the release and continued scrolling through her inbox. Crap, crap, and more crap. When she switched to her AOL account she found another e-mail from her ex, Charlie O'Donnell.

> *Hey Kit—*
> *I'm glad I found you. I'm back in the area, briefly, but Bitchsword is scheduled to play the first few dates of the Women of Rock Tour. Rumor has it a certain Philly girl garage band will be on the second stage? It will be great to see you. The tour should be interesting. I hear there are all kinds of politics already between Showgirls Entertainment and the evil Sheer Strait empire, but I'm sure things will work out once everyone starts making money. I'll definitely track you down in Camden.*
> *Charlie*

Kit stared at the e-mail, reading and re-reading. "I'll definitely track you down in Camden." The tone could be interpreted multiple ways. Was it an old friend looking to reconnect? Or was it Damien trying to trick her using an alias e-mail address?

No, she decided. Sleep deprivation had made her paranoid. She deleted the e-mail, switched back to her work account, and set up an auto-reply telling the computer world of her professional demise. Then she quickly packed up her cubicle.

When she opened the door to the parking lot, she squinted in the bright sunlight. When her eyes had adjusted, she saw that her car was still only one of a few in the lot. As she walked across the macadam carrying the few personal items from her cubicle, she noticed Ronni's beat-up old Pinto slathered in band bumper stickers, Deirdre's spotless SUV, and a dark car she didn't recognize. She'd just clicked the remote to unlock her door when something caught her eye.

New York plates.

Panicked, Kit opened the car door, dove in, slammed it shut, and clicked the locks. She pulled her phone out as she started the engine, peering toward the car. It appeared to be empty. It was probably just a record executive, she told herself. They came here all the time. If this was the car that had hit Keri's it would be damaged, and this one seemed intact. But she couldn't overcome the anxiety she felt as she dialed the daycare.

"New Dawn, good morning," a woman's voice answered.

"Hi, this is Kit Greene. I was just checking to make sure Elinor is all right."

"Hi, Kit, it's Holly. Elinor's fine. Are you?"

"Yeah, sure." Relief flooded through her. "I left work early today, so I'll be there shortly to pick her up. I just wanted to let you know."

"Oh, okay. Your father just called."

Kit paused. "Really? Did he say what he wanted?"

"He just wanted to make sure Elinor was all right, too. She's a lucky girl to have such a caring family."

"And you're sure it was my father?"

"He said it was."

Kit hung up and sped out of the parking lot, running through several yellow lights on her way to the center. Her father had never called there before. She wasn't sure he even had the number.

✱ ✱ ✱

When she pulled up to the daycare, she jumped out of the car and ran into the center and up the stairs. She was so relieved to see Elinor sitting in a circle of friends as the teacher led them in a round of "Itsy Bitsy Spider" she could have cried. Elinor squealed and kicked her legs and arms when she saw Kit.

"Hi sweetie," Kit said, sitting down with her and giving her a hug.

She waited while the kids sang a few more songs then lifted Elinor onto her hip.

"Want to come home with Mommy?"

"Papa," Elinor said.

"She's been asking for him all morning," Holly said, pulling a tissue from a box and wiping one of the many runny noses.

"We're staying with a friend for a few days before the tour."

Holly cocked her head. "Are you sure everything's okay?"

"It's just a little hectic getting ready for the tour, that's all."

Holly tickled Elinor under the chin. "Are you still coming to play at my house tomorrow?" she asked.

Kit had forgotten about tomorrow. "Holly," she said, "I need to tell you something." She leaned out of earshot of the other teachers and children. "I received a threatening letter from Elinor's father recently," she whispered.

"Oh no. What did he say?"

"He threatened to take Eli—" the words caught in her throat, and she swallowed back tears. She paused to compose herself. "I just have to be careful, that's all. That's why I'm leaving her with you tomorrow, and not my dad."

Holly looked concerned. "Do you think this guy would come to my house?"

"No," Kit said, trying to sound convincing. "He doesn't know where you live or anything about you. He only has my home address."

Holly looked at Elinor and wrapped a small curl around her ear. "Poor baby," she said.

Kit swallowed again. "I'll call you tomorrow morning. I really appreciate your help."

"Of course," she said. "I'm glad you told me."

On her way out, Kit stopped at Elinor's cubby to get her craft projects and parent information sheets. A white envelope sitting on top of the papers caught her eye, and she opened it.

> *Hi little girl,*
> *You are so cute. I can't wait to meet you in person. I think you have Daddy's face—the same one your whore of a mother spit on when she lied about you. Don't worry, honey. We'll meet very soon.*

Kit dropped the envelope, crumpled the letter into her pocket, and ran to her car, frantically looking over her shoulder as she strapped Elinor into her seat.

She drove straight to the police station.

CHAPTER 24

There were a few officers standing together in the station when Kit carried Elinor into the waiting area. She walked over to the group.

"Excuse me," she said.

The three young men turned toward her, then looked her up and down. Kit was suddenly embarrassed by her magenta-tinted hair and tattooed arms.

"I need to file a harassment complaint," she continued. "Can you tell me where I can do that?"

The youngest of the officers smiled, a bit flirtatiously.

"I can help you," he said. "Why don't you follow me back to my office?"

He smiled at his coworkers then led Kit down a bright hallway, past a series of small offices. The stench of burned coffee hung in the air.

She followed him into an office and sat down on a cracked leather chair. He walked around a cluttered desk, hoisted up a belt cluttered with weapons, and sat down.

"What a cute little girl," he said, smiling again.

Kit held Elinor a little tighter. "I'm getting some threatening letters from my daughter's father," Kit said, "and I'm afraid he might hurt her or me. I wanted to find out what my legal rights are in this situation."

The officer leaned back in his chair, cupped his hands behind his head, and propped his heavy black boots on his desk.

"Do you share custody with the father?" he asked.

Kit fidgeted. "No. I didn't think he even knew about my daughter."

The man took his feet off the desk and leaned forward. "And why is that?"

"Well, we didn't have much of a relationship, and my daughter was a bit of a surprise." Kit flushed.

"So his name isn't on the birth certificate?"

"No," she said.

"Well, I'm sorry to tell you, but if he is her father he has a right to some sort of custody or visitation rights—unless you can prove he's mentally unfit in some way. But even then you'd have to let family court decide that."

"What if we're in danger now?" Kit fought the urge to cry. She had to stay strong. She pulled the note from her pocket and handed it to him. "This was left at my daughter's daycare. I think he may have called there, too."

The officer shrugged. "Unless he hurts one of you, or attempts to hurt one of you, there isn't much we can do."

"I think he may have tried to hit my car," she said. "I'm in a band, and my drummer was in a bad hit-and-run accident after our rehearsal the other night. The car had New York plates, and witnesses said it just pulled out of an alley beside the building where we practice."

This seemed to get his attention. "If he followed you there, why didn't he hit your car?"

Elinor picked up a pen from the man's desk and began to draw on Kit's jeans. Kit clicked it shut and let her play with it.

"I don't know. It was dark, and my drummer has a similar car to mine. Maybe he didn't see us come out."

"Why didn't you see anything?"

Kit thought back to the night. "Parking was tough so I had to park a few blocks away. It was a one-way street that took me in a different direction, so I didn't drive back past the studio where my drummer was parked."

"Were you drinking alcohol before you drove home?"

Kit flushed again, thinking. Did they bring beers that night? No, they were too stressed about prepping for the Hamilton show. It was the practice before that where she did shots at the bar with Margo before driving home to her baby daughter. She hoped her face didn't reveal her shame.

"No," she said, maybe a bit too defensively.

"I see."

Kit continued, determined. "I've received two threatening letters—one at my home and now this one at my daughter's daycare. My friend was involved in a suspicious hit-and-run and was badly hurt. I've had to move my daughter out of her own home, and we're afraid to leave the house. I have to go to New York tomorrow with my band, and I'm terrified to leave my daughter alone. There has to be something I can do."

The officer sighed loudly and crossed his arms on his desk. "Let me tell you what I'm hearing, miss. You're trying to hide your daughter from her own father, and you're surprised that this might make him angry. You're in a band and travel around while someone else watches this daughter you're so concerned about, and now you want the police to come in and clean up your mess." He paused for effect, his thin lips curling into a cruel grin. "Unfortunately, miss, we just don't have the staff to handle these kinds of requests, but there are social services that do. If you'd like, I can call a friend of mine there and arrange for a visit."

"No," Kit said quickly and stood up. The pen Elinor had been holding fell to the floor with a light clink. "No, thank you. You've made yourself very clear."

She walked past the men in the waiting area and out through the front door before she let the tears erupt. Elinor stared at her mother, confused. Kit tried to smile and kiss her daughter on the cheek, but Elinor remained concerned.

"It's okay, baby," she lied.

She clicked Elinor into her car seat then climbed into the driver's seat, looking around the street again for strange cars as she did. Seeing none, she pulled her phone out of her purse.

"Dad," she cried into the phone. "I need your help."

* * *

Her father agreed to meet Kit at a café near his house. When Kit arrived at the dark, cozy coffee shop, she saw both her father and her sister sitting stiffly in the corner, enormous mugs of coffee on the tiny table before them.

She carried Elinor over and sat down.

"I thought your sister should come, too, since she can tell us exactly what she told Skip," her father said.

"I am so sorry, Kit," Nikki said. "I had no idea just mentioning your situation would get back to Damien."

"What exactly did you tell him?" Kit asked. She was no longer angry, just numb.

Her sister looked thoughtful. "I know I told him you were back at home with a baby." She looked at Kit and held out her hand to touch Elinor's cheek. "But that's it. It was just a quick little thing, and then he mostly started talking about himself and all of his band successes, blah blah blah." She paused. "That, and he did say Damien had sort of lost it." She looked at her father and then back at Kit. "He knew you had kind of a thing with Damien, and I guess he passed it along as interesting trivia. He did say he hardly ever saw Damien anymore. I really don't think he put your baby and Damien together." She picked up her coffee and took a sip.

As Nikki spoke, Kit was surprised that her father stayed calm, nodding his head as he listened to the details of Kit's sordid sexual history as if it were a stock report.

"So," he said, "he knows you and Elinor live with me, and he knows where that is thanks to Skip." He practically seethed his name through his teeth. "It also sounds like he may have followed you to daycare, and maybe even to work. We're in a unique situation, though. We're leaving for a few weeks. That could be enough time for him to lose interest, or disappear, or start another project."

"Or find you," Nikki said.

He gave her an angry look. "That's not helpful, Nikki."

"Shouldn't you file a restraining order or something?" Nikki asked.

"With what evidence?" Kit said. "All I have is a bunch of speculation. Based on my experience at the police station, that won't hold up legally."

Her dad interrupted. "On the tour, Kit and Elinor will be surrounded by people, and I'll be there the whole time. I think it will be the safest thing to do. We just need to make a plan for tomorrow when she goes to New York."

Nikki looked at Kit. "You're going to New York in the middle of all this?"

Kit blushed. "I shouldn't."

"Of course you should," her father said, loud enough to cause the pierced café cashier to turn and look at them. He lowered his voice. "How many times do you get to go on national television?"

"Excuse me?" Nikki asked.

"Yeah, we might play on D.J. Hamilton tomorrow," Kit said. "It's not definite—only if there's enough time after Margo is interviewed. But yeah, maybe."

"No, way!" It was Nikki's turn to be loud.

"Yes," her father said, "and this jerk isn't going to prevent her from having that opportunity."

Kit raised her eyebrows. She'd never heard her father talk like that before.

"It's only one more day," he continued. "Kit, you should stick with your plan to take Elinor to Holly's house. I can go over and make sure everything's all right."

Kit hugged Elinor close and tickled her with her nose.

"Thanks, Dad," she said. "By the way, did you call the daycare today?"

Her father lifted his mug. "Nothing wrong with a granddad checking in on his little girl once in a while."

Kit smiled, feeling safe for the first time in days.

CHAPTER 25

Thirtieth Street Station was busy for a Tuesday. Margo sipped her coffee and admired the historical landmark—the statue of an angel towering over one end of the station and the soaring ceilings carved with ornate designs typical of the Beaux-Arts period. Commuters buzzed around her, descending and ascending the many numbered staircases, and the old-fashioned train schedule clicked off arrivals and departures above her head.

She scanned the crowd for Kit, but face after face remained anonymous. Kit had left the house long before Margo that morning—of course her kid had been up at the crack of dawn again. According to the plan, Kit was meeting her dad at a gas station somewhere, switching cars, then dropping her daughter off at a babysitter's house before driving to the station. How long could that take? Margo looked up at the enormous clock ticking away on the wall. Their train was leaving in ten minutes.

She decided not to wait. Their track had not yet been announced, but she wanted to get in position to race the hordes of New York travelers to a good seat. She stood and lifted her heavy bag over her arm and grabbed her guitar with her other hand. She had packed five different outfits and was still unsure that any would be just right. Some were casual but sexy; some were formal and sexy. All of them showcased her best asset with plunging necklines, but now she was starting to worry that they were too plunging. She hoped they had a decent makeup artist who could cover the bags under her eyes.

She walked closer to the sign and stared intently at the New York train information, ready to sprint toward her track at its command. There was a tap on her shoulder and she turned to see Kit, who looked frazzled.

"Sorry. This whole bait-and-switch game took longer than expected."

Margo heard the click of a spinning schedule above their heads and looked up. Track 12. "Let's go."

The two women joined the stampede toward Track 12. The crowd of passengers snaked quickly into a long queue, and once the Amtrak employee removed the thick red rope, the stairs clogged with people cramming to be the first ones on the train. Margo descended with the masses, losing Kit in the process. She walked down the tight aisles, scanning for available seats, her large bag banging against seatbacks and elbows. Finally, near the snack car, she saw Kit. Her worn duffel bag was holding the seat next to her and she was arguing with every passenger that tried to steal it. Margo slid her guitar on top of Kit's bass in the storage rack above their heads.

"Good lord," Margo said as she plopped into the seat, squeezing her large bag under her feet.

"I know—it's crazy. Glad I don't have to do this every day."

Margo watched as the last of the Philadelphia crowd emptied from the platform and the train pulled away from the station. A large man stood in the aisle next to her, bumping her knee with his briefcase. She squeezed closer to Kit.

The train emerged from the dark tunnel and daylight streamed in through the windows. They passed an endless stream of row homes in the distance before leaving the city behind. Margo leaned back and closed her eyes. She would have over an hour to relax.

"So, do you think Ronni will be all right?" Kit said. "I mean, if there's time for us to play."

Margo nodded, hoping Kit would get the hint.

"I hope so," she continued. "I'm really nervous. You do this all the time, but I've never been on television. I hope I don't totally fuck up."

"You'll be fine," Margo answered, eyes still closed.

"At least we'll have some time to practice," she said. She paused. "We will, right?"

Margo nodded again.

"So, do you feel ready for tonight?" Kit asked

Margo looked at her old friend. "I know you're excited, Kit, but I'm exhausted. I'm just going to take a little nap."

"Oh." Kit blushed. "Okay, sorry."

Margo closed her eyes again, letting the rumble of the train lull her to sleep.

CHAPTER 26

As the train pulled into New York's Penn Station, Kit gathered her bass and duffel bag and squeezed into the aisle behind Margo. The train ride had been fine, but as the mass of passengers pushed her out of the train, the rumbling white noise of the station brought back memories of less pleasant times. Before Elinor, she'd made regular trips to Philadelphia's big sister city to see bands and hang with friends of friends. It was during one of those trips that she'd seen Damien.

It had been a weeknight. Now that she had Elinor, she couldn't imagine burning so much energy on any night of the week. But back then she was living in her own place. She would leave right after work, party all night in the city, and take an early train home in time to shower and return to her job at a medical publishing house.

On that particular night she'd been feeling especially low. Her attempts at starting a new band after Broad Street had been a disaster. Margo had started dating a local newspaper journalist, so Kit saw very little of her. Her sister was still screwing her ex-boss, and Kit hadn't had a steady boyfriend since she and Charlie broke up. Self-pity was not a good appetizer for New York City. Nothing made Kit lonelier than a crowd.

She was supposed to have met friends at The Continental to see Rockzilla, a tongue-in-cheek metal band that had been generating some buzz. Her friends never showed up, so Kit drank. Beer after beer after beer. By the time the band started, things were a bit fuzzy. She didn't know Damien was Rockzilla's guitarist. He'd shown up late and gone straight on stage. When he came over to talk with her after the show she was so glad to have someone to talk to, to pay attention to her, that she tried not to think about his history with Charlie, about how he'd started as a guitarist for Charlie's band and then convinced the other members to throw Charlie out. In her alcoholic haze, talking to this tall dark-haired man with light eyes after sitting alone at the The Continental all night, she'd all but forgotten how pissed off and even verbally abusive he'd been when Charlie's new band started getting better gigs and better write-ups.

Damien had been a familiar face when she needed one. She'd gone back to his apartment. He'd told her about the excitement of living in New York and played some of his own material on his acoustic guitar. They got naked. She did not remember discussing birth control.

That one night stretched on—into Bloody Marys the next morning, calling in sick to work, drinks in the Village, drinking more beer at a show his band played in Tribeca the next night. When her phone died she didn't bother recharging it. She was happy to disappear for a while.

Thinking back, she knew there were signs that Damien was not quite normal. The other band members didn't seem to like him very much. He had some very strong opinions on things that didn't seem based in reality—like his belief that the government was trying to poison society by dousing all foods in saturated fats. But, at the time, he was warm, temporary comfort.

It was on the third day that Kit's sister got a message to her through a mutual friend. Their mother was dead.

"Let's try and find a cab." Margo's voice interrupted her memories.

Kit blinked, re-acclimating herself to the present and to the busy station. "Sure. I don't feel like dealing with the subway."

They merged onto yet another crowded escalator that carried them up to the street and the cacophony of horns and chatter and hawking street vendors. They waited in a long line until they were finally standing beside their personal golden chariot. The driver tossed their bags and instruments into the trunk and Margo gave him the address.

The cab wove through the busy streets as they made their way up to Fifty-Third. Kit stared out the window like a fish, not quite sure if she could breathe outside of the safety of the quiet cab. It had been so long since she'd experienced the kind of intensity she watched through the window.

When they arrived at the theater, Kit was disappointed when she saw the marquee sandwiched between a camera shop and a fast-food chicken restaurant. The building was smaller than she'd expected, with a tattered Art Deco front. She'd expected grandeur and lines of waiting fans screaming to see the show. In fact, very few people were mingling in front of the entrance, and the guard who stood by the door looked bored.

Margo stepped up to him. "We're on the show tonight. Can you tell me where we need to go?"

The man pointed to the corner of the building. "Around there," he said flatly. "1697."

Kit and Margo exchanged glances, shrugged, and walked around the corner, where it was quieter still. They found the number 1697 on a dirty glass door, and inside another bored guard sat in an old folding chair.

She turned a cold glare in their direction. "Yes?" she said.

"Margo Bevelaqua," Margo said. "We're on the show tonight."

"One moment." The woman stood and shuffled to a phone that sat on a small desk. She dialed, spoke into the receiver, then hung up. She shuffled back to her seat and sat down.

"You're early. Come back in an hour."

"Shit," Margo grumbled. "Can we at least leave our things here?"

"No," the guard said. She returned her attention to her tabloid newspaper.

They stepped back outside. Kit's bass felt heavy on her shoulder. "Let's get something to eat," she suggested. "We've got time."

"Okay," Margo said. "Something light. I don't need a gut tonight."

They found a small deli that had decent salads and an open

table. They crushed their things as close to the wall as they could and sat down.

"I don't think I've ever played completely sober before," Kit said, crunching on her salad.

Margo looked up. "You know, you're right. I never even thought of that. They probably have booze in the greenroom, but maybe we should pick up a little extra confidence booster."

"Alcohol always seemed to make our gigs go smoother," Kit said, smiling.

They finished their salads and lugged their bags and instruments down Broadway until they found a small store with a neon "Spirits" sign in the window. They tucked a small bottle of Jim Beam into Kit's guitar case then headed back toward the theater.

The same guard greeted them with the same lack of enthusiasm. She reluctantly picked up the phone to announce their arrival.

A few minutes later, a young redhead in a blue suit emerged from the dark hallway that led into the building. She greeted them with an extended hand and a bright white smile.

"Hi!" she said, shaking each of their hands. "I'm Melanie. I'll take you back to the waiting room, where you'll meet our producer, Nancy Klein. Please follow me."

She turned and led them down the long corridor. Kit's heart pounded as they passed open office doors where young people talked on phones and typed on computer keyboards. Writers? Interns? She wasn't sure who they were, but they all seemed to be doing something important.

They were ushered past this chaos and into a pleasant waiting room with a television in one corner. D.J. Hamilton photos and posters and awards covered the walls.

"Wait here," she said. "The producer will be here shortly. You're a little early."

As the door shut behind her, Kit turned to Margo.

"Can you believe we're here?" She felt woozy with elation and nerves. D.J. Hamilton himself could be just feet away from where they were sitting. She looked around at his many representations on the wall. In one photo, a young D.J. Hamilton displayed his famous wild brown hair and bearded grin, his arm wrapped around Richard Pryor, clearly before he'd been hit with MS. In another photo

Hamilton was joking with that animal guy as a giant white cockatoo gripped his shoulder.

"This is a little surreal," Margo admitted.

Kit was glad that Margo also seemed intimidated.

As they sat staring at the television, Kit's mind was spinning with possible scenarios of how the night would go—many of them ended in embarrassing disaster.

Stop, she scolded herself. Everything will be fine. You've played the song hundreds of times. Well—at least dozens. She started doing the math to take her mind off her anxiety. They had practiced once a week for two years, adding in two shows a month . . .

The door opened and Ronni burst into the room, looking much cooler than Kit felt. "Hey, gals!" she said. "Holy shit!" Her eyes panned the walls. "This is too much."

She plopped her bag onto a small loveseat and boldly walked around the room, running her finger along awards on the walls, picking up trophy-like statues from the end tables and turning them over to examine them. Her blatant disrespect for these items made Kit nervous.

"Did you take the train in?" Margo asked.

"Nah," Ronni said, grabbing a handful of candy from a bowl on a glass coffee table. She continued to look around the room as she spoke. "I drove in with some friends. They're trying to scope out tickets for tonight's show as we speak. Oh! Here's a phone. My cell totally died on the way up."

She walked over and picked up the receiver of a green phone that sat in one corner of the room. She listened for a moment, then started dialing.

"Maybe you shouldn't be doing that," Kit suggested.

Ronni cocked her head. "Who's going to care? I have to call my roommate. She's gonna totally die when she hears where I am." She continued punching buttons, hanging up, punching more buttons. "Shit, I can't get an outside line. Oh, hello? Um, yeah, I'm one of the guests tonight and I'm trying to make a call."

Kit wanted to strangle her. She was sure Ronni would get them kicked off the show before they even got a glimpse of the stage. She glanced at Margo, who was flipping through a magazine.

"Great, thank you," Ronni said. She smiled triumphantly

at Kit. "Piece of cake," she said. She dialed again and paused. "Charlotte! Guess where I am! Yeah, I'm really here. Looks like the guy is a total egomaniac—he has pictures of himself all over the place."

Kit heard the low rumbling of voices in the hallway. It sounded like two women, and the volume swelled until she was sure they were just on the other side of the door. Panicked, Kit walked over and hung up the phone.

"What the—" Ronni said.

"Someone's coming," Kit whispered.

Moments later, the door opened and a well-dressed woman entered, accompanied by the same redheaded page. The woman seemed a little surprised to see how many people greeted her.

"Good afternoon," she said. "Which one of you is Margo?"

Margo stood and offered the woman a confident outstretched hand. "I'm Margo. It's nice to meet you."

"I'm Nancy Klein, the show's talent coordinator. We spoke on the phone. Would you follow me, please? I'll take you back to wardrobe." She looked around the room again. "I'm afraid guests need to wait in here or out front. I can see that you all get tickets for the show."

Kit panicked.

"Actually, they're in my band," Margo said. "You mentioned we might be playing tonight."

A hint of surprise rippled across the woman's professional mask. "Oh, I forgot about that. I meant to discuss that with the segment editor, but . . ." She paused and looked at Kit and Ronni. "I guess you can come back with me, too. We'll see what kind of time we have."

Kit's enthusiasm dissipated into embarrassment as she and Ronni followed Margo, the only one truly wanted in this pack, down the hall toward the famous green room.

CHAPTER 27

Margo was disappointed in the green room. It was only slightly larger than the waiting room and furnished with the same generic leather couches. A crystal bucket of ice sat next to a selection of small soda and water bottles on a long table. Where was the champagne? She thought surely there would be an open bar in a D.J. Hamilton greenroom.

There were also two silver trays of food—one filled with cookies and pastries and the other with small sandwiches. A small television hung from the ceiling in one corner.

"You can leave your things here while we go to makeup," Nancy said. She moved her eyes over Margo's casual attire. "Will you need to change your clothes?"

"Of course," she said. "I brought a few things." She kept her bag over her shoulder while Kit and Ronni deposited their things on the floor.

Nancy looked at her watch. "We have a little less than an hour. I guess I can take you back now."

"What should we do?" Kit asked.

Nancy looked at her, wrinkling her nose slightly. "Wait here. I'll find out if we have time." She turned back to Margo. "You did send a demo to our segment editor, right?"

"Yes, of course," Margo lied.

"Okay, I'll check with him. You must have some powerful friends to have gotten on the show on such short notice." She stared hard at Margo. "Follow me," she said. She turned on her heel and marched out of the room like a drill sergeant.

The makeup room was not much different than the one at Contemporary Living—there were just more chairs. Each one faced a similar small table illuminated by a mirror ringed with round lights. Two young women in black looked up with anticipation when she walked in, but their excitement faded when they saw she was only a small celeb. Margo missed Peter.

"Effie, this is Margo," Nancy said. "I need you to work on her. She needs to change, too, so help her with that. I'll be back in about twenty minutes to get her." She walked out, closing the door behind her.

Margo resented Nancy's patronizing tone but stood patiently while Effie sauntered over. She was tall and rail thin, with big exotic dark eyes, poker-straight black hair, and explosive red lips. Margo was sure she had to be an aspiring actress.

"Follow me," she said. She led Margo to the back of the room, where smaller dressing rooms were pocketed along the back wall.

"You can get changed in there." She pointed randomly to one of the dressing rooms.

She turned away and slunk back to the other girl, her hand already on its way to her face for a whispered evaluation of Margo.

Margo stepped into the dressing room and closed the door. She unzipped her bag and began pulling out her options, shaking the slight wrinkles out of each one. First was the black dress, simple, a little snug, low cut. Maybe too simple. Next she pulled out a black skirt with a colorful form-fitting top. She could wear it with tights and high black boots. Too casual? A sleeveless tight dress paired with a bright tailored jacket was next. She could accent this with a scarf or necklace. This was the winner so far. She pulled out the last two outfits and rejected both of them. She wasn't thrilled with her choice, but it would have to do.

As she undressed she felt the film of New York clinging to her skin and wished she could take a shower. She reapplied perfume and deodorant before stepping into the dress and pulling it up and over her shoulders. She looked in the mirror. Her stomach curved out a

little more than she liked, but overall the fit was flattering. She put
on black stockings, then a chunky necklace, and finally the jacket.
She looked again in the mirror. While the jacket hid her stomach, she
didn't look very urban guerilla.

There was a tiny knock on the door. "Are you almost ready?"
Effie sounded bored and impatient.

"Yep, be right out." She glanced again at the mirror. Fuck it,
she thought. She looked pretty good, and she could always remove
the jacket if she was feeling bold.

When she opened the door Effie looked up and motioned
with her head to follow her to one of the vacant seats. She sat down
on the cold vinyl chair, causing it to spin slightly until she caught
herself with her foot.

Effie began her work with the enthusiasm of a funeral home
director, pulling Margo's hair back with a headband, wiping off her
old makeup with a cotton ball doused with remover, applying new
makeup without questioning Margo's usual colors.

"Greens and browns always work pretty well," she offered,
hoping Effie was not painting a harsh turquoise above her green eyes.

"We'll make you gorgeous, don't worry."

Margo wanted to slap her. Instead, she tried small talk. "Who
are the guests tonight?"

Effie's face lit up. "Jake McGinty. I'm hoping I get to do him,
but it depends when he shows up." She looked over at her coworker,
sitting in the corner filing her nails.

Jake McGinty was the current Hollywood hottie, starring
in successive bad romances that attracted young, swooning girls like
Effie. Margo considered him another bland blond who would fade
faster than his perfectly aged jeans.

"Anyone else?" Margo asked.

"Yeah, that psychic from New Jersey—and you, I guess."

"No musical guest?"

"I guess not. I think the psychic's going to do some gag with
D.J. or something. I really don't know for sure. Look up, please."

Her touch was cold, not the loving hand of a friend to which
she was accustomed. Margo was anxious for her to finish so she could
return to the green room.

CHAPTER 28

Kit was ready to kill Ronni, who was bouncing around the green room fondling various items despite Kit's protests. She took experimental bites from just about everything on the platters and tossed what she didn't eat into a small trashcan.

"Put that down," Kit said for about the twentieth time. Ronni was harder to manage than Elinor, who was hopefully secure and happy at Holly's house. She suddenly wished she could be holding her in her arms instead of scolding this immature excuse for an adult.

Ronni was holding a swirl of blue glass that was surely worth thousands of dollars. She was spinning it in front of her eyes, the blue light twinkling across her face.

"I wonder what it's made of," she said.

"Something you can't afford, I'm sure," Kit said. She stood up, grabbed the object from Ronni's hand, and replaced it on the end table.

Ronni rolled her eyes again and smiled. "You really should lighten up, Kit."

Kit glared at her. "Don't forget who invited you here." Her voice trembled slightly. She felt this whole dream was now as fragile as paper; the slightest disturbance might send it crumpled to the wind. No one wanted them on the show. No one knew who she was, or who the band was. Their invitation to be on the tour was based on the faith of The Venturas, who hadn't seen them play in years. And she'd travelled over a hundred miles away from her daughter, who was at risk from her deranged father, to chase this elusive dream. For what, she wondered miserably.

As the minutes ticked away in the empty green room, she grew more and more convinced that this Hamilton experience was a foreshadowing of the weeks ahead, and that Ronni was the bull in this china shop.

The door opened and Nancy Klein led in a smiling man who looked vaguely familiar. He was short and stocky, with thick dark hair and matching eyebrows. The aroma of his cologne flooded the room. When he looked at the two women, his smile faded.

"Who are you?" he asked them.

"These two are in Margo Bevelaqua's band," Nancy said. She turned and looked at them. "I'm sorry, I didn't catch your names."

"I'm—" Kit began.

Nancy waved her hand. "Doesn't matter, just introduce yourselves to Bob. I'm running late."

"Do you know if we're playing yet?" Ronni asked.

"Not yet," Nancy said, her voice fading as she exited the room. "I'll know more soon."

The door closed behind her, sealing the three in silence.

Mr. Cologne looked them both up and down, pausing to take in Ronni's tight jeans and perfect petite chest. He burst into a synthetic white grin. "You forgot something," he said.

"Excuse me?" Ronni said.

"You left something important at home, and now you're worried about it."

Ronni paused, then smiled. "Hey—you're that psychic guy from the Sci-Fi channel!"

He shook Ronni's hand. Kit noticed chunky gold rings on almost every finger. "Bob Tenerelli, nice to meet you . . ."

"I'm Ron—"

He quieted her with a thick finger to his lips. "Wait." He clung to her hand and closed his eyes dramatically. After a moment, they snapped back open. "Rhonda."

Ronni shot a quick smirk toward Kit and smiled back at Bob. "How did you know?"

He brushed off the mock compliment with a shrug. "So, tell me, Rhonda. What is it you forgot?"

Ronni walked over to her drum bag and began sorting through it. Kit didn't mind being invisible. Fraud or not, she didn't want this guy anywhere near her head. She'd seen parts of his show a few times while flipping channels on the rare occasions she had time to watch TV. He usually stood in the center of bleacher-style seats filled with sad people. He "read" their thoughts and told them nice things about dead people they loved. She resented how he exploited these people.

"Looks like I have everything," Ronni said.

"Were you expecting a family member to come to the show, maybe a younger sibling?"

Ronni looked up. "No . . ." she said uncertainly.

"I definitely get the feeling of a missing child."

Kit panicked. "I have a daughter."

Bob turned his dark eyes toward her. His pupils blended into deep charcoal irises and they seemed to bore through her.

"Is she," she said, pausing to lick her dry lips, "is she okay?"

Again, Bob's face cracked into a blinding white grin. "Oh, she's fine. I knew I got the sense of a child. You left her home today, with a family member?"

"Well, sort of. A childcare worker she knows very well." Kit wanted to call that instant, to hear the sound of her daughter in the background, happy and playing safely.

Bob extended his hand and Kit took it.

"I'm Kit," she said. His skin was rough—the hand of a carpenter or mechanic.

"Of course you are." He smiled but did not release her hand. He cocked his head slightly, as if he'd suddenly noticed something about her, a memory triggered.

Just as Kit could no longer resist the urge to pull her hand away, the door opened again and Nancy walked in with Jake McGinty. Kit gasped.

Jake was clearly accustomed to this reaction. His dirty blond hair was strategically mussed, his tan skin buffed to accentuate an attempt at bad-boy stubble, his casual clothes worth more than Kit's car. He was a man who had made it, at the ripe old age of twenty-two. He looked annoyed.

"We're so sorry about your dressing room, Jake," Nancy was saying. "They told us they'd have those pipes fixed by now, but there's still water everywhere. You'll be very comfortable here, I assure you. I can get you anything you want."

"You can get my fucking manager on the phone," Jake snarled. He heaved himself into a chair, lit a cigarette, and sulked.

"Just let me know what you need," Nancy continued, unfazed. She turned to Kit and Ronni. "Good news, girls. It looks like we'll have time for you to play tonight. I talked to the segment producer. He thinks we can give you about a minute and a half."

Kit gasped again, but this time it was internal—an involuntary lung constriction. Panic. She attempted a smile, a look of confidence, but the effort was irrelevant. Nancy was gone.

CHAPTER 29

Effie scraped makeup onto her skin until it tingled with raw abuse, and when Margo was finally released from her cold talons she felt both relief and anxiety. Leaving the makeup room brought her one step closer to meeting D.J. Hamilton and to being watched by more viewers than her entire run combined. Of all those millions, there was one in particular she wanted to impress. She had known Harry less than a week, and already she wanted to make him proud of her. It was ridiculous.

She followed another young page back to the green room, where she was surprised to find that Kit and Ronni had been joined by a tacky Italian guy and none other than Jake McGinty himself. Jake was everything Margo had imagined—as beautiful as the rich celluloid that had given him birth. He was clearly not happy to be stuck there with them and didn't even bother to offer her a polite smile when she entered the room.

"We're going to play!" Kit fairly exploded with the news.

This did not make Margo feel better. She had begun to quietly hope there would be one less thing to worry about. It was all she could do to keep a concise internal monologue of stories she would tell tonight. "That's great," she said. She forced a smile and then remembered the little helper in a bottle tucked away in Kit's case.

"Be careful," the tacky Italian man said to her.

She turned. "Excuse me?" She recognized his face.

He smiled and offered his hand. "Bob Tenerelli."

She shook it. "Nice to meet you. I'm Mar—"

"Margo, I know," he said. His smile grew wider. "I'm a big fan."

Margo was familiar with this kind of leer, but his was different somehow—more intimate. She pulled her hand from his and looked over at Jake, who was still slouched in a chair, flipping through a *Star* magazine. He was clearly not a fan.

"Can you believe it?" Kit said. Her wide-eyed enthusiasm somehow made Margo even more nervous. Kit glanced at the psychic, then back at Margo. "I have to make a quick call. I'll be right back."

"Never pick a man who's prettier than you are." Ronni's voice sang softly into her ear behind her.

Margo shook her head, newly annoyed by Ronni's adorable ethnicity and feeling white and dull and old next to her. Ronni smiled and nodded toward Jake, who had his feet up on a coffee table and was talking loudly into his phone. "Perfect song for someone like that, huh?" Ronni said.

Margo ignored her and walked over to sit on the couch next to Jake. She would be noticed. When he finished his call, she leaned over and offered her hand. "Margo Bevelaqua."

He looked down at her hand, then back up. "I don't shake hands. Germs."

Margo fought the urge to wipe her hand against her nose and rub it in his face. Instead, she dropped her hand into her lap. "I understand. I get freaks all the time wanting to do more than just shake my hand."

He stared at her, amused that she would compare her celebrity to his.

"Oh yeah," she continued. "Just last week, I had a fan letter smeared with his personal greeting card."

Jake's lip curled. "Who are you?"

"Not a big fan of gardening, huh?"

Jake raised his eyebrows and shook his head.

"I'm the Garden Princess of the Contemporary Living Network. Lucky you—you're surrounded by cable television!" She nodded toward the psychic, who was leaning close to Ronni and staring down an open fold of her shirt.

"That guy helped a friend of mine," Jake said. Margo was startled by his sudden vulnerability. He was gazing at the psychic, remembering. "He lost his brother." He paused. "No, his brother died. I hate when people say you lost someone like you have no idea where they went. His brother was in a car, and then someone hit that car and killed him."

Margo looked at the psychic. She found it difficult to imagine him comforting anyone.

"My friend went to his show," Jake continued, "and this guy helped him talk to his brother. I still think it's bullshit, but it made him feel better."

Margo wasn't sure how to respond. She stole another up-close glance at this flawless species. From his hair to his manicured nails to his scuffless shoes, this was perfection incarnate. "People look for comfort in those situations," she said.

Her words seemed to snap him out of his thoughts and he looked at her, surprised to still see her there. He returned his attention to the magazine, mumbling insults about the various celebrity photos. Margo went over to Kit, who was putting her phone away.

"Everything okay?" she asked.

"Yes." She raised her eyebrows in the direction of the psychic. "That guy freaked me out. He knew I'd left Elinor behind."

"But she's all right?"

"Yeah, she's fine. My dad actually got to the babysitter's house a little while ago to help take care of her. One less thing to worry about, I hope. Now I'm just down to one huge worry."

The door opened. Nancy was back.

"We have about fifteen minutes until dress rehearsal. Jake, you'll be up first, then Bob, then Margo. The band will have to set up before taping. You can keep your stuff backstage until we're ready." She looked at Kit and Ronni. "If you need to change, you should do it now. Margo can tell you where the dressing room is. Okay, I'll be back in a few minutes to get you, Jake."

"I can't get hold of my manager—is she here yet?" he asked.

"Oh, shoot. I did get a call from her, sorry. She's running late, but she said she should be here in time for your segment."

The door closed.

"Fucking cunt!" Jake shouted, throwing his phone across the room.

Everyone else froze as the sound of the phone hitting the wall echoed in the silence.

Bob walked over and placed a gentle hand on his shoulder. Jake shrugged it away. "She's stuck in traffic," Bob said calmly. "She'll be here soon."

Jake rolled his eyes and turned toward the wall. "She would have called."

"Her phone died."

"She has all my material. We always do a run through before I do these stupid talk shows."

"I don't know about you guys," Margo piped up. "But I could use a drink." All eyes were now on her.

Kit smiled, opened her case, and released the Jim Beam. She uncapped it, took the first swig, then passed it to Margo, who followed suit. She walked over to Jake and held out the bottle.

"Alcohol kills germs," she said.

He stared up at her, then at the bottle. He reached out and emptied a few large swallows into his perfect mouth.

CHAPTER 30

When Nancy came back a fast fifteen minutes later, Kit was already feeling a little buzz. Nothing debilitating, just the hint of confidence she needed.

"Jake, you ready?"

"Ready!" he said. He winked at them and followed her out the door.

"I should get changed," Kit said. "Ronni, did you want to change?"

"Nah," she said. She'd returned to her curious touch-every-thing-in-the-room mode and Kit realized it didn't bother her as much as it had half an hour ago.

"I'll show you the dressing room," Margo said.

Kit picked up her bag and followed Margo down the hall. In the makeup room, a tall thin woman was leaning close to Jake's face. Another tall thin woman scowled in the corner.

"Hi gals," he said.

"Hey, Jake," Kit said, tingling with the thrill of recognition.

Margo pointed her to a row of doors. "You can get dressed in any one of those."

"Come in with me," Kit said. The liquor had made her feel warm toward Margo, remembering the days when they spent hours before a gig choosing the perfect outfits.

Margo smiled. "Sure."

The two women squeezed into the small room. Margo had to press herself against one wall to give Kit enough room to lean down and sort through her suitcase. Suddenly, Kit straightened up with a jolt.

"I just realized something," she said. "What if Damien sees me on television? He'll know we're on the tour."

"I hate to tell you this, but it's not exactly a secret."

"Right. Of course. What the hell am I doing?"

"Kit, you and Elinor are going to be surrounded by security at all times. Damien isn't the only nutty fan out there, believe me. Don't let him ruin this for you." Margo opened the door a crack, peeked out, and then popped her head back into the small dressing room. "Let's make you look fabulous. I saw a rack of clothes against the back wall down there. We should check it out."

"How can we get to it without those makeup girls noticing?"

Margo rubbed her fist against her right eye, smearing mascara and eyeshadow. She smiled at Kit and walked out, leaving the door ajar.

"Hey, Effie, can you fix this eye? Sorry, I got something in it."

Kit heard an exasperated sigh and footsteps. When she looked out a moment later, both women were hunched over their work in great concentration. She tiptoed over to the rack, grabbed a few quick outfits from the large selection, and whisked them back to the dressing room. The gowns were beautiful, but most of them, designed for anorexic Hollywood, were much too small. A few were too large, but she found two that looked perfect. She stripped down to her underwear, pulled a short black sequined dress over her head, and wiggled into it. It was a little snug, but flattering. She smiled at herself in the mirror. She thought she actually looked like a star.

The door opened and Margo slipped in, her makeup returned to its previously overdone state. "You look awesome," she whispered. "But you can't look better than me. Let's see what else we have here." She began flipping through the gowns Kit had hung on the dressing room hooks.

"What if someone notices?"

"We play dumb. This is your first time on television—you can't be expected to know everything."

Margo wriggled into a long red gown that shimmered in the fluorescent lights. Kit helped her pull the zipper closed. When Margo turned around, Kit smiled. She looked stunning.

"I think we found us a winner," Margo said.

Kit quickly touched up her makeup and they slipped out of the dressing room and past the makeup artists, who hardly seemed to notice them. Jake had left, and the two tall women were huddled in excited conversation.

CHAPTER 31

Margo giggled with Kit as they scurried back down the hall to the green room, but she felt her giddy buzz dissipating. Reality was setting in, and time was running out. She would be called out shortly for dress rehearsal, and she was growing less mentally prepared as the moments passed.

Back in the green room Ronni was curled up in a corner chair hugging her shins, head on her knees, listening to her headphones. The only sign of life was an index finger tapping out the silent beat. Psychic Bob rested on the long couch, his head back against the wall and his feet propped up on a coffee table. Jake was gone.

When Margo and Kit closed the door behind them, Ronni looked up. Her face split into a grin. "Holy shit!" she said. "Where did you swipe those?"

This roused Bob, who sat up to inspect the transformed glamour girls.

"Very nice, ladies," he said with a sneer.

"Well, Bob," Margo said. "Will we get away with it?"

He cocked his head. "I'm not sure. Might need to wet the old whistle again to tap the senses."

"I might need to tap the senses myself," she said. "Kit?"

Kit pulled the bottle out of her bag. "Not much left," she said.

"I thought they usually keep booze backstage." Margo said.

"D.J.'s a notorious teetotaler," Bob said. "The official story is that he doesn't want his guests inebriated during their performance, but I sense he's in A.A."

"Whatever," Margo said. "We have a problem that needs solving, and I think we should send our new drummer out to get some more before the show."

"Why me?" Ronni whined.

"Because you're new," Margo said, "and because you owe us at least one."

Ronni sulked but did not protest further. Kit twisted off the cap and took a long swig. She passed the bottle to Margo, who did the same and handed it to Bob. He drank deeply and handed the near-empty bottle to Ronni.

"Great," she said. She finished the contents and ran the back of her hand against her mouth. Before she had time to twist the cap back on the bottle, Nancy opened the door. Ronni slipped the bottle behind her back, as subtle as a jackhammer.

Margo arranged her smile and turned to Nancy, expecting to be scolded.

She glanced up from her clipboard. "Margo, you're up," she said.

"Great," Margo said with a forced smile.

She glanced back at Kit, who smiled warmly. "Go kick some ass," she said.

Margo followed Nancy as she walked down the corridor, eyes focused on her clipboard. She heard the slow swell of noise—music and voices—as they approached the backstage area. The space was dark and cluttered with equipment, and Margo glimpsed light through a slit in a heavy black curtain.

Just before they reached this opening, Nancy thrust her hand back against Margo. "Wait," she whispered.

The sound was now coming into focus. Margo heard D.J. Hamilton's familiar hearty laughter, and then Jake said something she couldn't hear. Another sincere laugh from D.J., and then some parting words of appreciation. The band music bloomed and Jake slipped through the parted curtains, pausing to whisper in Margo's ear.

"Got any more hooch?" he asked.

She could smell the strong sting of whiskey on his breath and realized she was wearing the same oral perfume. She slipped her thumb into her bra, searching for her breath strips, but felt only skin. *Crap*, she thought, realizing they must have fallen out when she changed her dress.

"You're next," Nancy said, pushing her into the light of the stage.

CHAPTER 32

Margo blinked in the lights and shivered. It was freezing, and her nipples instantly stood at attention. She walked across the stage toward a smiling D.J. Hamilton—the man who had lived in two dimensions on her late-night television through high school and college and into adulthood. Here he was, in the flesh. She tried to remember to smile. He was just a man. He took a dump like everybody else, and now he was wrapping his warm soft hand around hers in a firm sensual handshake and she had to keep thinking: *Smile, smile. You're Margo Bevelaqua, intimidated by no one.* But she had trouble believing this now. He was taller than she thought he'd be, and he smelled fantastic—clean and a little spicy and—shit. *Smile, smile.*

She followed him to the desk that had also lived for so long on her television and sat on an ice-cold leather chair.

"You can relax," the legend, D.J. Hamilton, was saying to her. "This is just rehearsal. No need to freeze your face into a perma-grin."

"Thanks," she said, not removing the smile from her face. "It's great to meet you."

"So," he said, looking down at some index cards on his desk. *He doesn't know who I am,* Margo thought. Although this didn't surprise her, it did bother her. "Your gardening show has been doing really well, and you've developed an audience not typically known for gardening. How do you do it?"

"A lot of tight clothes," she heard herself saying with more confidence than she felt.

And there was that big laugh from the legend's gut. It was forced and insincere, but she was incredibly grateful for it. As abruptly as it started, it stopped.

"That's fine," he said, straight-faced. He turned toward the huge looming cameras in front of them. Behind the cameras, she saw the dark figures of large men silhouetted against the empty theater. "Bill, how are the lights on this dress? Are you getting too much glare?"

"It's okay," a husky voice said from one of the silhouettes.

"You sure?" he asked again. He turned and stared at Margo's breasts. "I've seen these throw a lot of hot spots at the camera."

"The dress looks just fine from here," the voice said again, followed by a chuckle.

Margo sat up straighter, comfortable now that she had regained her usual role in front of the camera. *The camera is your best friend.* "Harry's words swam in her head.

"Hey, watch where you put that dolly," she joked to the anonymous voice, shifting her body slightly sideways to appear slimmer. She turned her attention to D.J. "Don't worry. We've done all kinds of fabrics on my show, and I've never had a glare problem." Her heart was returning to its usual pace. "Not that I garden in cocktail attire that often, but it's happened."

He looked at her differently, she was sure. His soft blue eyes glinted behind his expensive glasses. "Formal horticulture? I like that. I dabble in plants a bit myself." His tone had changed. They were having a normal conversation, like two normal people. Not in front of millions, but just the two of them.

"You seem like a root vegetable kind of guy," she said.

He smiled. "Is it that obvious?"

"You have what you need, D.J.?" a woman's voice echoed electronically around them. He looked toward a control room illuminated from above the empty auditorium. Margo followed his gaze and saw Nancy and some other technicians staring down at them. D.J. gave her a thumbs-up.

"We need to bring her band out to get a sound check."

Nancy's voice echoed around them again.

D.J. turned back to Margo. "That's right," he said. "Nancy tells me you have a little musical number to do for us, too. You're quite the multitalented young lady."

She leaned toward him flirtatiously, aware of how the gesture augmented her breasts. "Some people think so."

"Margo," Nancy interrupted again. "Please go backstage and get set up."

Margo stood, smoothed out her dress, and walked slowly back across the stage.

CHAPTER 33

"Hurry up," Kit whispered to Ronni.

She rolled her eyes with bored exasperation. "I'm working as fast as I can," she said. Kit took a quick peek onto the stage to see if anyone else heard. She saw Margo lean over to D.J. Hamilton and then stand up and walk toward them. She looked beautiful in that red dress—confident as always.

When Margo reached them she scowled at Ronni. "We're on in a few minutes," she said.

"No problem," Ronni said. "I'm almost ready."

A man with a long blond ponytail emerged through the stage curtain. He extended his hand to Margo. "Hey," he said in a husky soft voice. "I'm Vic. I'll help you get a sound check. Just bring your stuff out to the stage and we'll get you set up with amps and mics."

They followed Vic with their guitars. The stage was smaller than Kit expected.

"Bass," Vic said to her. He pointed to a shadowed corner where an amp was set up. "We're going to set you up to the side here so the cameras won't see you until the band is on. Margo, you can stand here. We want you up front, obviously."

Kit set up her guitar and strummed the strings until a low thud emanated from the speaker. She looked over at Margo. Vic was standing closer to her, straightening her guitar straps against her breasts, looking her up and down to see if the star was presentable.

Ronni finally emerged from behind the curtain—the tiny girl pulling a comically outsized set of drums. Vic waved her into another corner. We're just the back line, Kit thought, all about supporting the star. She tried to stay focused. Shadowed or not, she would still be on television. She gazed up at the lights, thinking about the one viewer she hoped would not be watching, and decided it might not be a bad thing to not be so visible. As Margo had reminded her in the dressing room, she and her daughter would be more protected on the tour than they would be if she remained a lowly employee at ASMP.

"Okay," Vic said. "We'll do a quick sound check, then you guys can play the song. We're only going to have about a minute and a half, so you'll need to trim it. We'll start with guitar. Margo, can you strum a little?"

Kit waited while they tweaked and fiddled with Margo's sound and checked Ronni's drums with quick snaps of toms and bass drum, adjusting the volume. Finally, a voice boomed from the control room above: "Bass." She thudded through the simple bass line of the verse in "Ugly Men."

Margo turned toward Ronni and Kit. "Let's cut out the second verse—that should make the time. We should all come in at the same time, too, to shave off a few seconds."

Kit stared at Margo and the huge army of cameras that loomed just behind her. She searched for the song structure, trying to remember where the second verse fit in around the bridge. Did it come before or after the second chorus? Just as she opened her mouth to ask, Vic's voice boomed through the studio again.

"Let's go!" he shouted.

Kit panicked, praying she would remember the structure when the moment arrived. Ronni lifted her sticks dramatically, clicked off a four count, and came crashing down into a confident intro. Kit started playing, but it took her a few beats to get into step with the rhythm. Margo started roughly as well, but she caught up after a few beats. She stepped to the microphone earlier than usual, but Kit thought that was okay. She followed along.

"Never pick a man who's prettier than you are," she sang confidently into the microphone.

The monitor mix was amazing, Kit thought. She had never

heard each instrument more clearly or more well defined. They played through the verse without any problem. When they reached the chorus, Kit stepped into her microphone to sing harmonies. Her first note was rough, the remnant of whiskey and phlegm caught briefly in her throat, but it cleared up as she pushed through it.

After the chorus, Margo started into the verse chords, and Kit followed, but then Margo suddenly switched and began playing the bridge. It was a noticeable stumble and Kit struggled to catch up, the alcohol clouding her memory. Ronni dropped the beat too but managed to pull it back together. Kit's hands started sweating despite the ice-cold temperature of the room, and she had trouble clutching the pick between her fingers. She focused all of her remaining concentration on remembering the rest of the song, feeling the ominous eyes of the dead cameras upon her. Soon they would be alive, drinking in and broadcasting her ineptitude, and the whole world would see she was a fake.

Focus, focus, she told herself as she stepped up to the mic again. This is fun. Really.

They finished the song without any additional flubs—but without much enthusiasm either. Kit leaned over to turn off the amp, imagining Vic's cynical stare.

"That sounded pretty good," Margo said.

Kit shook her head in disbelief. "You're kidding, right?"

Margo looked as if she'd been slapped, and Kit immediately regretted her negative tone. She knew from long experience that expressing criticism before a show was never a good idea with Margo, who relied so on praise for her performance.

"I know, we did kind of fuck up the bridge," she said.

Kit knew it was up to her to be the cheerleader. It was the role she often played in the old band, with the old Margo.

"Actually," Kit said, "it wasn't that bad. We were just rough on the bridge because we had to cut it short. We'll map it out before the show. It'll be fine."

Margo smiled. "Yeah, sure. It'll be fine."

"All right!" Nancy's eyes were still glued to her clipboard. "Now I need you to go back and wait in the green room. The show will start taping in less than an hour. You can leave your equipment here."

"No problem," Margo said. She put her hand on Kit's arm and nodded toward the drummer. "I think Ronni has to run a quick errand first. Let's go."

When Margo whispered to her, Ronni scowled. "Now?" she whined.

"Now," Margo and Kit said in unison.

CHAPTER 34

Back in the green room, all of D.J.'s guests for the evening were together again and the new, larger, bottle was being passed from mouth to mouth—the effort to clean it growing less enthusiastic with each round. Ronni, Bob, and Kit were squashed together snugly on the couch with Bob happily in the middle, while Margo and Jake lounged on large high-backed chairs on the other side of a glass coffee table littered with magazines and rapidly filling ashtrays. The air in the room had changed from celebrity weigh station to dive bar, thick with smoke. The television hanging in the corner had been turned on, and the taping had begun. Hamilton was doing his monologue, and Margo was trying to watch it, but her companions kept interrupting her concentration.

"You guys sounded awesome at rehearsal," Jake slurred as he struggled to tap a cigarette from his pack. Margo lit another cigarette and handed him her lighter, which he clicked three times before producing fire.

"You think so?" Ronni said. "I thought we sucked."

"You were fine," Bob said, cupping Ronni's knee with his hand. "You have nothing to worry about. I see all good things in your future."

Margo turned away from the television, annoyed by Bob's relentless implications about his power. "I don't get it, Bob," she said.

"Are you a fortune-teller, or can you talk to the dead?" She was feeling quite buzzed now, and time seemed to be slowing down, her purpose in this room drifting into puffs of smoke.

"Are you mocking me, Ms. Bevelaqua?" Bob teased, leaning forward without removing his hand from Ronni's knee.

"It's a valid question," Kit said, turning a heavy-lidded glance toward the psychic. "On your show you just talk to the . . . well, you know, pretend to help people."

Margo tried to imagine what was going through her mind. Did she want to talk to her mother?

"I can help people, Kit," Bob said seriously.

"So how does fortune-telling fit in?" Margo asked. "Do you think Jake here will win an Oscar for that surfer romance he just did?"

"Hey," Jake said, scrunching up his perfect face. "That film made a shitload of money."

"I can safely say that Jake will continue to be successful in the near future," Bob said. "In the box office, anyway."

"What does that mean?" Jake asked.

The door opened and Nancy walked in, pausing to cough and swat her hand in front of her face to wave away the smoke. Margo held her breath as Nancy glanced over at the bottle of whiskey, currently resting on the floor by Jake's feet. She was suddenly back in high school, caught by the principal with a bottle of booze.

"Jake, you're up," she said.

"Already?" he asked. "Where the fuck is Elisa?" He looked down at his phone. "Oh, shit, my phone died." He threw his head back in a ridiculous cackle.

Nancy crossed her arms. "Now," she said.

Jake leaned toward Margo in a conspiratorial whisper. "I better go, huh?" he said. He laughed again.

Margo pulled a new pack of mint breath strips from her purse and handed him one. "Take this," she said. "You'll be done before you know it."

Jake left the room and Margo turned back to the television. There was a commercial on, and she realized she had no idea where they were in the show.

"God, that man is beautiful," Kit said with a sigh.

The commercial was over, and the show was back on. Hamilton sat at his desk, leaning into the microphone to introduce Jake.

"Our first guest tonight has just completed another smash hit with 'Surf's Up,' now in theaters," Hamilton's tinny voice said from the television screen. "Please help me welcome the star of 'Our Last Date' and 'Pretty Fella' . . . Jake McGinty!"

The band launched into a rendition of Roy Orbison's "Pretty Woman" as Jake strutted across the stage, hands crammed in his pockets, ignoring the shrieking young females in the crowd. When he pulled his hand out to shake Hamilton's hand, Margo's leopard-print lighter sprung from his pocket and went sputtering off the stage. Jake followed it with his gaze, shrugged, and followed Hamilton back to the desk.

The shrieking continued for some time in fits and starts, and when it finally stopped Hamilton leaned toward Jake in a friendly gesture.

"Welcome to the show," he said.

Jake nodded.

"So," Hamilton continued, "I hear you're a big golfer."

"Yep," Jake answered.

"I heard you had an interesting golfing experience in Florida recently." Hamilton waited for an answer, but Jake was staring at the audience and smirking. He waved toward the camera, releasing more shrieks from the audience.

Hamilton looked at the audience and grinned, then he turned back to Jake. "Why don't you tell us about it?"

"An alligator ate my balls." The audience laughed. Catching himself, Jake continued. "I mean ball. An alligator ate my ball." He giggled stupidly.

Hamilton laughed along, undeterred by Jake's nonchalance. Margo was impressed.

The interview limped along in the same painful pattern—Hamilton trying to make Jake seem interesting and Jake continuing to come off as another shallow pretty face. Finally, after what seemed an eternity that included a movie clip, the interview was over and the screen went black.

"Well," Margo said, "that was pretty bad."

Bob had begun pacing the room during Jake's interview, running his chubby fingers through his dark hair, leaning into a small mirror on a table to check his face. His skin had become splotchy with patches of red, and a shiny film glistened on his forehead.

When Nancy led Jake back into the room she turned to Bob. "Okay, Bob," she said, "follow me."

When he turned from the mirror, Nancy looked displeased. "We need a quick stop at makeup," she said as she whisked him away.

Jake sat heavily on the couch. "That was bad," he said. "I can never do this shit without Elisa."

"You were fine," Margo lied.

Kit chimed in. "Of course you were. You were really funny."

Jake reached behind the couch for the whiskey bottle. "No one gives a shit what I have to say anyway," he said, taking a long swig.

"Hey," Margo said, sitting down next to him and putting her arm around his neck, "be grateful you have an audience. Believe it or not, most guys don't watch my show for the planting tips. There are just two reasons I have a show, and I don't care. I'm doing what I want. That's all that matters."

Margo wasn't sure she actually believed this, but she had to for now. She had to get out there and be the Margo B. that everyone expected. The truth was, she was feeling a little sentimental. It had been a long time since she had just sat and talked with friends. It was probably the whiskey, but she enjoyed sitting next to Jake, a completely inaccessible stranger under any other circumstance, and comforting him.

"Thanks," he said. He rested his head against her arm and they sat in silence as they watched the television, waiting for their new friend Bob to do his thing.

CHAPTER 35

Kit was getting drunk. Too drunk to play a song on D.J. Hamilton. Too drunk to call and check on her daughter again. But she was having a blast. She felt confident that Elinor was safe with Holly and her dad, she would have plenty of time to sober up, and she was hanging out with Jake McGinty. Not too bad for a nobody from the 'burbs.

She sat down next to Margo and Jake on the couch, the three feeling the warm embrace of a shared buzz. Ronni was sitting on the floor, tapping the rug with her drumsticks. The television came back on. The camera zoomed in on Hamilton, still sitting at his desk.

"Our next guest has developed quite a following for his unusual work," he said to the camera. "Bob Tenerelli likes to chat with the dead." A slight chuckle from the audience. "And tonight, we have a little treat. He's going to demonstrate his psychic talents for us right here, live and unedited. Would you please welcome, the Jersey Psychic himself, Mr. Bob Tenerelli!"

The screen cut to Bob walking across the stage, nodding to the applause. He looked much better than he had a few moments earlier. His skin was clear and uniform and his smile brimmed with sober confidence. After exchanging a few pleasantries and dead jokes, D.J. invited Bob to "do his magic" and Bob walked to center stage, where a spotlight illuminated him spookily as the house lights faded.

"Good evening," he began, his voice smooth and calming. "Tonight I'm going to do something a little different." The camera moved in closer to his face, and his dark eyes looked even darker. "I'm going to make connections with people who are still on this side. There are people right here in this audience who have connections with others and don't even know it." Bob closed his eyes and held his fingers to his forehead, concentrating. "I see a . . ." he hesitated. "I see a group of relatives. They haven't seen each other in a very long time. They are . . ." He paused again, scrunching up his face. "Brothers!" His eyes popped open and the lights brightened. He pointed to the audience. "Ladies and gentleman, I give you D.J. Hamilton's long-lost brother, Hal!"

The camera cut to the audience, where a D.J. Hamilton look-alike sat hunched over a beer can, a baseball cap with a large bill shading his face. When the camera zoomed in on him, his eyes darted wildly as the audience laughed and clapped. He stood up in mock panic, looked frantically around the room, and squeezed out through the row of people.

"Mom always loved you best!" he shouted at the stage before sprinting up the aisle and out the door.

The camera returned to a close-up of Hamilton, standing as if he planned to stop him. "Hal!" he called. "Don't go! You still owe me forty bucks!"

The camera cut back to the closed door. He was gone.

"Thanks, Bob," Hamilton said. "We haven't seen Hal since the bowling scandal of '92."

The camera returned to Bob. "No problem, D.J."

"Do you think there might be any more connections here?" Hamilton asked.

"Oh, yes," Bob said. The lights dimmed again and the camera zoomed in on him. "This next family has . . ." His eyes widened again, as if he'd seen something very important, and then he smiled. "Actually, this is good. This couple has traveled some distance to be here tonight to see a very special person who I've had the pleasure of meeting backstage." He glanced over at D.J. "This isn't planned, but hopefully I won't screw things up here."

Kit glanced at Margo and Jake. They all sat up straighter, hypnotized by the screen. Ronni stopped tapping her sticks.

"Would the Bevelaquas please stand up?"

"Oh my god," Margo gasped.

The camera cut to a pan of the audience and came to rest on Orlando and Vincenza Bevelaqua, who had jumped from their seats and waved frantically. Vinnie looked just as Kit remembered her. Her hair, dyed the color of champagne, was teased into a high helmet and was in stark contrast to her too-tan skin, which clung tightly to her bony arms and chiseled cheekbones. She wore bright pink leather pants and a short-sleeved white shirt tied up to reveal a flat brown stomach. Orlando wore a bright blue Hawaiian shirt, open at the neck to display a gold chain hidden in a jungle of hair.

Kit looked over at Margo. Her face had gone pale, her mouth parted in a prolonged gasp. Kit had seen the Bevelaquas' effect on Margo a few times before, and she was amazed at how they could reduce their confident daughter to a quivering adolescent.

"Surprise!" Vinnie shouted into the camera.

CHAPTER 36

Margo could not believe her eyes. She watched in stunned silence as her parents, miniaturized into a small box, somehow managed to attain new heights in embarrassment. She wanted to flee, to dash down the corridor and out the door so she could blend into the New York crowd and disappear. She always felt this urge when her parents were around.

Hamilton was back on camera, looking a little surprised by these enthusiastic, uninvited guests.

"Well," he said, regaining his composure. "This is a surprise. I suppose we'll need to bring out our last guest a bit early."

"Oh, shit," Margo said, just as the door flung open and Nancy appeared, frantic.

"Margo," she said, panting. "We have to go!"

"Ladies and gentleman," Hamilton was saying from the screen, "please help me welcome the very lovely host of the Contemporary Living Network's *Guerrilla Gardening*, Miss Margo Bevelaqua!"

Nancy rushed Margo down the hall toward the stage. Margo's head was spinning from the whiskey. The sound grew louder as she neared the open curtain and the light and the cold. She wasn't ready; she hadn't checked her face or her lipstick or sucked on a breath strip. *This isn't fair*, she thought. But before she knew it she was onstage and the audience was clapping and she tried to remember once again: Smile!

D.J. Hamilton was walking toward her with a welcoming grin while Bob remained center stage. Her parents were still jumping up and down excitedly in the audience right in front of her, as if they'd just been selected for *The Price Is Right*. It had been bad enough seeing them on the screen in the green room. Now they were real, and loud, and horrible.

You're Margo B., she told herself. They can't control you anymore. This is your moment, not theirs. Don't let them take it from you.

"Hi, honey!" her mother shouted from the audience.

Hamilton reached her and leaned in for a long embrace, his beard scratching against her ear. "We had no idea they were here," he whispered. "Do you think you can control them?"

She nodded, but he didn't release her.

"I want you to know," he continued, "that I only bent the alcohol rules because I like you. Don't disappoint me."

He released her from his embrace with a huge smile that Margo suddenly feared. She forgot about the millions of viewers and her parents shrieking in the audience.

Hamilton led her over to Bob, who smiled at Margo. The applause had faded, and the three stood on the stage. Goosebumps erupted on her naked arms.

"Looks like you made a genuine connection here, Bob," Hamilton said. "I guess we should bring up Margo's surprise. Mom, Dad, do you want to come up here?"

The audience clapped again as Orlando and Vinnie shoved their way through the row to reach the aisle. They jogged over to the stage and walked quickly to the threesome, squeezing Margo into an embarrassing group hug.

Hamilton held out his hand to Margo's father first, who shook it enthusiastically.

"What's your name?" he asked.

"I'm Orlando, and this is my wife Vincenza," Orlando said, gesturing toward Margo's mother.

"Interesting names," Hamilton commented. "And where are you coming from?"

"We came all the way up from Boca to see our little girl!"
Vinnie said. "And doesn't she look gorgeous?" She turned to the
audience and encouraged them to applaud. "Oh my god," Vinnie
continued. "We haven't been on stage since, what, honey, '83?"

Orlando put his hand to his chin thoughtfully. "I think it was
'84."

"Are you sure?" Vinnie said.

"I think it was that show in Newark, remember?"

"It doesn't matter, Dad," Margo said.

"Were you performers?" Hamilton asked.

Oh god, Margo thought. He took the bait.

"Yes!" Vinnie said with a huge grin. "Remember Parallel?"

Hamilton shook his head.

"'Can't Fake that Smile?'" Orlando prodded.

"Oh, sure," Hamilton said. "I remember that song!"

They're stealing my moment, Margo thought, like they always
have. Her whole childhood came back in an angry rush—being
crammed on buses with strangers and dressed up and displayed like
a finely tuned instrument that her parents had crafted with their very
own talented hands. She stood on stage, the invited guest, disappearing behind the chaos that was her parents.

The bandleader started tinkling the piano keys, and moments
later the band was playing the melody that had made Margo's life
hell—the annoyingly perky "Can't Fake that Smile." Her parents
started shifting back and forth in time with the beat. Oh no, please
don't sing, Margo thought. But it was too late. Hamilton pulled a
microphone from the guitar player's stand and handed it to Orlando.
This gesture amplified her parents' choreography, and her mother
began clapping to the beat with wild, overly dramatic gestures. The
two leaned together into the mic, and it was all over. They were
singing their song, erasing Margo.

"*You came to me with that big boy smile,*" Vinnie sang. "*I asked
you if you wanted to stay a while.*" She took the microphone from
Orlando and began flirting with her husband as she sang. It was
their stage routine, lifted straight from the pages of Sonny and Cher.
Margo stood watching and fuming, forgetting about her nipples, her
buzz, and the pasty film of whiskey on her tongue.

"*You told me that you loved me but I couldn't believe,*" Vinnie sang, now running her long pink nails across Orlando's chest. She made her way over to Hamilton and put her hand on his shoulder and leaned close. "*Until you kissed me, baby, I thought you just might leave.*" Hamilton was smiling, genuinely, letting Margo's mother sing close to his ear. "*But when I looked into your eyes I knew you were wild, 'cause no one with a face like yours could fake that smile.*"

Hamilton turned to the camera. "We have to take a break!" he said loudly over the music. "Stay tuned for Parallel's daughter, Margo Bevelaqua!"

The music continued as the lights went down, and Hamilton walked over to Margo.

"Not bad, kid," he said. "Might be a tough act to follow. Come on over—we'll get you some coffee."

Margo followed him to his desk, leaving her singing parents behind her. She was grateful for the mug of coffee a crew member handed her. Hamilton paced behind the desk, drank some coffee, reviewed a few cards on his desk. After a few more moments, a producer signaled the return of the show and Hamilton sat back in his chair, cleared his throat, and waited.

The eye of the camera woke with a red glow, and the audience applauded on command.

"Welcome back," Hamilton said with another large grin. "Well, we just had quite a treat from the parents of my next guest. Margo Bevelaqua is the star of *Guerrilla Gardening*. She'll also be touring this summer with her all-girl band on the Women of Rock Tour." There was some applause and whistling at the mention of the tour. "So, Margo," he said. He turned toward her and reached his arm out so it touched her chair. "What was it like growing up with famous parents?"

"They weren't famous," she said, before she could stop herself. "They had one hit. That's it." She didn't want to sound bitter. She was here to win over her audience, to convince them to follow her to Sundays, to save her show. But the acid that churned in her stomach was hard to ignore.

"Still, you must have had some interesting experiences," Hamilton continued.

She knew he was trying to make her sound interesting, like he did with Jake, as he did with all of his guests. And she knew her time here was limited. She could be pissed later.

"Oh, we had many interesting experiences," she said. "I learned how to pass a joint around the room without burning my fingers when I was about five. That was a big hit with the musicians." There was a nervous chuckle from the audience. "I could fetch beer, and I knew which performers liked which brand. I can still remember the labels, because I always thought they matched the people that drank them somehow."

Hamilton chuckled, trying to encourage the audience to join him. "Really, can you give us an example?"

"Well," Margo began. She thought back to that world, sitting on the floor of the bus while the musicians and roadies towered around her, sipping cans of beer and chain smoking. "Gary Glitter always liked Miller beer, and the gold can matched most of his outfits. It was the seventies, after all. I won't name the person who liked Mickey's Big Mouth—his body was kind of the same shape as the short, stout bottle."

"Clever. So why didn't you become a professional musician like your parents?"

She took a sip of her coffee, which had already cooled to mouth temperature. "That arena is pretty full already. I just do it for fun. Personally, I'd rather be gardening." She wanted to steer the subject back to her show, to mention the time change.

"I find that hard to believe. You look more like a stage gal than someone who enjoys weeding."

"Well, I'm lucky. I managed to combine both talents into a TV show—which, by the way, is moving its time slot to Sunday after-noons in the fall."

Hamilton smiled. "Smooth." The audience chuckled again.

"Hey, I do what I can." She felt her control resurfacing. "If I don't give the plug, they make me do all the fertilizing on the show. I like to garden, but there's a reason I do it with plenty of willing interns." She held up her hands, showing the audience her painted nails. "Have to watch the manicure."

They laughed.

"As long as you're plugging, what cities will the tour hit first?"

Margo's mind went blank. "You know, D.J., that's a very good question. I will definitely have to fire the intern who was supposed to give me that information. I know we're playing in Camden on Friday.

People can go to the Women of Rock Tour website to get all the information about shows in their area."

"Sounds great," Hamilton said. "And I know we were hoping to hear your band play tonight, but unfortunately we've run out of time. So check out Margo's band on the Women of Rock Tour, and tune in on Sunday afternoons in the fall to see Guerrilla Gardening, starring Margo Bevelaqua, on the Contemporary Living Network. Ladies and gentleman, a big hand for Margo Bevelaqua!" He held his hand toward Margo and the audience applauded. She sat and smiled, full of mixed emotions: gratitude mingled with disappointment that they wouldn't get to perform, anger at her parents for robbing her of this opportunity, relief that the whole experience was behind her. As the applause faded, and D.J. shook her hand, and someone came to lead her away, her thoughts turned to Harry. What would he think of her performance tonight?

CHAPTER 37

Kit stared in shock at the announcement that they wouldn't be playing. They hadn't even mentioned the name of the band. Margo's obnoxious parents had eaten into time to which she was entitled. She watched as Margo walked offstage and the credits began to roll, swallowing her last opportunity to play even one note on television. She would never have this chance again.

Margo walked through the door. "I am so sorry," she said, but Kit didn't believe her. It wasn't fair. Margo already had celebrity, fame, opportunities. She'd been embraced by D.J. Hamilton and sat in the chair that had held the butts of many a famous celebrity.

Margo sat on the couch next to Jake. He was dozing, his head flopped back, his mouth slightly open. Ronni seemed indifferent to the disappointing news and was back on the phone with a friend.

"It's his fault," Margo said. She pointed to Bob, who was sitting on a chair across from the couch, his feet propped up on the table. "How did you know they were there?"

"I told you I'm not a fake," he said.

Margo lit a cigarette. "Bullshit. I bet that Nancy bitch planned the whole thing to embarrass me."

"She didn't," Bob said with a shrug. "I did a little research on you when I heard we were going to be on the show together. I read about your parents and their hit song and saw some pictures of them.

Who can forget that hair? I had no idea they would actually be here, but when I saw them in the audience, I couldn't help it. I thought it would be funny. And it was."

Before Kit could complain, there was a knock at the door, which opened immediately.

"Honey!" Vinnie's shrill voice cut through Kit's fading, groggy buzz like a knife.

Vinnie and Orlando rushed in to pounce on their daughter. "Oh my god, honey. You were fabulous!" Vinnie embraced her dramatically.

As Orlando gave Margo a big hug, Vinnie looked over at Kit. "Oh my goodness!" she cried. "I can't believe this is Kate! You look so different."

"Kit," she corrected her. "How are you, Vinnie?"

"Vincenza, please, dear. You wouldn't believe how many old farts are named Vinnie down in Florida. God knows I don't want to be mixed up with them!"

Vinnie grabbed Margo's hand. "Can you believe they knew our song, honey?" she squealed. "That D.J. Hamilton is such a nice man to let us sing."

"Well," Margo said, "your song made the show run long so our band couldn't play. How did you even get tickets?"

"Oh, you know how persuasive your father can be," Vinnie said. "When we found out you were going to be on the show, he made some calls and told them who we were, and poof! We were heading to New York!"

"Whatever," Margo said. "We have to pack up. Where are you guys going now?"

"Anywhere we want, honey," Orlando said. "We sold our house in Florida and bought a Winnebago." He smiled wide. "We've decided to take our act on the road again!"

Margo's eyes grew wide. "Excuse me?"

"Yep!" Vinnie said. "Surprise again!"

This was not good news, Kit thought. With Margo's parents on the loose, they could show up at any show on the tour, any time.

"I need to get home," Kit said. She was growing more exhausted by the moment.

"We'll give you a ride!" said Orlando. "We've got plenty of

room for your equipment, a running toilet, and plenty of beer. Who's in?"

* * *

Margo was not happy. To say that history was repeating itself was an understatement. She was living the ultimate bean burrito of repetition. She was back in a large vehicle with her parents. Towering equipment vibrated threateningly as the Winnebago rumbled down I-95 toward Philadelphia. Kit, back in her faded jeans, was sulking in the corner of the Winnebago's built-in couch, staring out the window at the fading New York skyline.

Margo didn't have the energy to cheer Kit up, but when she couldn't tune out her parents' loud conversation from the front about how the Hamilton show was the big break they needed to launch the tour, she decided to go sit next to her.

"Pretty weird day, huh?" she asked, sitting down and pulling a Diet Coke from a cooler that sat by her feet. "Want one?"

Kit nodded and accepted the offering. "Yep. Pretty weird." She clicked back the tab and a small spray of caramel foam spurted from the can's mouth.

"At least we were able to direct people to the tour website. That will definitely get more people out to see us."

"Maybe. Although since Hamilton never actually mentioned Broad Street I'm not sure how they'd find out about us."

"Didn't he?" Margo asked. "Oh shit. I should have said something. I was so flustered by the whole thing with them—" She gestured toward the front of the cabin. "I didn't even know what I was saying. Sorry."

"I know. It's not your fault." Kit sipped her soda. "I've seen similar things happen all the time on that show. I'm just feeling sorry for myself."

The truth was, Margo really wasn't that sorry. Of course it wasn't her fault, and if anyone should be pissed she should be. She was the one who had been humiliated on national television. She wasn't even sure she'd watch the show that night—she didn't want to see how ridiculous her face looked as she gaped at her parents' performance. She'd worked so hard to leave them in the shadows of her life and thought she was finally safe with them tucked under a palm tree down south.

The radio suddenly grew louder from the front seat.

"Honey!" her mother shouted over the music. "Remember this song?"

She turned up the radio louder still. A sticky sweet bubblegum riff blasted from the tinny speakers.

"Peppermint Rainbow!" Orlando called back, turning around to talk to them. "We played with them a couple times in upstate Ohio. Remember?"

"Dad, please watch the road!" Margo pleaded.

Orlando smiled and turned back around. Nothing ever seemed to faze her parents, Margo thought. She remembered being worried about that, even as a child.

Vinnie unbuckled her seat belt and stumbled back toward Margo and Kit. She plopped down on the floor at their feet.

"Time to celebrate, I think," she said, digging her long pink nails through the cooler's melting ice. She found a can of beer and pulled it out, shaking off large drops of cold water before popping it open. "Don't you girls want a beer?" she asked. "You're rock stars now! Time to start living the life."

"Then why are you drinking?" Margo asked.

Vinnie smirked. "Funny girl! Come on, honey, why are you being such a sourpuss?"

"I have a headache, and Kit has to go home to her child. Some people think you should be sober for parenting."

"Okay, now, be nice. Kit, don't you think Margo should be nice to her mother? I bet you always are."

Margo wanted to toss her mother into oncoming traffic. She knew about Kit's mother, and it was just like her to forget something so important.

"She's dead," Kit said quietly.

"Oh my god," Vinnie said. "I forgot. Oh, honey. I'm so sorry." She stood up, squeezed herself between Margo and Kit, and put her arm around Kit's shoulder.

Her strong, musky perfume pinched Margo's nose, and she moved over to avoid squeezing against her thin hips.

"That must be so hard," Vinnie said. "Especially with a little baby at home. You need your mom for stuff like that."

Margo looked at Kit, who was wringing her hands in her lap.

"Mom," Margo said, "Kit doesn't need to think about that right now."

"Of course she does!" Vinnie said, startling Kit into looking up. "Kit, you need to think about her every day. You don't want to erase her. She had a whole life with you and before you and you should never pretend that didn't happen. That's when it gets sad." She pulled Kit tighter. "I lost my mother young, too, and it killed me. Just killed me. And I tried to push her out of my mind over and over, but she kept coming back, asking me to look at her—and finally I did. I looked at her all over again, especially after I had this little girl here." She put her beer can on the floor between her feet and wrapped her other arm around Margo. "I looked at her, and I realized how amazing my mother was. Of course she wasn't perfect, but she was still amazing."

Margo had forgotten about her grandmother. She'd never known any grandparents, and she never thought about her parents missing them.

The three women let the sounds envelop them—the rumbling of the huge gas-guzzling Winnebago, the tinny radio singing happily from the front, the hum of passing cars. Margo let her mother keep her arm around her.

CHAPTER 38

When Margo finally arrived home that night, she could barely drag herself up the stairs. They'd had to stop to pick up Elinor and listen to long reports from the babysitter and Pierce detailing the many inane things the child had done all day while Vinnie and Orlando cooed over the kid the whole time. Then she had to wait for Kit to say goodbye to her dad and explain the whole Hamilton mess. The whole ordeal felt like it took hours.

As Kit was unloading a sleepy Elinor and all her equipment into the house, her parents had begged Margo to go out with them—they certainly wouldn't watch the show in Margo's living room. But she had absolutely no desire to sit at a public bar while they tapped strangers on the shoulder and pointed proudly to the television. They'd stayed at Margo's long enough to compliment her condo in their usual backhanded way. ("What a beautiful kitchen," her mother had said, "I bet it would look great without all that clutter."). After Margo watched them drive off toward Center City in the Winnebago, she dragged herself upstairs to change into sweatpants. She washed her face, removed her contacts, put on her old glasses, and grimaced at her reflection in the mirror. She was too tired to care. Out in the hallway, she heard Kit taking Elinor to their room.

Back downstairs in the empty living room she checked her phone messages. There were a bunch of missed calls, but only one voicemail. It was from Harry.

"Hi," he said. "Just checking to see how the show went. I can't wait to see it. I may actually be back in town tonight. I know it's late, but I wondered if you might want to watch it together."

Margo saved the message and sighed. The thought of making herself presentable and worrying about what she would see on the show, especially in front of Harry, was daunting. But the thought of his soft skin against hers again held great appeal.

She pulled an open bottle of Pinot Grigio out of the refrigerator, poured herself a glass, and sat at the kitchen table enjoying the quiet. She would call Harry back, but first she just needed to be alone for a little while. As she reviewed the emotional roller coaster of the day's events, her mind kept returning to potentially embarrassing moments. Public moments. She had won an audience with her show, but now these strangers would glimpse an intimate interior that she hadn't wished to reveal to anyone.

After finishing the wine she still didn't have a plan, but she dialed Harry's number.

"How was it?" he greeted her.

She smiled. "Am I really the only private number who calls you?"

"Nope. I've just been answering that way all day. It's amazing how much information I now have about people. So, how was the show?"

"It was, um—interesting. You'll see it all tonight—I might need some consolation when it's all over."

"Will you?"

The tingling returned. How could he do that to her with so few syllables? "I guess so. What time do you get back?"

"Actually, I'm back now, but I have to take care of a few things. Is eleven o'clock too late? I can come to your place, if you want me to."

She looked at the clock. She had less than half an hour to prepare. "That would be nice."

Margo gave him her address and returned to her bedroom to look for something to wear, but when she saw her bed and the thick billowy comforter and soft inviting pillows, she decided to lie down. Just for a few minutes.

* * *

In her dream, Margo was hiding. She knew she was in Philadelphia, but she didn't recognize where she was. The alley was dark and she heard noises—maybe rats or a homeless person—but she couldn't see anything. She knew she was in danger, so she stood against a brick wall and held her breath and stayed as still as she possibly could, but then there was a bell. A fire engine? A school bell? It rang and rang, and when she opened her eyes the sour taste in her mouth reminded her that she was sleeping and now Harry was here and she wasn't ready.

She jumped out of bed as the doorbell continued to ring. She checked the clock: it was quarter past eleven. Had he been out there for fifteen minutes ringing the bell? She ran to the bathroom, quickly put in her contacts, dabbed on a little mascara, sucked on a glob of toothpaste, and ran a red lipstick over her mouth. The mirror revealed a woman who had just woken up and was trying to hide it. A deep red crease cut across her right cheek, and her hair was pressed down on the same side. *Oh, fuck it*, she thought. In the hallway she collided with Kit, who had obviously just woken too.

"Who is that?" she asked. "The noise will wake Elinor."

Margo shot her an angry look. "I'm expecting someone. Just go back to bed."

The doorbell rang again, and there was a cry from the guest room.

"Shit," Kit said. She jogged back down the hallway.

Margo ran down the stairs, almost tripping on the last one. She stumbled over to the door and pulled it open.

"Sorry I'm late . . ." Harry paused, taking in Margo's appearance. "I'm sorry, were you sleeping?"

Elinor's cries from upstairs grew louder.

"Can you tell?" She motioned him through the door. "Come on in. I just meant to lie down for a minute, and I fell asleep. It's been a long day."

Harry glanced up the stairs. "Am I interrupting something?" he asked.

"No. My friend's staying here for a few days. Long story."

Harry hesitated. "I can leave. Really. I called when you didn't answer the door, but there was no answer. I shouldn't have come."

"Do I look that terrible?" Margo asked.

Harry smiled and stepped through the door, wrapping his arms around her. "You look adorable."

They were a contrast—Harry in a suit and Margo in sweats, but she felt safe with the prickle of pricey wool against her skin. She wrapped her arms around him, too, and before she knew it his lips were pressed against hers, parting gently to tickle her tongue with his. Mint swirled between their mouths and Margo felt a deep chasm spread open like wings and Harry was removing his coat but still kissing her, and his skin was so warm and soft.

"Oh, sorry."

Margo, startled out of the moment, turned her head to see Kit and Elinor descending the stairs.

"I just need to get to the kitchen," Kit said, scurrying past them.

Margo's passion cooled to an entirely different emotion. She turned back to Harry. "Sorry."

"I should go," he said, removing his arms.

"No!" She was surprised by her vehemence, but she wasn't about to let Kit blow this. "They'll go back upstairs in a minute, I'm sure. Have a seat. Do you want a drink?"

"Sure. Scotch, if you have it."

He hung his coat on an antique stand by the door and sat on the couch.

In the kitchen, Kit was spooning some purple goop from a jar into Elinor's mouth.

"Sorry," Kit said. "Since she's awake, I thought if I gave her something to eat she might actually sleep a little later tomorrow." She raised her eyebrows. "So, who's the hot old guy?" she whispered.

Margo peered over her shoulder, then leaned closer. "He's my boss. I don't know—it's weird. We only actually met the other day, but he's already sent me flowers and taken me out to breakfast."

"He's got kind of a George Clooney thing going on."

Margo smiled. "You think? I couldn't put my finger on it."

"Oh yeah, totally hot."

Margo glanced back over her shoulder, put a finger to her lips, and lowered her own whisper. "Hot, and probably bored right now. Listen, would you mind hanging upstairs after you're done?"

Kit shrugged. "I was kind of hoping to watch the show tonight."

"There's a TV in my room—you can watch it there."

Kit looked disappointed. "Okay, no problem."

"Thanks, you're a doll."

Margo poured a Scotch for Harry and another glass of wine for herself. Harry was flipping through one of her coffee table books—a large book on photography.

"Who's Rudolfo?" he asked.

Margo sat next to him and handed him his drink. She looked down at the inscription beneath a photo of the handsome Latino: "To Margo, Never forget Argentina—Love, Rudolfo."

"History," she said, and sipped her wine. She picked up the remote and flipped on the television.

They sat in silence as the tail end of the local weather played out on-screen. Margo wanted to reach out to him but was conscious of Kit and the baby in the next room. After a small eternity, she heard footsteps and turned her head. "Goodnight," she said quietly.

Harry stood up and offered his hand. "Harry Thomas."

Kit smiled. "Kit Greene. Nice to meet you. This is Elinor."

Harry did the obligatory chin tickle. "Hi cutie," he said.

"Well, I'm off to bed," Kit said. "Have fun."

Once Kit was upstairs, Margo nestled closer to Harry. She wasn't ready to feel this comfortable with anyone. She barely knew this man—a man who was clearly used to getting what he wanted. What was it about him that drew her so strongly? It was more than the money or the power. There was something about him that just seemed so . . . stable. That was the word she'd been unable to find before.

On-screen, Hamilton had progressed through the monologue and the painful Jake McGinty interview, and Margo felt her stomach clench as they neared her segment. She held Harry's hand as they watched yet another beer commercial.

"Good to see Jake McGinty is living up to his cliché," Harry said.

Margo laughed. "He's actually a pretty nice guy."

The commercial faded to black and Hamilton was back, introducing Bob.

"Oh, I've seen this guy," Harry said. "He's a great cold reader."

"Yeah, he was entertaining," Margo said, "but that's not the really interesting part." She squeezed Harry's hand in hers. "I had no control over what you are about to witness. Please don't hold it against me."

Harry lifted his eyebrows and smiled. "No nudity I hope."

"Worse." She released her grip, internally wincing in anticipation.

On the screen, the fake Hamilton brother was scampering down the aisle, and the real Hamilton was calling after him. After a few moments, the camera returned in close-up to Bob's shadowed face, his dark eyes glowing creepily in the dim lighting.

"Oh, yes," Bob said into the camera. "This next family has . . ." His eyes widened, and Margo thought there was genuine surprise in them. "Actually, this is good," Bob said. "This couple has traveled some distance to be here tonight to see a very special person who I've had the pleasure of meeting backstage. This isn't planned, but hopefully I won't screw things up here."

"Here we go," Margo said, her chest constricting. She clutched a throw pillow to her stomach.

"Would the Bevelaquas please stand up?" Bob's small voice said from the television.

Harry looked at Margo. "The Bevelaquas?"

Margo nodded. "More like the Munsters. Again, I would like to remind you that I had absolutely nothing to do with this."

And there were her parents, standing and waving, a confused audience applauding tentatively. A few moments later, Hamilton was leading a stunned pre-recorded version of herself onto the stage. She studied her entrance critically, looking for evidence of the thoughts that had flooded her memory at that moment, but she was surprised at how hard it was to read this taped version of Margo. She actually looked pretty cool about the whole thing. Margo watched herself standing, smiling, as her parents were brought on stage and started singing with the band.

Harry began to chuckle. "That's great!" he said. "Where did they find those actors? They're perfect."

Margo looked at him. "They're not actors."

Harry's smile faded, and then he seemed to catch himself and he smiled again, but it was different. "Oh, really? They certainly are . . . entertaining."

"Don't sugarcoat it. They're insane. It's something I'm comfortable hearing since I've been saying it my whole life."

Harry watched the rest of the song in silence, and Margo grew nervous. Her parents weren't only narcissistic—they were also tacky, and crass. Margo knew they could never fit into Harry's world.

When the song was finally over, the television once again faded to a commercial and Margo and Harry sat for a moment in silence.

Margo felt naked and miserable. "The good news is, I only see them once or twice a year," she said.

"That is good news," Harry said. "Mind if I get a glass of water?"

She stared at him, unsure how to interpret his tone. "I'll get it for you. Would you like another drink instead?"

Harry looked at the clock on the wall. "I'd better not. I have an early meeting."

Great, Margo thought as she walked into the kitchen. He's already working the early meeting excuse.

"Well, I'm getting a drink," she said. *He may as well think I'm an alcoholic, too*, she thought.

She stood in her kitchen, the ceramic tile floor cool under her bare feet. She poured herself another glass of red wine and Harry a tumbler of ice water. *They're all the same*, she thought, *no surprises*.

When she returned to the living room, Harry was sitting up, his back stiff against the couch. She handed him the water and sat on the other side of the sofa.

"Thanks," he said. He was staring at the screen, and Margo watched herself back on again, sitting next to D.J. Hamilton. She had seen herself many times on television on her own show and on some daytime talk shows, but they were all low-rent cable fluff. This was different.

They watched as the on-screen Margo joked about her childhood. She was pretty impressed with the confidence she portrayed. She looked like she belonged in that chair. As Hamilton continued to ask questions, Harry glanced over, raised an eyebrow, and patted the space next to him. This gesture lifted a weight from her. She placed her wine glass on the end table and moved closer to him.

"Well, I'm lucky," she was saying to Hamilton. "I managed to combine both talents into a TV show—which, by the way, is moving its time slot to Sunday afternoons in the fall."

"Nice," Harry said.

Margo chuckled. "Yeah, it was a little awkward, but I knew my mission."

Harry turned and kissed her. "You're good," he said. "I knew it immediately."

She wasn't sure exactly what he was referring to, but soon her own television voice talking about the tour she would be on in just a few days was fading into the background and she was wrapped in Harry's arms again, their clothes were on the floor, and she was lost in the swirl of his kisses and caresses. She forced her mind to stay in the moment, to allow herself to enjoy it for as long as it lasted. She was tired of always questioning everyone's motives. It was nice just letting herself feel good for a while.

CHAPTER 39

As she sat alone in Margo's room watching her cool, confident friend chatting easily with D.J. Hamilton, the same Margo who was at this very moment curled up downstairs in the arms of a rich and handsome older man, Kit tried not to feel sorry for herself. She couldn't even remember when any man had looked at her the way that Harry looked at Margo tonight. Certainly not since her pregnancy.

As the Hamilton show ended, her emotions shifted from excited memories of meeting celebrities to crushing disappointment that their opportunity to play had been stolen. It seemed unreal that, only hours earlier, she'd been standing on the stage, inches from D.J. Hamilton's desk. As the credits began to roll, the camera panned across the studio audience and there, in the corner of the screen, she was sure she saw him. It was only a flash—a puff of long dark hair, a snapshot of a band T-shirt, but in her gut she knew who it was. Damien had been in the audience.

CHAPTER 40

Kit tossed and turned all night, the image of Damien haunting her sleep-deprived anxiety. She replayed the moment over and over in her mind. The camera had gone by so quickly—it could have been anyone. Certainly lots of other people had long dark hair and wore grungy band T-shirts. Was she just getting paranoid?

She lay in bed, watching the cruel digital clock click through the minutes and hours of the night until Elinor woke up shortly after sunrise.

She changed Elinor's diaper and carried her downstairs. The living room was in obvious sexual disarray: the couch pillows were tossed around the floor, the coffee table had been moved to accommodate two horny bodies. Kit sighed and carried Elinor into the kitchen.

As she poured eggs into a pan and chatted absentmindedly with her daughter, she ran through the coming weeks in her mind. Their first meeting with The Venturas' tour manager was scheduled for later in the morning. Broad Street had met The Venturas, one of Kit's favorite bands, at one of their early gigs at a Chinatown club. She had practiced bass lines to their albums and played their songs over and over in the hope that, through osmosis, she could write a song half as good as one of theirs. Opening for The Venturas that night in Chinatown was the beginning of a string of successes for

Broad Street.

She scooped the eggs onto Elinor's plate and blew on them until they were cool enough. They would be on the road tomorrow—leaving it all behind.

Hopefully that would include leaving Damien behind, too.

* * *

Several hours later, Kit and Elinor were playing in the straightened-up living room when Margo finally descended. Her hair was wet from a shower and she was buttoning her shirt, sleep still pressed into her cheeks.

"Morning," she said, walking straight into the kitchen. "Is there any coffee?"

"We're supposed to be there in an hour," Kit called. "Can we pick up some coffee on the road? I still have to drop off Elinor at the babysitter's."

"I won't be long," Margo called back. "I'm almost ready."

A few minutes later Kit followed her into the kitchen. "I think I saw Damien in the audience on Hamilton last night," she said.

Margo snapped her head around. "What? Impossible."

"I'm hoping I'm crazy, but when the camera panned the audience at the end of the show, for a split second I saw someone who looked exactly like him."

The coffee maker finished brewing and Margo poured herself a large mug. "Look, sweetie, no offense—but I think you're losing it. You can't just walk in and see the show. You have to get tickets months in advance and answer all kinds of trivia questions, and even then there's no guarantee. Basically, he would have had to get the tickets before we were even booked."

"What if he knew someone who could get him on the show, or said he knew you, like your dad did?"

Margo shook her head. "I seriously doubt it."

"I'll see if I can find someone who recorded it. Maybe I can pause it and get a better look."

"I'm sure everything is fine," Margo said. "We have our meeting today, and then we're out of here tomorrow, so why don't you try and relax?"

Kit shrugged. "I guess you're right. This whole thing is making me a little nuts."

"Don't worry about it. I'll go finish putting on my makeup and we can head out."

* * *

Kit waited in the living room with Elinor, packed and set to go, while Margo meandered around the house, taking her time getting organized to leave. As Kit had feared, they were cutting it close by the time they dropped Elinor off at Holly's house and were finally headed to the meeting.

Margo took a piece of paper from her purse and unfolded it. "Okay, looks like this place is in Northern Liberties. Probably the best way to go from here is down Vine. This will be interesting—I have no idea what to expect in terms of the arrangements and practical details."

"I just hope they can give us some money for hotels and food," Kit said. "I don't need much, but I definitely don't want to sleep in my car with my dad and Elinor."

Margo gave her directions as the car rumbled across the cobblestone streets of the historic district. They headed toward Northern Liberties, a hipster area of restored warehouses.

They arrived to find a dimly lit room with painted windows and a hazy glow of smoke. It appeared to be an office, with a beaten-up desk in one corner and old chairs and couches scattered around the room. Kit recognized The Venturas' drummer first. Mandy was masculine and stocky, with stringy black hair that hung in her face. She sat next to Paula, the lead singer, a trashy-attractive blond with thick black eyeliner that contrasted with her little-girl ponytails. The bass player Daria, a plain but attractive brunette wearing jeans and a black T-shirt with a small diamond glinting from her nose, stood in a corner. Kit didn't recognize the two men in the room.

As she scanned the group, she realized there was no one here like her. Everyone here was still able to party and be cynical and tell the world to fuck off. As a mother, she no longer had that option. It surprised her to realize that not having that freedom anymore didn't really bother her.

"Hey, guys!" Margo greeted the crowd.

The shorter of the two men walked over to them. He had thick dark hair and a muscular build. Although he wore jeans and a T-shirt, he looked anything but casual. Kit could smell the spice of his cologne.

"Steve Knoll," he said stiffly, grasping first Margo's hand then Kit's. "You must be Margo and Kit."

"Guilty," Margo said.

"Well, it's great to meet you both," he said. "I'm The Venturas' manager. I'm sure you remember the band—"

He swept an open arm toward the room behind him and Margo and Kit exchanged hugs and air kisses with the three women.

Kit greeted Daria last. "How've you been?" Daria asked. "I haven't seen you since, what, that Ohio gig?"

"I think that was it. It's great you guys are still doing it. I miss it."

"We're still waiting for those big checks to roll in, but we have enough to get by. I have to share a house with three other people, but it's worth it. What's new with you?"

Just as Kit was formulating a creative way to describe her situation, Steve interrupted.

"Okay," he began, clapping his hands to get everyone's attention. "Let's get started."

The room stilled as everyone sat back down, many lighting cigarettes. Kit sat next to Margo on an old red couch.

"As you know, we're getting together here today to kick off the Women of Rock Tour. The first show is tomorrow night at the Tweeter Center, right across the bridge in Camden, New Jersey. The tour will be running for about eight weeks, but The Venturas are only playing the first three due to a prior European commitment. They were asked to invite an opener to join them for the tour, and out of the kindness of their hearts, they asked Broad Street."

Paula clapped loudly, knocking her cigarette ash to the floor. Margo and Kit smiled in her direction.

"We'll play seventeen shows in three weeks, and I have a printout here of the cities we'll be playing."

He paused to distribute a copy of the list to everyone in the room. Kit scanned the list—from Camden they'd move up the coast to New York, Hartford, and Boston, then west to Columbus, south to Nashville, further west to Denver, then down to Austin. It looked impossible.

"So first, logistics," Steve continued. "The Venturas will be getting $700 per gig, and they can give $75 of that to Broad Street. This money will cover all of your expenses, including transportation and housing, less the fees for the booking agent, tour manager—and myself, naturally."

Kit calculated. They would have only $1,275 to pay for gas, hotels, and whatever else for the next month. Her heart quickened as she tentatively raised a hand. "That probably won't cover our expenses," she said. "Is that figure set in stone?"

She felt Margo's eyes on her and glanced around to see everyone staring at her.

Steve's smile was cold. "This is an amazing opportunity, Kit. Some bands don't get paid anything to do this."

Kit swallowed. "I'm grateful for this opportunity. I'm just asking."

"I wish you could all get paid what you're worth, believe me, but this is coming from Showgirls, not me. I know the budget is a big concern for this tour and finances are very tight." Then Steve smiled and his worried expression cleared.

"There will be other ways for you to make money," he said, looking down at Kit. "My advice to you is to bring lots of CDs to sell, T-shirts, hats, whatever. Honestly, you girls are at an advantage and a disadvantage by not being represented. You don't have anyone getting you bigger money, but whatever you get you can keep yourselves." Steve turned away from Kit. "As I was saying, The Venturas will be getting their guarantee, plus their rider and per diem, from the label. Making sure this all happens will be your tour manager, Graham."

Steve gestured toward the guy sitting by a metal desk. Kit thought he looked young, maybe early twenties, and he was dressed more like a Deadhead than a rocker. He wore a baggy flannel shirt and torn jeans and his hair was buzzed short against pale skin dotted with a few freckles. Homemade beads were tied around his wrist and neck. When he stood and smiled Kit thought his eyes seemed to light up, and his slightly crooked teeth reminded her of a little boy, genuine and innocent.

"Hey, everyone," Graham began, his voice soft and musical. "Thanks so much for coming here to my office today. When Steve called me about working with you guys, I was really flattered. I've been a big fan of The Venturas for a long time, and I also remember seeing Broad Street a few times—back in the day, so to speak. You gals can all really rock."

Kit was flattered that he knew their band.

"I've managed a lot of tours since I started doing this," Graham continued, "everything from metal to country to reggae, and I've gotten pretty good at it. As you know, I'll be the one making sure everyone gets paid and has a working amp and new strings and sound checks—and all that stuff that can be such a pain in the butt."

Kit loved that he said "butt" instead of "ass." She found herself trusting this guy, and the singsong of his monologue drew her in.

"I'm also an excellent driver, and I'll be making sure The Venturas arrive safe and sound wherever we go. You'll mostly like me, but sometimes I'll have to wake you early for the occasional radio interview."

There was a groan from the lead singer, Paula, who was making a face.

"I'll try and keep that to a minimum," he joked. "I know your usual tour manager is on maternity leave, and it will be a little strange having me around, but I really think we're going to have a good time." He pushed his hands into his jeans pockets. "Are there any questions?"

"Yeah, are you single?" Paula asked. She laughed and jabbed the drummer, Mandy, in the ribs with her elbow.

Graham smiled, nonplussed. "I couldn't do this job any other way."

Paula and Mandy laughed and Kit tried to silence the pang that burned slightly in her stomach.

"Anything else?"

"I assume you'll be taking the same $1,000 a week?" Paula asked.

"That's my usual fee, yes," Graham said.

"We've worked that all out," Steve interrupted. "Graham has an excellent reputation, and you girls will not be sorry to have him along. As you well know, managing tours is a lot of bullshit, and Graham can handle it. So, if there are no more questions, let's talk about tomorrow."

The group spent another hour reviewing times and locations. The show would open on the second stage with a local act that would vary at each tour stop. Bitchsword, Charlie's all-girl death metal band, would follow with the first main stage act. After they finished, Broad Street would play for twenty-five minutes on the second stage while the main stage prepared for Ginger Snap, the lead singer of a defunct super-girl group who had recently launched a solo career. The Venturas would follow Ginger Snap's set on the second stage for their short set, then the show would conclude on the main stage with The Crocodiles, who had just released a mega-hit after years of gathering a primarily underground following, followed by the headliner, Sam Starr.

Kit glanced over at Graham occasionally as Steve spoke. He leaned over the list studiously, jotting notes in the margins. She noticed his handwriting was childlike, with small blocky letters. She hoped he might look in her direction, but he kept his attention on his paper.

As Steve continued to list the many back-to-back shows, Kit began to wonder if she could sustain the energy night after night— especially with a daughter who still woke at five every morning. She'd need to work this out with her father sooner rather than later.

After getting all the details, Kit and Margo said their goodbyes. Although Kit was relieved to be getting back to Elinor, she cast one last backwards glance at Graham, who was on the phone and hunched over his desk.

"Wow, Paula put on some weight," Margo said as she buckled her seat belt.

"Really? I didn't notice." Kit sighed. "What did you think about the whole money thing?"

Margo shrugged. "I'm cool with it. Like Steve said, we can always sell some T-shirts and CDs. Don't we have like a thousand CDs left from before?"

"Yeah, something like that," she said, picturing the tall pile of boxes gathering dust in her basement—reminders of her career cut short.

"So, we'll bring those along," Margo said. "And I'm sure we can wrangle up some shirts to sell."

"We're leaving tomorrow."

"I know," Margo snapped. "I'll go online tonight, put in an order, and have them delivered to my friend Peter. He can ship them to us wherever we are."

"Glad you have it all figured out."

Margo turned and glared at Kit. "What's your problem?"

Kit fought the desire to explode. She didn't have Margo's money, or freedom, or success, and she couldn't understand how Margo could be so blind to their differences. She took a deep breath. "I'm just concerned about how I'm going to afford this trip," she said.

Margo's face softened. "We'll be fine. Hey, your dad won't mind if I smoke in his car, will he?" She cracked a window and lit a cigarette.

"I know this probably sounds crazy," Kit began, "but what about having your parents drive us? We could crash in the Winnebago so we wouldn't have to worry about paying for a hotel every night, and I'm sure they'd love to live vicariously through us."

Margo took a long drag from her cigarette, and as she exhaled the smoke sailed through the window. "Sorry. There is no way I could deal with having them along."

Kit stared at the road in front of her. "Would it kill you to have a little sympathy for my situation?"

Margo shifted around in her seat. "Excuse me? Do you think I enjoy being woken at dawn every morning? I didn't create your situation, Kit. You did. I've been nothing but supportive. When are you going to grow up?"

"Oh, like screwing loudly while I'm right upstairs is so grown up?"

Margo laughed. "You have some nerve. It's my house. If you don't like it, turn up the television."

Kit drove silently, the excitement about the tour draining away like bath water. "You're right," she finally said. "I have fucked up, and I shouldn't ask you to do anything for me because I haven't been much of a friend." She turned onto Holly's street. "I just feel like this is my last chance to do something I love. I know that's not your responsibility. You have a great life, because you created it. I wish I could be more like you."

She pulled the car into the empty driveway. A note taped to the front door flapped gently in the breeze.

"What the hell . . ." Kit said. She ran up to the door and tore off the note.

Meet us at the same place we went to the other day. —Dad

Margo came up behind her. "What does that mean?" she asked.

Kit didn't answer but ran back to the car.

* * *

When Kit, breathless, burst through the door of the coffee shop, she saw Elinor, Holly, and her father sitting at the same table where they'd been when Kit told Nikki and her father about Damien. Holly looked pale and shaken.

Kit pulled Elinor into her lap with a kiss. "What happened?" she asked.

"It was probably nothing," her father said. "Holly thought she saw a suspicious car driving in front of her house."

"I'm sure I'm completely overreacting," Holly said, twisting a paper napkin in her hands. "I think I'm more nervous about this whole thing than I realized."

"What kind of car was it?" Kit asked.

"It was dark, with New York plates," Holly said. "A big old man car. I'm not good at makes. But it drove past twice that I noticed, and I just panicked and called your father."

"Did you get the plate number?" Margo asked.

Holly shook her head. "I didn't think anything of it at first, but then when I noticed the New York plates the second time I saw the same car, I remembered what Kit had told me." She took a drink of water. "Like I said, I'm sure it was nothing."

"Well, we're not taking any chances," Margo said. "I know some local cops. I'll make sure they pay extra attention to my house tonight. Tomorrow, we're out of here anyway."

Kit smiled at Margo, relieved and surprised by her concern.

"Thanks."

Margo shrugged. "Dr. Greene, do you want to stay at my place tonight too?"

"No, thanks, Margo," he said. "I have some final packing to do."

"Okay. I just need to call my parents to make some travel arrangements," Margo said.

Kit caught her eye, more grateful than words could say.

CHAPTER 41

Margo dropped her purse onto an end table and went straight into the kitchen to brew a fresh pot of coffee while Kit took Elinor upstairs for a nap. As it percolated, she went out to the garden and lit a cigarette. She was already more than halfway through her first pack of the day. She was annoyed that she'd been trapped into asking her parents about driving the band. Even if she could escape to a hotel every night, her parents would still be with them every day of the tour. But she did find this whole stalker dad thing a little creepy, and Kit was clearly not in charge of the situation. She took another drag of her cigarette.

She was also irritated because she hadn't heard from Harry since he'd left the night before. She prided herself on the wall she kept between herself and most men, but there was something about Harry that made her dare to fantasize about a normal life—a house in the woods, a real relationship, maybe even a kid.

She shook her head. She was stupid for even considering a relationship with Harry. This tour would be good for her. She needed some time away to think about him.

When her phone rang and she saw it was an unfamiliar number, she answered it quickly and hopefully.

"Hi honey!" her mother chirped. "I'm calling from my new cell phone. I can call you from just about anywhere now!"

Margo sighed. "Hi Mom."

"You'll never guess where we are."

"Vegas, getting discovered."

"Very funny. We happen to be standing at the Tweeter Center in Camden. Do you know how big this place is? Oh my gosh, honey, your father and I are so excited for you. If all the venues on the tour are like this, you are in for some serious fame!"

Margo sighed again, more loudly this time. "Mom, do you think you and Dad would like to drive the band?" she asked flatly. She held the phone away from her ear slightly, in anticipation. Her mother's predictable squeal came moments later.

"Orlando!" she called. "Margo wants us to go on tour with the band!"

Margo reviewed the logistics briefly as her parents passed the phone back and forth between them, asking questions and talking over each other. She asked if they could be at her house by noon the next day.

"Sure thing!" her mother said.

Her father took the phone. "What do you need us to bring?"

"Lots and lots of alcohol," Margo answered.

He laughed and relayed what Margo had said to her mother. She squealed again in hysterics and grabbed the phone from her husband. "Oh, you," her mother said. "We'll go to that big store we saw on the drive over here and get everything we need. Toilet paper, soap, shampoo . . ."

When Margo hung up the phone she lit yet another cigarette. The thought of being on tour again with her parents was more than depressing. She'd definitely need to treat herself to some nice hotels along the way.

Back inside, she logged onto her computer and began searching for hotels, moving down the list of cities on the tour. She started her search in New York City, the first real stop away from home. She could probably deal with one night in the Winnebago, and she could always take a cab home from Camden if her parents were really driving her crazy.

She scrolled through the many options, enjoying the fantasies of bubble baths in luxury tubs, room service, champagne on week-nights just for the hell of it. She finally settled on a place in Midtown, close to Fifth Avenue for some last-minute shopping before they went on to Hartford. She called the hotel, got a voicemail, and left her name, phone number, and credit card information.

As she hung up the phone, she felt a little less anxious about climbing into the cramped Winnebago. She knew she had an escape.

❋ ❋ ❋

After dinner, Kit said she'd turn in early. Margo was wide awake, so she decided to open a bottle of wine. She walked out to the garden, sipping the cool Chardonnay. Again, her thoughts turned to Harry. Who was he to screw her then not even call before she left for three weeks? That's what she got for letting down her guard. She lit a cigarette and drank some more, and before she knew it she'd emptied the glass and was pouring another. Her head was beginning to buzz, which only amplified her anger. She was not some stupid intern he could just screw and walk away from.

She pulled out her phone and scrolled through the recent call list. She found Harry's number from a full three days ago, when he'd called to set up his breakfast date with her like she was some complimentary prostitute that came along with his title. Asshole. Before she realized what she'd done, her thumb had pressed his number and her phone was automatically dialing the last person she wanted to talk to right now. She could have hung up, but she couldn't stop herself from bringing the phone to her ear, from listening to the ring and wondering where the phone was, what it was interrupting, hoping it was something very important. She took another gulp of her wine as it rang twice, three times, four, five, and then switched over to voicemail.

She listened as Harry's voice lied to her, assuring her he was unavailable. He knew she was calling. He always knew when she was calling.

She clicked off the phone and drank more wine. Get a hold of yourself, Margo, she whispered into the darkness of her garden. You're starting to get Fatal Attraction here, and it's not necessary. No one's worth feeling like this.

She scrolled through the numbers again, found a more comforting one, and chose it.

"Hello?" Peter said after a few rings. Margo heard music and the pulsing swell of a crowded room in the background.

"Hey, sweetie. It's Margo."

"Margo? Hey! Hold on a second, I can barely hear you."

Margo waited while Peter rustled on the other end of the line, already regretting interrupting his good time. The noise grew muffled, and then Peter's voice was back. "Hey, stranger!" he said. "I thought you'd be gone by now."

Margo's cheeks were suddenly damp, and she realized she was drunk and feeling sorry for herself and had no right to impose that on her friend.

"No, I'm not leaving until tomorrow," she said, slurring slightly. "I just wanted to say ciao, babe."

There was a pause. "Are you okay?"

"I'm fine."

"No you're not. What's up?"

"Nothing."

"You're lying," Peter said. "You always get lonely after the season wraps, but listen, you're about to go on a national tour where you'll be a rock star and you'll have to beat off the gorgeous guys with your guitar. Just leave everything behind and enjoy it."

"I miss you already," she said.

"You miss me because I'm the smartest person you know, and no one knows you better than the man who chooses your makeup. Listen, I love you. Have a blast, don't think about the station or flowers or any other goddamn horticulture shit. Just sit back and enjoy the rock cliché."

Margo thanked him, said her goodbyes, and hung up the phone. She blew her nose and walked back inside to dump the rest of the wine down the sink. She brought some leftover dinner up to her bedroom to eat in front of the television. There was no one to criticize her for spilling food, or for leaving the dirty plate by her bed, or for sleeping in her clothes. She only had to answer to herself.

CHAPTER 42

Kit was up at the crack of dawn on Thursday morning trying to consolidate the small mountain of Elinor's supplies: portable crib, stroller, clothes, toys, books, special foods, kid-friendly dishes and silverware. Even after she'd weeded out superfluous items and focused on Elinor's favorites the pile still looked like it would fill an entire Winnebago.

When Margo came downstairs she groaned at the pyramid that sat by the door.

"I know," Kit said. "How can such a little person take up so much room?"

Margo rolled her eyes and walked into the kitchen.

Kit was prepared to take a little shit. She was excited to finally get away and on the road—and to start playing live again.

She peered out the front window. The street was quiet, her father's car parked in front of Margo's house just another reminder of the threat she'd been living with for two weeks now. Kit had watched the patrol car pass by several times before she finally fell asleep the night before. She was still nervous, but she felt like they would be safe in the crowded Winnebago.

The phone rang.

"Can you get that?" Margo called.

When Kit answered a man's quizzed her. "Who is this?"

"Kit. Who's this?"

"Hey, Kit! It's Orlando. You ready for your big day?" Before she had time to answer, Orlando continued. "Vincenza and I are sitting here at Penn's Landing, enjoying the view of the river."

Penn's Landing, Philadelphia's underdeveloped waterfront, had a stage, some bleachers, and not much else. Kit knew the view consisted of the Camden aquarium and prison, along with a few big ships rocking in the water. Only Orlando and Vinnie would find this enjoyable.

"Great," she said. "Are you coming over soon?"

"Of course!" He paused and his voice trailed away. "What?" he asked. "It's Kit." His voice came back loud and clear. "Hold on, Kit, someone wants to say hi."

"Hey, girl!" Ronni shouted into the phone. "You ready to rock out or what?"

"Ronni? What are you doing there?"

"Hangin' with Parallel! These guys are totally awesome. We went out last night and saw some friends of mine play, and these guys can totally party. This trip is going to be awesome."

Kit closed her eyes. In her vision of their entourage, she'd forgotten about Ronni. She'd assumed that Ronni would tag along in her own car with the dozens of friends she was always touting. The huge Winnebago was growing smaller by the moment.

"Yeah," she said. "Awesome. Listen, put Orlando back on the phone, I need to give him directions from Penn's Landing."

✳ ✳ ✳

Almost an hour later, the camper arrived. Kit, who couldn't wait to leave Margo's house where she clearly wasn't welcome, had waited on the front stoop with her daughter. Elinor had woken up screaming in the middle of the night, waking an angry Margo in the process, and it had taken Kit almost an hour to calm her down. Kit was worried about Elinor waking up everyone in the Winnebago, too, but at least she would have her father's help.

But now Elinor was wide awake, pointing at every bus, bird, and taxi that passed. Kit tried to remain calm as the minutes ticked away. As the Winnebago rumbled down the quiet street, Kit could make out Orlando and Vinnie's silhouettes through the large windshield, broken by the reflections of trees against the glass. Vinnie was waving wildly and Orlando began honking the horn. A cluster of blackbirds leapt from the solitude of a large oak tree, flapping their wings to escape the commotion. Kit couldn't help but smile. She lifted Elinor to her hip and met the camper in the driveway.

Vinnie popped out first. "Oh my goodness," she said, wrinkling her nose and tickling Elinor's cheek. "Look how pretty you are today! Elinor, you are too gorgeous!"

Elinor giggled, her round cherry cheeks dimpling with a smile. Kit had to agree—her daughter really was beautiful. She had dressed her up in mini rock wear, with little embroidered bellbottoms, a purple ruffled shirt, and a matching barrette to pin the brown curls back from her face.

Moments after Vinnie had announced that she had to pee and disappeared into the house, Kit heard another car pull in behind the Winnebago. Her heart skipped a beat until she saw her father coming around the back corner of the Winnebago, a box of CDs under his arm, his tattered green suitcase in the other, and Nikki backing out of the driveway with a wave.

"Nice of her to say hello," Kit said.

He looked at the Winnebago with a scowl. "This is what we're traveling in?"

"Yeah, isn't it great?" she said. "A little camp-like, but it'll be fun."

"I can't say this was in my retirement plans. I always hated those old farts who sold their homes and drove to Florida in these things."

"Hello again, Pierce." Orlando came up behind them and extended his hand.

Pierce looked Orlando up and down, from his teal floral shirt to his white Oxfords. "Orlando. Good to see you again."

Orlando pumped his hand and Vinnie came out with bags of Elinor's things and greeted Kit's father. Kit stared at the contrasting figures, the withered academic with the faded pop stars. Other than lost dreams, these three had nothing in common.

"Where's Ronni?" Kit asked as they loaded Elinor's luggage into the camper.

"She's meeting us at the Tweeter Center," Vinnie said. She grunted as she lifted the portable crib into the Winnebago.

"Here, I'll get that," Kit said, taking it from her. "Sorry about all the stuff."

Orlando surveyed the scene, crossing his arms over his belly. "No problem. We'll make it work."

*　*　*

Even though Margo had only had a few glasses of wine the night before, she still had a dull headache that sucked every ounce of her energy. And for what? A guy? This was not her style, and she vowed it would be the last time it happened.

She was packing the last of her things into the new leopard luggage set she'd treated herself to when the phone rang. She grabbed the phone from her nightstand without looking at the number. "Yeah?" she said.

"Good morning, Margo. It's Harry."

A jumble of emotions rose within her, but the strongest one was anger.

"Sorry I haven't had a chance to call," he was saying. "It's been a crazy time, wrapping the season and dealing with all the time changes. Anyway, I know you're leaving today and I just wanted to wish you well."

"Thanks," Margo said.

"Are you all packed?" he asked.

"Yep."

"Are you angry I haven't called you?"

"Yep."

"Sorry. I thought you'd have so much going on you'd barely notice my absence."

She didn't buy this. They'd had sex. That should warrant even a brief day-after phone call.

"I've been busy," she lied. "In fact, my ride is here, so I probably should get going."

"I don't want you to leave angry." He paused. "I miss you already."

He had turned on that voice, the one that was deep and soft

and touched Margo unwittingly. She closed her eyes and tried to stay focused on her anger.

"You don't even know me," she said. "I'm not sure what you're used to, but I don't like to play games." This was, of course, a lie. She played games all the time, but she refused to be on the receiving end of this one.

"I think I know you pretty well," he said. "You're tired of the exhausting dating scene and you're looking for something more serious." He paused. "So am I."

"And you're not at all concerned about the moral ramifications of dating your employee?" she asked.

"There are only ramifications if things sour," he said. "I don't think they will."

Margo shook her head. "You sound pretty confident."

"It's my job."

She laughed. "I'm not sure what I'm getting into here, but I have to admit I'm intrigued."

The blare of a horn outside interrupted her. She peered out the window to see the behemoth vehicle filling her driveway and she flinched at the sight of her brightly colored parents waving wildly up at her.

"I'll call you soon," she said.

"I'll look forward to it."

She picked up her purse and opened her wallet one last time to check that she had all of her credit cards. She wanted to make absolutely sure she didn't have to camp out with this entourage if she didn't have to. If everyone was driving her crazy, she decided she would take a cab back home from the Tweeter Center. She hadn't heard back from the hotel in New York yet, but she could try again later.

Her mother was at the bottom of the stairs when Margo came down, lugging a heavy leopard suitcase behind her. "Can you believe this?" she squealed as she greeted her daughter with her usual overly enthusiastic air kisses. "It's so exciting!"

Her father bounded up the steps and started grabbing suitcases. "All right," he said. "Let's get this turkey roasting!"

Margo followed them out and said hello to Pierce.

He smiled and gestured toward the camper. "Your chariot

awaits."

She was shocked at how much stuff had been crammed into the Winnebago. Bags and suitcases of various shapes and sizes were piled high in the corner next to the back bunk beds. Bags of chips and six-packs of beer and a 48-roll package of toilet paper were all piled into a small mountain next to the beds, and stuffed animals and picture books were already strewn across the floor.

Kit handed Elinor to her father and squeezed past Margo to tidy up the mess. "Sorry," she said. "Elinor was getting a little fidgety. I think she's excited."

"No problem," she said as she looked in vain for somewhere to put her own bags.

"There's room up there, honey," Orlando said, pointing behind the driver's seat.

She shoved her bags into the space between the driver's seat and a bench that ran perpendicular to the wall. There was another anchored seat behind the front passenger chair that had a baby car seat chained to it with the seat belt.

"All righty, then," Orlando said. He slammed the side door shut and stepped over Margo to get to the driver's seat. "Is everyone ready to rock and roll?" he called over his shoulder.

"Where's Ronni?" Margo asked.

"She's meeting us there," Orlando said. He twisted the key in the ignition to spark the roaring engine to life, snapped on the radio, and found the oldies station. A Stevie Wonder song drifted into the cabin. "Perfect!" Vinnie said, and he turned up the volume.

Kit had strapped Elinor into her seat and was crouched on the floor next to her. Margo sat on the bench behind her father and watched out the window as her home faded from view, and then her street, and then Philadelphia. Individual buildings morphed into skyline as they crossed the Ben Franklin Bridge into Camden, New Jersey—the former home of Campbell's Soup and RCA had sunk into deep economic recession after those companies left. Margo's fellow passengers all chattered around her with excitement, amplifying the dull thumping in her head. She closed her eyes and leaned her head back, waiting for the aspirin to kick in.

CHAPTER 43

Kit's legs were falling asleep from crouching so long beside Elinor, trying to entertain her with books and toys as she squirmed in her car seat. The radio's blasting volume reminded her of how loud live music could be, and she realized she should have brought ear protection for her daughter.

She glanced over at her father and was surprised by how comfortable he looked. He was sitting on a bench in the back, a New Yorker magazine draped open across his lap as the Winnebago bounced and rattled through the desolate streets of Camden.

As the Tweeter Center came into view, rising above the horizon, it provided an odd contrast to the immediate surroundings. Orlando turned down street after street, following the small signs that directed them to the Center. With each turn, the megaplex filled more and more of the window until they were face to face with it and driving through a massive, empty parking lot littered with beer bottles and empty cigarette packs. When they came to a small white building close to the entrance, an old black man with a long white ponytail walked toward them. He was carrying a clipboard.

Orlando rolled down his window. "Good afternoon, brother!" he called.

The man raised his eyebrows. "May I help you?" he asked in a low, rumbling voice.

"I certainly hope so!" Orlando continued. "I'm the tour manager for Broad Street, and we're trying to figure out where to unload our gear."

The man looked at his clipboard and ran his finger down a list.

"Broad Street," he said, peering into the back window. Kit and Margo waved at him, smiling. "What's she?" he asked, pointing to Elinor. "A backup singer?"

Orlando glanced over his shoulder and laughed. He turned back to the man. "Good one! Actually, she's our bouncer. You don't want to mess with her."

The man laughed too. "All right, you want to head over there." He pointed toward the entrance. "You'll see a small driveway just past the gate. You'll want to follow that around to the back of the stadium. You'll see other tour buses there. You can park in any empty space marked with yellow, not red. Those are reserved for the main acts. Once you're there, anyone can show you where to load in."

"Thanks, my man," Orlando said again cheerfully.

"Anytime, brother," the man said with a smile.

As they drove off, Margo said, "Dad, can you knock off the 'brother' crap? It's not 1960, and you sound like an idiot."

"Honey!" Vinnie said.

"Oh, don't worry about her," Orlando said to his wife. "She's just too young to understand."

Margo looked at Kit and shook her head. Kit smiled. She was happy and relieved to share a joke with Margo. She'd been uncomfortable since the moment she'd set foot in Margo's house. Margo clearly did not like children—something she hadn't considered—and she felt guilty about bringing Elinor on the tour.

Orlando negotiated the large vehicle down the narrow driveway between a metal fence and towering metal studs that supported the huge stadium. When they rounded the corner, Kit saw a handful of tour buses parked in the prestigious red parking spots and other smaller vehicles scattered around the dirt lot. She recognized the huge purple star splashed across the largest of the buses: Sam Starr's signature. She was breathing the same carbon-monoxide-tinged air as the queen of punk—a tall wisp of a woman who combined poetry and music to develop a completely unique sound that had ignited an entire women's movement in rock. Kit wondered how Sam felt watching this movement devolve from girl power in the eighties and early nineties to flat-bellied girl toys in the new millennium. It was another reason Kit was proud to be included on this tour. Except for Ginger Snap, who had been the lead singer of the girl group the Sugarbees, the other bands all wrote their own music and played their own instruments.

The other buses were unidentified and had blackened windows, and Kit felt a twinge of anxiety as she scanned the people milling around the parking area. Many of the guys, with their long hair and battered band T-shirts, could have been Damien. She hadn't realized what a cliché he was.

Orlando pulled the Winnebago into the yellow space closest to Sam Starr's bus. Kit peered up at the blackened windows above them and felt humbled and lucky and terrified.

Orlando clapped his hands together. "Everybody out!" he said, pushing himself out of his chair and back into the main cabin. "Let's go see what we need to do here."

Kit unbuckled Elinor, who also stared wide-eyed out the window, and carried her out of the camper. The haze of dust that the Winnebago had kicked up lingered in the air.

Margo pressed her hands into the small of her back and stretched. "Shit," she said. She glanced sideways at Kit and Elinor. "Oh, sorry. That bench killed my back."

Kit smiled and shrugged, but Margo walked off anyway. Kit carried Elinor over to her father. "Can you take her for a few minutes while I figure out what's going on?" she asked.

He reached out for her, but Elinor leaned into Kit and hung on tight.

"It's all right, honey. Papa is going to play with you for a few minutes. I'll be right back." Elinor started to cry, but Kit handed her to her father anyway. "I promise, sweetie, I will be right back." She wailed more loudly.

"Go ahead," her father said. "She'll be fine."

Kit walked away, closing her eyes and trying to block out the sound. She followed Margo toward the back of the stadium, where a huge opening led into the darkened area under the stadium seats. She could hear the swell of voices rising as she stepped into the darkness, blinking the sun out of her eyes until she could make out shadowy figures. Graham, The Venturas' tour manager, approached them. Kit smiled, but he reached out to shake Margo's hand.

"Hey, Margo," he said. He glanced at Kit. "Hi," he said, and returned his gaze to Margo. "You guys can bring your stuff in here. There's a hallway that leads to the second stage. It's a bit of a haul, but there's a dressing room where you can make yourselves at home. Did you send out your rider to Showgirls Entertainment?"

Kit had no idea what he was talking about.

"I've been in touch with them," Orlando said from behind them. He walked forward, extending his hand toward Graham. "Orlando Bevelaqua, tour manager for Broad Street. We're still working things out, but I'm sure we'll come to an agreement," he said.

Graham looked between Orlando and Margo.

"Yeah, we took your advice, Graham," Margo said. "We figured it would be better to have someone looking out for us, too."

"Oh," Graham said. He reached a tentative hand out to Orlando and introduced himself. "You do know the terms of this opportunity for Broad Street, right?"

"I've heard the offer, yes," he said. He looked at Kit and Margo. "Why don't you girls start bringing your things in? Let me talk to Graham for a few minutes."

Kit smiled and walked with Margo back out into the sunshine. "What was that about?" she asked.

"God only knows," she said. "My father's up to something. He may be annoying, but he can negotiate a killer rider. We always had the best stuff in our dressing rooms when we went out on tour. When I was a kid he used to get a case of crayons and paper delivered for me. When I got older, he'd get packs of double-A batteries so I could play video games or whatever. And we always ate very well too.
"

"Good," Kit said. "Maybe he can wrangle up some diapers for me."

"I wouldn't be surprised."

Kit didn't see Elinor or her father around the Winnebago. She scanned the vast lot but saw only strangers milling around, smoking cigarettes, carrying instruments.

"Let's grab our guitars," Margo said. "Maybe we can find

some roadie to help us with the amps."

"Okay," she said. She stopped and turned, slowly, looking in all directions. He was probably in the camper, she decided, trying to keep Elinor out of the sun. She jogged to the vehicle but found it empty.

Margo pushed her way into the cabin and grabbed her guitar. "I guess I can take something else," she said.

"I'll be right back," Kit said. She's around here, somewhere, she repeated to herself. How can two people just disappear? She went around the side of the stadium, more ugly thoughts filling her head with each passing moment. She's fine, she said over and over, she's fine. But a louder voice scolded her for thinking it was a good idea to bring her baby into a public place where she could so easily be spotted. As she was heading down the long stretch to check the other side of the massive stadium, she heard her father's voice call her name from behind. She turned but didn't see him.

"We're in here!" he called again, and she saw his arm waving from a crack in the darkened window of Sam Starr's bus. Flooded with relief and a tinge of wonder—what was her father doing in Sam Starr's tour bus?—she ran around to its open door and stepped inside.

The bus, gutted of seats, was decorated with plush couches, soft red lighting, and stacks of stereo equipment. Elinor was sitting on Sam Starr's lap, holding onto a huge pendant that dangled from her neck. Sam had weathered significantly since the iconic soft black and white photo of her signature seventies album in which she sat cross-legged on a beaten chair, a cloud of cigarette smoke streaming from her small mouth and wrapping around her like an embrace. She was still thin, with long dark hair, but her soft face had become hard, cut with the lines of rock life. The sight of this megastar stopped Kit's breath for a moment.

Sam looked up at her, her deep brown eyes still as soulful as they'd appeared on the album cover.

"Is this your little girl?" she asked.

Kit nodded.

"She's beautiful," Sam said, turning her gaze back toward Elinor, who was still hypnotized by the large black stone on Sam's necklace. "It's been a long time since my daughter was this little. My baby's graduating from college this year."

Elinor finally sensed her mother's presence and turned toward her. "Mama," she said with a smile.

"Hi honey," she said, reaching out and lifting Elinor from Sam's lap and kissing her on the cheek. "I'm Kit," she said to Sam.

"I'm Sam. It's nice to meet you."

"We were baking in the sun," her father said, "and this woman was kind enough to offer us a break. I hope you packed sunscreen."

"Yes, Dad," Kit said, embarrassed. "I packed sunscreen."

"You're lucky," Sam said. "My parents would never have come on tour with me to take care of my kids."

Kit never thought of Sam having children or doing anything remotely ordinary. She'd read about her tours through Europe and Asia, her work with Arab women who had been wrongly imprisoned, her advocacy for HIV education in Africa.

"Did you bring your kids on tour?" Kit asked.

"Usually. It was tough. I'd have to rely on my manager, who was always busy juggling a thousand other things. Then, when I had my son, it was too much to ask anyone to take care of them for me. Sometimes I hired someone to come along with me, but too many times I left them at home with my mother. I missed a lot doing that," Sam said, gazing at Elinor.

Out the window, Kit saw Margo standing alone, looking around.

"I better go help Margo," Kit said.

"Go ahead," Sam said. "We can stay here. If that's all right with you, Pierce."

Pierce? Sam Starr was already friendly with her father, who had no clue who she even was.

"Sure, that's fine," he answered, leafing through a music magazine.

Kit felt odd handing her child back to a stranger, but there was something about Sam that she innately trusted. She kissed Elinor on the cheek again. "Mommy's going outside for a little while, and then I'll come back. Okay? You can stay with Papa and Ms. Starr."

Elinor nestled contentedly in the lap of this music legend, rubbing Sam's smooth black pendant between her tiny fingers.

* * *

Margo stood sweating in the hot sun. She had yet to spot any roadies who might help lug her equipment, and she'd be damned if she was going to carry it all herself. And now Kit had disappeared. Her head was pounding from the wine and the heat, and she grew increasingly irate as she looked around for her bass player. When she saw Kit emerge from Sam Starr's tour bus she strode toward her.

"Where the hell have you been?"

"Sorry," Kit said. "I couldn't find Elinor and my dad. What's up?"

"What's up is the dressing room where we have to cart all our shit is like three miles away and there isn't a single Diet Coke in there," she said. "And I can't find anyone to help, let alone some kind of cart to haul it all down there."

"Hey, guys!" They turned at the sound of the familiar perky voice. Ronni, with a gang of twig-like followers in tow, was bouncing toward them. There were two girls, also small and Asian, and a short, thin white guy with a tall pompadour.

"Perfect timing," Margo said. "We need help carrying our stuff to the dressing room. Follow me."

She led them to the camper. She was in the midst of assigning pieces of equipment to each person when Orlando popped his head in the door.

"Hey, don't carry that stuff!" he said. "We've got roadies to help us with that."

Margo peered around her father, who had been joined by four sweaty men. She recognized the redhead immediately. It was Kit's ex-boyfriend Charlie. She glanced over to see Kit's reaction and caught her surprise.

"Hi Kit," he said with a warm grin.

The two stood awkwardly. "Hi Charlie. You found us pretty quickly."

"I told you I would, didn't I? We're here to help you out," he said, gesturing toward Orlando. "This guy told us you needed a hand, and when I found out the one and only Broad Street was here, I rounded up the boys."

Orlando began barking orders to his new militia.

Margo interrupted him. "Hey, Dad, what did Graham say about the money?"

"Piece of cake, darlin'," Orlando said. "I got you up to a hundred bucks a show, plus a very comfortable rider. You should be proud of your old man."

Margo smiled. "Thanks. I knew that sounded like a bullshit deal when they told us about it."

✳ ✳ ✳

The farther they walked into the depths of the stadium, the cooler it was. Margo watched the scurry of men carrying lighting and musical equipment, worker ants carrying out the thankless work of putting on a rock show. The Broad Street crew passed several doors and finally arrived at one marked "2B." The room had been transformed since Margo checked it out less than half an hour earlier. There was a large metal tub filled with ice, beer, water bottles, and soda. A spread of sandwiches sat on a table.

"How the hell did you get this here so fast?" Margo asked her father.

"Oh, I just convinced The Venturas they had enough to spare."

Margo plucked a bottle of water from the tub. "Nice. I thought I was going to have to get Ronni to run out and get us stuff at every show."

"What's that?" Ronni asked as she entered the room with a drum throne.

"Oh nothing," Margo said. "Look what The Venturas gave us."

"Excellent," Ronni said. She made a beeline for the sandwich platter and began picking through them.

"Ronni," Kit said, "those are for everyone, so maybe you don't want to be pawing all of them."

Ronni gave Kit a bratty smirk and pulled two sandwiches from the top of the pile. "Hey, guys," she said to her friends. "Dig in!" She took a large bite out of a small triangular sandwich.

Margo saw Kit roll her eyes and carry her bass over to a free corner of the room while Charlie stood uncomfortably in another corner. Margo already felt alone with her old friend who gave all of her attention to her baby, and now her old boyfriend had turned up on the tour as well. She looked at Ronni chomping down more triangles, crumbs gathering at the corners of her mouth, her friends joining her and laughing like toddlers who had broken into the cookie jar. Margo was alone on a rock tour with her parents. Again.

CHAPTER 44

Although it felt awkward, Kit was glad to see Charlie again. He looked good. He'd lost some weight and shaved his goatee. The sun had darkened his pale skin and his light eyes looked even bluer. Despite the years on the road, he still had a boyish face dotted with freckles, though there were lines forming at the corners of his eyes and at the curves of his mouth. There was something about him that she found calming, which only amplified her guilt over sleeping with Damien. She had no idea how to bring up Elinor.

They walked out into the cool, dark corridor, leaving the others behind in the dressing room. Ronni was already getting on her nerves, and she was working hard to ignore her. She was here to have fun, not to babysit her drummer.

"You really look great," Charlie said, his voice stretched by the reverb of the cavernous hallway. "I like your hair long."

"Thanks."

Their heels clicked along in silence.

"So," Kit said, "how was Europe?"

"It was great. Busy, very little sleep, but still fun. I had a few days to rest at home, and now we're right into this tour. But I love it. I can't complain."

As they neared the exit and the bright sunshine, the temperature rose. Kit tried to imagine Charlie on tour with Bitchsword. She smiled at the contrast between his innocent red hair and freckles and the Satan-worshipping wardrobe of the all-girl death metal band.

As they walked toward the Winnebago to make sure they hadn't left anything behind, Kit glanced over at the Sam Starr bus. She stopped, oddly embarrassed, and turned to Charlie.

"There are a few people I'd like you to meet," she said.

Charlie looked toward the bus. "Wow, do you know her? She's amazing."

"I do now."

She led him around the bus and stepped into the air-conditioned interior. Sam was sitting with Elinor on an army blanket spread on the floor, letting her sift through colorful guitar picks. Her father was still reading the music magazine, but his feet were propped up on a chair. Elinor looked up from her task.

"Mama!" she said, and crawled toward her.

Kit glanced at Charlie to gauge his reaction. He stared at the small child squirming hurriedly toward them, then looked back at Kit.

"You've been busy," he said, a trace of anger in his voice.

"Yeah, she was a little surprise," Kit said, lifting her daughter from the ground. "This is Elinor."

Her father grunted from behind his magazine.

"We've been having a great time," Sam said as she unfolded herself and stood up. "Your daughter is adorable."

"Thank you. Sam, this is my friend, Charlie."

Sam shook Charlie's hand.

"It's a pleasure to meet you," Charlie said. "I'm a huge fan. But I guess you hear that all the time."

"I never tire of it," she said with a smile.

"And you remember my dad," Kit said.

Charlie walked over and shook his hand. "It's nice to see you, sir."

Her father looked Charlie up and down, from his dusty steel-tipped boots to his sweaty T-shirt. Kit resented the judgment in his eyes.

"You still a musician?" her father asked.

"Nope. Just a lowly roadie."

"Hmmm."

Kit interrupted. "So, can you help me get a snack for her, Dad?"

He looked out the window at the parking lot shimmering in the heat. "I have a headache. Can you bring her bag over here? It's better to feed her in the air conditioning anyway."

Kit pursed her lips, angry and embarrassed at being corrected so publicly.

"It's fine, Kit," Sam said. "They can stay here as long as they want."

"Thank you, Sam," she said. She glared back at her father, who was calmly flipping the pages of his magazine. "I'll walk her over with me and come back in a bit. You are really being very generous, and I appreciate it." She looked at Charlie. "Do you want to come with me?"

He shrugged but followed her back out of the bus.

Kit carried Elinor back into the hot sun toward the Winnebago. Before they reached the camper, she felt Charlie's hand on her shoulder. It stopped her, and she let the weight of it comfort her for a moment before she turned around.

"So, where's Elinor's dad?" he asked.

"I don't want to talk about it," she said.

He shook his head. "Same old Kit."

"What does that mean?"

"I better get back. I'll see you later."

He turned and walked back to the Tweeter Center. She wished she could follow him, to let him comfort her like he used to, but instead she stepped up into the camper to get her daughter a snack.

CHAPTER 45

Several hours later, the temperature was still high even though it was late afternoon. As quickly as Margo dabbed powder onto her face, it moistened and left her skin shiny with specks of flesh-colored chunks that she had to wipe off with a tissue. Her sleeveless silk top was also dampening under her armpits. She tried not to think about how much she'd paid for it and the fact that she wouldn't see a drycleaner for weeks.

She stared out from a shaded corner of the small stage at the ocean of empty seats and felt a slight twitch of anxiety. It was one thing to stare into a camera and know theoretically how many eyes were on the other side, but it was another to see those people physically in front of you. Their stage was significantly smaller than the main stage, tucked in a far corner of the grounds at a distance from the main act. The first band, a local act that would vary at each tour stop, would play the smaller stage at five o'clock, and then Bitchsword would go on the main stage around 5:30. The smaller stage performances served as a sort of glue during the main stage turnover time, playing short sets while the main acts broke down one band and set up the next one. Broad Street would follow Bitchsword, and then Margo would have to sit through Ginger Snap on the main stage, back to see The Venturas on the second stage, and then watch the final main acts, The Crocodiles and Sam Starr.

It's going to be a long night, Margo thought.

She looked around at the vendors pitching small tents on the lawn, the roadies and sound people putting the final touches on the stage equipment, and the other musicians milling around. Almost everyone seemed significantly younger—black-clad men and women with punk scowls on their faces.

She felt alone and was glad when she saw Kit walking toward the stage.

"Hey, Margo, sorry," she said, a bit out of breath as she climbed up on stage with her. "My dad's already completely useless. Sam Starr was actually helping me change Elinor's diaper." She chuckled and shook her head. "The whole thing is crazy. She's like nuts for my kid."

Margo smiled but she was annoyed. She'd been a huge Sam Starr fan as a kid. Her music, which was completely different from her parents' music, with its dark lyrics and experimental melodies and rhythms, had gotten her through some hard times. And now Kit was hanging out in her tour bus just because she reproduced.

"So," Kit continued, "what's going on here?"

"All right, ladies!" Orlando strode toward the stage with Vinnie and the two Venturas managers. They climbed up the steps to the stage and Orlando crossed his arms and looked out to survey the grounds. The rest of the Venturas were walking slowly toward the stage. "I think we've worked out all the bugs," Orlando said with a big grin.

"Hey," one of the black-clad girls called from the wings, "you're that guy from the D.J. Hamilton show!"

Orlando puffed up his chest and reached back to put his arm around his wife. "Did you get to see that? You're a lucky girl."

Others turned around to look and recognition spread across many of their faces.

"I thought you looked familiar!" said Mandy, The Venturas' drummer.

A small crowd began gathering around Orlando and Vinnie as they launched into their familiar monologue about the old days.

"Dad!" Margo said. "We need to figure out the equipment. Can you help?"

Orlando smiled at his daughter. "Of course, my princess."

"That's your dad?" asked Paula.

Margo nodded and sighed.

"Cool! No wonder he's such a hard ass. He's probably done this like a million times."

"Now, Paula," Vinnie said, touching Paula's arm. Her pink nails glittered in the stage lights. "It's probably closer to a half million. Don't make us into dinosaurs!"

Paula smiled and Vinnie and Orlando laughed.

"Dad, please," Margo said again.

Orlando turned to his audience and lifted his eyebrows. "The boss is calling."

They continued to finalize equipment sharing and lineup. As Margo tuned her guitar, tested her microphone, and adjusted the amp's volume, she did her best to ignore her parents' growing popularity. Not one person mentioned her show, but just about everyone seemed to have seen the Parallel comeback on D.J. Hamilton.

CHAPTER 46

A crowd slowly began to filter into the Tweeter Center—mostly scantily clad young people, and mostly women. Kit tried hard to stay focused on getting ready to play, but she couldn't help scanning the audience that started filling the empty seats in front of their stage, expecting one of the many punkers to morph into Damien. In her mind, he'd become taller, darker, more menacing than he probably looked in real life. She began to wonder if she'd even recognize him.

She also kept thinking about Charlie. He seemed so cold, but what should she expect? She'd cheated on him, dumped him, and had a child. What would he say when he found out Damien was the father?

Things had started falling apart when Charlie got some jobs on the road. She knew he would be faithful to her. He was an old-fashioned romantic who used to send her letters and unusual gifts from the places he visited. At the time, the gifts hadn't been enough for Kit. When Broad Street broke up she lost her identity, and self-pity led her to make many less-than-wise decisions.

"Bass." A man's voice boomed from several large speakers that skirted the front of the stage.

Kit glanced to the side of the stage and saw the soundman staring at her. She nodded and adjusted the volume on her guitar.

She plucked at the strings rhythmically, silent at first, and then the volume began to swell as it bled into the cables and out of the many speakers stacked on the stage and dangling from the scaffolding above.

"Okay, guitar."

Kit watched Margo as she began to strum. She looked nervous, and this made her feel better. They'd always felt their closest connection to each other right before a show.

"Thanks, guitar. Drums," the soundman said.

Ronni was in position on the house drum kit, ignoring the rest of the world as always. She was in tight shorts and a tank top, her skinny arms and legs working their way around the kit as she tuned and tested. She thumped on the huge bass drum with her tiny foot and snapped the stick on the snare drum, then each tom-tom. She was solid and confident, and Kit envied how easily it came to her.

"Let's run through one," the man said.

"Let's do 'Ugly Men,'" Margo suggested.

Ronni clicked off four, and they launched into the familiar song. As Kit played, her fingers felt stiff from not practicing for a few days. The sun was pressing hard against her skull and she began to feel lightheaded, distanced from herself. She watched her fingers move through the motions, but she felt as if she were watching from the audience.

"Okay." The soundman's voice boomed through the speakers. "That's good. Let's get The Venturas up here."

Kit pulled her bass strap over her head, unplugged her bass from the amp, and walked it to a guitar stand in the corner of the stage. She saw Graham standing next to the soundman, leaning close in a conspiratorial pose. She was impressed once again by how kind, almost innocent, Graham seemed.

Her eyes wandered over the growing crowd in the stadium. The sea of green seats that wrapped around the main stage was filling in, and the vast lawn behind the seats was quilted with blankets. Kit felt nervous as she saw their increasing numbers, and she worried about Elinor in the heat and the crowd. She decided to tell her dad about the band's air-conditioned dressing room.

On the walk back to Sam's bus, she watched a group of young girls giggling as they carried big sloshing cups of beer in both hands.

They reminded her of herself in a previous life, when she and Margo would play neighborhood outdoor festivals and drink beer until dawn and then sleep the rest of the day away until they rose with raging hangovers and ordered pizza.

As she neared Sam's bus, she heard someone call her name. She turned around and saw Daria talking to Graham. Daria waved her over.

"Did that bass amp sound weird to you?" Daria asked. Graham was looking at her—finally seeing her, Kit thought, wanting her opinion. She tried desperately to remember playing just a few minutes earlier, but she couldn't recall how the amp sounded.

"Yeah," she lied, "it sounded a little strange."

"I thought so, too," Graham said, staring at her with his deep blue eyes.

Kit noticed his slightly crooked teeth again, the way they turned in like a child's before braces. She imagined his mouth on hers.

"I hope I didn't blow my speaker," Daria said. "Maybe we should try using yours, Kit. Is it back in the dressing room?"

"Actually, I left it in the Winnebago," Kit said. "I can go back and get it if you want."

"I'll come with you," Graham said.

"Cool," Daria said. "I'll meet you guys back at the stage. I have to help Paula."

"No problem," Kit said, her heart racing.

She walked in silence with Graham, aware of the crunch of their feet against the dirt and grass, the warmth in the air.

There was no one in the Winnebago, but the doors were unlocked. Graham followed her into the cabin, where the curtained windows dimmed the bright sun. Kit's amp was tucked in a corner beside a mountain of baby supplies. She pulled it out, but when she turned around Graham was in front of her.

"I can get that," he said. His hand touched hers for a moment before he took the weight of the heavy amp from her.

"Thanks," she said.

"You guys sounded good out there," he said, not moving.

"Thanks again." She felt stupid and awkward, like she should say more, but her vocabulary had disappeared. They stood silent for what felt like an eternity, waiting for something to happen. Graham lifted his free hand slowly, mysteriously, like he might stroke Kit's cheek. The door burst open.

"Oh, hi!" Ronni said as she jumped into the cabin. "I left some of my hardware in here."

Graham turned around. "What do you need?" he asked in a tone that erased the moment completely.

"Oh, just my other pedal. It's here somewhere." She pushed past them and started digging through a pile of her clothes. "It's probably under a pile of diapers."

Kit envisioned her hands around Ronni's skinny neck, her eyes bulging like a cartoon. "Maybe if you didn't throw your shit everywhere you wouldn't have this problem," she suggested.

"Here it is!" Ronni said, pulling the V-shaped metal bass drum pedal from under a stack of bags, sending them toppling over. "Okay, see you guys later!" She raced out the door.

"Yeah, we should probably get back," Graham said.

Kit sighed. "Yeah, probably."

Back out in the warm air, Graham picked up his pace to catch up with Ronni, leaving Kit in the dust. She veered back toward Sam's bus, feeling the sting of rejection. You're a mom, she scolded herself. A role model. You can't pick up your old life and sleep with men who have no respect for you. Life's supposed to be different now.

* * *

Margo was growing annoyed by Kit's frequent disappearances. Before a show had always been their favorite time. They'd share a few beers, mock the other bands, calm each other down. Her parents were no help. They were still sharing tour war stories with anyone who would listen, so Margo decided to head back to the dressing room and get a beer alone. Very few faces in the crowd glanced at her in recognition.

She'd only been away from work a few days, but she found herself missing her show, the respect she had among the staff, the control. Her father had taken over her band, and she didn't have the energy to fight him. Though she hated to admit it, he was doing a better job than she could.

She spotted Kit in the distance and waved. "There you are!" she called. "Do you need a beer as badly as I do?"

Kit hesitated. "I, um . . ." She paused. "I kind of didn't want to be too far from my dad in case he needs me."

Margo sighed. "You brought him along to help, right?"

Kit shrugged. "Yeah."

"Then let him help. He's fine. He's done this before, plus you have your new best friend Sam Starr to keep an eye on them."

Kit glanced back at the parking lot.

"Look," Margo said, "all I'm saying is that you're never going to be able to relax and enjoy this if you hover over them all the time, and your dad will never be able to figure things out if you're always second-guessing him."

"I guess so."

"Great, then let's go have a beer."

Kit followed Margo back to the dressing room. Margo recognized Ginger Snap, the redhead from the defunct super-girl group, who was surrounded by assistants asking her questions and jotting down notes as they walked hurriedly through the corridor. A week ago this had been Margo—powdered and pampered and respected. Now she was sweating through her two-hundred-dollar silk shirt and there was not an intern in sight.

They opened the door to the dressing room to find her parents making out on the couch. Her mother's long tan leg was wrapped around her father's back, and they jumped in surprise at the sound of the door.

"Jesus," Margo said. "Really?"

Vinnie unwrapped her leg and smoothed her hair. "Honey, you should be happy your father and I still love each other so much."

"I'm thrilled," Margo said. "But I'd be happier if you took it to a hotel room."

Orlando laughed, wiping the pink lipstick from his mouth with a handkerchief. "I'm too busy making sure you girls get everything you deserve, like nice cold beer." He stood up and pulled two bottles from the tub full of ice. He handed one to each of them, then took two more for himself and Vinnie.

They sat down and Margo enjoyed the chill of the air-conditioned room.

"I did hear a little bad news today," he said. "It looks like Cincinnati and Chicago canceled the shows."

"Why?" Kit asked.

Orlando shook his head. "Who knows? They're saying ticket sales are low for the tour, but I'm sure it will be fine. It'll give us a little time to rest between gigs. I thought you gals sounded good today. The bass amp is still a little funky, and your vocals were lost in the mix, but I'll stand next to that guy and make sure he makes my girls sound perfect."

"They're using my amp now," Kit said. "Graham took it over to them."

Orlando slapped his knee. "Well then they should pay a rental fee! The crap they're paying you girls, they can't just burn out your expensive amp!" He stood, agitated.

"It's all right," Kit said. "We share equipment all the time. I'm sure Daria will get hers fixed."

Orlando sat back down and took a long swig from his beer. "We'll see what happens." He looked at his watch. "The first bands are probably starting now. We should head out and check out the competition."

There was a knock on the open door. Margo turned to see Harry, looking uncomfortably casual in khaki shorts and a polo shirt.

"Am I interrupting anything?" he asked.

CHAPTER 47

Margo stood, her head swimming with mixed emotions. She was grateful that he'd come to see her but slightly embarrassed by his appearance.

"Hi," she said. "This is a surprise. Come on in."

He smiled, stepped in, and extended a hand toward Orlando.

"Mom, Dad, I want you to meet a friend of mine, Harry Thomas."

The two men shook hands. "Orlando Bevelaqua. This is my wife, Vincenza."

Harry shook her hand. "Nice to meet you both," he said. "Hello, Kit."

"You must have some convincing story to get past security here," Orlando said with a wink.

"Yeah, I know a few people," Harry said.

"Harry runs the cable station, Dad," Margo said. "He's my friend and my boss."

Orlando and Vinnie exchanged glances.

"Gotcha," Vinnie said. She touched her husband's arm. "We were just heading out, weren't we, honey?"

"Oh, yes!" Orlando said. "Kit, care to join us?"

Kit stood up, leaving her beer on the floor by her feet. "No, thanks." She walked toward the door. "I'll catch up with you guys later."

"Okay!" Vinnie said. "You two take your time."

Orlando looked at his watch again. "But not too much time! You're on in about an hour."

When the door closed behind them, Harry pulled Margo into him for a long kiss, and any apprehension Margo had about his presence there disappeared.

"Sorry," he said as they separated. "I couldn't help myself."

"Anytime. Want a beer?"

"Actually, yes, I would."

Margo pulled another beer from the tub and handed it to him. She sat down on the couch and motioned for him to sit next to her. But he sat in a chair next to the couch instead.

"I have something I need to tell you," he began.

Margo slumped back into the couch. "I hate when things start like that." She lit a cigarette.

Harry put his beer on the table, untouched. "I guess there's no way to say it, except to come out and say it. I am, technically, married."

Margo took a long drag on her cigarette and blew it out above Harry's head. "Technical marriages are always the most difficult."

"Please don't joke," Harry said. "I'm only telling you because I really care about you."

"I wish I could say I was flattered."

He reached for his bottle and took a small sip, then rested it on his knee. He kept his eyes on the floor.

"I met my wife in college and we got married young—too young. I didn't really know her that well. I just thought she was different, and interesting, and I was drawn to that. She had this strength that I really admired." He looked up at Margo. "In some ways, you remind me of her when she was young." He paused, then returned his gaze to the floor. "Anyway, it wasn't long into the marriage that her episodes began. It started with the cleaning. She cleaned constantly. I didn't think anything of it at first—I thought she was just enthusiastic about having her own place for the first time, but it got worse and worse. If I put a glass of water on the kitchen counter, she'd run over and wipe up the mark. She'd wake up at six in the morning and start vacuuming. I'd come home from work at the end of the day and she'd still be at it. Even through all this she seemed okay in public, but then her fear of germs started escalating. She got bladder infections because she refused to use any bathroom other than her own. Eventually, she stopped going out altogether."

Margo wrinkled her brow, trying not to smirk at the image of some frantic woman dragging a vacuum cleaner back and forth as she mopped her damp brow with a monogrammed handkerchief. She crossed her legs. Harry's story didn't make any sense. How could he hide something this big from the many gossipy mouths at the studio?

Harry took another sip of beer. "Things got worse still. She wouldn't go out, but she was afraid to stay home alone. I missed lots of work, just as I was being considered for a promotion. We were one of the first shows to have an African-American lead, and . . ." he trailed off, staring at the wall behind Margo. "Anyway, it became impossible to live like a normal couple. We stopped seeing family and friends; she stopped getting out of bed. It was just . . . bad."

Margo tapped her ash into the ashtray next to her.

"She's in an institution," he continued. "She has been for almost ten years. She's on medication, and she's better, but she's still not capable of living in the real world, so to speak."

"So," Margo said, taking another long drag on her cigarette. "Let me get this straight. You're married, but no one knows about it. Your wife was put away and, again, no one knows about it."

"I've been very careful with my personal life. I've changed studios twice since this all happened, and I just stopped talking about it. I have some close friends who know, but they're real friends and they respect me enough to keep it private."

Harry got up and sat next to her on the couch. He placed his hand on her knee, but she kept her hands occupied with the beer and what remained of her cigarette.

"There have been other women along the way," he said, "but you're the first one I've ever told."

Margo took one final drag from the cigarette, the last of the spark sizzling toward the filter, then stamped it out in the ashtray.

Harry touched his hand to her face and turned it toward him. "Look, this is something that I have to live with, but it's not something you have to live with. I've wanted a divorce for years, but I'm afraid what that might do to her. I'm only telling you because I take you seriously. I'd like you to be a part of my life. Please just think about it for a while. We've got plenty of time."

Margo looked into his deep brown eyes. She was almost positive there were flickers of sincerity. She wanted to believe him. Her mind wandered again to her image of the two of them tucked inside a normal life. A crazy wife didn't fit so neatly.

"I thought not calling me was bad," she managed to say.

"That was bad, and I'm sorry. I know we just met, but I wanted to get this out of the way. As you know, there just aren't many sincere people in this biz. You're the first person I've met since Patty who may actually like me, not my title. I'm sick of show biz people."

"I'm not sure if you've seen my show," Margo said, "but I am one of those people."

"No you're not. Not really."

Margo smiled, denying the concern in her gut, and let Harry kiss her. Maybe it would all work out, just like in the movies.

CHAPTER 48

The crowd continued to grow, and Kit tried to stay calm as she waited for Margo to meet her behind the stage. She was annoyed that her George Clooney guy had just shown up, right before their show, and that Margo had just melted—like the band meant nothing.

Kit watched as the first act, a young blond, set up her guitar, stool, and lone microphone. She couldn't imagine being onstage alone, so naked, without even amplification to hide behind. The girl was confident; clearly she had done this many times before. She tested the microphone, strummed her instrument one last time to ensure she was in tune, then hopped onto the stool, her legs dangling.

"Hi everyone," she said into the microphone. A few people looked up at the stage, but most were just walking past on their way to the vendor's area. "I'm Felicia, and I'm honored to play with all of these incredible women." Kit heard a few small pockets of polite applause, mostly from the other bands waiting to play. "My first song is, basically, a love song. It's called 'Fifty-Four Spring Garden Street.'"

Oh no, thought Kit. She knew this type—the singer-song-writer who culled the adolescent tirades of her diary for lyrics.

"You had the cat, I had the dog," she sang. "Together we could have laughed through it all. But you went to the gym, and you never came home. Little Mister Pepper had to bury his bone."

Kit did her best not to chuckle. Where was Margo? She

couldn't believe she was witnessing this alone.

"Fifty-four Spring Garden Street," the girl continued. "We lived at Fifty-four Spring Garden Street . . ."

She went on—and on—with this literal musicalization of her life with Mister Pepper's father. Her next song was a variation on this theme, though she had moved from Spring Garden Street to another location with the pets. The music wasn't bad, if a bit derivative, but the unintended comedy of the lyrics amazed Kit.

As she launched into her final song, Margo and Harry joined Kit.

"What did I miss?" Margo asked.

"Only another Sarah McLachlan wannabe," Kit said. "She was seriously singing her address history."

"Hysterical."

The three stood silently. The singer thanked the audience, who replied with slightly more enthusiastic applause. When she was finished, Kit turned toward Margo and Harry, who both seemed tense.

"So," Harry finally said, "where's your little girl?"

"Luckily she's sleeping right now," Kit answered. "My father's watching her for me."

"Is she napping in Sam Starr's bus?" Margo asked.

"Yep. Some new nanny, huh?"

"I remember Sam Starr," Harry said. "Her first album was great."

Margo and Kit exchanged a glance. They were both impressed.

When Vinnie and Orlando reappeared, Kit noticed with a smug smile that Vinnie's hair was a bit flat and her makeup had been redone.

Together they walked over to the main stage to check out The Crocodiles, who put on a strong short set of power pop punk. The summer night had finally cooled and, thanks to a beer from the dressing room stash, Kit was beginning to feel more relaxed. Even Margo and Harry holding hands didn't bother her too much. They had about twenty minutes before they would head back to the second stage and start setting up for their set, and Kit was getting that performance anticipation mashup of fear and excitement. That's when she spotted her father pushing Elinor in the stroller. Kit looked from her daughter to the massive speakers that were stacked on the main stage.

Kit tossed the remains of her beer into a trashcan and walked quickly over to her father. "What are you doing?" she asked.

"Mama!" Elinor said, reaching for her.

Kit lifted her into a hug. "Hi honey," she said.

"I'm taking your daughter for a walk," her father said. "Or did you want me to keep her cooped up in a bus all day?"

"Of course not," Kit said, glancing again at the stage. "It's just that this next band is going to be extremely loud and I'm worried about her ears."

"Mama," Elinor repeated, patting her mother's back lightly.

"I agreed to help," her father said. "I did not agree to be a prisoner. If you want me to be Elinor's caretaker while you're off drinking with your friends, then you have to let me make some decisions. I did raise you and your sister, remember?"

"No, Dad, I don't remember that."

"I know your mother did most of the work. And I know I was busy with school. But don't imply that you were abandoned by me, because that isn't true."

"Whatever, Dad. All I'm asking is that you be careful. This is obviously not an ideal environment for a baby."

"Do you want me to take her home?" he asked.

"Of course not, just . . . just please be careful." She felt the familiar burn of frustration. How did he always manage to incite that? "Why don't we walk over to the other stage together? We're on after this band."

"No problem. I've never seen you play before."

Great, Kit thought, another opportunity for him to criticize me.

✳ ✳ ✳

Margo was holding hands with her boss. She couldn't remember the last time she'd held hands with anyone. High school, maybe? Donny Schmidt, who'd been hers for those glorious few weeks. Margo with her bad teenage hair and Donny with his bad teenage mustache, swinging hands as they strode through the halls, girls turning their jealous stares in her direction. She'd been so proud to hold his hand.

And now she was clutching the hand of a man in khaki shorts and a polo shirt in a sea of black T-shirts and tattoos. She could tell some of the people staring at them recognized her from the show and some couldn't figure out where they fit in this scene. She was happy that Harry had stayed, but she was still reeling from his confession. There were so many things about his story that didn't make sense.

"All right, ladies!" a large woman with spiked hair shouted from the stage. "It's time for some serious female empowerment shit. All the way from Seattle, give it up for . . . Bitchsword!"

The crowd applauded—some pockets with more enthusiasm than others. Four girls with long dark hair and matching black Bitchsword T-shirts strode onto the stage. They all wore thick black eyeliner, pale makeup, and black lipstick. The music kicked in with the drums, and the volume was deafening. Even though they were outside, with no walls to slam the noise around, Margo felt engulfed in the wave of noise. The guitarist stepped up to the microphone and began singing—sort of. It was more like wailing, high-pitched and painful, and soon the keyboard player and bass player joined her in strange operatic harmonies.

Margo glanced at Harry, who was no longer pretending to enjoy the music. She squeezed his hand—trying to talk was useless—and pointed to the smaller stage. He nodded.

When they arrived at the second stage, Orlando and Vinnie were talking to Paula.

"Hey, Harvey!" Orlando greeted Harry with a slap on the back. "You guys have enough time together back there?" He smiled and winked.

"Harry, Dad," Margo said. "His name is Harry."

"Oh! Sorry, old man."

Margo cringed.

"No problem, Orlando," Harry said. "I get that all the time."

"I think we have everything under control," Orlando said. "We've got the drum kit tweaked for our little Ronni, Kit's bass rig is EQ'd perfectly and buzz-free, and I've got my baby's vocal mics up in the mix and dripping with reverb, just the way she likes."

"I'm looking forward to hearing it," Harry said, smiling at

Margo.

"Yeah, no pressure," Margo said. "Just playing for the first time in front of my boss and a couple hundred people."

"You'll be great as always, sweetie." Orlando rubbed his hands together. "Who wants one last beer before you gals get up there?"

CHAPTER 49

Bitchsword finally brought their dissonant, screeching cacophony to a loud and painful climax. A large part of the crowd had fled their seats during the performance and lingered instead in the vendor area throwing Frisbees, talking, eating, and drinking. Many were also heading over to the second stage to kill time before the next main stage act, The Crocodiles.

The summer sun was sinking into the Philadelphia skyline across the river. Kit found a vendor selling earplugs, stocked up, and brought them over to her dad and Elinor. She twisted a pair and poked them into her own ears to convince Elinor that wearing earplugs was super fun and then twisted another pair into the tiniest diameter possible and pushed them gently into Elinor's ears. After Elinor shook them out of her ears a few times, Kit was able to distract her with a freebie squeegee ball long enough to get the earplugs into position. She handed another pair to her dad.

They had reached a truce—she'd agreed that he could let Elinor watch Broad Street play as long as they stayed safely outside the piercing cone of sound created by the speakers.

As they joined Margo and Harry back near the stage, Orlando came bounding over.

"Come on, girls!" he commanded. "Quit yakking and get your butts on stage!"

Margo glanced at Harry. "Charming, isn't he?"

"He reminds me of someone," Harry said.

"Very funny. Come on, Kit."

Kit turned to her father. "Okay, I need to go. It'll be a quick set, but if Elinor gets fussy I won't be offended if you have to leave."

"Got it," her father said.

She kissed Elinor on the forehead, climbed onto the stage, and grabbed her bass from its stand. As she checked that she was still in tune, she was peripherally aware of the crowd building in front of the stage. But she was more anxious about her father watching her play. She knew he'd dissect their inane and suggestive lyrics, filtering them, as he always did, through his professorial pretension.

She cast a glance over the audience and spotted an even more frightening reality: a petite woman in dark glasses and a large floppy hat had joined Elinor and her father. Sam Starr was going to watch them play. The woman whose musical poetry had carried her through many of her adolescent struggles was about to witness her simplistic garage rock. She blushed and chastised herself for criticizing the blond acoustic singer. Her own lyrics hardly rose above bathroom graffiti. She leaned toward Margo. "Sam Starr's here," she whispered.

"What? Where?" Margo, still tuning her guitar, scanned the audience.

"Over by my dad."

"Oh shit. It's bad enough I have my boss watching me."

"Your boss?"

"Well, you know, date—whatever."

Kit smiled at this slip. Margo was just as nervous and excited as she was, and she felt better. "Well then, I guess we just have to kick some ass," she said.

Ronni had hopped up to her drums and was banging away as she warmed up, drawing attention to herself.

"Were we ever like that?" Margo asked.

"Never."

"Thank god." She nodded toward Kit and Ronni and stepped up to the mic. "Hey, everyone," she said. Her voice echoed through the massive speakers above their heads. A hush rippled through the crowd as people turned to the stage. Kit saw her father lift Elinor onto his shoulders so she could see her mom.

"Thanks for coming out today!" Margo continued. "We're Broad Street, and we're here to rock your world!"

Ronni clicked her sticks enthusiastically over her head four times and slammed them down onto the drums. Kit and Margo met her there at exactly the right moment. Kit's bass sounded amazing—thick and powerful. This sound system was far superior to anything she'd ever played through at a local club. It was almost disjointed, the connection between her small pick and the massive wall of noise it created. She felt her body responding, moving with the beat. She caught Margo's eyes and the genuine smile she flashed her before she stepped into the microphone and started singing another Broad Street favorite, "It's Not My Fault."

Kit stepped into the microphone to sing, staring ahead but at nothing, above the heads of the people in front of her.

It's not my fault, that you love me
You got caught, thinking of me . . .

Kit was in the song, in the moment, letting the music wash through her. They sounded good—really good. Ronni's drums were full and powerful, Margo's guitars were splashed in the mix and, despite the thick texture of their instruments, the vocals were clear. Was this what it was like to be a pro?

When they reached the end of the song the audience applauded—not the rousing cheer Kit had hoped for, but sincere enough. She scanned the crowd for Sam and her dad, but the audience had swelled and she could no longer spot them.

"Thanks!" Margo said. "That was a little song about one of Kit's many fan boys."

Margo glanced back over her shoulder at her and Kit nodded and smiled.

Ronni clicked off the next song, "Action Girl," another fast and loud one that Kit always enjoyed playing. She closed her eyes and focused on the thumping repetition of her bass, as rhythmic as a heartbeat. She was strangely reminded of being in the hospital, ready to give birth to Elinor, all alone as her father waited outside, her sister too busy with her own children to stay, wires attached to her large belly as a machine monitored Elinor's heartbeat in loud pulses, the only sound in the room. Elinor had become so real to her then, a part of her and not at the same time.

She looked out over the audience. She still saw only strangers, and despite everything she felt disappointment. She wanted her father to see why she had given up everything else, to see how happy she was on stage making music. She'd hoped he might see, and agree, that this was where she belonged—not in graduate school or in some corporate job.

Margo was singing the verses to the audience, selling them as she always did. She was great at fronting the band—smiling, dancing, and joking between songs. She was a natural, and that was why there was no Broad Street without Margo. Margo turned to her and smiled. For thirty short minutes, they owned this stage and this crowd and it was ten years earlier and they were still best friends.

* * *

Margo tried not to look at Harry as she revived her old Broad Street vamp. She had forgotten the energy of a live audience and was savoring the adrenaline as she sang and played. Her performances in the television studio were so controlled, with all of the decisions—from where she should stand to what she should say—planned ahead. The unpredictability of the stage was raw and exciting. She felt connected again, and she realized that was what she had missed.

She glanced back at Kit again, but she seemed preoccupied, scanning the crowd—probably worrying about the baby again.

Margo easily found Harry in the sea of black—he was smiling, seemingly unaware of how he stood out in this crowd. She liked that he seemed so comfortable with himself and wished she could be more like that. She caught his eye, gave him a flirty wink, and kept singing.

He raised his eyebrows and pointed at his chest. "Me?" he mouthed.

She smiled and turned her attention back to the people in front of her—some watching, most talking and only half-heartedly paying attention. She was determined to win them over.

She belted the final notes of the song and lifted her guitar neck to play the crescendo. When the final drum roll ended, the crowd paused before clapping intermittently. There was one high-pitched whistle, from Harry, and Margo blew him an air kiss.

"This next one," she announced, "is one of the first songs we wrote in Kit's living room."

This was their one instrumental, a short surfy song reminiscent of Dick Dale. Margo started on guitar, following Ronni's time on the kick pedal, then Kit hopped in for a measure, and finally Ronni came in with the full kit. It was simple and upbeat, like all of their songs, and Margo realized she could never write a song like this now. It wasn't that she was so unhappy, but the simplicity of the music was so young. She would probably overthink its structure, adding complicated bridges or changing the chords to something more unusual.

The song ended with a few flubs, but nothing that noticeable—especially since virtually no one in the audience seemed to know their music.

The rest of the set went surprisingly well, considering how few practices they'd had. As much as Margo hated to admit it, that was largely due to Ronni's solid drumming. She kept the time consistently and even managed to bring Margo and Kit back to the right place when they wandered. She was also fun to watch, with her twirling sticks and bouncing long black hair.

When they reached the end of their set, most of the crowd was still there—despite the many distractions of vendors and flying frisbees and Ginger Snap's band setting up loudly on the main stage.

"Thanks for coming out today," Margo said to the audience. "We're Broad Street, and we have CDs for sale if you want to come up after the show." She pointed to her father, who was standing next to a box of their old CDs and waving one in the air. "Stick around for The Crocodiles and, of course, the fabulous Venturas!"

There were a few loud cheers from the audience at the recognition of these names, and then some house music started up from the speakers as the soundman put on a CD, signaling Broad Street to exit the stage.

"Pretty good show," Margo said to Kit as she wrapped a cord around her arm.

"Yeah," Kit agreed. "I just wish my dad could have heard it. I didn't see him at all after the first song."

"He'll have plenty of opportunity to see you again."

"I know," Kit said. "It's all right. I had a blast. And—" She leaned in to whisper. "Ronni was actually pretty good."

"She was. Let's not give her too big an ego, though."

Kit smiled. "Agreed."

As if on cue, Ronni bounded over to them. "You guys rocked!" She punched them both lightly in the arm.

Margo rubbed her arm. "Yeah, that was a decent show. Good job back there."

"Hey, thanks! I was so into the music, it's just so simple balls-out rockin'. The audience kind of blew, but who cares? We're going to win the crowds over all the way to Texas!"

"That's the plan," Kit said.

"Need a hand?" Harry had climbed up onto the stage and was standing behind her.

"Are you offering?" she asked.

"Of course!" he answered. "I actually have gotten my hands dirty on occasion."

She looked at his smooth hands and manicured nails. "I find that hard to believe."

"I can grab my stuff, thanks," Kit said as she walked away.

Margo was sorry to see her go. She wanted Kit to hang out. And she still wasn't sure how to handle Harry's confession. She needed time to digest it.

Harry put his arms around her waist and pulled her close. "You looked really hot up here," he whispered in her ear.

She felt the bite of an uncontrollable sexual urge. "I bet you say that to all the rock stars," she said.

"Maybe we should carry your guitar back to the van," he suggested.

She looked up at him, the naked lust in his eyes, and couldn't help but melt a little. What was it about this man? He was like no one she'd ever dated. It had been a long time since she'd felt out of control like this.

"Maybe we should," she said.

She handed him her guitar, stuffed the last of her cords into a small suitcase, and led Harry off the stage toward her parents, who were standing at a table with their CDs, hawking them to everyone in earshot.

"I'm just going to run a few things back," she told them. "Can I have the keys?"

The scent of grilled meat from the food trucks hung in the air. Walking briskly with Harry at her side, carrying her guitar, Margo felt giddy with lust. She ignored the staring eyes as they walked through the crowd.

When they reached the Winnebago, Margo unlocked the side door and the two stepped up into the dark, warm interior. The camper had baked in the sun all day, and Margo instantly felt sweat beading under her arms. She glanced at the bunk bed with rumpled sheets and remembered her parents' unkempt appearance earlier. She pushed the image of them rolling around on this bed, naked and disgusting, from her mind. As a child she had found them like that too many times, and the memory turned her stomach.

As she was trying to refocus, she felt Harry's arms again snaking around her waist, his lips nuzzling her neck. His skin was already damp from the airless room, and the warmth of his body made her claustrophobic.

"It's too hot in here," she said, pulling away. "Let's go back outside."

Even in the dim light, she could see the disappointment in his eyes. "I'm not going to see you for a long time," he said. "I think I'm just starting to realize how much I'm going to miss you."

She looked into his dark eyes and realized she would miss him too. She peered out the front window. There were still people milling around the parking lot, carrying equipment, smoking, talking, but she spotted a small patch of woods nearby.

"Come with me," she said, taking Harry by the hand.

She locked up the camper and led him toward the woods, away from the crowd. Ginger Snap's shrill vocals faded as they walked into the deep shadows of towering evergreens. Margo looked behind her, past Harry, to see if they could hide sufficiently in these shadows. She kept walking until she felt secure enough to stop and kiss him deeply, her tongue exploring the sweet mint of his mouth. He pulled her closer and she felt his erection against her leg. She pulled her skirt up and turned her back toward him, leaning against a tree as Harry lowered her panties and lifted himself up and into her. He felt incredible. It was raw and exciting, the scratch of the bark against her hands and face as he pumped in and out of her, wrapping his hand around the front of her and massaging her breasts, the blood surging from her head to between her legs as she grew dizzy with passion. They were both moaning, the song of raw lust drifting among the soft call of birds and distant music. Her head grew lighter as she felt herself falling to the ground with Harry, their bodies cushioned by the soft pine needles.

They lay for a few silent moments as Margo stared at the elegant shapes of evergreen painted against the dusky pink sky.

"So," she said, "do I get a raise?"

"I think you've raised enough already, thank you very much." He rolled over and propped his head on his hand. "I could get used to this."

Margo smiled.

"I have to admit," Harry continued, "I was a little jealous watching you on stage, thinking about all the other people in the crowd who were having the same sexual fantasies I was having."

"You're the one I'm lying here with."

"Yeah, but . . ." He paused. "I can't help it. I want you all to myself."

"You have me, for now."

Harry pushed himself up, pulling up and zipping his shorts. Margo sat up and rearranged herself, removing stray leaves from her panties.

"I'm serious," he said.

"What do you mean?"

He leaned back on his hands. "I wish you didn't have to go on this tour."

His suggestion irritated her. "I'll be back soon. I'm sure you have plenty of things to keep you busy between now and then."

Harry stood and brushed off his shorts.

Margo craned her neck to look up at him. "What, are you mad? You're the one who's married, in case you forgot."

He gave her a long look, then sat down next to her again. "You have every right to be mad," he said. "I'm just asking you to give me a chance. What do you have to lose?"

"Let's see . . . my job? My dignity?" she said, crossing her arms over her bent knees.

"What about your future?" Harry asked.

She glanced down at their bed of pine needles and thought

about the interns and the empty nights. She was tired of being alone.

"I'm not very good at this," she admitted.

Harry smiled. "Me neither. I'm sorry I said anything about the tour. I'm not usually the jealous type. Clearly, we both have to figure out how to have a normal relationship in an abnormal situation. But, I'm game if you are."

Margo kissed his cheek. "I love a good challenge."

CHAPTER 50

Kit finished packing up her equipment and wandered toward the main stage where Ginger Snap and her band were launching into a perky pop song. Kit stood on tiptoe to see the woman in bright pink skipping around the stage, her outfit flowing behind her like a butterfly. The former power-pop star began clapping her hands above her head, and sections of the audience near the stage joined her. She skipped around some more before grabbing the microphone from the stand and starting to sing in a high-pitched, nasal voice.

Ronni stood nearby with her yappy little friends who were all laughing and slapping her on the back. As Kit looked around for her father, hoping she wouldn't see Damien, a few strangers stopped to tell Kit they enjoyed the show.

Her rumbling stomach reminded her she hadn't eaten since early that morning, and she headed for a hot dog stand.

"Kittimany!" her father called from behind her.

He was still pushing Elinor in the stroller, a shrouded Sam Starr still at his side.

"I enjoyed your set," Sam said from behind her large dark glasses.

Kit flushed. "Really? I mean, I didn't think you guys were watching."

Elinor was reaching for her, so Kit bent down and lifted her into her arms, still trying to digest Sam's compliment.

"We walked back away from the speaker," her father said, "but we could hear everything. Elinor was even clapping along. It wasn't too bad."

Kit smirked at him. "Gee, thanks, Dad."

"Hey, you know this isn't my kind of music. I like things a little more complex."

Kit was not about to debate the merits of rock music with her father. She turned her attention to Elinor, tickling her with her nose and bouncing her on her hip.

"Your drummer is impressive," Sam said. "I can't remember ever having that much energy. Back in the Sex Pistols tour days we'd go days without a break, sometimes playing two and three shows a night. I don't know how we did it."

"Youth," her father said. "It's a very powerful stimulant. I used to read my poetry at Beat happenings in the Village, hanging out until three, four in the morning." He smiled at Kit. "That was long before I met your mother and started teaching."

Kit looked back at her father, surprised. He'd never mentioned this previous life. She knew he was born in Brooklyn, but she'd heard very little about his life before he met her mother.

Ginger Snap was working her way into another bright song about boys—at least Kit thought that's what the squealing vocals were about.

"You were a Beat?" Sam asked.

"I don't want to date myself, but I think the hair gives it away." He ran his fingers through his white hair. "Yes, in my former life, before I accepted my adult responsibilities. I even had a bit of a following in the Village. I read a few times at the Howl Festival. Corso and Ginsberg used to stay and have drinks with us afterward." He paused. "That was a long time ago."

Kit couldn't believe what she was hearing. Her father, the stodgy old professor, hung out with Allen Ginsberg?

Sam tilted her head to look up at him. "I'd like to hear some of your work."

Kit watched her father look at Sam, a woman at least ten years his junior, and was quietly disgusted by the obvious attraction between them. First Margo and Harry, now this?

Kit sighed as she watched The Venturas set up, only half listening to this stranger/father talk poetry to Sam Freaking Starr. It was all so surreal. After what seemed an eternity, Ginger Snap thanked the cheering audience, and soon The Venturas' drummer was clicking a four-count with her sticks, and the band exploded with their first song.

Kit held Elinor in her arms as she bounced to their music. The Venturas were still one of her favorite bands. Even though she kept her distance and tucked the earplugs carefully into Elinor's ears, she could tell the band kicked ass just as much as they had when Broad Street had played with them years before. Daria was an amazing bass player, and Kit strained to watch her through cracks in the enthusiastic crowd. Elinor smiled and clapped, swept up by her mother's enthusiasm.

The Venturas soon reached the end of their short set and were packing up their equipment. Kit walked over to congratulate them, but fans quickly surrounded them, so she instead found her father and Sam.

"I'm going to get something to eat," Kit said.

"Oh, okay," her father said. "Sam, are you hungry?"

"I have plenty of food back on the tour bus," Sam said. "Why don't you all come back? We can all get something to eat and I can relax a little before my show."

Kit looked at the charred hot dogs that hung from slowly spinning spokes. "That sounds good, thanks," she said.

She strapped Elinor back into the stroller and followed Sam and her father back toward the bus, pausing to squeeze fresh plugs into Elinor's ears as they neared the main stage where The Crocodiles were singing their first song.

As they neared the bus, Kit saw Margo climbing out of the Winnebago wearing a different outfit. She waved.

"I'll meet you back at the bus, Dad," she said. She pushed the stroller over to meet Margo. "Look at you with a new outfit on. That good, huh?"

"I just had a very weird experience," Margo said. She was gazing into the distance towards a large patch of trees.

"Where's Harry?" Kit asked.

"He left." Margo shook her head. "I don't know about him,

Kit. I'm a little freaked out. Turns out he's married, but his wife's in a nut house."

"What? How could you not have heard about that at the studio?" Kit asked.

"That's what I keep wondering," Margo said. "I don't know what to think. I was really attracted to him, but now . . ." She paused. "I don't know. I'm all fucked up." She looked down at Elinor, who was staring up at her with wide eyes. "Sorry, kid. I need a drink. Want to join me?"

"We were on our way to get something to eat in Sam's bus. Want to come along?"

"Sure," she said.

Inside the tour bus, Sam was sitting cross-legged on the floor and her father was on a plush red loveseat. Sam had an unwrapped turkey sandwich at her feet and was just lifting half of it toward her mouth.

"Hey," she said. "Help yourself to food." She gestured toward a refrigerator behind the driver's seat. "There's beer in there, too."

"Thanks," Kit said. "This is Margo, our lead singer."

Sam smiled at her. "Nice to meet you. You put on a hell of a show."

"Thanks," Margo said.

"You must be starving," Sam said. "Dig in!"

The refrigerator was filled with sandwiches, salads, beer, soda, and bottled water. Kit thought about grabbing a beer, remembered her father's presence, and grabbed a water instead, along with a turkey sandwich. Margo took a beer and ignored the food.

The three of them—Kit, Margo, and Elinor—sat on the floor with Sam. Elinor crawled over to Sam and started playing with the paper wrapping from her sandwich.

"Don't do that, honey," Kit said, reaching out to pry her fingers from the paper.

"It's okay," Sam said. She smiled at Elinor. "I can share."

She broke off a piece of her sandwich and handed it to Elinor, who began to examine it closely. They ate in silence for a few moments. Margo, taking deep swallows of her beer, seemed lost in thought. Kit was worried. Harry's story seemed so surreal, and she'd seen Margo fall for the wrong guy more than once.

Minutes later, Margo stood up and walked toward the refrigerator. "Mind if I have another one?" she asked Sam.

"Help yourself," Sam said. She sat up, brushed off her behind, and crumpled the remains of her sandwich, along with Elinor's crumbs, into the paper. She looked at her watch.

"I'm down to less than an hour before my show, so I'm going to retire to the back of the bus to do my usual routine." She looked at Pierce. "That means I'm going to get stoned. Anyone who wants to join me can."

Kit couldn't believe her ears. Her face flushed as she looked at her father to gauge his reaction. But instead of looking shocked, as she expected, he looked curious. "I'll come back with you," he said.

"Dad!" Kit said. "What about Elinor?"

"I think you can have a turn watching her for a while."

"Margo?" Sam said.

"Sure, what the hell," Margo said.

The three disappeared behind a paisley curtain, leaving Kit and Elinor alone. She looked down at her daughter, who still had sandwich crumbs stuck to the corners of her mouth.

"I guess we're taking a walk, sweetie."

* * *

Sam's offer was just what Margo needed, she thought, even though it was odd getting stoned with Kit's father.

The back room was dim and a U-shaped couch lined the red walls. A small table in the middle of the room was littered with various smoking paraphernalia. Sam reached into a carved wooden box under the table and pulled out a large bag of leafy pot. Margo watched as she expertly pulled a rolling paper from a small matchbox-sized dispenser, creased it, filled it with weed, and rolled it into a neat joint. Margo looked over at Pierce, who was watching with curiosity. Sam put the joint to her lips, pulled a star-emblazed lighter from the table, and lit it. Sparks danced as the thin paper caught on fire. Sam inhaled then quickly blew on the end to extinguish the flame. She took another drag then passed it to Pierce.

He took it gently with his fingers, and Margo noticed how old his hands looked, spotted and wrinkled.

"It's been a while," he said with an uncharacteristic smile.

He lifted the joint to his lips and inhaled, then began to cough violently. He held out the joint as he leaned over his lap, his back convulsing with each new bout. Sam released the joint from his hand, handed it quickly to Margo, and went over to clap him gently on the back.

"Don't worry, Pierce," she said, "It happens to the best of us. Your virgin lungs are just protesting."

Margo hesitated, unsure if she should take a drag or help Sam. For all she knew, Pierce could be having a heart attack. She waited, and after a few more bouts of coughing he straightened up, hand over his chest, and started to laugh. Really laugh. His face grew redder as he chuckled, his blue eyes tearing. Margo had never seen him laugh.

"That was embarrassing!" he said at last.

Sam still had her arm on his shoulder, waiting. "Not at all," she said when he'd caught his breath. "We have plenty of time to perfect it, trust me."

Margo watched the two of them—Sam, petite and weathered, was still significantly younger than Pierce, whose white hair and professorial demeanor contrasted with her long dark hair and tattoos. They were night and day, winter and spring, and yet there was definitely a connection between them.

"Not sure how much I'll be practicing," he said, "but I'm always up for a challenge."

They both looked at Margo, who realized she was now holding a quenched joint.

"Oh!" she said, pulling the lighter from the table. "Sorry."

She lit the end and inhaled, the thick, sweet smoke coating her throat. She exhaled and instantly felt the warm buzz in her ears. She passed the joint to Sam and leaned back on the couch. It had been a long time since she'd gotten stoned. It had been her drug of choice in college and soon after, but after the band her sources had dried up and she'd focused on alcohol and an occasional prescription painkiller instead. She missed the fast, no-calorie alternative of marijuana.

Sam took a drag and handed the joint to Kit's father, who managed to toke with minimal coughing this time. Then the joint was back in Margo's hands, and round and round it went until all that was left was a tiny remnant of burned paper. Margo could feel the glaze of her eyes and the sticky coating on her tongue and reached for her beer to finish the last of it.

The curtain parted and a thin, balding man walked in. He raised his eyebrows when he saw Margo and Pierce and turned to Sam. "Which mic did you want to use tonight?" he asked.

Sam nestled her small figure into the couch and stretched her thin arms above her head. "Let's use the EV," she said, "unless you think it will be too warm for outdoor sound."

"Nope," the man said. "That should be fine." He disappeared back through the curtain.

"My ex-husband," Sam said indifferently. "Poor guy can't find a job in this ageist market."

Margo looked at Pierce to see his reaction. His eyes were slightly red, but he looked more in control than Margo felt. "That's nice," he said after a pause. "You're a good person."

Sam laughed, and Margo could have sworn she saw her blush. She didn't think people over fifty blushed. "Many people would disagree with you, Pierce." She nodded toward the closed curtain. "Including him. But thanks." She looked at her watch. "Oh shit. I better get going."

"Thanks, Sam," Margo said as she stood up with her empty beer can. "Do you need help with anything?"

"Nope," she said. "That's the great thing about being around forever. People don't ask you to lift heavy things any more."

"Okay, well," Margo said, "it's been fun, thanks. I'm looking forward to hearing your set." Walking back into the night air, she was grateful for the darkness that hid her guilty eyes.

From the main stage she heard what sounded like The Crocodiles playing their big hit. She walked toward the music, breathing in the mixture of cooked food and cigarette smoke, but the image of the woods kept replaying in her head: the feel of the bark against her skin, the pine needles under her back.

She pulled her phone from her purse and called Peter. After several rings, she heard his outgoing message followed by the beep.

"Hey, babe," she said quietly, looking around her unnecessarily. "It's me. Listen, I wonder if you could check . . ." She paused. "Um, this is strange, but I think Harry may be married. I don't have

Warren's number, but he might know. If you can ask him discretely, I owe you one. Yes, I know I already owe you a million, but this is important. Thanks, sweetie."

She closed the phone, unsure what other steps to take. The music swirled around her and people milled in random patterns like ants looking for lost crumbs. As she got closer to the main stage she looked around for Kit but saw only her parents. Orlando and Vinnie were dancing in the audience, mingling and laughing and living as if they didn't have a care in the world.

* * *

Elinor was getting tired, but Kit wasn't about to take her back to Sam's bus where her father was getting stoned, a fact she still couldn't quite get her head around. She kept her daughter amused by oohing over Frisbee players and the dazzling lights of the many varied vendors that dotted the grounds, and finally she spotted Margo and her parents.

"Hi sweetie!" Vinnie called to Elinor. "Want to come to Auntie Vincenza?"

She held out her long thin arms and Elinor stared at her bright pink fingernails curiously. Kit handed her to Vinnie, and Elinor was surprisingly open to the transition. Vinnie began bouncing her and Elinor squealed.

"Okay," Orlando said. "Let's go check out the big Starr!"

They walked down to a grassy area closer to the main stage as they waited for Sam's roadies to set up the minimal backing band. The enormous Tweeter Center lights illuminated the grounds like daylight. Kit smiled as she watched Elinor, still clutched in Vinnie's arms, taking in the varied sounds and colors with wide eyes. It was nine-thirty, far past her daughter's usual bedtime, but the stimulating environment kept her entertained. Kit hoped this also meant she would sleep later tomorrow morning.

A voice calling out through the speakers drew their attention back to the stage. "Hey, everyone!" A young blond, the lead singer of The Crocodiles, was at the microphone. "I've been given the very special privilege of introducing one of the early pioneers of the New York City punk scene. Sam Starr has blended poetry with rock n' roll for over a quarter of a century, from her indie single 'Where's Larry?' in 1972 to her 2002 Grammy-nominated 'Dusted Eyes.' Please help me welcome one of our founding mothers, the incomparable Sam Starr!"

The crowd erupted into cheers and applause. Kit surveyed the scene—almost every seat was filled and the aisles and perimeter areas were packed with people. She saw her father strolling briskly from the side of the stadium. She called his name several times, waving her arms over her head, until he finally saw her.

"Glad you could make it," she said.

He shrugged and watched the stage, an odd grin on his face. Sam walked onto the stage, looking even more petite against the backdrop of piled Marshall amplifiers. From where Kit stood, she looked much the same as she had on her seventies album cover.

"Hello, Camden," Sam said in a low, smooth voice. The crowd cheered, and she waited until the noise died down. "Thanks for coming out tonight. It's an honor to be headlining with such a talented group of women."

The crowd cheered again, and Sam signaled the drummer, who began a low beat on the bass drum.

"We're going to kick off the set with a song off my first album," she continued. "It's called 'Number Games.'"

The applause and cheers swelled again and Kit watched as Elinor clapped along with everyone else. She wasn't sure if Elinor could see her new friend on stage or if she was just swept up in the excitement, but she was proud of her little girl. She touched her cheek and reached out for her. Vinnie handed her back, and they swayed as the music started. Orlando and Vinnie began dancing like ridiculous teenagers, holding hands as they swirled their heads around. Even Kit's father tapped his foot along with the music. Only Margo seemed out of sync with the moment. She was staring at the stage, her eyes glazed and distant.

CHAPTER 51

All Margo wanted to do was to go home to her condo, open a bottle of wine, and relax in her garden. Why did she put her stuff in the Winnebago? She should have thought through her plan to go back to her condo after the show, but her head had been so foggy this morning, she hadn't been thinking clearly. Now she had to figure out the logistics of getting her bags and finding a cab late at night with a bunch of drunks at the crowded Tweeter Center, only to wake early and rush back to New York. The whole idea of these logistics exhausted her. Maybe she should just suck it up and crash in the Winnebago. She could treat herself to a hotel tomorrow night.

She also knew the real source of her melancholy was Harry's confession, and Sam's dreary lyrics did nothing to improve her mood.

When Sam and her band finally left the stage to loud applause after their final encore, Margo was ready for a drink.

"I'm going to head back to the dressing room," she announced to Kit.

"That sounds good. I'll come with you. Let me just talk to my father a minute."

Talk to her father, check on the baby—this theme grated on Margo's nerves. "No problem," she said with a forced grin.

She waited, only half listening, as Kit negotiated with Pierce. Elinor was tired, and Pierce agreed to take her back to the camper to put her down for the night. Kit suggested he could relax and read one of the new novels he'd brought along. Margo watched the family—Elinor's affection for her mother and grandfather and Pierce's love for his granddaughter—with envy. She couldn't deny the desire she had for this kind of family relationship, which only amplified her disappointment in Harry. Would she ever find a decent guy? And if she did, would her fibroid disease prevent her from even considering this June Cleaver role? The whole idea was ridiculous. Her thirst grew more powerful.

"Ready?" Kit said when the two had walked away, Elinor tucked back into the stroller.

"Don't forget us!" Vinnie said. "I'm ready to party!"

"Super," Margo said.

Back in the dressing room she tried not to think about the confession Harry had made, or about the striking contrast between the stark beige walls and beaten up furniture and her comfortable dressing room in her TV studio. She was a touring musician now, she thought. She would have to accept these compromises.

She went directly to the tub of ice, which had been restocked with cold beer, and retrieved one. She opened it and started drinking.

"Hey, Dad," she said, "did you get us anything stronger than beer?"

"Do you think I'd forget my baby's favorite vice?" He pulled a large bottle of Tequila from a paper bag.

"You deserve whatever we're paying you," she said, walking over and taking the bottle from him.

Margo filled four paper cups with Tequila. She could hear the sizzle of the strong alcohol eating away at the cup's wax lining as she lifted the drink to her lips and swallowed quickly, the familiar burn swimming down to her stomach.

More shots followed that one, and Margo was soon on her way to forgetting all about Harry as she enjoyed the shallow arguments over the day's musical performances while chain smoking and sipping cool beer. Her parents sat on the couch together, and then her mother moved to her father's lap, giggling. As a child Margo used to cringe at this embarrassing display of affection, but now that she was drunk it didn't bother her so much.

Daria knocked and popped her head in the door. "Hey, guys!"

she said. "Mind if we join you? Our room is getting a bit crowded with annoying people."

"Sure!" Orlando said, popping his head from behind Vinnie's bleached blond hair.

"Thanks!" Daria came in with a few people she introduced as local friends—two women and an attractive young guy named Nate. Margo sat up a little straighter and said hello.

They all grabbed beers and sat down. Margo managed to guide the new guests so that Nate was sitting next to her. While the group launched into simultaneous conversations, Margo turned to the kid. He wasn't perfect—he had a slight blemish on his cheek and he chewed his nails, but he was certainly a promising diversion.

"So, what do you do, Nate?" she asked.

He shrugged and looked into his beer. "Not much. Paint houses, mow lawns, that kinda shit."

"Hey, at least you're working," Margo said. He was shy, too. She liked that.

He looked up at her. "You have that TV show, right?"

"Yes! Have you seen it?"

There was another knock on the door, and Margo looked up to see The Venturas' drummer, Mandy, along with their manager, Steve, and the other one, their tour manager.

"There you are!" Steve said. "Mind if we come in? Paula's on one of her rampages and it's getting ugly over there."

"Of course!" Orlando said, and the three walked in, already holding beer cans, and sat on the floor.

Margo returned her attention to Nate. "Anyway, you were saying?" she said.

"Oh, I just asked about the show. Yeah, I watch it a lot." He took another swallow of his beer. "You look even better in person."

"You're sweet," she said, placing the palm of her hand briefly on his knee. "Thank you."

"Do you guys want some Tequila?" Orlando asked the managers.

"I would love some," Steve said. "I actually have a little gift myself, if anyone's interested."

He pulled a bag of weed from his breast pocket and leaned into the circle. "If I opened this in the other room Paula would smoke the lot of it herself."

"Bring it on, my friend," Orlando said. "It's not my cup of tea, but make yourself at home."

Margo watched as Steve pulled out a bowl and tapped the pot into it. He tapped the leaves down, lit it, took a long toke and then handed the pipe to Kit. She shook her head and passed it to the tour manager, who was sitting by her feet. He took a toke and handed it to Daria. Margo was next, and she inhaled deeply for the second time that day. The smoke amplified her Tequila buzz. She closed her watering eyes for a moment before handing the bowl to Nate.

"Thanks," he said, touching her hand as he took the pipe.

The conversation continued to spin around Margo as the substance euphoria lifted her spirits, inspiring her to focus on one thing. She knew Nate was willing to participate. She'd seen his type too many times not to recognize the growing lust in his pants, the sexual energy that heightened as they got wasted together. She glanced at Kit, who seemed on a quest of her own with the tour manager at her feet. What's his name? she wondered. She'd heard someone say it just a few minutes ago, but it was gone. Oh, well, she thought, it's not important.

✳ ✳ ✳

Kit was having a good time. She knew Elinor was safe, asleep in the Winnebago under her father's watchful eye. She had just played in a concert with some of the biggest influences on her music, and she was enjoying her conversation with Graham. As the Tequila settled into her, he became increasingly attractive. Each time his blue eyes looked up at her and he smiled with those crooked teeth she felt herself tingle. He was definitely flirting with her—but he also seemed to be flirting with Daria, so she wasn't sure if this was his style or if he just liked bass players. Kit returned his flirtation when he was talking to her, and when he was talking to Daria she talked to Steve, leaning in to let her long hair brush against Graham's neck. As the evening wore on, she went from lightheaded to confident to outright loud. She wasn't the only one—the room buzzed with conversations that drowned out the music blasting from the speakers in the corner. As she emptied yet another can of beer, she realized she needed to empty her bladder.

She leaned down toward Graham. "I'm going to find the bathroom. Can you save my seat?"

He smiled. "Gladly."

As she stepped over him, she stumbled and caught herself on a chair. She giggled. "Whoops!"

Out in the crowded hallway, she lost her bearings. She remembered the restrooms were nearby, but she couldn't remember which way she should turn. She stood stupidly, looking both ways, as strangers jostled past her.

"You look lost," a voice whispered from behind her.

She turned to see Graham's sweet face. "A little, yeah."

"Follow me." He took her hand in his own, warm and strong, and led her through the crowd until they reached the restroom doors.

"Thanks," she said, giving his hand a squeeze. "I can probably find my way back."

"I'll wait here for you just in case," he said with that adorable smile.

Two women were making out in the corner by the sink. "Sorry," she said. She darted into an empty stall and locked the door.

When she was done she walked straight to the sink, careful not to interrupt the romantic moment next to her. This wasn't easy, as they were moaning and groping, and curiosity drew her eyes sideways to sneak a peek. She didn't recognize the women, but the one pinned against the wall opened her eyes and caught Kit's stare. She stopped kissing the other woman for a moment and tilted her head so she could see Kit better.

"I know you. You're in that band," she said.

Kit hesitated. "Yeah," she said, "Broad Street."

The other woman, a tall, Goth chick with jet-black hair and alabaster skin, turned around. "Cool set," she said.

Kit opened her mouth and was about to thank her when she noticed the familiar band logo on her black T-shirt: Rockzilla. Damien's old band.

Stunned, Kit backed out of the bathroom, the buzz of alcohol making everything seem surreal and dangerous. The girl in the T-shirt laughed, her blood-red lipstick a sharp contrast to big, pointy teeth. As the door swung closed and the scene before her began to disappear, she felt arms around her. Graham grabbed the door, pausing to look into the room where the girls had resumed kissing. Then he let go of the door and pulled Kit into a long kiss.

She didn't react at first, surprised and uncertain that his lips and tongue were actually a part of her, but then she remembered he was there and she had wanted him to do this all day. She let him push her out of the crowded hallway, away from the ladies room, and through another door where the scent of urine and mothballs choked the air. She stopped kissing him long enough to realize they were now in the men's room. The room was empty, and she didn't care—it had been so long since she'd been this free, without restrictions and responsibilities and obligations, and she let Graham push her against the cold tile wall and put his warm hands up her skirt and into her panties. She was so lost in the moment that she didn't hear the door open, didn't hear her name at first. By the time she realized someone was looking at her and she'd pulled away from Graham, she saw only the back of Charlie's head as the door swung shut behind him. And she remembered all the bad decisions she'd made and all the good things Charlie had done for her and the moment was gone. She was back to her old self, the one who did nothing but disappoint the people around her.

"What's wrong?" Graham said, his voice a breathy whisper in her ear as he continued to push himself against her.

She pulled away, pushing her skirt back down. "Sorry," she said. "That was a friend of mine. I have to go."

She didn't look up to see the expression on Graham's face. She kept her head down as she walked out, drunken tears already threatening to spill over as she realized it wasn't freedom she craved, but self-destruction—something she thought she'd given up the day Elinor was born. Fresh grief overwhelmed her as, in this moment of terrible clarity, she understood that this toxic desire still lingered in her gut, waiting for the soft caress of alcohol and loneliness to bring it back to life. She wanted to be home, and sober, and in her own bed with Elinor safely next door.

She saw Charlie in the distance and called to him, but he couldn't hear her—or didn't want to. He moved down the hallway, wading through the tide of strangers until he disappeared into the crowd. She wanted to follow him, but she didn't have the strength.

She wanted to go see her baby daughter, but she was too wasted. So she wandered back to the dressing room and returned to her empty seat.

Only Daria acknowledged her return. "What happened to you?" she asked.

Kit realized she hadn't fixed her makeup or hair after the restroom tryst and quickly smoothed her hair. "Oh, it was really crowded in the restroom," she lied.

Daria nodded skeptically, and Kit ran her fingers under her eyes to swipe away stray mascara and pushed her lips together to even out any remaining lipstick. She looked over at Margo, who was getting chummier with the good-looking kid. She fell back against the couch, exhausted, willing the buzz to cool so she could go and get some sleep.

When Graham returned a few minutes later, fresh shame flushed her cheeks. He avoided Kit's eyes but returned to his seat on the floor between her and Daria. Kit watched as Daria grabbed Graham's shoulder, squeezing tightly with her black-painted nails.

"Where've you been?" she whispered through clenched teeth. She gave his shoulder a shake and turned her glare back toward Kit.

Kit felt the force of what she'd done like a punch in the gut. Maybe she hurt other people even more than she hurt herself with her self-destructive behavior. In her stupidity, she'd managed to crush Charlie as well as ruin her friendship with Daria.

But she wasn't finished. "I had no idea," she said. By the time she realized what she had said, it was too late.

"Fuck you both," Daria said. She pushed her chair back and stormed out of the room.

Silence fell over the room as everyone watched Graham stand up and follow Daria out the door.

Margo broke the silence with a loud laugh. "Damn, girl, what did you do?" she asked.

Everyone else joined in her laughter, and the noise pulsed in Kit's buzzing ears. She felt drenched with fatigue.

"I'm going to bed," she mumbled.

She wove her way through the crowded hallway once more and fstepped into the nighttime air, cool and sweet with the scent of summer. Although there were still band members and roadies lingering outside as well, their voices and music didn't bounce off the stadium walls as they did inside—instead the sounds melted into the night and Kit breathed deeply as she made her way back to the Winnebago.

Inside the cabin, she could only make out silhouettes in the dark. Her father's low snoring drifted from the lump on a single bed right next to the portable crib. Kit slipped into the tiny bathroom to wash off the evening. She brushed her teeth vigorously in a vain attempt to remove the taste of Graham's kiss and tried to wash away the girls in the bathroom and the incessant reminder of Damien and the pain she continued to cause Charlie as she rinsed her face. She tied her hair back to keep the thick smell of smoke away from her nose.

She tiptoed back to the crib. Elinor was curled in a ball, her arm wrapped around the worn blue teddy bear she'd had since she was born. The sight of her sweet innocence emptied Kit of everything negative and filled her with an overwhelming love that made her catch her breath. She kicked off her sandals and lifted her daughter into her arms. Elinor stirred, and she kissed her on the forehead and carried her over to a small bunk bed in the back of the cabin. She lay down on the bed, cocooning her daughter in the crook of her arm, and let the powdery scent of childhood lull her to sleep.

CHAPTER 52

Margo was naked, and her pounding skull a loud reminder of her situation. Although she was awake, it was several moments before she could gather the courage to open her eyes. She felt the crumbs on the dirty sheets underneath her and the scent of cigarettes wafting from the naked boy who lay beside her. *Shit*, she thought. What had she done? Harry's face drifted to her mind and she was overwhelmed by shame.

She wanted to leave without being seen and run to the closest shower, but the boy was already stirring, rolling over toward her, putting his heavy, sweaty arm over her breasts. She peeled her eyes open and winced at the bright sunlight that burned through the tattered shade in the window.

"Hey," Nate said. His rancid breath turned her stomach.

She wrapped herself in the sheet and pushed herself to sitting, knocking his arm off her. "What time is it?" she asked.

He rolled onto his back. "Jesus, my head hurts," he said.

"Do you have a clock?"

He looked at her and raised an eyebrow. He was young—at least ten years younger than she was. *God*, she thought, *I hope he isn't a teenager.*

"Yeah, hold on," he said as he rolled over. "It's only eight o'clock. Let's go back to sleep." He flopped onto his back and flung his forearm over his eyes. "I need to sleep."

"Then sleep. I have to go." She looked over the side of the bed but saw no sign of her clothes. She scanned the small room but saw only the dirty laundry of a young man.

"Where are my clothes?" she asked curtly.

He removed his arm from his eyes and smiled slyly. "Don't you remember?"

She pulled the sheet tighter around herself. "Remember what?" she snapped.

He ran his finger up her bare arm, sending chills down her spine. "You put on a little show for us in our living room. The garden princess went back to nature last night—it was great."

Margo searched for memories to support this horrifying statement but found only large chunks of missing time. She remembered partying in the dressing room, then getting into a van with some people and going to someone's house, where she did more shots of Tequila. That was when things began to get fuzzy.

"I have to go," she said. "Would you please be a gentleman and get my clothes?"

He sighed. "Yes, my princess."

He strutted naked across the room. He had the thin, muscleless body of youth—when you could drink cases of beer and eat dozens of cheesesteaks and suffer no consequences except a little gas. He returned moments later holding her clothes in front of his genitals. He tossed them to her and jumped back into bed.

"Who said chivalry was dead?" she asked, slipping her clothes on under the covers. He grunted and flung his arm back over his head.

Once she was dressed, she turned one last time to face the appalling lump on the bed next to her. "Thanks," she said. "Remember to watch me on my new Sunday time slot."

Nate peeked out from under his arm. "Only after football season," he said.

✳ ✳ ✳

Once outside, she realized she was back in Philadelphia. The neighborhood was unfamiliar, but she could see the tip of the skyline above the row homes. She walked to the corner and looked up at the street signs. Walnut and 40th. She was in West Philly, and finding a cab would probably not be easy. She looked in her purse and saw that she had less than ten dollars in her wallet—not enough for the cab ride back to Camden. Her phone was dead. What a way to start the tour.

She walked a few blocks to a supermarket with an ATM. She tried two hundred dollars, but the machine spit out a receipt telling her she had insufficient funds. Confused, she tried sixty but got the same result. How could that be? She knew she had plenty of money in her checking account. She ejected the card, checked that it was the right one, and reinserted it into the machine. The same thing happened. She put the card back in her wallet and massaged her aching temples.

She could take a cab anyway, she decided, and borrow the fare from her parents when she got back to the stadium. Out on the street, a few sideways glances from passersby made her realize how clearly her wrinkled stage clothing announced that she had not slept in her own bed. Finally, a yellow cab crested the horizon and pulled over. She gave the driver the address and nestled into the cracked leather seat. She would call her accountant as soon as her phone was charged. He could figure out what was going on. When she closed her eyes, all she could see was Harry's face. Despite all he had confessed, she felt as if she had betrayed him.

CHAPTER 53

Kit and Elinor woke when a slice of sunshine slipped under the shades of the Winnebago. Her father was snoring heavily and Orlando and Vinnie lay pressed together on a small cot across from him. There was no sign of Margo or Ronni, for which Kit was grateful.

She carried Elinor into the tiny bathroom, where she managed to squeeze them both into the shower. As a slippery Elinor squirmed, Kit untied her hair and leaned her head back in an attempt to rinse the last of the stale smoke from her follicles. She felt groggy, but not as hungover as she'd expected. She'd woken with a new positive spirit. She would make a few apologies, and if Daria wanted to stay angry with her, that was fine. Graham was the one who had approached her, after all. Charlie was a more delicate matter.

Wrapped in towels back in the cabin, Kit found them both clothes to wear for the day. They'd be heading to Randall's Island in New York this morning, a venue that had hosted Lollapalooza and Ozzfest and many other large musical extravaganzas. In her groupie days she'd spent many weekends there, drinking herself into enough confidence to approach the bands. She made it backstage about half the time, which was more than enough opportunity for embarrassing behavior.

Noticing that her father's bed was now empty, she peeked out the window. He was standing in the parking lot in his pajamas and an old robe, hands stuffed into his pockets, staring at Sam's tour bus.

As she dressed herself and Elinor so they could join him outside, she glanced at the clock. It was almost ten o'clock—yet there was no sign of Ronni or Margo.

"Morning," she said as she stepped out of the Winnebago.

"Papa!" Elinor cried.

Her father reached out for her. "Good morning, beautiful girl," he said, giving her a kiss. She giggled as he tickled her with his gray stubble. He looked at Kit. "What time did you stumble in last night?"

"It was late, Dad."

"Hmm."

They stood in silence, staring at the abandoned grounds. Empty beer cans and bottles were strewn across the beaten grass. It was hard to imagine that, just hours earlier, the place had been buzzing with activity. It was as empty and silent as a graveyard—only a few tour buses remained in the midst of the garbage.

"Want to go wake up Aunt Sam?" her father asked Elinor.

"Aunt Sam?" Kit said. "Aren't we chummy now?"

"Come on, honey," her father said to Elinor as he made his way over to Sam's bus.

Kit was mortified. He looked old and unkempt—and who was he to honor strangers with familiar titles with her daughter? She jogged to catch up with him.

"Elinor needs breakfast," she snapped, reaching out to snatch her daughter away.

"I have some baby food with me," he said. "Sam invited us over last night."

Fuming, Kit followed her father and daughter.

He knocked on the smoked windows of the folded door, and moments later it opened. Sam, wrapped in an old kimono, her long dark hair tied into a knot, smiled. "Just in time for eggs," she said.

Kit forced a begrudging grin, annoyed that Sam had made Elinor's favorite breakfast.

* * *

When Margo opened her eyes, the gray-blue beams of the Ben Franklin Bridge were sailing above her head. She sat up and turned to see the skyline disappear behind her for the second time in as many days. Knowing she wouldn't see that familiar scene for weeks, she missed it already.

The parking lot at the Tweeter Center was empty, and it wasn't until they got closer that she saw the gate was closed. The cab driver stopped.

"I can't go no farther," he said.

"You can if you want to get paid," she said. She got out and walked to the security gate. She was relieved to find that the same man was guarding the lot and remembered her.

In the tour bus parking area she instructed the driver to wait. The Winnebago cabin was dark and empty except for the blanketed lump of her parents. She shook her dad by the shoulder. He rolled over with a moan, his face creased by the pillow.

"You okay, honey?" he said hoarsely.

"I'm fine, Daddy. Where's your wallet?"

He squinted and looked around the messy room. "I have no idea. Vincenza, sweetie, do you remember where I put my wallet?"

The cab driver began honking. Margo did her best to ignore it.

"I think it's in your pants pocket," Vinnie said sleepily. "Why? What's wrong?"

"Nothing, Mom, I just need to pay a cab driver and I'm tapped out."

"Oh." She pushed herself up on one elbow, her blond hair pressed flat on one side, and looked around the room.

The cab driver laid on the horn again, the shrill sound cutting through the sleepy air. Margo peered out and saw noses pressed against the windows of some of the tour buses.

Orlando, dressed only in Mickey Mouse boxers, rolled out of bed. His large hairy stomach sagged generously over the waistband.

"I know it's around here somewhere," he mumbled as he began to sort through the piles of clothes and toys.

"Where's Kit?" Margo asked. The drone of the horn was constant now.

Orlando stood up and crossed his arms over his belly. "I have no idea."

Margo glanced out the window again toward Sam Starr's bus. "Don't worry about it. I'll be right back."

She walked over to the door of Sam's bus, holding her finger up toward the cab driver—which made him stop honking his horn. She rapped loudly and blushed when Sam opened the door.

"I am so sorry to bother you, but I was wondering if Kit might be here."

"We're in here!" Kit called.

"Come on in," Sam said with a welcoming gesture. "You look like you could use a little help."

As she stepped up into the cabin, Margo remembered that she was still wearing yesterday's clothes and makeup and she blushed again, embarrassed for Sam and Pierce to see her this way. It took a moment for her eyes to adjust to the dim interior.

"Hey," she said. "I am so sorry to bother you, but does anyone have fifty bucks I could borrow? It's a long story, but you've probably heard my new friend out there—he's a little impatient."

"I've got it," Sam said. She pulled three twenties out of her wallet. "Tell him to keep it."

Margo hoped it was too dark for Sam to see how red her face was. "Thanks, Sam. I'll pay you back as soon as I get to a cash machine, I promise."

Sam shrugged. "Don't worry about it. I know where you live."

Margo smiled and strode back to the cab as the driver started blaring the horn again. A few people shouted obscenities out of their bus windows. She shoved the money through his window. "Don't you know who I am?" she said. "Of course I'm going to pay you, jerk."

The man looked her up and down and laughed, threw the cab into reverse, and spun out of the lot back towards Philadelphia, leaving Margo in a cloud of dust.

She didn't have the energy to yell at him or wave her fist in the air and will him off the bridge on his return trip. She was exhausted, stinky, and humiliated. She wanted only to shower and wash off the last 12 hours and make a fresh start in New York.

CHAPTER 54

Kit sat on an empty cooler and surveyed the cramped quarters. Everyone was back in the Winnebago and Orlando barked orders and checked off items on his imaginary clipboard. Ronni, listening to messages on her phone, ignored him. Margo was curled on the couch with a blanket pulled up over her ears, her phone plugged in at her feet. Kit's father read, and Elinor banged a stray drumstick happily against Margo's leopard suitcase. The Winnebago that had looked enormous when Kit first saw it, with its stacked bunks, kitchen, bathroom, and cabinets, now seemed no bigger than a walk-in closet.

"Okay!" Orlando said, looking around one more time. "We'll take the turnpike up to the GW Bridge, then we'll follow the Cross Bronx to the Major Deegan to the Triboro Bridge, and go from there."

"Nobody cares, Dad," Margo said, her voice muffled under the blanket. "Just drive. It's getting late."

Orlando looked at his watch. "Holy crap, you're right." He clapped his hands. "Let's roll, people!"

Back in the driver's seat, he started the rumbling engine. Kit looked out at the nearly empty lot—most of the other buses had left already—and wondered where Charlie was. She had paid a quick visit to the Bitchsword bus after breakfast, but the girls told her he hadn't

come back last night. She hadn't been able to switch off the flood
of memories that seeing Charlie had stirred up for her, and most of
those memories filled her with shame. When Charlie's roommate Ben
cheated on Kit, and left her at parties, and slept with her only when
it fit into his schedule, Charlie was there to be a good friend. When
they dated, Charlie had been kind and thoughtful. But Kit was cursed
with the affliction she shared with many of her female friends: the
constant attraction to the wrong guy, the dangerous guy, the elusive
goal.

Kit spent the three-hour drive entertaining Elinor in her car
seat with toys and books while the rest of the cabin read or slept.
Orlando and Vinnie sang along with—and without—the radio all the
way to New York. When she saw the skyline appear on the horizon,
she pointed it out to Elinor.

"That's New York City, honey," she said. She did not say,
"That's the place where you were conceived in a drunken stupor."

Orlando sang as he negotiated his way through the busy
streets of New York, back onto the expressway and across the Triboro
Bridge. He was still singing as he followed signs to Randall's Island.

Kit looked out the side window as Randall's Island came
into view. It was an open, sprawling slab of dusty field that had been
well used for other concerts. There was a main stage and a smaller
second stage, as at the Tweeter Center, though on Randall's Island the
vendors were scattered over the large property.

After parking the Winnebago, Orlando left to investigate
equipment load-ins and Kit unfolded her cramped legs and carried
Elinor outside to stretch. A few minutes later Margo stumbled out,
tired and hungover.

"Here we go again," she said as she stretched and surveyed the
grounds.

They stood in silence for a moment, and Kit realized this was
the first time they'd been alone together in days. "Did you have fun
yesterday?" she asked.

Margo looked at her with a weary expression. "Do I look like
I had fun?"

"Actually, yes."

Margo laughed. "If I keep having fun like that, I'm going to
end up getting arrested. Did you see how young that guy was?"

"Sixteen will get you twenty," Kit joked.

"You were looking pretty chummy with that tour manager guy. What's his name?"

"Graham."

"Man, did Daria look pissed about that."

"I had no idea they were seeing each other. Who knows if they even are? The worst part was that Charlie caught me kissing him in the men's room."

Elinor was wriggling and heavy in Kit's arms, but she didn't want to put her down on the blacktop littered with cigarette butts and shards of broken glass. "Let's go look at the tree over there," she said, pointing to a small patch of grass under a large oak tree.

Kit and Margo sat with their backs against the tree while Elinor crawled through the grass, plucking blades and examining them. A light breeze caught Kit's hair and wrapped it in wisps against her face.

"Oh, crap," Margo said, pulling her phone from her pocket. "I totally forgot to call my accountant. There's more shit going on with my bank account—that's why I couldn't pay for the cab this morning." She looked at the display. "Oops! Three new messages. I don't even know when it died—yesterday sometime."

Kit watched as Margo listened to her messages, furrowing her brow. When she'd listened to them all she exhaled slowly. "Okay. Wow."

"What's up?" Kit asked.

"My makeup guy asked around for me and he says he doesn't think Harry's really married."

"Why would he make that up? If anything, you'd think he'd say he wasn't married when he was."

"Who knows? Honestly, Kit, all I wanted was a normal relationship with a grownup. I can't be sixty years old and still screwing teenagers."

"Why not?" Kit said with a smile.

Margo sighed. "You don't understand. You have a family. And I—" She raised her eyebrows towards the Winnebago. Her parents were chasing each other around the camper, laughing. "I have that."

Kit glanced over and grinned. "I think they're great."

"Sometimes I just wish I had something a little more normal."

"I think you'd get bored with normal."

"Maybe. But why would Harry lie about being married?"

"The whole thing does sound a little extreme," Kit said. "Like it's taken right out of a scene from *Jane Eyre*. Wife goes crazy, gets locked up, heroic husband stays married to her."

"It does seem like something from a bad Lifetime movie." She punched a number into her phone but hung up after a pause. "Shit, I keep getting his answering machine. I need a computer."

"I think I saw one in Sam's bus," Kit said. "I'm sure she'd let you use it."

Kit thought she'd spotted Sam's bus heading down the long driveway toward the band parking lot, but as it came closer she realized it was The Venturas bus, which was also black, though smaller.

"We should head back," she said. "The Venturas are here, and I may as well get used to the dirty looks now."

"Oh, fuck them," Margo said. "They're stuck with us now. Daria will just have to deal with it."

As they walked back toward the Winnebago Kit watched The Venturas stepping down out of their bus—first Paula and Mandy, then Graham and Steve. There was no sign of Daria.

Kit averted her eyes from Graham and walked quickly to the Winnebago. She heard the rumble of another vehicle as Sam's bus pulled up alongside them.

Kit was happy for the excuse to put off that first awkward encounter with The Venturas. "There's Sam now," she said. "Let's see if she'll let us use her computer."

*　*　*

Margo's stomach was in knots. Peter had left two messages— the first letting her know that he'd received her message about Harry, the second one confirming that he hadn't been able to find any evidence of his marriage. The last message was from her accountant, who still hadn't gotten to the bottom of what was happening. He thought that maybe someone had accessed her credit card information from a Web purchase, though that didn't explain why all of her cards were maxed out—which usually only happened when a wallet had been stolen. Although this sounded bad, Margo still had all her cards in her purse and it sounded like a problem that could be fixed. She decided to call the accountant back later. The many questions about Harry were the real source of her anxiety.

She followed Kit to Sam's bus, and within minutes she was logged onto the Internet. Sam left to stretch her legs, taking Elinor with her. Kit sat next to Margo as she typed her search into Google. She started with Harry's name and scrolled through the results until she found what she was looking for: a list of all the shows with which Harry had been associated. These shows, dating all the way back to a Nickelodeon game show Margo had watched as a kid, reminded her again of their age difference. Harry's headshots aged gracefully as she dissected his resume.

"Oh my god," Kit said over her shoulder. "This guy's been around forever."

Margo recognized the names of some of the more successful shows interspersed with many failed pilots. "Okay," she said, "we're looking for a clue, for a plot that sounds like Harry's lie."

"What about that one?" Kit asked. She pointed to a title on the screen: *The Ugly Truth*. When she clicked on it, a description of the made-for-TV movie and cast list popped up.

In The Ugly Truth' *teenager Juliet Winter explores her family's dark secret. Juliet knows something is wrong with her mother, but her father won't talk about it. Her mother, once an active socialite, becomes increasingly withdrawn until she's no longer able to leave her bedroom. David Winter continues to deny his wife's problem, clinging to the hope that she will soon get better. But Juliet knows her mother needs help. With the aid of a sympathetic school counselor, she gets her mother the profes-sional attention she needs and uncovers a dark secret—the years of abuse her mother suffered as a child at the hands of her own father. The Ugly* Truth *is a classic tale of denial and acceptance, told with the empathetic authority of a concerned daughter.*

Margo stared at the screen. "Gee, this sounds kind of familiar," she said.

"What are you going to do?" Kit asked.

The ugly truth was, Margo had no idea. Would Harry really have made up some melodramatic story to tell her? And if so, why?

"I'm going to call my accountant," she said finally. "And then

I'm going to play a rock show. After that, I'll probably get drunk again."

Kit put her hand on Margo's shoulder. "I'm sorry."

The light weight of Kit's touch comforted Margo. Harry Thomas could kiss her sweet ass.

"Let's go make some music," she said.

CHAPTER 55

The arrangements in New York were similar to those in Camden. Broad Street's sound check had gone well, since they had replicated the setup from Camden, and Margo stood with Kit and her parents watching the other bands run through their sound checks. It was only about four o'clock, but the audience had begun to trickle in, establishing small properties with blankets over the sun-scorched lawn. Paula and Mandy were definitely giving Broad Street the cold shoulder, but they still hadn't seen Daria.

The air was cooler today, perfect for an outdoor show, and the blue sky stretched above them. Orlando and Vinnie had already set up their improv Broad Street store-in-a-box, and Margo was passing time by commenting on the bad fashion of some of the local hippies.

When Daria finally appeared, she walked directly over to Orlando. "Is it all right if I use your bass amp again today?" she asked. "I still haven't gotten mine fixed."

Orlando smiled. "Of course! It's all set up and ready to go."

"Thanks," she said. She walked away without another word.

"Cold," Margo said to Kit.

Kit nodded.

Margo fished her ringing phone out of her purse. "I have to take this," she said. "It's my accountant. I'll be right back."

"I'm going to go check in with my dad," Kit said. "I'll see you later."

Margo walked behind the stage where it was quieter. "Hey, George, what did you find out?"

"It's not good."

"What do you mean?"

George's deep voice was soft, concerned. "Someone has purchased thousands of dollars worth of merchandise with your credit cards and your debit card, and the bank has placed a hold on your account due to suspicious activity."

"So what are you going to do? I need money."

He paused. "I've contacted the fraud departments of the three major credit bureaus, filed a police report and a complaint with the FTC, and I've closed those accounts that I can, but you'll need to make some calls yourself."

Margo groaned. "How am I supposed to deal with this when I'm on the road?"

"Don't worry," George said. "I'll make it easy for you. Can you check e-mail?"

"Yeah."

"I'll e-mail you all the information you need. The person I talked with at the FTC said these things can take some time to resolve, so you'll need to be patient."

"And what do I do for money in the meantime?"

"You do have some stocks you could sell."

"In this market? I'll take a huge loss." Margo's palms were sweating.

"You have one account that's pretty liquid. I can get you about a thousand, but you'll probably need to think about selling some stocks. How much do you think you'll need in the next few weeks?"

Margo's head was spinning. Her final paycheck for the season had been deposited last week, totaling over ten thousand dollars. She wouldn't be collecting another one until they started filming again. How could so much money just disappear?

As she paced behind the stage her parents came back into view. She sighed. There would be no four-star hotels, no plush robes at night, no hot baths—only a crowded Winnebago with her parents, three generations of Kit's family, and a perky drummer. In the space of a phone call Margo had been launched back to her world before there was money, and all of the anxiety that went with poverty came back to her in a rush.

"Just make sure I have enough to cover my bills until I get back," she said. "I'll make whatever calls I need to."

"No problem," George said. "I'll keep you posted."

Margo hung up and walked in a daze back to her parents.

"What's wrong, honey?" Vinnie asked.

"I'm fucked."

She explained the situation as both her parents listened carefully.

"How could this happen?" Orlando asked. "You say you still have all your cards?"

Margo shrugged. "Yes, but who knows? I guess people who know how can hack into accounts on the Internet and get all the information they need."

Orlando rubbed his chin. "I'll call Carl, our money guy down in Boca. I'm sure he'll know what to do."

"Thanks, Dad," Margo said. "My accountant's handling every-thing that can be handled. I'll need to make a few calls, but I'm sure it will get cleared up. I just need to sell some stocks so I can get through this, which sucks."

"You'll do no such thing," Vinnie said. "We'll cover you." She put her arms around her daughter and squeezed. "You can support us in our old age. Okay?"

Margo smiled. Her parents never had a lot of money. Their apartment in Downingtown had been small and rundown and they never took vacations. They never discussed it, and they'd never seem ashamed of their lack of things. Margo had always found this, as well as everything else about her parents, baffling. But she realized as she stood between them now, their arms around her, that she'd begun to feel different around them. Crazy as they were, she was actually starting to enjoy their company.

"Thanks, Mom," Margo said, squeezing her mother's thin shoulders. "I'll definitely pay you back as soon as things get back to normal."

Vinnie waved her offer away. "You just keep playing good music. Let your father and I take care of the rest."

* * *

Kit arrived back at the Winnebago to find it empty. She tried not to panic, but she felt a cold sweat break out. Relax, she told herself, you're in a public place. Nothing can happen. They're probably in Sam's bus, just go find them there. She closed the door behind her and headed toward the bus with the purple star.

She felt a tap on her shoulder and spun around.

It was Damien. He had the same long dark hair, pale white skin, and pockmarked face, and he wore the same tattered rock clothes. She stood stunned, her mind racing. She had to find Elinor.

"Are you the bass player for Broad Street?" he asked.

The question confused her. Was it possible he didn't recognize her?

"I am," she said.

"My bass player forgot her head, and we were wondering if we could use yours."

"Well, sure, I guess."

Damien cocked his head and squinted. "You look familiar. Have we played together before?"

"I don't think so . . ."

"Kittimany!" Her father's voice called from behind, and she knew without looking that he would have Elinor. She stood for a moment paralyzed, terror-stricken. She took a deep breath and turned around.

"Mama!" Elinor squealed from her stroller.

Kit lunged towards her, but something stopped her. An angry fist was clenched around her wrist. Damien pulled her into him.

"Do you really think I don't know you?" he whispered into her ear. He tightened his grip. "I've been watching you for a long time, you stupid bitch. Should we tell your little girl who I am?"

Before she knew what was happening, she was on the ground. She saw Damien pull a flash of metal from his pocket. He walked toward Elinor, while Kit pushed herself to her feet and ran after him. He turned and hit her sharply across the side of her head with a gun. The blow knocked her to the ground again and she felt warm blood seeping down her cheek.

"Dad!" she screamed.

She watched her father jump in front of Elinor and her heart sank as she struggled to get to her feet. He looked so old and helpless. But then she saw a flash of red and two bodies crashing to the ground. She struggled up and ran over, holding her head. Charlie had one knee pressed against Damien's chest, the other pinning his armed hand to the ground. Kit kicked the gun out of his hand. Charlie stared at Damien then looked up at Kit, a question in his eyes.

Damien took advantage of the moment to push Charlie off his chest and jumped to his feet. Charlie grabbed hold of his leg and tackled him again, shoving the side of Damien's face into the dirt.

Damien, helpless, shifted his eyes to look up at Kit. "Want to tell old Charlie why I'm here?" he said.

Kit's face grew hot. She couldn't breathe.

"That'll teach you to fuck with me, Charlie," Damien spat.

"What?" Charlie said.

"Thanks to you I had to leave town, go to New York to find someone to play with. Everyone in Philly thought I was taboo. The least I could do was fuck your ex-girlfriend."

Kit was stunned. This was about a band rivalry? All of the fear and running and hiding—for a fucking band rivalry?

She walked over and kicked Damien in the ribs, hard. He groaned and curled his legs under Charlie's weight.

"That's for Elinor, you piece of shit," she said.

Security guards were suddenly surrounding them, rolling Damien over, handcuffing him, bagging his weapon. Charlie stood motionless, staring, his hands still clenched into fists.

Kit walked over to him. "Are you okay?"

Charlie bent over, flushed and winded. "I think so. Are you? Your cheek is bleeding."

Kit reached up to the sting on her face, her heart still beating wildly. "I'll be fine."

They watched as the cops walked Damien away. "What a dick," Charlie said.

"I'm so sorry," Kit said. "I was stupid. And feeling sorry for myself. And still missing you." She turned toward him. "I've been a real shit to you, and you never deserved that. Thank you, Charlie. Thank you for everything you've done for me."

Charlie smiled. "That's what friends are for."

Kit's father came over with Elinor and wrapped Kit into a hug. Sam followed behind him with a damp washcloth and pressed it against the slice in Kit's cheek. "Are you okay?" she asked.

"I am now," she said.

CHAPTER 56

Margo watched from the second stage area as a group of security guards ran from the main stage over to the band parking lot.

"What's going on?" her father asked.

"Let's check it out," Margo said.

She and her parents walked quickly toward the parking lot. When the scene came into view, she was shocked by what she saw: some tall, scruffy guy getting taken away in handcuffs, Kit and Charlie staring at him, Kit's hand on her bloody cheek, Kit's father and Sam running toward them, Elinor clutched in her grandfather's arms.

Margo ran over to them. "What happened?" she asked Kit. "Are you okay?"

Kit pointed toward the guy in handcuffs. "I wasn't crazy."

Margo looked back at the tall, black-clad figure, his head up, defiant.

"Damien?" Margo asked.

"Damien."

Kit held the cloth against her cheek as she told the security guards what had happened over the past two weeks: the notes, the threats, even the attempt at filing a police report. They wrote it all down, took her information, and said they would keep her posted. When they turned to Charlie to ask some questions, Sam briefly interrupted.

"I'm going to take her to my bus," she said, and one of the guards nodded an approval.

Pierce brought Elinor inside Sam's bus and Sam went in to get her first aid kit. As Kit and Margo sat and waited on the steps of the bus, Kit gazed at the commotion before her, a glazed look in her eyes. "I am such a fuckup. I hurt everyone who cares about me."

"You are a bit of a fuckup," Margo said, grinning. "But you're a great mom."

Kit turned. "Do you really think so?"

"I can't event count how many times you've ditched me in the past few weeks because you were worried about your kid."

"Sorry."

"I know it can't be easy. How many kids can say they have a rock star for a mom?"

"I can name one."

"Right. And look how well I turned out."

"I probably can't have children," she confessed. The words fell from her mouth before she was prepared for them.

"What?" Kit asked. "Why?"

Margo pulled a cigarette from her pack, paused, then replaced it. "I have fibroid tumors," she said. "That's the female trouble I didn't tell you about after our first practice that night. It means it would be difficult, if not impossible, for me to have children. And the older I get, the more impossible it becomes."

Kit reached out and touched Margo's knee. "I'm sorry."

"It's nothing to be sorry about," Margo said, twirling the pack of cigarettes in her hands. "It's fairly common. I'm not sure I want to be a parent anyway. But it's hard, especially when I see how much you love Elinor. I just feel pressured—mostly by myself. I guess that's why I was so drawn to Harry. He's the first man in a while who seemed like he might be a decent candidate for fatherhood. But, of course, I was wrong as usual."

"You'll find someone."

"You know," Margo replied, "I'm not so sure I care anymore."

"You have us," Kit said.

Margo slung her arm around Kit's shoulder. "I'm glad," she said at last.

They sat for a while, each lost in her own thoughts, until Sam came back out with the first aid kit and cleaned Kit's wound. Vinnie came over with Orlando, who had his arm around Charlie.

"This guy is quite the hero," he said, and Charlie's face went red. "I hear you pinned that jerk down like a pro."

"I've been a roadie for a while," Charlie said. "You get an instinct about assholes I guess."

"Well, the security guards were all impressed. That jerk's probably going to be charged with aggravated assault and more. Nice work, son." He clapped Charlie on the back.

"Thanks." Charlie blushed again. "Kit, if you're okay, I better get back to help the band."

Kit smiled and nodded.

Margo looked at her watch. "Shit. We need to start getting ready, too." She looked at Kit. "Are you still up for playing?"

Kit touched the bandage on her face. "Do I look more rock with this thing on?"

"Definitely." Margo smiled. "Where the hell is Ronni?"

"Who knows?" Kit said. "She always manages to find us in time."

CHAPTER 57

Margo was ready to play. She had bottled up so much
emotion that she knew only the squeal of a loud guitar would set her
straight. She and Kit were back on stage, tuning and testing the mics
as they waited for Bitchsword to finish playing on the main stage.

"Told you," Kit said to Margo. She pointed toward their
drummer, who approached with her usual pack of friends in tow.
"She always finds us in time."

"Hey, gals!" Ronni said as she climbed on stage. "Shit." She
looked at Kit's wounded cheek. "What happened to you?"

"Bar fight," Kit said.

"Ha! Good one."

Ronni sat down and worked her way around the kit like a
pro, tuning and twisting the drums until they met her approval.
Margo and Kit looked at each other and shrugged. Yep, Margo
thought, I was that young once, too. They put the final touches on
their equipment as the Bitchsword set screeched to a dramatic conclu-
sion. Margo tuned one last time, and the soundman approached her.

"You're up," he said.

The crowd from the main stage was already beginning to
scatter in different directions, and a small audience was growing
in front of them. Margo felt a surge of energy, the challenge of
converting a group of strangers into Broad Street fans.

When Kit and Ronni were ready, Margo stepped up to the microphone.

"Thanks for coming out today everyone," she said. "We're Broad Street, and we're here to rock your world."

This cued Ronni to click off four, and they were off again, into the first song. Margo strummed her guitar and swayed her hips to the catchy rhythm of Kit's bass. It felt like old times. The whole day had felt like she was going backwards—not regressing, but reliving a time before her minor celebrity and money and solitude. Youth.

"Things work out for me," she sang, "always get it for free; powers that be, all come to tea, don't you wish you were me?"

She stepped back from the mic to strum a few angry chords, which Ronni accented with splashy cymbal crashes in perfect time. She kept her eyes on her guitar, not ready to face the judging eyes before giving them all they needed to be converted.

"Got no plan to steal your man," she continued, "I got a better tan. I'll win the race, in your face. Don't you know your place?"

She and Kit sang together: "How do I do it? How do I do it? Things work out for me."

She loved singing this song she'd written when she was feeling particularly insecure one night. It reminded her that music was power—the power to make you something you're not, to trick your psyche into a new persona. Music was magic.

She let herself assume the role of the narrator as she moved her hips and smiled at Kit and surrendered to the feeling that engulfed her. When they reached the end of the song, the crowd applauded. There weren't a lot of people, but Margo enjoyed their enthusiasm. It felt real and alive.

The rest of the set progressed almost flawlessly. When they flubbed, Margo plowed through without getting flustered. She could forget about Harry and her finances and screwing the young boy. Her head was filled with the moment.

The crowd continued to grow, and they cheered more enthusiastically after each song. By the time they'd reached the final song, Margo noticed people bopping their heads with the music and she knew they'd won them over.

She glanced over at Kit and knew that she was feeling it too.

Something had changed since yesterday—not one big event, but a collection of smaller ones that seemed to have erased the missing years. Margo even tossed a congratulatory smile toward Ronni, who nodded her head as if she actually appreciated it.

* * *

Kit was loopy with adrenaline as they packed up their equipment. It had been a long time since she had clicked with Margo the way they had in that set. It had been hard work getting there, but it finally felt like the real thing. It reminded her of the early days of Broad Street, and she wanted to savor the moment.

As Ginger Snap's catchy pop launched from the main stage, Kit carried her bass over to Margo, who stood with her parents.

"Great set, girls!" Orlando said, pulling Kit into a careful hug.

"Thanks," Kit said.

"Excuse me." A young woman, petite and very pierced, touched Kit lightly on the arm. "Hey," she said in a soft voice. "You guys really rocked. Where are you from?"

"Thanks!" Margo said. "We're from Philly."

"Cool, cool." She nodded. "My name's Sarah McGinnis. I'm a reporter from *Rolling Stone* magazine and we're doing a piece on the Women of Rock Tour."

"Really?" Vinnie said enthusiastically. "Then you definitely need to cover these girls. They're going to be the next big thing!"

"Mom, please," Margo said, shooting an angry glare in Vinnie's direction.

"Well," Sarah said, clearing her throat. "I'd like to do that. I know Margo is a bit of a celebrity already, so I came to check out the band—and I have to say, I'm impressed."

"Well, thank you," Margo said.

Kit sighed, ready to be shoved into Margo's shadow once again. She tried to stay positive as the reporter asked Margo a series of questions about her experience, and influences, and other predictable journalistic fare. She stood with what she hoped was an attentive look on her face, her mind wandering, until she heard her father call her name. He and Sam were walking towards them, Elinor in his arms. Her first instinct was to wonder why Elinor wasn't napping. Then she wondered why they were carrying her instead of pushing her in the stroller.

"Excuse me," she said to the reporter and started to make her way toward her father.

But he held his hand up. "Wait," he said. "Stay there." He put Elinor on the ground a few feet away from Kit. "Go ahead, honey. Walk to Mommy."

Kit froze as she watched her father let go of Elinor's hands, still up in the air for balance. She stepped forward once, twice, three times, her pace accelerating as she neared her mother. Kit watched with a mixture of pride and disbelief. Her baby, the child who had been safe inside her only months ago, the huge decision that changed her life, was now beginning a journey of her own. Kit squatted and reached her arms out to Elinor, who toddled into them with a huge satisfied smile on her face. Kit wrapped her arms around her.

"Good job, sweetie," she said into Elinor's ear, squeezing her tightly. "You are Mommy's big girl. I am so proud of you." She kissed her repeatedly on the cheek, and then Elinor pushed herself out of her mother's hug.

"Walk, walk," she said.

Kit put her down and Elinor tottered back to her grandfather, who swept her into his arms as Sam applauded.

"Is that your daughter?"

Kit turned to see the reporter standing next to her.

"Oh . . . yes."

The reporter raised her pierced eyebrows. "You bring your baby on tour with you?"

"Well, I didn't have much choice," Kit said, flustered and embarrassed. But she looked over at her daughter, and her father, and Sam, and her shame disappeared. This was her family, and she was proud of them. "But my father is along to help, and this experience has already been great for Elinor."

The reporter lifted her small pad and scribbled some notes.

"How do you juggle being a mom and a rock musician?" Sarah asked. "It must be hard with all the late nights and noise and everything."

Kit shrugged. "I don't know. I love my daughter, and I think I'm a better mom because I haven't given up on my other interests. I think it's healthy to keep my life balanced, and I know she's having a great time, too."

Kit wondered how this stranger would interpret her decision. She envisioned the headline: "Irresponsible Parent Exposes Toddler to Noise and Drugs." But she didn't care. The only people whose opinions mattered were right here, and she knew they supported her.

"And isn't that Sam Starr over there with your father?" the reporter asked.

"Yeah," Kit said. "We all just sort of hit it off with her."

The reporter scribbled some more. "If you don't mind me asking . . ." She pointed to her own cheek with a pen. "What happened?"

"Bar fight," Kit said. The reporter looked shocked. "Just kidding," Kit continued. "I fell, nothing exciting."

The reporter laughed, a bit nervously, and then asked her more about her life as a musician and mother. Kit enjoyed being in the spotlight and wondered briefly how Margo, who was standing a few feet away with her parents, felt about it. But she was also aware that by talking to this woman she was missing some of Elinor's big moment. She wondered if feeling torn like this was part of the life she was choosing, part of what this reporter, who was clearly too young to understand, should write about women in rock. Kit certainly didn't have these answers.

After the reporter was finished asking Kit questions, she took some pictures of Kit with Elinor, then of Kit with her dad and Sam, then with Margo and her parents. Kit positioned herself so her wounded cheek was hidden from the camera as much as possible. She felt a bit silly, but she enjoyed the stares they received from passersby.

"Thanks," the reporter said. "Is there a number I can call if I have more questions?"

Kit gave her Margo's number, assuming that was the contact she was most interested in, shook the reporter's hand, and watched as the petite girl disappeared into the crowd.

"That was cool," Margo said, appearing at Kit's side. "I can use all the publicity I can get."

Kit smiled. Some things will never change, she thought.

"Mama!" Elinor called again. "Walk, walk."

Kit squatted again as Elinor walked toward her and then she

scooped her up into another hug.

As she perched on Kit's hip, Elinor pointed at Margo. "Ma-go," she said.

"Do you want to go to Margo?" Kit asked.

"Ma-go," Elinor said, reaching out her arms.

"Is that okay?" Kit asked.

"Of course!" Margo reached out her arms and Elinor slipped into them. Margo held her stiffly, as if she might crumble if she moved. Kit thought she saw Margo's eyes tear slightly.

Elinor began to play with Margo's necklace. "Ma-go," she repeated.

"You are pretty cute, kid," Margo conceded. "I can't believe you're walking already. You might be doing back-ups by the end of the tour."

Ginger Snap was reaching the end of her set, many in the audience clapping above their heads in time with the skipping redhead. It wasn't a full crowd, but it was a good audience, receptive. Kit and Margo watched from a distance until Kit's father came over and told them he was going to keep Sam company while she got ready to perform. Kit looked at Margo and back at her father. "Have fun, Dad."

"Let's go check out The Venturas," Kit said. "It'll be fun to see how long Daria can go without speaking to me."

They walked over to the second stage as The Venturas were setting up. When she saw Kit and Margo, Paula looked back at Daria with a sneer. Kit refused to be a part of their petty jealousy. In her mind, she'd done nothing wrong.

The Venturas kicked into their set, as strong as ever. Kit pushed plugs into Elinor's ears and stepped away from the speakers.

"This next one goes out to some ex-friends," Paula said into the microphone as they moved into their second song. "They know who they are."

A few seconds in, Kit figured out they were playing "Hit the Road." She knew it was directed at her.

"Let's go," she said to Margo.

They walked away from the stage, back toward the dressing room, as The Venturas' angry lyrics faded behind them.

"I told you once, I told you twice; now I'm sick of being nice. Bye

bye, baby; bye bye . . ."

✳ ✳ ✳

Back in the dressing room, Margo and Kit found Ronni with her pals, once again raiding the sandwich tray. Margo was still feeling good. The moment Elinor said her name, something had clicked—like a flash illuminating the subject of a photograph. She suddenly noticed that Elinor was a small person, not a generic child with too many things that got in Margo's way.

"Good set, gals," Ronni said, her mouth full of sandwich.

"Thanks," Margo said. She got two beers out of the cooler and held one up with a questioning look at Kit.

"Oh what the hell," Kit said.

Margo handed her the beer and Kit put Elinor down.

"Show our friend Ronni what you learned how to do today," Kit said, and Elinor looked at her, confused. "That's Ronni over there, the one with crumbs all over her face."

Ronni waved wildly.

Elinor looked toward Ronni and her group of friends and clung to her mother's leg.

"It's okay, honey," Kit said. "You don't have to do anything you don't want to do."

Margo stood up, leaving her beer on the coffee table, and walked across the room. "Elinor, come here," she said, dangling her necklace as temptation. "Walk over to Margo."

Elinor looked at her mother, who nodded, and she waddled over to Margo, who picked her up and hugged her. The others were applauding enthusiastically when Orlando stepped into the room, a serious expression on his face.

"I have some bad news," he said.

Margo looked at him, frozen in a magical moment with Elinor.

"Let me guess," Kit said. "The Venturas want us off the tour."

"That I could deal with," he said. "This is worse. The tour's been cancelled."

He unfolded a letter and read:

A MESSAGE FROM SUSAN MCKEOWN
To all my Fellow Musicians,
It is with a heavy heart that I inform you of the Women of Rock Tour's disbandment. I hope you can forgive me for not providing you with the summer you counted on. I tried hard to keep the tour on course, but due to huge financial losses we are unable to recover. This is a sad time for the musical community, under the influence of big corporations and bottom lines.
I value your talents and look forward to meeting you again. With genius like ours, they can't hold us down for long.
Susan

"Well," Margo said, "that sucks."

CHAPTER 58

One week later, Kit was in her father's kitchen, making dinner. She was back to some old routines, but nothing felt the same. Since their abrupt return to Philadelphia, after her rock tour fantasy had been cut short like an umbilical cord, she didn't feel as badly as she'd expected. When the tour was cancelled, Charlie decided to move back to Philadelphia. He was still job hunting and apartment hunting, but he'd already been to visit a few times. Even better, he and Elinor made each other laugh. Comfort. That was Charlie, and that was exactly what Kit had wanted.

Still, she had to admit she was disappointed that the tour had been canceled. She hadn't bothered to call about her old job, and she had no plans to look for another one. She was writing some new material for the band, and she knew she could pick up some freelance proofreading work. Her father had been surprisingly silent about this. Perhaps it wasn't so surprising, though, since he was in the stupor of romance with Sam, with whom he had spoken every day since she'd returned to her New York apartment. Kit glanced at the clock as she put the final touches on the lasagna she was making for Sam's first visit. She was due to arrive at any moment.

Kit put the lasagna into the oven and sat down on the floor to play with Elinor. Her daughter handed her blocks and together they built, demolished, and rebuilt a tower until Kit heard the crunch of gravel outside.

Kit stood and looked out the window. A large old Mercedes pulled into the driveway. Her father was at the store buying wine for their dinner, so Kit brought Elinor outside to greet Sam.

"Hi!" Sam said, holding out her arms toward Elinor. "Can I give you a hug, sweetie?"

Elinor squealed in delight and let Sam wrap her arms around her. Sam smiled at Kit.

"How are you holding up since tour interruptus?"

Kit shrugged. "Okay, I guess. Want some iced tea?"

"Sure." Sam carried Elinor to one of the weathered wooden rocking chairs on the porch and Kit went into the kitchen.

She'd made homemade iced tea the way her mother used to, dark and strong with lots of mint. It was strange to repeat this routine with this new woman, but it didn't feel like a betrayal. She liked Sam. She thought her mother would have liked her, too. And it was good to see her dad finally happy again.

She filled two tall glasses and returned to the porch. Elinor was still snuggled in Sam's lap. Kit sat in another rocking chair and they rocked silently, listening to the song of cicadas. It was high-pitched and monotone, with an otherworldly echo that Kit found soothing.

"Your mother created a beautiful garden," Sam said.

This observation hit Kit hard. Sam could have said anything about the house, or her mother's tea recipe, or her choice of curtain fabric. But the garden was sacred, an intimate labor of love that was as organic as birth.

"It meant everything to her," Kit finally said. "I mean, except for us."

Sam smiled at her over the top of Elinor's curly head. "Your mother would be proud of you, Kit. I know your father is."

Kit let these words wash over her as she gazed at the garden that continued to thrive even though Kit lacked her mother's talent. She thought of all the work her mother had put into it, and into her.

The phone ringing inside interrupted her thoughts. "Excuse me," she said to Sam.

"Did you see the article?" Margo said as soon as Kit picked up the phone.

"What article?"

"Oh my god, Kit. You're going to get such a big head over this. Remember that *Rolling Stones* reporter who talked to us that day in New York?"

"Yeah."

"She did a feature article on you. Well, the article is kind of about the tour and kind of about the band, but mostly it's about you, and how you brought Elinor along, and how cool that was, and how you hang out with Sam Starr—and a bunch of other stuff to inflate your ego."

Kit sat down on a kitchen chair.

"Not only that, but I got a call for you on my cell. Some Hollywood type who wants to talk to you about buying your story."

"What?"

"I'm not making this up. It gets even better. My dad called me this morning to tell me that he's been in touch with Susan McKeown, and she wants to help us set up our own tour with The Crocodiles. Something smaller, but they think they can get it together pretty soon. What do you think?"

Kit walked to the living room and watched her father pulling into the driveway behind Sam's car. There was a spring in his step as he walked up to the porch and greeted both Sam and Elinor with a kiss. He looked younger than he had for years. "Kit?"

"Oh, sorry. Yes, of course I'm interested. I was just watching my roadies. I think they'd be up for it."

"Excellent. I'll have my dad go ahead with the arrangements."

Kit smiled. "I couldn't have done it without you."

Margo laughed. "I know."

* * *

Margo hung up the phone. Kit needed this, she thought, and I need it too. She knew it would be good publicity for her show, but strangely enough, that was low on her priority list at the moment.

The authorities had identified the source of her credit card issues. It turned out the thief was Jimmy, the intern she had screwed near the end of the season. Her recollections of that night were fuzzy at best, but she remembered he had bitched about a bunch of college loan debts and how he thought she was so lucky she didn't have to worry about that kind of stuff. Of course it seemed obvious now that she shouldn't have left her purse in the bedroom when she went to take a shower the next morning. He must have copied down the numbers of her debit and credit cards, including all the expiration dates and CVV numbers. It was a stupid mistake, and one she vowed she wouldn't repeat—for more reasons than losing money.

She decided not to press charges, since she was happy to have the situation resolved—and eager to keep that whole unfortunate night with him as much under wraps as possible.

She'd also been avoiding Harry's calls for days. He'd left messages on her cell phone and her home phone. He'd heard the tour had been canceled and was wondering how she was doing. She wasn't quite ready to jump back into that mess yet.

After talking to Kit and giving her dad the go-ahead to make the arrangements, Margo poured a glass of wine and wandered out to her garden, soaking in the familiar smells and colors. It was good to be home, but it would also be good to be on tour, even for a few weeks. Her parents had volunteered to drive them all again and mentioned that they might try to get a few gigs themselves along the way. She didn't have to bunk with them in the Winnebago now that she had the resources to avoid it. But she thought she might tag along anyway.

The doorbell rang, and Margo walked inside to look out the window. It was Harry.

"Shit," she said, putting down her wine and pausing to check her face in the hall mirror. She took a deep breath and opened the door.

"Hi," he said, a bouquet of roses in his hand.

He looked good, and Margo felt the familiar rush of desire race through her.

"Hi," she said, not moving from the door.

"Mind if I come in?" he asked.

She stepped aside and walked into the living room. "Want a glass of wine? I'm having one."

"Sure, thanks."

He followed her into the kitchen and placed the roses on the counter. She poured him some wine and put the flowers in a vase.

"Come on out," she said. "I'm enjoying my garden."

They walked out to the garden and sat down.

"You've been avoiding me."

"Yes, I have."

"Why?"

Margo looked into his deep dark eyes and felt the weight of the doubt and anger that had been plaguing her since his confession over a week before. She no longer cared that he was her boss.

"Because I think you're lying about your wife. I read about the show you produced that happened to have a very similar story line as your life. And, I think you're focused only on publicity and sex and don't really care about me at all—at least not very much."

Harry sat back in his chair and crossed his legs. "Hmmm. Interesting."

"Interesting?" This was the last response she expected.

He leaned forward, elbows on his knees. "Has anyone ever told you, Margo Bevelaqua, that you have a little trouble letting your guard down?"

"No," she lied, remembering Peter's words.

"Margo, I know what I told you is a lot to absorb. I've managed to keep my wife out of the picture for a long time, and no one at the network even knows about her. I wanted to protect her. But now I want to protect you too. If you don't want a relationship with me because of my situation, I understand. But things are different now that I've met you, and I want to make some changes. I've talked to my wife about some of this already, but that's between her and me. What's between you and me is that I think I'm falling for you, and I think I can see us old and gray together, you sneaking off to smoke cigarettes while you work on your garden, me pretending I don't know you're doing this."

Margo smiled, in spite of herself.

"In fact," Harry continued, "maybe you wouldn't need to work anymore. I thought maybe we could even put your show on hold for a little while."

"What?" Margo sat up so abruptly her wine glass wobbled. She steadied it.

"I just think you deserve to relax a little, that's all."

She leaned toward him. "I worked my ass off to make that

show what it is."

He looked surprised. "I thought you wanted a normal life."

Margo looked out over her asters, the blooms exploding purple next to a bonfire of daisies. She thought about when she planted them last year, thinking these hearty plants would be good for an urban garden, and she thought back to when she introduced the idea on her first episode last season. She also thought about the arrangements she'd made with a local lawn care service to ensure these blooms would be well kept while she was on tour. Rock and roll gardener. This was the life she'd earned.

"I thought so too," she said. "But it turns out my life is pretty good right now."

"Oh," Harry said.

"That doesn't mean I can't enjoy a glass of wine with a friend."

"Friend?"

"For now. We can see how it goes."

Harry leaned back in his chair and took a sip of wine. "You should know I'm used to getting what I want. I am a major TV executive, you know."

"So you keep reminding me."

"How about dinner soon?"

"I'm going on another tour, but maybe I can squeeze you in."

Harry paused. "As friends?"

"We'll see."

Harry chuckled. "Margo Bevelaqua, you will make me crazy."

"You won't be the first."

They sat in silence, and Margo was surprised at how little she cared whether or not it would work out with Harry. She'd thought that all she wanted was a traditional family of her own, but now that it was within reach she wasn't so sure. Maybe without realizing it she'd bought into an ideal picture society had painted for her. Maybe the fear that she couldn't have children had pushed her into thinking she needed a child to make her complete somehow. She wasn't sure. But she was sure she wasn't cut out to be a traditional housewife. And she was also sure that for now she was content to be a rock star and a TV celebrity. She thought of her crazy parents, and Kit and Elinor, and Peter, and her fans, and all the people she'd met who might be part of her life if only she let her guard down a little. She wasn't alone anymore.

"*Things work out for me* . . ." The Broad Street lyrics ran through her head. Would they work out for her? She breathed in the sweet scent of the garden she had created and was pretty sure they would.

Acknowledgments

Come As You Are is a bit of an exercise in time-travel. It's the sequel to *Broad Street*, which came out in 2008 and takes place in the mid-1990s. *Come As You Are*, published in 2016, takes place in 2006. Confused? I was, too, so my first thanks go to my editor, Tara Smith, whose thoughtful eagle eye helped me travel back to this odd era in music, 2006, and ensure I wasn't referencing inaccurate pop culture like the iPhone one year before it was released.

A huge thank-you to Carla Spataro, for all she's done to support me and so many other writers. I am proud and grateful for the work we've done together with the help of our passionate volunteers through our nonprofit, Philadelphia Stories.

I'm also grateful to my musician friends, especially Margo's muse, Lynette Byrnes, and Elisa "Chi Chi Boom" Steingruebner. Our adventures in the band Mae Pang inspired many scenes in *Broad Street* and helped me to create characters that lived large enough in my mind that I wanted to continue to tell their stories.

I also want to thank my fabulous writing group: Julie Odell, Tony Knighton, Jim Zervanos, Kath Hubbard, and Nathan Long. They are all incredibly talented, and our monthly meetings encourage me to keep writing despite the many obstacles thrown in my path.

None of this would be possible without the support of my husband, "Rockbottom" Rob Giglio, who tolerates my crazy ideas with the perfect encouraging words and humor. We're also lucky to have one very cool kid, Dexter. Love you guys.

Thanks also to my family and friends who support me in all the many hats I wear. I feel very fortunate to be surrounded by so many smart, creative, and passionate people.

Finally, I want to thank my dad, who understood and shared my passion for writing and was the first person I called whenever I had news to share or needed advice. Pierce Greene is largely inspired by my father's no-nonsense intelligence. I miss him every day.